'Brilliantly twisty, a sharp, sinister and addictive read'

'Tension oozes from the pages'
i newspaper

'A fab debut with two twisted women at its core'
Prima

'Utterly compulsive reading'
Jenny Blackhurst

'An original and chilling
portrayal of twisted relationships'
Debbie Howells

'A fantastic psychological thriller . . .
We couldn't put it down'
Take a Break

'Taut and suspenseful'
Heat

THE
DAUGHTER

Michelle Frances has worked in television drama
as a producer and script editor for several years,
both for the independent sector and the BBC.
The Daughter is her third novel, following
The Girlfriend and *The Temp*.

ALSO BY MICHELLE FRANCES

The Girlfriend
The Temp

THE
DAUGHTER

MICHELLE FRANCES

PAN BOOKS

First published 2019 by Pan Books

This paperback edition first published 2019 by Pan Books
an imprint of Pan Macmillan
20 New Wharf Road, London N1 9RR
Associated companies throughout the world
www.panmacmillan.com

ISBN 978-1-5098-2154-9

1 3 5 7 9 8 6 4 2

A CIP catalogue record for this book is available from the British Library.

Typeset in Sabon LT Std by Palimpsest Book Production Ltd, Falkirk, Stirlingshire
Printed and bound by CPI Group (UK) Ltd, Croydon, CR0 4YY

Visit www.panmacmillan.com to read more about all our books
and to buy them. You will also find features, author interviews and
news of any author events, and you can sign up for e-newsletters
so that you're always first to hear about our new releases.

For Livi and Clementine

'A mother is the truest friend we have, when trials heavy and sudden fall upon us; when adversity takes the place of prosperity; when friends desert us; when trouble thickens around us, still will she cling to us, and endeavour by her kind precepts and counsels to dissipate the clouds of darkness, and cause peace to return to our hearts.'

Washington Irving

'Fortune favours the brave.'

Translation of Latin proverb

PROLOGUE

A tiny, perfect wave flopped onto the absurdly beautiful beach. A few seconds later it was followed by another, then another, in a faultless rhythm, the warm water seeking out Kate's toes as she stood at the edge of the turquoise ocean. She looked up at the horizon, the blue of the sea merging with the sky. She lifted her sunglasses, checking out the colours both with and without the tinted lenses. Which was more incredible? Glasses up. Glasses down. Impossible to choose.

Plip! Plip! went the water, in a pattern repeated over time eternal. And then suddenly, a rogue wave came too quickly, a double time *Plip! Plip!* that upset the rhythm and, in doing so, altered the flow forever. At one point, Kate had thought her life was set on a predictable path, that she was going in a direction that would never change. Then, quite unexpectedly, everything was thrown out of sync. Even now, she thought, twisting the ring on her finger, no one knew what was in store. You just didn't know what was going to hit you next.

ONE

2017

'It's the police,' said Kate, looking out of her kitchen window. She jerked the stuck wooden blind to get a better view. Across the close, Iris struggled with arthritic fingers for a full minute trying to unlock her porch door. Two police constables, a man and a woman, waited outside patiently as Iris glanced up through the glass with a flustered smile.

'Bloody little shits,' said Kate.

'They look quite well behaved to me,' said Becky, peering over Kate's shoulder.

'You know what I mean. The little buggers who've been graffiti-ing the back of her fence. Ripping holes in it. They should pick on someone their own size. Or age. Oh, thank God, I was just about to go over.' Kate felt Iris's relief as the door finally opened. She could tell by the way Iris was gesturing that she was being overly apologetic, in the way her generation often are, not used to needing help, not wanting to be a burden. Iris looked up and Kate threw her an encouraging wave. Iris nodded, then disappeared back into the house, the police removing their hats before doing the same.

'Jam?'

Kate turned to see Becky grab two slices of toast that had just popped up and start to butter them.

'Yes, please.'

'Now, you sure you don't want any help later?' asked Becky.

'I thought it was hard for you to get away? The big scoop that's too top secret to even tell me about.'

'You're right. All exposé journalists should discuss their story first with their mothers.'

'Oh, go on, give us a clue. Is it someone famous? An actor caught with a washing-up bottle and a goldfish?'

Becky stared. 'What the heck . . . ?' She shook her head. 'I don't want to know. You know I can't tell you what I'm up to . . . not yet anyway. I have to get my story first, get all my facts straight.'

'Can you at least tell me where you've been disappearing off to?'

Becky, taller than her mum, held Kate's head and kissed the top of it. 'No. So. Later?'

'I thought I'd try steak.'

'Pie?'

'Fillet.'

Becky whistled. 'He *is* special. Or is that for me?'

'Of course, you too.'

'I can't wait to meet him.'

'He can't wait to meet you.'

4

'Maybe I'll question him.'

'He's not hiding anything. He's just a bus driver. You don't have to do your investigative journalist routine.'

Toast ready, Becky handed one slice to her mum. She spoke solemnly. 'Remind me. How many dates have you two had?'

Kate giggled. 'Are you worried about his intentions?'

'Does he open doors? Walk on the outside edge of the pavement? Take his shoes off when he comes to the house?'

'He's not been yet.'

'OK, his house?'

'He has a pair of very fine slippers. Moccasins. With fur lining.'

'I will not rise. It's just . . . it's been a while since you've seen anyone. I mean, I know you've had dates since I was conceived . . .'

'I should hope so. That was twenty-one years ago.'

'But there's not been anyone truly significant before.' Becky paused. 'He's the Big One. I can sense it. It'll never be you and me again.'

Kate laughed and touched Becky's cheek. Gave the reassuring smile of a parent. 'It'll always be you and me. And that's a promise.'

Becky smiled sheepishly. 'Sorry, I'm used to it being just the two of us.'

'So, now it can be the three of us. Sometimes.'

'And I'm chuffed to bits, you know that. Tim sounds wonderful . . .'

'He is. Do you know, he texted me a picture of dawn this morning when he was out on his route.'

'. . . and romantic.'

'Oh, and I meant to say, he's bringing the wine tonight.'

'. . . and generous.'

'All right, no need to go overboard. Anyway, you don't have to worry. Do you think I can't tell a plonker when I see one?' Kate pointed at Becky with her toast. 'I tell you, I spotted that little tyke in the electrical aisle before security even realized he had a bloody drill up his jacket.'

Becky stopped chewing. 'Please God, tell me you haven't been tackling shoplifters?'

'Well, security weren't doing anything about it.'

'He might have had a weapon! A gun!'

'Don't be daft. It's B&Q.'

'It's south London,' said Becky sternly.

'I was fine. Anyway, he got a cracked fibula – that was the ladder that fell on him, not me – the store got its drill back and I got a bonus. Fifty quid,' she added drily.

'Are you short?' said Becky, a small, worried frown appearing. 'Because I am going to pay you back. Every penny.'

'And I've told you, you don't have to. It wasn't like I did much—'

'You did *everything*,' insisted Becky, not for the first time.

Not enough, thought Kate, but kept it to herself. Her eye caught the clock on the wall. 'Hadn't you better go?'

Becky looked up. 'Yikes, I'm going to be late.' She grabbed her bike helmet and backpack from the hall and threw open the front door, stopping just briefly to fling her arms around her mum. Kate pulled her cardigan tight over her faded T-shirt and jeans and watched as the side-alley door clanged and Becky wheeled out her bike. She covered her shoulder-length auburn hair with her helmet, threw one leg over the crossbar and started to pedal, the wheels making tracks in the frost.

'I'm doing chips!' called Kate, as usual her heart swelling as she watched her daughter cycle off.

Becky lifted a hand without looking back. 'Great! See you at seven!'

'Love you!'

'Love you too! And not just because of the chips!'

TWO

Becky flew down the steep hill, bracing herself against the February cold that made her eyes water. It was a big day today. And not just because she was meeting her mum's boyfriend. She smiled as she recalled the sensational news of the morning – fillet steak! Never in her entire life had Becky known her mum to buy fillet steak. But Tim seemed to have won her over. Ever since he'd come on the scene, her mum had blossomed.

Becky wondered what she'd make of him – what they'd make of each other. She felt a wave of protectiveness wash over her and smiled to herself. He'd better be good, or he'd have her to deal with.

She slowed the bike and swung into the road leading to the station. As she dismounted, her thoughts turned to the other big event of the day.

Her interview. She was up for the position of reporter – at the most highly regarded free-thinking newspaper in the country. An opportunity people would cut off their right arm for. It was a big step up from her trainee post – and a permanent role. She wanted the job so much she got a physical ache in her chest every time she thought about it, which was almost constantly.

Becky had something planned to convince her boss she was the right candidate: an investigative story that she'd sourced herself, something she was doing on the quiet. Her pulse quickened as she thought of her story. It was explosive – well, it would be when she got her hard-fought-for last piece of evidence tomorrow.

Her secret source. He was finally going to tell her. Then she could reveal to them all what she'd been investigating – her mum, her boss, the whole darn world. This story was her coup, a piece to blast Piers – the competition – out of the water. There was only one job. And two trainees hungry for it.

Becky waited on the platform with the crowds of grey-clad commuters. She had to beat Piers. Her mum's comment that morning, something that came up every now and then, was a trouble-maker of a sentiment that broke her heart every time it surfaced: her mum thinking she'd not done enough through her childhood, feeling like she'd let her down or something. It had been hard, there was no denying it, but Becky knew her mum had done her best.

Getting this job was her way of showing her mum she'd done all right.

THREE

'So, have you had the fence people round?' asked Kate. She knelt by Iris's back door, holding a tower bolt against the frame, and marked the screw holes with a bradawl. She liked doing things for her, it gave her an opportunity to pay back this woman who had helped so much over the years, who had been the mother Kate had never had.

'They can't come until tomorrow, they're too busy,' said Iris, lowering herself into a kitchen chair; the last few inches of her descent were an uncontrolled plunge, and her relief showed at having made it safely. 'All these high winds we've been having. They say there's a shortage of panels.'

'We've got loads in the shop,' said Kate, then wished she hadn't. There was nothing to be gained by highlighting that the fence company were spinning Iris a line. 'I'm sure they know what they're doing,' she added quickly.

Iris raised an eyebrow. 'Sound like a bunch of fibbers to me.'

'If they don't turn up tomorrow, I'll get onto someone else. There's a bloke who comes into the shop quite a bit. Seems decent. I'll get his number.'

'Thanks, love.'

Kate took a sip of chestnut-coloured tea from a mug decorated with an assortment of garden birds. 'The police find out who it was?'

'How can they? But I know they're from the college. Every year we get trouble. Some new bunch, hanging out at the park, causing mischief, smoking those funny cigarettes. They're doing a door-to-door at least. See if anyone's seen anything, had any bother. Did they come to you this morning?'

'I had to go to work. They'll probably catch up with us later.'

'Weren't you working at the weekend? I thought you were cutting back your hours, now Becky's left university.'

'Back down to five days, week after next.'

Iris patted Kate's shoulder. 'Good. You worked all the hours God sent to get that lovely girl of yours an education, a proper start in life.'

Kate shrugged. 'She's the one who got herself a trainee-ship on a respected national paper. Beat all those others. Over two thousand applied, apparently.' She picked up her drill. 'This is the noisy bit.'

The conversation lulled as Kate screwed the bolt securely to the door.

'She still working hard?' said Iris, once the screech had subsided.

'I hardly ever see her. She's investigating some major story. Top secret.'

'I remember when I used to mind her for you and she'd be outside on her pink bike with those tassels on the handlebars. Taking all her teddies for a ride. One by one. Once round the tree and back again, then it was the next one's turn. Always fair and square. She was always like that. Hated meanness or anyone taking advantage.'

'There you go,' said Kate, sliding the bolt back and forth. 'One at the top, too. Although I really don't think anyone'll try anything.'

Iris moved her gold-rimmed glasses from their resting place on the top of her maroon-rinsed hair and placed them on her nose. She looked across at the door. 'Makes me feel better, anyway. Now, hadn't you better get home before your shopping spoils?'

Kate stood and gathered her grocery bags and tools. 'Becky is meeting Tim tonight.'

'First time?'

'Yes. I was fine this morning, and now . . .'

'Bit nervous?'

Kate nodded.

'Oh, I'm sure they'll get along. They're both very lucky. You're a good sort, love. Thanks for popping by.' Iris started to hoist herself out of her chair.

'Please don't get up. I'll see myself out.'

'Do you mind sticking Constanza back in the window on your way out?' The porcelain flamenco dancer in a flame-red dress was Iris's sign – she put it in the window at night and it was taken away in the morning. That way, Kate knew she was OK.

'Course. Ring if you need anything.'

'I will. Don't forget my invite sometime. I want to meet this fancy fella too.'

Kate leaned down and gave her a peck on the cheek. 'It's a date.'

A bag in each hand, Kate walked through her front door, kicking it shut behind her. She slipped off her shoes, then went into the kitchen and lifted the grocery bags onto the worktop. She took a little peek inside, delighting in things she hadn't been able to afford for a very long while; in fact she'd never been this extravagant, not without getting items from the discount shelf. The fillet steak, a packet of the 'upmarket' frozen oven chips, double cream and fancy chocolate to make a mousse. She placed them all just so in the fridge, and then, noticing the bin needed emptying, tied up the black sack and made her way out of the side door to dump it in the wheelie bin. She was just about to turn back when an unmistakable odour wafted down the garden.

Frowning, she walked across the small patch of grass to her back fence. She sniffed again. Two or three young male voices sounded from the other side. There was a narrow path there that led to the high street and the college, the same path that backed onto Iris's house. Very quietly, she lifted the faded, tatty kiddy's plastic table that had been Becky's when she was small. She carefully placed it against the six-foot fence, then stepped up and peered through a small knothole near the top. Three lads were standing on the other side, loitering, swaggering. Looking suspicious by way of not doing very much at all. They passed round a joint – the source of the smell that had trespassed under Kate's nose.

She popped her head over the top of the fence. 'Got yourselves lost, boys?'

The dance of the guilty, limbs flying like puppets with their strings suddenly pulled. Coughing, spluttering, fingers burned from hiding the ciggy behind a back, one jumping so far he fell into some stinging nettles.

Kate hid a smile.

'Shit!' said the one who would now have a rash on his hand.

One of them had a zigzag shaved into his hair, around the back from one side to the other. He glowered at her. 'What do you think you're doing, lady? You nearly give us a heart attack.'

'The ciggy'll do that. After the asthma, lung cancer and low sperm count.' She noticed the crest on their school uniforms, blazers worn with the sleeves rolled up. 'Whaddayasay, I don't tell your headmaster about your little extra-curricular here, if you answer me some questions.'

Three stony faces stared up at her.

'Why don't you grab my cock?' said Zigzag.

'I didn't bring my tweezers.'

'Fuck this,' he retorted and started to walk off, the others following.

'Hey, quitters! I hear Mr Hodgson is very keen to improve his lower-than-low Ofsted rating – in fact he's been shipped in specially to do so – which means, boys, I'd expect he's a little trigger-happy with the letters home, the detentions and even –' she winced – 'the suspensions.' The boys had stopped walking. 'All I'm asking is for you to tell me what you know about the damaged fence a little way up.'

'It wasn't us,' said Nettle Burn.

'But you know about it?'

Zigzag shrugged. 'Saw it.'

'Any idea who it was?'

'Couldda been anyone.'

'Ah, yes. I had deduced this myself. But . . . was it *anyone in particular*?' Kate smiled expectantly at them but all she got in return was shoes scuffing at the gravel, eyes swivelling to the sky. 'I'm sure Mr Hodgson doesn't really want to hear about your funny cigarettes, bet he's got enough to do, eh? New term and all that.'

'We ain't grasses,' said Zigzag sullenly.

'Or there again, maybe he's a bit bored. Waiting for the phone to ring.'

'Fucking 'ell . . . why don't you hassle that lot what bus-in from the Western estate,' he mumbled angrily, walking off. 'Come on, lads.'

'What about a name?' called Kate, but they carried on, their shoulders hunched. 'Thanks, boys! By the way, you're not bunking off, are you? Has class finished?' she added as an afterthought.

They ignored her.

'Honest boys don't do that,' she said, half to herself. 'Just don't.'

She watched them disappear around the corner and then

climbed down. Brushed the fence dust off her hands. It wasn't a guaranteed identification, but it was a start at least. She'd call the college in the morning.

Making her way back into the kitchen, she put on an apron and started to separate the eggs. Then she saw a text had come through from Becky while she was outside. 'Leaving now. See you (both!) soon. X.' Kate smiled, then switched on the radio. It was a nineties show, and she sang along to an old Blur track.

She liked living in this suburb of south London. It had a strong sense of community, even if it was a bit rough around the edges. People generally looked out for one another, you'd recognize faces in the street and say hello, and there was always a summer fair in the park; more cheap candy floss and tacky bric-a-brac stalls than gourmet ice cream and homemade crafts but it was something. It was all she could afford anyway, when she moved to her tiny two-up two-down twenty-odd years ago. The rent had eaten up just over half of her small salary from the garden centre, the first of a succession of dead-end jobs.

It wasn't the way her life had been planned. Kate's mother, Dervla, a strict working-class Irish woman, had insisted on an all-girls Catholic school when Kate was growing up, her determination silencing Kate's dad's wish for something more mainstream. It wasn't posh, just authoritarian and stuck in the sixties. Dervla had become increasingly more severe as her miscarriages had come along. Kate was the first baby, but she had four unborn brothers and sisters and ultimately remained an only child.

It wasn't a particularly happy home to live in, and once she was allowed to go to her first-ever teenage party, she felt the relief of freedom as she realized that the world was an easier, more opportunity-laden place than she'd believed. In the giddiness of the moment, she'd been flattered into losing her virginity. The new-found freedom was short-lived. Her Catholic upbringing meant an abortion wasn't something she had the courage to face, and so the baby would be due in the middle of her GCSEs. She managed to attend some of her exams, but it was difficult concentrating when you were eight months pregnant and a curious specimen amongst the rest of the girls. She hadn't been especially academic, but she'd been better than average, she would've got something. But with next to no grades, there would be no A Levels and no university. Her mother was struck dumb by her disappointment and her father was cowed into giving her barely more than a sympathetic smile when he could. The baby's father was not much more than a kid himself and Kate didn't even tell him.

It was a miserable, silent nine months while she worked weekends at the local garden centre, saving every penny she could. Then beautiful Becky had been born and she'd fallen in love with her. Two days later, Kate left the hospital and moved into the tiny house a few miles along from where she'd grown up. Her father had signed a lease for two years on her behalf (until she was eighteen) but he was unable to pay all the rent. Becky could only afford to stay off for four months and then she had to work full-time, leaving Becky with Iris. Her newly retired and newly widowed neighbour had been a godsend; she'd refused to accept anything but a token amount of babysitting money and only that to spare Kate's pride, but it had still broken Kate's heart as she'd wanted to be with her baby.

Becky's grandparents had missed Becky growing up, so it had been just the two of them, mother and daughter. Christmas cards had arrived, but Kate could tell her father had signed for her mother too. She would reply and occasionally drop in a photo of Becky, but there was never any acknowledgement of these. And then the cards had stopped altogether when Becky was six.

Having missed out on a future herself, Kate was determined that Becky would have the best possible opportunities she could afford. She worked two jobs to keep the house. She shopped at the charity stores and took advantage of whatever little perks she could from her jobs. Damaged vegetable plants from the garden centre that she'd nurse back to health and harvest a crop come the summer, leftovers from the Thai restaurant where she waitressed that were headed for the bin, and when she started at the home-and-garden centre, she took as many DIY courses as she could fit in so she never had to pay for any maintenance.

There had been little time for dates: a fling with the manager at the Thai restaurant that had ended badly when she'd quickly tired of his fantasy of shagging in the storeroom, and a few others, no one memorable. In fact, it had been more hassle than it was worth explaining about Becky, which made most twenty-somethings, and even thirty-somethings run a mile. And then, only a few weeks ago, Tim had come into the DIY centre to ask for advice. He'd been surprised at first to see a woman behind the desk (as was every man) but he'd done a good job of hiding it and had listened quite intently. She'd schooled him on the intricacies of fitting window flashings, and he'd asked her out. And for the first time in years, it felt like she had a chance to do something for herself; it was her turn.

Kate appraised her handiwork: the chips were laid out on a tray and the chocolate was in a bowl ready to melt. She went upstairs to shower and wash her hair – the same shade of auburn as Becky's. As she dried it, she smiled ruefully at the early grey strands, then tucked them in so they couldn't be seen. She spent very little time deciding what to wear; in all honesty, there wasn't a lot of choice. A clean pair of jeans and a top Becky had bought her for her birthday with money from her first pay packet. It was deep purple silk with sheer sleeves and it was the most beautiful, most expensive, most sensuous thing Kate had ever owned. She still approached it as something she hadn't yet got to know as it hung in her wardrobe, but when she put it on, it paid her compliments like they'd been friends for years.

The doorbell rang, and she ran downstairs. This was it, the night she'd been waiting for; introducing her boyfriend to her daughter. Not just a fling, but an actual, proper boyfriend, and then she realized: he was her first. At her grand old age of thirty-seven! Sometimes she couldn't quite believe it was real; she'd met a man who was reliable, fun and someone who she felt would get on with Becky, *plus* she fancied the pants off him. Life was lighter around him, and at the same time more fulfilling somehow, and with a bolt, she suddenly realized she was in love. A grin appeared on her face at this new understanding and she took a breath, fluffed out her hair in the hall mirror and opened the door.

Tim produced a large bunch of yellow tulips from behind his back. 'For you.'

'Thank you.' She kissed him long and hard and pulled him inside. She liked holding his hand. He was stocky, solid in a comforting way, and despite still being in his thirties had thick, short silver hair and a shadow of grey stubble covering his extra quarter of a chin. It was starting to rain and she shut the door on the encroaching dark and noticed the bag over his shoulder.

'Did you bring your toothbrush?'

'Not just that.' He pulled out a roll of fabric and let it unravel. Flannel plaid in a dark green.

'Flipping heck! Tell me you don't wear those.'

'You know I don't. Pyjamas are my mother's idea of a Christmas present. And . . . seeing as I'm spending my first night here, I want to be suitably attired should I get up in the night. Don't want to be embarrassing anyone on the landing. Actually, the only person I'd probably embarrass is myself.' He looked around. 'Is Becky here yet?'

'No. Probably still on the train. But she's dying to meet you.'

'Likewise. Need a hand?'

'Yes please.'

He followed her into the kitchen and she threw him an apron. 'Can you whisk?'

He looked at the egg whites in the bowl and the chocolate. 'What's this?'

'Mousse. Or it will be.'

His bright-blue eyes lit up. 'How did you know?'

'You like it? It's Becky's favourite, too.'

'Can I just stick my head in the bowl?'

Kate laughed. 'There's this fallacy that women are mad about chocolate, but in my limited experience, it's the men who are the addicts. I have friends who have to hide it from their husbands.'

'That is so cruel.'

'Ten pee bet right now that you always keep a stash in your cab.'

Tim laughed. 'I need something to soothe a day's endless ding-ding-dinging of the bell. Someone today went mental. Just because the stop was closed. Like it's my fault! And the announcement was on.' He imitated the automatic-voice system. 'This bus is going on diversion . . .'

A movement outside made Kate look up. Two police constables, a man and a woman, were heading down the path. She groaned. 'That is such bad timing. They're here to ask about Iris's fence. Across the road,' she explained. 'It's been vandalized. I'll just be a sec.'

She went to the front door and opened it as they arrived.

'Are you Miss Kate Ellis?' said the policeman. The policewoman stood next to him.

'Yes.'

'Can we come in?'

'OK, but I've only got a couple of minutes.' She gestured back towards the kitchen. 'I'm in the middle of cooking.' She smiled. 'Got a special thing tonight.'

They came in and stood in the hall. 'Is there somewhere we can talk?'

Kate hesitated. She'd rather just get it over with quickly, so she could get on, but didn't want to seem rude. 'Sure,' she said, leading them down the hall. 'Come into the living room.'

'Would you take a seat?' asked the policeman. Kate gave a minuscule frown, but she did as they asked. The PCs sat down too.

'I'm police constable Simon Andrews and this is police constable Elaine Harwood from victim support.'

'Oh, it's not my fence though, it's Iris's. I've not had any trouble.' Kate smiled and then she noticed that the two faces in front of her were different to those she'd seen out of the kitchen window that morning.

'We're here because of your daughter, Becky Ellis.' The policeman paused and she saw he looked nervous. 'I'm afraid I have some very bad news for you. Your daughter has been involved in an accident and I'm sorry to have to tell you that she has died.'

For a moment it didn't compute. Long seconds went by while the words travelled round and round in Kate's head. She looked from the policeman to the woman, but their expressions remained sombre and only then did something hideous begin to explode inside her. Pain and panic in a vicious ambush.

'What?'

They didn't answer, instead they were both looking at her to see how she was reacting, and she felt a sudden rising hysteria and anger at their subtle, microscopic observation. They were following the rules, their training, and she knew she couldn't give in, couldn't make it real. *Don't cry.*

The policewoman spoke. 'I am so sorry.' She went to reach out a comforting hand and Kate flinched. The police-woman awkwardly withdrew.

'Everything OK?' said Tim, who had appeared in the doorway.

'Is this your husband?' asked the policeman.

'I'm a friend,' said Tim, coming into the room. 'What's going on?'

Kate looked up. 'Have you left the chocolate melting on the stove?' She got up hurriedly and headed out the door. 'I need to check it.'

They followed her into the kitchen, watching her uneasily as she did her best to ignore them.

'Miss Ellis, do you understand what we are saying?' asked the policewoman, her voice suffocatingly gentle.

Kate felt herself get angry again: *do they think I'm an imbecile?* She looked at them directly for the first time. 'I want to see her,' she said defiantly. She didn't believe them, it was a mistake. They agreed instantly, and their lack of resistance unsettled her.

'See who?' asked Tim.

'Becky. They're saying she's dead.' She saw him reel and, distracted, she wondered if she should put the eggs back in the fridge before she set off, so they didn't spoil. She heard the policeman quietly repeat the news about the accident to Tim and then felt him take her hand and she looked up at him, confused and grateful.

They both followed the policeman and woman outside and the man opened the back door of the car for her to get in. Tim ran around the other side and got in beside her and she stared out the window the entire journey. It was pitch black now and still raining. The wind was blowing stronger. She remembered the weatherman saying there was a high chance of sixty-mile-an-hour gusts that night and she watched as trees buckled, resisting losing their branches. She watched as they fought to cling on.

It was a long drive, only a few miles but they had to confront the Friday-night traffic. They arrived at the hospital and Tim got out first, then ran around to open her door. She climbed out just as the wind whipped up and she was almost blown against the car. Tim took her arm and tried to shield her from the rain as they followed the policewoman towards the entrance, bright lights spilling out onto the wet pavement. It was no calmer inside; a melee of people seemed to fill the place, jostling, crowding. Looking back to check she was still following, the policewoman set off.

Kate walked down the brightly lit corridor. The lights hurt, offered no cover. She noticed how the glare didn't seem to bother anyone else, and she passed people, both medical staff and ordinary people like her, and couldn't understand why they weren't squinting. Some of them even smiled, caught her eye, as they stood aside to let her pass and she found herself getting angry at them. She didn't need her path cleared as she walked down this corridor, she didn't want to get there any faster, and she looked away. Told herself again that it was all a gruesome mistake. And it could be, it *was*. She hadn't seen Becky yet and so of course it was possible, entirely possible. Her train was probably delayed, God knows it happened often enough and there was never any phone signal just outside Victoria station so it wasn't as if Becky could call her. Or she'd forgotten, she'd got so wrapped up in that story, she'd forgotten to come home early. For a fleeting moment, she felt sorry for some other poor mother who hadn't even been told the awful news, and now she, Kate, would see that woman's daughter first, some poor unknown girl, knocked off her bike and killed.

They suddenly stopped, which seemed odd to Kate as this corridor was the same as any other.

'Would you mind just waiting here a moment?' said the policewoman, indicating some chairs lined up against the wall, and then she went through a door in front of them. Kate and Tim sat, their hands joined over the wooden arm-rests of the low-slung, wipe-clean chairs.

'This way, please,' said the policewoman, reappearing at the door. She held it open, so they could enter what was a consulting room. A doctor was sat behind a desk, but got up quickly as they came in. He offered them more seats and sat down again on the other side of the desk to them.

The door closed and the quiet was instantaneous.

'I'm very sorry,' the doctor said, and then seemed at a

loss for what to say next. With no further condolences to add, his next words felt cruelly blunt. 'Are you ready?'

Kate saw them waiting for her. It took her a moment to stand. She didn't want to go into the room that was being indicated, just off this consulting room. Then the policewoman opened the door and her legs seemed to propel her forward of their own accord, obeying the rules and requests of this hideous nightmare she was in. *It's a mistake*, the voice inside her tried to say, but it had dimmed so she could hardly hear it. Something in her throat was stopping her from breathing properly.

'Please don't move the sheet,' said the policewoman, making eye contact with her. 'It's very important.'

They waited for her to go in first and Kate felt Tim take her arm.

She stepped inside, and an animalistic moan pulsated out of her. Becky lay on a high bed, a sheet up to her neck, eyes closed. *My baby, my beautiful baby*, Kate thought, and she broke free from Tim and touched Becky's head, stroking her cheek, her forehead, with her thumb. There was a cut just above her eye and she suddenly noticed her hair wasn't covering it because they'd brushed it but the parting was on the wrong side. She had an urgent need to put her back together and she smoothed her fine auburn waves back the way they should be. There, now she looked like Becky, but in a sudden moment of horror Kate realized that wasn't what she wanted, and she felt her head fall next to her daughter's and she wept and wept.

*

They'd sat in another consulting room for over three hours before Tim softly suggested he take her home.

The taxi driver had instinctively known something terrible had happened, or maybe Tim had told him, but either way he mercifully stayed silent. Tim sat next to her on the back seat and she was aware of him glancing her way every few minutes, a worried and compassionate frown creasing his brow. After a while, the landscape grew increasingly familiar. They passed Trinity Primary, where Becky had gone to school, and Kate had a sudden image of her running towards her from the classroom on one of the rare occasions she'd been able to pick her up, Becky's arms outstretched and full of paintings and her book bag and water bottle as she'd hurled herself at her mum. Tim's hand landed softly on hers and she blinked, once, and the school was replaced by the park where Becky would go mad for the swings, taking herself higher and higher until Kate got worried and wasn't able to restrain a quick 'Careful!' The swings were now hanging idle in the wet dark, with just the occasional twitch as the wind whipped through the play area.

The taxi driver took another turn and then they were in her road, pulling up near the house. Tim paid and then ran around to open her door but this time she'd already done it. The taxi driver waited until she'd got out and then he turned his car around quickly, as if he was embarrassed and wanted to be away from whatever it was that had been inflicted upon them, and after a few seconds the tail lights disappeared as he drove around the corner.

'What the . . . ?' said Tim urgently and Kate looked up. 'Wait here,' he instructed and then ran up to the front door – which was already open – and then he was in the house and she couldn't see him anymore. A sudden glow spilled out onto the street as he switched on the hall light.

Kate followed and tentatively stepped into her hallway. Nothing had changed. She took another step, past the kitchen and then on into the living room where the police had sat just hours before.

It had been ransacked. Papers tipped onto the floor, books scattered. Recoiling, she backed out. 'Tim?' she called out, frightened.

'Upstairs,' he shouted, then added quickly, 'Don't come up.'

But she already had done and was standing behind him at the entrance to Becky's room. He tried to take her arms and steer her out, but she pushed him away. Like downstairs, the room had been turned over. The walls suddenly spun, and she grabbed the door frame. Becky's clothes, books, personal possessions all strewn across the carpet. She stared numbly as Tim punched at the wall.

'The bastards,' he cried, 'the fucking little bastards.'

Right at the edge of the room near the radiator, half-buried under some clothing, was a faded, almost threadbare oval of cloth: an ear. Blue Puppy had been snuffled and stroked and spent the majority of his early years tucked under Becky's nose as she caressed his ear with her finger. Becky had been so attached to him, Kate had always referred to him as her second child. She stepped haphazardly through the mess, quickly needing to get to Blue Puppy, and then clutched him to her. When she turned back and saw Tim, the look of pity and anguish on his face was more than she could bear.

FOUR

1995

She was mooing like a cow. A low, guttural groaning that spewed out of her body, along with a large number of fluids; in fact everything seemed to be emitting out of her except for this goddamn baby.

Christ, she was scared.

Even more so by the worried, tense faces that she glimpsed in short flashes when her eyes actually managed to focus on something, for most of the time the walls rippled, floated around the room, like those in a horror movie.

'I'm going to be sick!' Kate suddenly shouted out, a brief moment of lucidity, which brought a second of relief, despite the fact she was retching into a cardboard tray that an anonymous hospital worker held at her face. Why would you be relieved to feel nausea, to vomit? Was it because it was a reminder you were still alive?

When would it end?

The door opened. The long-awaited anaesthetist. Kate was propped up. Her back swabbed. She was told, instructed, *commanded* to keep still. The severity of the

tone indicated that if she didn't, there might be dire conse-
quences. How could she keep still when she was speared by
pain right through her abdomen? Held down on her back,
writhing in agony?

When would it end?

Then, a call. Urgent mutters. Barely controlled panic in
voices. Something was wrong.

'I need more time,' pleaded the anaesthetist.

'There is no more time!' hurtled back the reply from
someone at the polar opposite end of her ravaged body,
somewhere down by her spreadeagled legs.

It was like you read in the newspapers, magazines. The
awful thing that always happened to someone else, not
you. This time it *was* happening. The baby wasn't going to
make it.

People were doing things to her, shaving her, rapidly telling her she was going into theatre, bizarrely gaining her
permission. What? She had to sign! A nightmarish scrawl.
A joke. On her. Then suddenly—

Leaving them all behind. She was going under. Somehow,
despite knowing the outcome wasn't going to be good,
there was a sense of calm, peace.

Relief.

Dark.

Eyes open. A different view. Hospital still, but somewhere
else. The panicked people all gone.

Almost immediately, a nurse appeared. Tall with bobbed
dark-blonde hair, the same age as her absent mother. From

her position lying down, Kate could see the nurse was carrying something tiny in her arms, which she promptly laid at Kate's breast.

'She's a natural already,' said the nurse delightedly, as the small creature began to suckle.

Dazed, Kate looked down.

A baby!

Her baby.

She looked again.

It really was a baby!

'Is she all right?' she said quickly, the nightmare flooding back.

'Course!'

'I mean, they'd tell me if anything was wrong with her?'

The nurse looked shocked. Laid a tender hand on Kate's arm. 'She's perfect,' she said. 'Scored very highly in her Apgar. Nine out of ten.'

It sounded good, whatever it was.

Oh my God, she had a baby.

Her first visitors were two school friends, Lara Tomlinson with her enviable poker-straight white-blonde hair and her sidekick, Megan Taylor. They came onto the ward with a CD Walkman shared between them, but the single set of headphones rested on Lara's head, with Megan bent sideways to listen in. They were singing lightly to The Rembrandts' 'I'll Be There for You', which was swiftly interrupted and replaced by the sound of them freaking out at the noise of another baby screaming blue murder.

'How can you put up with that?' asked Lara as she approached Kate's bed.

Kate didn't want to explain that Becky made the same noise, although she was thankfully asleep at that moment. Lara and Megan leaned over the cot, cooing at how sweet she was.

'Did it hurt?' asked Lara.

Kate grimaced. 'Yes.'

'Don't think I could do that, push something that big out of my fanny.'

'You don't really have a choice.'

'Well you do . . .' started Lara loftily, leaving the rest of it unspoken: *if you don't get pregnant in the first place.*

Kate looked down at the bed and then sensed Megan nudge Lara as they offered up the CD Walkman. They shared the music with her, raving about the new series that had just started on Channel 4.

'Joey's soooo cute,' said Megan.

'How *you* doin'?' asked Lara and she and Megan burst into fits of laughter and Kate found herself smiling along even though she didn't know what they were talking about.

She attempted to get back into the conversation. 'How are the exams going?'

'Only chemistry and Latin left,' said Lara. 'Then the summer is all mine,' she drawled.

Megan nodded. 'We're going to the grammar in September. How about you?'

They were both looking at her expectantly, guileless, while Becky lay mere metres from them.

'Um . . . I'll probably give it a miss this year.' She saw them twig and glance over to the cot, and she smarted at their badly hidden pitiful looks. 'Got a full-time job lined up anyway.'

Lara sat up. 'Oh, right. Cool! Where?'

Damn, why had she said that? They were staring at her now, waiting for her answer. 'Garden centre,' she muttered.

They nodded again, pretending it was something good.

'It's just until I can get back to school,' said Kate quickly, knowing as she did that it would be almost impossible. Then suddenly Becky woke, and Kate was reminded of how such a small person could make such a piercing noise. She leaned over the cot and picked her up. Her two friends were watching, bemused.

'I need to feed her,' said Kate pointedly.

Lara and Megan still sat there, uncomprehending. Kate had no choice but to open the top button of her nightdress, her cheeks reddening as she did so. She tried to hide her enlarged breasts and cracked nipples but knew by her friends' horrified reactions they had caught a glimpse.

'Probably time we should be going,' said Lara suddenly, and Megan leapt up after her.

Kate watched them leave, knowing it would be a long time before she saw either of them again.

A day later, and in contrast to many of the ward's other grandparent visitors, her dad arrived without a cloud of balloons or weighted down by teddy bears. She'd wondered if he would come and couldn't help being overwhelmed by seeing him.

'Hello, love.'

'Dad.' Same old soft, brown eyes and slightly pinched face, worn down by her mother's anger, disappointment and sadness – feelings Kate herself had accelerated in her mother at an unbelievable pace from the moment she'd fearfully announced her pregnancy. (On a Sunday, with her mother just back from church, in the vain hope that some of the Lord's bountiful forgiveness was still lingering in her mother's scarred, hardened heart. No such luck.)

Her dad didn't look in the hospital crib at first, as if he was too scared. Then his eyes flicked across to it and his face lit up and, for a brief moment, Kate got a glimpse of how it was meant to be.

'She's as cute as a button, Katie.'

'Yeah?'

'Looks just like you did.'

He turned and smiled at her and all Kate wanted was to sink into her father's arms. But his smile faltered, and he glanced away.

'We're moving,' he blurted out.

A rising panic. 'What?'

'Back to Cork.'

It was like a punch to the gut. 'What about everything here? Your work?' She wanted to say *What about me?* but didn't.

'I've been offered a post at a secondary school.'

'That was quick,' she said accusingly.

He coughed. 'Maternity cover,' he said, embarrassed at the irony.

'When?'

He spoke but it was so quiet, she didn't catch it at first.

'Pardon?'

'Next month. I'm sorry, Katie . . . but your mother's sister – your aunt. She's ill. Your mother wants to be near her. It might not be for long. Just till she's on the mend.'

It was always the lies that were designed to spare you that hurt the most.

'You're leaving me.'

'Katie, you've already moved out.'

'I was kicked out.'

'Your mother has her faults, but she never did that.'

'Does not talking to me for seven months, *literally not one word*, not mean I was no longer there – in her eyes?'

As usual, his face clouded over, torn between the two women in his life. Kate didn't have the energy to feel sorry for him. Not anymore. The birth had taken it out of her, but it was something else too. A realization of who her father really was, of his profound weakness. She glanced at him in his brown corduroy jacket. He looked every inch the dusty maths lecturer, a man who withdrew from real life and hid behind his subject. Clinging to the only things he still understood, that never changed. Algebra. Statistics. Geometry.

He was looking at the brand-new changing bag on the chair next to her bed. 'It arrived then?'

'Yeah.' He'd posted it to her the week before, and she knew it was a secret parcel that her mother had known nothing about. Kate had come home from her job at the garden centre to find her new neighbour, Iris, had taken it from the postman to save her the mile-long walk uphill to the delivery office – something she would have found hard with the huge bump she was carrying. Inside were disposable nappies, Babygros, a blue puppy toy, £500 rolled up and tied with an elastic band, and a four-pack of Smarties, her favourite chocolate when she was little that her dad had always bought her as a special treat. It was this that had made her choke up, as it made her feel as if *she* were the child, not her imminent baby. And in many ways, she still was. The card had simply said, 'Love, Dad x.'

'I didn't know much about what to put in,' he said. 'The lady in the shop had more of a clue.'

He seemed to be looking for praise that he'd done the right thing.

'It's perfect. Got loads of stuff to keep me going.'

'Here's a bit more,' he said, tucking an envelope into the bag.

She knew it was money. And quite a bit of it, judging by the glimpse she'd got of the thickness of the envelope. She made a mental resolve to save it, put it aside with the other sum he'd given her. Suddenly she knew it was just from him, her mother didn't know about it.

'You ever think of telling her where to get off?'

'Katie!' he admonished.

'Do you?'

'She's lost four babies.'

'Foetuses. And one "baby" is still very much around.'

He said nothing, and her eyes still blazed.

'Did you ever consider . . . it might be difficult for her?'

said her dad gingerly. 'Trying for all those babies and failing, then you get one by accident?'

Her mouth dropped open with hurt and incredulity. 'So, she's jealous of me? Is that what you're saying?'

'No . . .' He shook his head, giving up. 'I'll write and send you things,' he said.

Kate nodded. 'She won't like it.'

'She won't know.' It was a rare moment of defiance from her father. *If only they weren't conducted in secret*, she thought angrily. *If only he had the balls to stand up to her.*

Her father indicated the crib. 'Can I hold her?'

'She's sleeping right now. Don't wake her.' Even as she said it, she knew that one day she'd regret her childish stubbornness. But she didn't retract her words.

He left soon after and, seemingly in protest, Becky began to cry. Kate picked her up and, as she fed her, Becky quieted.

'It's just you and me now,' said Kate to her daughter's tiny head, her voice catching. She swallowed back the tears, determined not to cry. Who was going to mop her tears anyway? It was a waste of energy. '*I'm* not going to leave *you*,' she said fiercely. 'Not ever. We'll do it, eh? Me and you.'

FIVE

2017

'Would you like to know more details about the accident?'
Sarah, the Family Liaison Officer, perched on the sofa, not
too comfortable, not too formal. Her mug of tea sat on the
table. She linked her fingers together on the tops of her
knees and her voice was soft with empathy.

It was what Kate had been dreading, and yet she had to
know. She nodded.

'Stop me at any time. If it gets too much.'

Kate quickly rubbed her face with her hands and realized
she was holding her breath. She made herself exhale.

'Becky was on her bicycle cycling south on Red Lion
Street—'

'Where's that?'

'It's just north-west of Chancery Lane underground station.'

'So, it was near her office?'

'Yes, about a mile away. A lorry was driving along the
same street. The lorry turned left in front of her path
and . . . she was trapped underneath. Are you OK?'

Kate blinked back her tears and nodded quickly. *Get it over with*, she thought; *I need to know*.

'You are aware of her injuries?' said Sarah, carefully.

'They told me she . . . she suffered massive internal injuries.' Kate's hands started to shake, and she held them tightly in her lap. Then she forced herself to ask the thing she'd been dreading. 'Was she . . . was she conscious? When she was under the lorry?'

Sarah paused. 'I'm sorry. Yes, she was.'

'How? Tell me how, exactly,' demanded Kate.

'Her pelvis was held under the wheels. She was able to ask people passing by for help.'

'Oh my God,' Kate started to sob.

'I'm so sorry.' Sarah placed a hand on hers. 'The investigation has already started,' she said. 'The police are appealing for witnesses.'

By spring, Sarah had become a regular visitor to the house. She was in uniform today, noticed Kate, with her blonde hair tied up in a high ponytail.

'Have you heard anything about the break-in?' asked Sarah.

'Nothing. The police have had no leads at all.'

'How about insurance?'

'I've filled in the forms. They only seem to have taken Becky's laptop, it was the only thing of any value and . . . I don't know . . .' She took a deep breath. 'It seems pointless claiming it.'

Sarah offered a sympathetic smile. 'Well, I do have some news.'

'Yes?'

Sarah took a preparatory breath before her announcement. 'The police have concluded the investigation and we are going to recommend to the CPS that they press charges against the driver.'

Tears threatened to well up in Kate's eyes. 'Thank God. What's the charge?'

'We are going to recommend Causing Death by Careless Driving.'

Kate frowned. 'Careless? What does that mean? It sounds . . . insubstantial.'

'There's a maximum sentence of three years.'

Her mouth dropped open. 'Three years?'

'I'm sorry . . . I know it might not sound adequate, Kate, but we have to go with the evidence, and also present what we think will enable the CPS to make a strong case.'

Kate was silent for a while, bludgeoned by yet more grief. She looked at the soft rain falling against the window. 'Can I see the evidence?'

'I'm sorry, but the investigating team don't want to disclose it.'

She looked up, taken aback, hurt. 'But it's my daughter. I need to know what happened. She was a good cyclist. She was responsible, she knew about the dangers of HGVs. She'd cycle on the quieter streets just to avoid the heavy traffic. She'd stay back when a lorry was turning – she *told* me this! Do you see? I still don't know what really happened.

Why it happened. Do you understand what I'm saying?'

Sarah gave a sympathetic smile but said nothing.

'I'm her *mother*.'

'I'm sorry, Kate, but in these cases, it seems hard . . . but the family is largely deemed irrelevant.'

She was so aghast, so demeaned, she was rendered speechless. It must be a mistake. But no, she could tell by looking at Sarah that it wasn't.

Kate tried to keep her faith in the justice system but a few weeks later, Sarah came to the house with news that shocked her further.

'I don't understand. She *died*. How can the CPS not press charges?' Kate stood up and went over to the kitchen window. Iris was watering the border at the front of her house. She'd planted a pink clematis there, for Becky, she'd said, and it was in full flower.

Kate knew Sarah was doing her best, but she found her calmness infuriating. Her shoulders were hunched aggressively as she listened to Sarah's response.

'They don't believe the case is strong enough. They don't think it will lead to a conviction.'

Kate spun around. 'What?'

'They've re-evaluated the evidence. They don't think it's strong enough,' Sarah repeated.

'I want to see the prosecuting officer.'

'That is possible. But the meeting would just be to explain their decision. The CPS don't have to justify it, nor, I'm afraid, are you able to challenge it.'

Breathing deeply to stop the pain and frustration over-whelming her, Kate forced herself to sit back at the kitchen table, opposite Sarah. She placed her palms quietly onto her knees. Appealed to her. 'But surely . . . he killed her. He says he didn't see her but that's not good enough, surely? How can that be an excuse? Why didn't he see her in his mirrors? And there was the sight test that he failed! What about that?'

'I'm very sorry, Kate, but the unfortunate truth of the matter is that the sight test was done three months after the accident.'

'So?'

Sarah looked uncomfortable. 'I'm afraid it doesn't prove that his sight was defective at the time of the collision.'

Kate was aghast. 'What? Why wasn't it done before then? On the day?'

'I'm afraid that's a question the senior investigation officer would have to answer.'

'I'm asking you.'

Sarah remained calm. 'I'll put that question to him for you.'

'You do that. The driver should have bloody seen her! Why didn't he? What was he doing? Where was he looking? I want to talk to him.' Kate had started pacing again and could feel herself getting hysterical.

'I'm afraid that's not possible.'

'Course not! Of course it's bloody not! I'm not allowed to ask or to say anything. Not allowed to question anybody. Not allowed to see any evidence. Not allowed to have an opinion. I just have to listen to all this bloody rubbish and . . .' She sat down suddenly, broken and deflated. 'She's my daughter, you know, my lovely, wonderful daughter.'

SIX

The summer passed in a haze of grief for Kate and, standing outside the courtroom, shivering in the cool breeze, she was suddenly aware it was the first autumnal day since Becky had died. Time was creating distance, but Kate didn't get any comfort, in fact it was the opposite. The pain and the longing became increasingly more acute as she was channelled further away from her daughter.

'You're sure you want to do this?' asked Tim.

'Yes,' she said. 'I want to see him.'

She meant the driver. She wanted to see what the man who had knocked down and killed her daughter was like. And there was another reason. Secretly, instinctively, she felt that the coroner would come to this inquest with the same sense of disbelief, of incredulity, that she had endured now for months. He would hear the witness statements and the police reports and conclude that this had all been dealt with incompetently and inadequately. He would recognize that someone had died, and this was the main point here, and it was inexcusable and this hideous, sickening powerlessness would be taken away from her.

They were led into the magistrates' court and the usher

showed them where to sit. There were one or two witnesses and a few officials already present but he – the driver – was not there yet. Kate had been told that here in the courtroom she would finally be able to ask questions. She clutched her bag on her lap. Inside was a piece of A4 paper. She'd written them down. She looked around the room, at the wooden panels and desks, behind which were chairs covered in a blue, woven fabric. The court was small and with a sudden realization she saw she'd be sitting close to the driver; only a few metres would separate them.

Then the usher came back in and a man followed him. He was medium-height, slim build. A neat beard covered his lower face, almost disguising a birthmark that ran across his cheek and down his neck. He had brown hair, cut short, which made it stick up a bit, and he looked as though he was in his late thirties. Dressed in an ill-fitting dark-grey suit that seemed to hang off his shoulders, he looked straight ahead. Then she saw another man was with him. Puzzled for a moment, she wondered if she'd got it wrong, but then she realized with a jolt that the second man was his solicitor. It wrong-footed her. He didn't deserve that, someone advising him on every word, every thought. Worse, she hadn't even considered getting any help herself. Such was her financial state, it hadn't even occurred to her.

She'd let Becky down. Again. She'd put her trust in the system, naively thinking seven months ago that it was so obvious the driver was in the wrong, justice would be served.

Tim put a hand on her knee as the driver sat down.

Trembling, she reached for him, and he curled his fingers around hers. She forced herself to stay locked in some sort of pseudo-composure, even though her heart was racing. She looked across, at first dreading it, but the driver didn't meet her eye. She carried on staring, convinced he would eventually glance over, until finally it dawned on her that he wouldn't and then she hated him for his cowardice. She didn't want him to have any part of this easy. She wanted him to see her pain, to know what he'd done, how he'd taken away the most precious person in her life. She wanted to go up to him and wipe that bland, tight-lipped expression off his face and shove him, punch him, scream at him over and over—

'All rise.'

The usher had spoken, and they all stood as the coroner came in. He had a bright tie on, turquoise and green, and Kate knew it was irrational, but it lifted her. It reminded her of a national newsreader who she admired greatly for his intelligence and candidness and his signature clothing was bright ties. It gave her hope.

As the inquest unfolded, Kate listened to the witnesses give their statements: the woman who had been passing when the lorry pulled Becky's bike under but had not seen anything as the wind and the rain on the night had meant she was holding her umbrella low to stop it turning inside out. She was the one who had called the emergency services, who had held Becky's hand until the ambulance arrived. The investigative policeman spoke of how the driver had been breathalyzed and was within the legal limits, how the indicator lights were working. He stated how CCTV confirmed that Becky had been fifteen metres from the lorry when the driver turned on his indicator but there was no CCTV of the actual accident site. As such, there were no witnesses to the event itself.

Then it was the turn of the driver.

'Mr Craven, if you could please state your version of events?' asked the coroner.

Kate watched as the driver spoke. He seemed calm.

'I was driving along Red Lion Street in a southerly direction, intending to turn left onto Sandland Street. I had taken a wrong turn and needed to get back onto Gray's Inn Road. I had my lights on and was travelling at eighteen miles per hour. I saw Miss Ellis in my mirrors. She was at least fifteen metres behind me. I put my indicator on then, as I approached the junction, I started to brake and checked in my mirrors again before performing my turn. I did not see Miss Ellis. I stopped as soon as . . . as soon as the accident happened.'

'And then what did you do?'

'I got out of my cab and went to the side of the road. I was told the emergency services had already been called so I waited until the police arrived.'

The coroner nodded. 'Thank you.' Kate then saw him look over at her. 'Ms Ellis, do you have anything you wish to ask Mr Craven?'

'Yes, Your Worship.'

'Please proceed.'

Kate trembled. This was it, her chance for the truth, for

clarity. She looked at the driver, but his gaze was down towards his hands. 'Why didn't you see her?' she asked.

He didn't speak. Instead, his solicitor looked up. 'My client has already said that he checked in his mirrors before turning left and did not see Miss Ellis.'

Kate bit back her frustration. 'I know that . . . but what I don't understand is *why*. In his opinion.'

The coroner interrupted. 'I should remind you, Mr Craven, that you do not have to say anything that may be incriminating.'

Just speak, pleaded Kate silently, *just tell me. Tell me what happened because I can't bear not knowing. You are the only person in the world who knows how it happened. At least give me this. Give me some explanation I can live with.*

She watched as the driver turned to his solicitor and they conversed in low voices. Then the solicitor looked up.

'Mr Craven feels that he has given all the information he can on this point and has nothing further to add.'

Kate felt something collapse, something die inside of her, and she knew the pain would never go away. She'd never know what really happened to her daughter.

She barely heard what was said in the last few minutes of the inquest, and it was only when Tim squeezed her hand that she saw the coroner look up from his notes and begin to speak.

'The deceased was Miss Becky Ellis who died at seventeen twenty-nine on Friday the twenty-fourth of February 2017 at the junction of Red Lion Street and Sandland Street in London. The means of death was collision with a heavy goods vehicle. My verdict is accidental death.'

Kate didn't see Craven leave the courtroom – she couldn't bear to and so she left as fast as she could, Tim taking her hand as they walked rapidly towards the train station. It was only as she was about to get on the train that she realized she'd left her jacket behind and cried out in dismay.

'I can't go back in there, Tim, I just can't.'

'It's OK, I'll do it,' said Tim and he walked with her back to the courtroom. Kate stayed outside, not wanting to be anywhere near the place, and she huddled against the wall as Tim went in to retrieve her jacket. *Please hurry*, she thought.

A man in a black leather biker jacket parked up his motorbike and, taking off his helmet, walked towards a street on the other side of the courtroom. He had a horse-shoe moustache and Kate frowned as she saw him approach Craven's solicitor, who seemed to be expecting him. But then Tim came back out and she quickly turned away. She didn't see the two men exchange a few words and the solicitor leave. Nor did she see the man in leathers pull out his mobile phone and dial a number.

'He got off,' he said briskly, his voice low. 'It's done.'

Message imparted, the man hung up, then walked back to his motorbike and drove off.

SEVEN

Tim was still with her at five o'clock that afternoon. He'd rung in to work to cancel his evening shift, claiming he was unwell. They'd gone back to Kate's house and he'd made lunch, then tea, and all of it had been left uneaten, the sandwiches still curling on the plates. He'd sat and asked if she wanted to talk but she didn't, she wanted to rage.

'Accident! How dare they. How dare they hide behind that word. It's not a bloody accident, accidents are unavoidable. It wasn't unavoidable, it was preventable. It had to be. There had to be a way of him seeing her. If you drive a lorry, you have to be able to see everything. Otherwise that lorry should not be on the road!'

'You're right. Of course you're right.'

'So why can't they see this?'

'I know it's awful, it's shameful, in fact . . . but they are following the rules.'

'If they are following all the rules and still this happens then the rules are wrong! Someone has to change the bloody rules.'

Tim was quiet and she stopped pacing up and down the living room, realizing how much she'd been shouting. She felt bad, but at the same time was angry at him for not ranting with her.

He stood and took her in his arms and she felt herself crumple.

'Do you want me to stay tonight?'

'Yes,' she said, crying into his shoulder. Then she pulled away and rubbed at the damp patch on his jumper. 'Sorry.' She caught his face, a glimpse of exhaustion, of worry. 'Sorry, Tim. To go on so much . . .'

He quickly smiled, reassured her. 'Don't be daft. I'm here to look after you.'

She woke the next morning feeling spent. Looking over at Tim, she saw he was already awake and was lying silently, staring at the crack in the curtains where the autumn sunlight was streaming through. She put a hand on his arm and he turned. He looked tired and she tried to remember who had fallen asleep first the night before.

'Morning,' he said.

She kissed him lightly on the cheek. Then she got up to go to the bathroom. Looking in the mirror over the sink, she saw that her once-few grey hairs now covered nearly half her head. Lines were etched around her eyes. Shadows fell under them. Something was missing. She tried smiling but the muscle movement in her face felt alien, so she dropped it.

She came out of the shower to find Tim had left the bed. Also, his clothes weren't where he usually put them, folded neatly on the floor on his side, his 'floordrobe' as he called it, and for a moment she panicked that he'd got dressed and was downstairs wanting to go home, but then she could hear him, making breakfast. She could smell bacon. *He must be 'helping me get my strength'*, she thought with a pang. It seemed like a lifetime ago that she would stay over at his flat and he'd lie in bed, enjoying watching her put her clothes on. They'd only been dating a few weeks before all this had happened. She was aware that it probably wasn't what Tim had signed up for.

She wasn't much in the mood for eating, and took her time getting dressed. She pulled on underwear and a T-shirt and that was about as far as her energy could take her. She sat heavily on the bed and wondered if the pain would ever go away.

Everyone else from the inquest had probably woken up that morning thinking of new things, something different. Now the inquest was over, the driver had dealt with the last of his inconveniences and could just get on with his life. Becky had been tidied away, the process had been *processed* and she knew she would never recover from it. It sickened her that no one had done anything, no one had changed anything, no one had taken responsibility. They had all just hidden behind the word 'accident'. Her head fell into her hands. The rules were wrong. There would have been a way for the driver to have seen Becky. There had to be. This happened far too often in London. *Why hadn't the lorry had the right mirrors?* she lamented. *Why hadn't the lorry had the right mirrors?* It seemed so simple. And if it weren't that, it would be something else simple. Simple compared to the way she was feeling.

She held her head, folded over onto her knees and wondered how long she could stay there.

It came to her so suddenly she launched herself upright. She nearly fell, had to grab the end of the bed while the dizziness passed. Then she heard Tim calling. Maybe she would have that bacon sandwich. She pulled on some jeans and made her way to the kitchen. He smiled when he saw her and switched the kettle on. 'Right, your tea is coming up. And I hope you're hungry . . .'

'Someone has to change the rules,' said Kate.

She saw him stiffen. 'You're right,' he said. 'I know that, you know that but, well, you've got to think of yourself, you can't fight 'em . . .'

'Why not?'

He looked at her worriedly. 'Kate, you've been through so much these last few months . . . maybe . . . maybe you just need to take a break from it all.'

'I can't. I can't just let her die and roll over when they tell me it was something unavoidable. It was avoidable, Tim. I've lost her and if I agree with what they say, then I'm as bad as them. My job was to protect her – *is* to protect her.'

He remained silent and she knew he disagreed. Thought she was acting irrationally. And in a way he was right. On the worktop was a plate with a just-made bacon sandwich. He sliced it and handed it to her. She looked around for another.

'Are you not having one?'

He hesitated, then looked at his watch, and the panicked feeling she'd had before came back.

'Tim . . . I know the last few months have been hard.

Hard on you, too. We'd only just met when Becky died . . . and you've been the one thing that's kept me going.' She smiled quickly. 'I didn't mean to say that – I mean, it's true, but I will be OK.' She paused. 'If you want to go. If it's all too much for you . . .'

He looked at her, mouth slightly agape. 'I need to call the depot. Check in about my shifts,' he said by way of an explanation for glancing at his watch.

Her mouth twitched. A smile. 'Sure?'

He pulled her to him. 'Of course I am, you wally. And if you want to pursue this . . . then I'm right behind you.'

She scoured his eyes. 'Really?'

'Abso-blooming-lutely . . .' he said, and relief flooded through her. Despite what she'd said, she didn't think she could be alone. In fact, he'd kept her afloat the last few months when she'd been overwhelmed with a sense of abandonment and total futility. Everything in her life up to that point had been about Becky, everything she'd done for years had been for Becky, in order to give her the chances that she herself hadn't had in life, and in one night her purpose had vanished. If Tim hadn't been with her in the mornings, he'd called her to make sure she was OK, that she'd got out of bed, got dressed. He'd given her errands, which had sometimes transpired to be unnecessary ones. And when she really couldn't face it, he'd held her, until the darkness let go of her again.

She took the bacon sandwich and wrapped it in some foil.

'What are you doing?'

'I'm late for work.'

His mouth dropped. 'You're working?'

She nodded.

'But I was going to take the day off – to, you know—'

She kissed him. 'You're wonderful. But I've realized I can only do this from within the company.'

'Eh? What company?'

'The lorry driver's!' she said, as if it was obvious. 'I've got three options: I become their safety director, unlikely; I buy the company, equally unlikely; or I buy just enough shares so I can go to the AGM.' Her voice wavered. 'Then I'll get a chance to speak.'

'You what?'

'This morning I realized I had already done the research, all those times looking at their website, trying to find out what might have happened. I've read every word there is to read about them. Including the notes from their annual general meeting. They have this section at the end: "Any other business". I am going to be any other business. And I'll ask them to change the rules. So, you see, I need to go to work because I need the money.'

He was still staring at her.

'To buy the shares,' she explained, then grabbed her bag and tucked the sandwich inside. As she headed to the door, she turned back to look at him. She smiled. 'Thank you, Tim.'

EIGHT

She worked every hour she could, every shift, every bit of overtime. The adrenaline kept her going and also a new, welcome strength. It was a feeling that, if she tried to look for it, locate it, it disappeared, but if she kept on going, did this thing she needed to do for Becky, she could sense it somewhere deep down, giving her some comfort. It was such a relief to be feeling something other than the inescapable, debilitating pain that she kept on working and thinking about buying the shares. When she was stacking tins of paint on the shelves, she would imagine herself going into a large conference room and sitting somewhere near the back. Listening. Waiting. Then it would be her moment. Would she stand up or stay seated? She composed various speeches in her head and none of them were quite right, but she still had time.

The money went into the savings account she had used for Becky's university fund and she watched every month as the number crept up. At first, she'd been afraid to find out how much she needed; a goal that was out of reach would topple her. Then one night she'd made herself switch on the computer and do some searching. The relief at finding out she only needed one share to attend was short-lived. Who would take anyone seriously who only owned a single share? So, she was determined to make as much as she could before the company's AGM.

Kate could smell Tim's cooking before she'd even opened the front door. It was nice knowing he was here, at her house, and she'd given him a key so that on the nights they met, he could come in early. He'd insisted on helping her, and if that meant making dinner when she came home late from work, that was what he would do. Tonight, they had invited Iris round and Kate could hear them chattering in the kitchen.

She kicked off her shoes and went to join them, kissing Iris on the cheek then going to hug Tim from behind as he pulled a lasagne out of the oven. She noticed a bottle of beer on the side.

'On the booze?'

'Yep.'

'Good. I could do with one.' She grabbed a bottle from the fridge and topped up Iris's wine while she was at it.

'Ooh, you'll get me all tiddly,' said Iris, but still held her glass out at full stretch.

'Dinner is served,' said Tim, wiping his hands on his apron.

'Great, I'm starving. I didn't have lunch today.'

He frowned. 'You need to look after yourself.'

'I'm fine. I've got you, haven't I?'

'Indeed, you have,' he said, wagging a finger, 'but you still need to buy a sandwich at lunchtime.'

Iris reached into her handbag as Tim started spooning lasagne onto plates.

'Before we start . . . I want you to have this.' She handed over a brown envelope.

'What is it?' asked Kate as she sat down next to her. She peered in and was met with a wodge of notes. 'Oh no, no, no . . . I can't take this.' She handed it straight back. 'It's your pension money.'

'I'm not leaving till you do, so you might as well, otherwise you'll be setting up a camp bed on the living-room floor. And I don't think my arthritis would like that very much.'

'But—'

'Shush,' said Iris, talking over her. 'It's only two hundred pounds but it all helps.'

'Two hundred pounds!' started Kate, but she was met with a stern look and knew arguing was futile. She also knew what a dent that would have made in Iris's income. 'I'm incredibly grateful,' she said softly.

'She was like a granddaughter to me, your Becky, so it's the least I can do. Now, who's for some peas?'

After dinner, once Iris had dozed off in the armchair, Tim and Kate snuck out of the living room to tackle the washing-up. The long day and the beer had got to Kate and she was quiet, happy to just dry the dishes as Tim methodically stacked them on the drainer. She leaned her head against his shoulder as she waited for the next item. 'Are you on the early shift tomorrow?'

'Yes. I'll be gone at five.'

She sighed. 'We never seem to see much of each other.'

'Are you working late?'

She nodded.

'I'll come and cook for you again.'

Kate was filled with such a rush of love, she pulled him away from the sink and wrapped her arms around his neck, then kissed him softly.

He smiled. 'That was nice.' He lifted his arms, but she still held on. 'I'm dripping.'

'Move in.'

'What?'

'Then at least we'll see each other whenever we're not working.'

Tim turned to face her. 'Seriously?'

'Why not? I know our relationship has had a funny start . . . we haven't even gone on many dates, well none, really, since . . . except that one time to the cinema . . .' She took a deep breath, suddenly realizing something. 'Sometimes I feel as if I don't really know anything about you. The accident eclipsed everything. I've been so distracted by it all.'

'Are you telling me you're asking a virtual stranger to move in with you?'

'Yes? Is that bad?'

'Usually not advised.'

'We'd save money too, living together. I could put more away!' She bit her lip, realizing what she'd said. 'Sorry.'

He smiled. 'Well, if you put it like that, how can I say no?'

NINE

2018

It was somewhere near here, thought Kate, gazing hopefully up at the trees. It had been almost ten years since she'd come to this park, just south of Crawley. When Becky had become a teenager, she'd declared herself to have outgrown it but before that they would come frequently. Actually, it wasn't so much a park as a wood, maze, cafe, petting farm and lake, all housed in 2,000 acres. She'd brought Becky here from babyhood – they'd get on the bus and escape the fumes and dirt of south London. At first, she'd push her in her pram, then later, Becky had toddled about while Kate took pictures of her hiding in the rhododendrons and exclaiming wide-eyed at the guinea pigs and lambs. Here was also where Becky had climbed her first tree – an ancient oak – and that was where Kate was headed now, as the tree had remained special to both of them; even when Becky had graduated to zip-wiring through the canopy, she'd always had to come here, just to say hello.

Of course, trees as well as children grow, and the area around where Kate used to come had changed dramatically.

Small saplings now acted as a gateway to the trees beyond, and up in the big old matriarchs, the mass of new leaves hid noteworthy branches. 'Becky's' tree had a prominent forked branch that split into two halfway up, and massive arms that curved upwards. When Kate finally saw it, she was reminded of how Becky had used one of those arms to lever herself up higher, getting three, four metres up into the canopy. Kate had only agreed to her climbing it if she promised to stay low, but Becky had gone higher when she wasn't looking and then promptly got stuck. Kate smiled as she remembered how she'd had to hitch herself up to go and rescue her, getting 'advice' from her seven-year-old daughter as she climbed, whose excuse for disobeying her mother's instructions was, 'I forgot'.

She looked up and saw the branch she'd had to coax her down from, near the little hollow in the trunk where Becky had imagined fairies lived. The same place where, on another day, Becky had climbed, more confidently this time, and planted a knife, fork and spoon in the damp cavity, that she'd snaffled from the kitchen drawer, 'so they can have tea parties', and Kate let her do it rather than hoist herself back up in the tree again. Some arguments were best left.

It was quiet here, as she was near the boundary of the park and not many people came this way. She'd been undecided, at first, as to where to go. She was tired of London, of having worked non-stop for the last few months, and needed a change of scene, to celebrate away from the house. For today was the day she had bought her shares.

Kate sat at the base of the trunk, opened her bag and

pulled out a sheet of paper. A receipt. She was now the proud owner of two thousand three hundred shares of Fresh Foods plc. She leaned back and looked up; she could see glimpses of the bright-blue spring sky through the green canopy.

'I did it, Becky,' she said, holding up the receipt. 'And not only that, I have an invitation to the AGM.'

Two squirrels chased each other through the branches and a flurry of flowers from the tassel-like catkins landed on her face.

'Oi! You know how to ruin a moment, don't you?' she shouted, then, feeling foolish and wanting to avoid an avalanche of pollen dust, got up.

Heading back to the populated area of the park, she spotted Tim. They'd arranged to meet by the lake after his shift had finished. It was full of boaters as the sun was out and numerous men were showing off their prowess with oars.

'Here,' said Kate, passing Tim the paper.

He opened it up and then stopped and pulled her into a hug, pressing her face into his shoulder.

'I can't breathe!' she said, but she was pleased he was so happy.

'You did it! So . . . what are you going to say?'

'I'll tell them who I am . . .'

'That'll be a shock.'

'And then I'll ask them to do everything they can to make sure it never happens again. Ask them to make changes. Look at all their vehicles and see what it is they need to do. I want them to make a proper project of it.'

'You sure you don't want me to come with you? You know, moral support?'

She squeezed his arm. 'I don't think it says "plus one" on the invitation.'

'OK, do your thing. Kick some ass,' he said, in a terrible American accent.

She laughed. Truth was, she didn't feel much like an arse-kicker. Kate considered herself street-smart, savvy. She'd had to be, being a single mum in a low-income job. She'd had no one to look out for her and Becky except herself. But now she was nervous. One hurdle had been crossed, another massive one lay ahead. She'd never owned a share in her life. She didn't know what happened at AGMs. How would she get the bottle to stand up in front of all those people? People who would know instantly that she wasn't some smart, educated businesswoman. She was a working-class girl who was completely out of her depth.

TEN

Kate gave her name to the young man in the nondescript white shirt and black trousers who stood at the doorway of the conference room in the nondescript hotel near a flyover in West London. She was handed a keypad as he ticked her off. She looked at him blankly. 'For the voting,' he explained and then he invited her to enter the room with a wave of his hand.

'Teas and coffees are on the side,' said the man and then he moved on to the person behind her – a man in wire-framed glasses. In fact, there were a lot of men here in this condensed space. Men milled around the coffee area, some talking in small groups, pontificating about . . . what? Shares? How much money they were making? The intricacies of restaurant-food distribution? More men were seated in the chairs laid out in rows, all facing a raised podium. Many were on their phones; some were reading sheets of paper. She had a sudden panic, as if she hadn't done her school homework. Was she supposed to have read up on something? She'd looked through the documents they'd sent with the invitation but none of it seemed to require any sort of response.

Kate went to get a cup of tea, ignoring the odd curious glance that came her way, and then looked for somewhere to sit. The top table was beginning to fill with what she presumed to be the directors, and so she quickly grabbed a chair. Unfortunately, the aisle ones were taken so she side-stepped past some knees to go about four spaces in, halfway back from the podium. She sat and listened, feeling alien in her new outfit. She had no idea what people – shareholders – wore to AGMs. Neither had the seventeen-year-old sales girl, but she'd seen a reality TV show where members of the public, usually young ones with over-inflated views of their ability, outdid each other for a position with a tycoon with a catchphrase. She was of the opinion Kate should wear a suit.

'It shows you mean business, gives you a sort of armour.'

Kate had looked at herself in the mirror. She could do with that, but wasn't convinced a blue pencil skirt and jacket with shoulder pads would provide it. And then the girl was tying a leopard-print scarf around her neck. Kate coughed.

'Sorry, was that too tight?' She slackened it, but the scarf was a step too far for Kate. She'd ended up buying the suit and a pair of shoes and had forced herself to apply a bit of make-up.

Now, she stuck the empty teacup under her chair and clutched the bag she'd bought in the charity shop for two pounds fifty to her stomach, trying to quell the butterflies that were somersaulting inside her, and listened to the man (another one!) who was speaking.

He was positioned in the middle of the group that had gathered and had stood to address the room. Gregory Hollander he was called, and he was the Chairman of Fresh Foods plc. He had tight brown curls peppered with grey and wore an expensive-looking suit. He cracked a couple of jokes in his opening speech and Kate wondered how long it had taken to write them, how prepared he was, and how he would react when she voiced her very unexpected request. It would be a while off, she realized, looking at the agenda, as there were presentations, voting and approval of accounts to get through first. It was incredibly dull and, in fact, one man fell asleep an hour in, his chin tucked into his chest, his arms folded.

At the coffee break she did her best to avoid everyone, not feeling in the mood for small talk as her nerves were growing as the morning wore on. She saw another woman – older – catch her eye; she was about to come over, but Kate couldn't face speaking to anyone and, in a panic, she turned her back, silently apologizing for her rudeness. She escaped to the ladies' and waited in there a full ten minutes until she knew it was time they were all back in their seats, then she slipped into the room and found her place.

At last it came. The Company Secretary stood and, in a slightly cautious voice, asked if there was any other business.

It was her chance. This was what she'd been waiting for.

No one else said anything. Kate found she was shaking. What was the matter with her? *Now! You have to speak now!* Was it the men? The fact she was one of only two women in a roomful of suits? She could handle men – she did all the time. She'd lost count of the times she'd had to explain that they *were* speaking to the DIY advisor. And only last week, seemingly unable to cope with this revelation, some idiot had made a comment about the size of her breasts and she'd been so annoyed she'd looked down and then screamed as if she'd never seen them before.

She could do this. She had earned her place here.

'Hello, yes, I have something to say,' she said. She stood up so quickly, her chair scraped back noisily on the floor. The sound rang out around the room.

'Yes?' prompted the Company Secretary.

'Last February, a girl – a young woman called Becky Ellis – was cycling in central London when she was knocked off her bike by someone driving one of your trucks. She was killed. Despite the coroner's verdict at the inquest, I don't believe in calling it an accidental death. It was avoidable. I'm convinced by this. I would like to ask you, all of you sitting up there, to look at ways of modifying your lorries so that it never happens again.' She paused and then remembered to add: 'My name is Kate Ellis and I am Becky's mum.'

ELEVEN

Silence. Should she sit or remain standing? Dozens of eyes were on her, but some were too awkward to meet her gaze. The sleeping man had woken up and was looking right at her. One of the directors was whispering in the Company Secretary's ear. Another looked deeply uncomfortable. Then one person started to clap, a spasm of noise in the room. The woman she'd snubbed. A rush of gratitude.

The Chairman – Gregory – stood. 'First of all, I would like to say how sorry I am for what happened. It was a great shock to all of us and we'd never had any accident before, nor have we since. That's not my way of dismissing your request,' he added quickly, 'on the contrary, I second your fellow shareholder's sentiment.' He indicated the lady who'd clapped. 'I think it would be very helpful for us to meet separately. Would you agree?'

Kate nodded.

'Perhaps in my office tomorrow? If you're free . . . my PA could confirm a time with you.'

He smiled, and Kate felt a tidal wave of relief so strong tears were pricking her eyes. She smiled at Gregory, at the room in general, not caring if anyone was looking. She clutched the back of the chair in front of her as her legs were distinctly wobbly and she was light-headed with a new, extraordinary fact. She'd done it.

She was conscious that she hadn't done *all* of it, as she followed Gregory's PA, Maddie, along a wooden-panelled corridor to his office in Belgravia the next morning. He hadn't promised anything at the AGM and she was braced for a fob-off, a business-speak reason why they couldn't change their lorries' design, which would be dressed up as something incomprehensibly technical but was actually down to money.

Kate didn't have another office-suitable outfit so, rather than repeat the suit, she was wearing her least-scruffy jeans and a shirt. Gregory met her at his office door as she approached and, when Maddie went off to make teas, he led her in. She sat in a club chair, he opposite. His trousers rode up and she saw his sock-clad ankles – a fine, dark-grey material with sheen, perhaps silk. A light-pink tie lay confidently over his belly; no middle-aged spread, he had the look of a younger man. He thanked her for coming and she noticed a quiet air of capability, of inner strength, of solidity. Despite herself, she found she was warming to him and she momentarily forgot the pre-rehearsed gags in his speech as here, now, there was something self-effacing in his very manner, the way he'd shaken her hand without being overbearing, his respectfulness around her; there was nothing grand or pompous about him at all.

He sat forward in his seat, held his hands together on his

knee. 'Before we get down to brass tacks, I just wanted to say how much I was impressed, moved, by what you did yesterday.'

'Thanks.'

'It was inspiring.'

'Thanks,' said Kate again. She smiled but gave nothing away. He sounded genuine enough, but she wasn't here for praise.

He seemed wrong-footed by her lack of response, ran his hands back along his thighs, sat up straight. 'Right. Well, I've already spoken to our Head of Transport and, as you may well be aware, we source our vehicles from an outside truck-haulage manufacturer . . .'

. . . so there's nothing we can do, finished Kate inwardly. She braced herself. *How dare he? How dare he publicly invite me in here on some pandering PR exercise to make his company look responsible and caring, and yet do nothing?* She knew it, she bloody knew it. She'd come so far; it had cost her so much. And all those months working . . . just to have the door slammed in her face. She kept her voice level. 'You know there's something about you, your type, that just winds me up.'

His eyes widened. 'Pardon?'

'Sitting there in your fine-leather chair, in your fancy suit, pretending you're so caring, that your company is not just about how much money you can make, giving me the fake pat on the shoulder and then doing some spin about complicated contracts and how it's just not your fault but you will look into it, you will not rest, except the minute I walk out of here you'll be ordering a coffee from your PA and moving on to the next item in your very busy money-making agenda, and you'll never even spend another nanosecond of your oh-so-precious time thinking about it, about the thing that killed my daughter—'

'We're investigating additional cameras and sensors for the trucks—'

'And even though you have the opportunity, *you*, Mr Hollander, you who has the power— What?'

'We already meet current legislation – of course – but we're doing a risk assessment on some additional features. Revising the front-passenger windows, too. We're hoping to have the entire fleet modified by the end of this summer. Maybe earlier. It's a question of how long the tests take . . . and, I'm afraid, the outside fitters. But I'm pushing for very little delay.'

Kate stared at him, dumbfounded.

'That's what you wanted, isn't it?' He seemed, again, wrong-footed by her silence.

She smiled, the first genuine one of the meeting. 'Yes,' she said. 'Yes, it is.'

'We feel responsible. I feel responsible,' he said, 'and I know nothing can bring your daughter back but what happened . . . it's never going to happen again. Not while I'm here.' He looked her straight in the eye. 'The driver, he's been dismissed.'

'He has?'

'Yes. Some time ago.'

Kate nodded tightly. 'Thank you.'

'There's one other thing. I was wondering . . . would you like it if I stayed in touch personally? To keep you updated with progress? The first set of results should be in in a few days.'

She smiled again. 'I would like that very much.'

TWELVE

Becky sat at her desk pretending to type, to be really engrossed in what was on the screen in front of her. It was positioned in such a way that her peripheral vision could still capture what was going on five metres ahead of her in her boss's glass-walled office, without having to look directly at it.

Terence Cooper was on the phone, as he had been for the last sixty-seven minutes. She was counting her lucky stars she could see in. He often enjoyed letting the metal venetian blind race down the window, then peering through, as if he were in some Hollywood investigation movie, and Becky had a sneaky suspicion he did this because it appealed to his ego, because Terence (never Terry) had a big ego. You kinda had to, to get as high up as he had in journalism. Granted, it was restrained, camouflaged by the passion he displayed for his craft and for rooting out a story about the scandal of the politicians' expenses, or covering the shock election win for Trump (something she'd been proud to have helped him on), but still, it was an ego. He knew he was good. And Becky was in awe of him. His thirst for ferreting out the truth inspired her, and that was the explanation she had all lined up should she get busted.

She risked a glance up – he was still on the bloody phone. Another glance at the clock: she had to leave in four minutes or she'd miss her train. Why didn't he finish the call, which should have been over twenty minutes ago, and go to his appointment that she knew he had in the diary at somewhere across the other side of town? Then she could get out of here. Becky was very aware some very difficult questions would be asked of her if Terence knew she'd spent several hours over the last few weeks not in the office, not doing her designated work, but doing her own rooting around.

She suddenly realized she was being watched. Piers, the other graduate, the one who was wealthy, who'd had no need of a scholarship, who'd been to Oxford. The one who was also going for the job of reporter, currently the only job opening at the newspaper. He always came to work in an impeccably crisp white shirt, which seemed to make his black skin glow with determination and superiority. He was looking at her quizzically and she forced a nonchalant, chin-on-hand perusal of her screen.

Hurry up! Hurry up! The clock ticked over another minute, the hand literally shuddering as it landed on the next black line. And then, miraculously, Terence put down the phone. Part of her worried he was so late he'd changed his plans, but he grabbed his jacket off the back of his chair and came haring out with a brief 'Got that research yet?'

'On it,' answered Becky immediately. 'Be ready by end of today.'

And then he was gone. She gave him two minutes – it was all she could allow – then casually picked up her ruck-sack from under her desk, with her things already packed away inside.

'Going somewhere?'

She looked up to see Piers hulking over her desk. She couldn't afford to wait, to pretend to be going to the toilet, she just didn't have the time.

'Only you seem to be leaving the office early.'

'None of your business,' she said as she stood. 'And I suggest you keep it zipped if you know what's good for you.'

'Feisty! I like that in a lady.'

'Not got time for this, Piers.'

'Hey, liking the dress,' he said as Darcy, the young PA, approached in a fitted red number.

She blushed and held out a Post-it. 'Phone number you were after.'

'Thanks.' Piers beamed at her and she blushed again, looking over her shoulder at him as she made her way back to her desk.

Becky ignored them both and made her escape.

Careful, careful, don't run any lights, she thought, pulling up quickly at a junction where the traffic lights had just turned red. Cycling in London was precarious enough without taking any stupid risks. She could still make it, if the light changed this side of Friday, and then it did, and she was the first away. Cars quickly flew past her and in another five minutes she turned into Victoria station. Three minutes to buzz her travel card and jump on the train – which she just managed as the platform dispatch guy blew his whistle. She was on!

There was a glimmer of real possibility about this story she was investigating, but it was early days. It wasn't anywhere near good enough to win her the job – not yet. She only had a few covert interviews, but Becky was determined to dig for that little thread, something that she'd pull on so it would unravel into something that would capture the public's imagination, that would cause a domino effect in the sphere she was investigating. This both scared and excited her. She hadn't told anyone yet. Terence would likely go ballistic, but she wanted to do her homework and find something concrete.

If she was honest, she wanted to go into Terence's office, tell him what she'd discovered and have him jump up from his desk. He'd admonish her (severely but briefly) and she'd take it on the chin because, after that, he'd be looking at her with a new kind of respect, praising her ability to find a story of such magnitude. She'd be summoned in to see the editor and Terence would describe her achievements in his usual pithy way, which just made them sound even more remarkable. And then she'd be offered the job of reporter, beating Piers fair and square. Becky allowed herself to linger on this fantasy for a moment and then smiled; it seemed as though Terence wasn't the only one with an ego.

She got off the train at Ramsbourne and, pulling her

scarf up over her mouth to protect against the cold, cycled the short distance to Hawthorne Lane and rang the bell at number twelve. This was the last of her interviews in the village.

The door was opened with a flourish. 'Hi!' A lady with cropped blonde hair beamed back at her.

'Hello, Mrs Stamp?' said Becky, holding up her ID. 'I'm Becky Ellis. From the *Herald*.'

'Grace, please. And excuse my appearance,' she said, indicating her apron and her white-dusted hands, 'but I promised the boys scones for tea. It's all about the cream,' she added by way of explanation, 'they're mad for it. Can we talk while I just finish cutting them out? Then I'm all yours.'

'Course,' said Becky, following her into the warm kitchen with its large range cooker. She looked about for 'the boys' but couldn't see any. 'Sorry to catch you at a bad time.'

'No, it's fine. Just busy, you know, now the kids are home from school.'

Becky smiled.

'So, living in the country, is it? Your article?' said Grace as she rolled out the sultana-studded dough.

'That's right,' lied Becky, leaning against the door frame.

'You can sit down, you know,' said Grace and then, just as Becky was about to, added, 'Actually, before you do, can you stick the kettle on?'

Becky followed her nod and, seeing a red kettle on the side, went to fill it.

'People from the city? Moving to the green?'

'You got it,' said Becky. 'For one of the Saturday supplements. So what happened to you? You fancied a change of scene?'

'We wanted a garden. Both Nick – that's my husband – and me. I was pregnant with the boys. We lived in Clapham at the time – nice common but it's not the same as having all this in your back yard.' Grace nodded out of the kitchen window.

Outside, it was already beginning to turn dark, the winter sun giving up its weak efforts, having barely got above the height of the dark, barren trees, whose branches were now silhouetted against the purpling sky. Becky could see the attraction – even in deepest winter there was a beauty in all that space. Beyond the garden was a large field patterned with fallow rows that still held the remnants of a recent snow flurry, the soft whiteness now turned to an icy filigree.

'Wow, fields right outside your window,' said Becky.

'Yes, we're very lucky.'

'Crops?'

'Uh-huh . . .'

'Which?'

'All sorts. Wheat, oilseed rape, winter beans. They all look beautiful, the colours on such a large scale, the bright-yellow rape, or my favourite is the wheat when it's got a bit of height and the wind makes patterns in it.'

'Is it ever left for pasture?'

'Not since we've been here,' said Grace, putting the scones in the oven.

'Do you manage to spend much time outside? Ever see it get planted – or the crops reaped?'

'Oh yes, all the time. I'm a right country bumpkin now – the boys too. We know all the stages in the crop cycle.'

Becky smiled. 'Oh yeah? Such as?'

'Well, you know, ploughing, then sowing, then spraying. Then you just keep your fingers crossed for the weather. If it's a dry spring the plants are never as big.' Grace gazed out the window. 'Yes, we're always outside. That's what we came here for.'

'So, the boys enjoy it?'

'You can ask them yourself.'

Becky looked up with keen interest as two five-year-olds came running in, clutching contraptions made of Lego.

'Boys, this is Becky and she's going to write about us in her newspaper,' said Grace.

'Why?' one of them immediately demanded.

'Because you have what seems like a huge amount of fun in the country,' said Becky, 'and I'd like to know about it.' She bent down to the boy's level and studied his face, his short hair – shorter than his brother's. Other than that, and the fact he was the tiniest bit smaller, they were identical.

'I have pets,' said the boy.

'No, we don't. Not real ones,' said his brother.

'Yes, I do,' retaliated the smaller boy.

'Whoa, easy, boys,' said Grace. 'Arnie, here, likes to keep worms.'

'We were going to get a dog but then Arnie got ill,' explained the other boy, John.

Becky knew this, as she'd already heard it from a neighbour in the village, but she pretended to be surprised.

'He's had leukaemia,' said Grace, 'but is in remission now.'

'Does that mean we can get a dog now, Mummy?' asked Arnie.

Grace knelt down to him and took his hands. 'We're just waiting to make sure you're one hundred per cent strong again first.'

'I'm strong. Look at my muscles!' Arnie flexed both arms, his eyes shut tight he was squeezing so hard.

'So you are! Now, why don't you two go and play because it's still a few minutes until scone time.'

'Is there cream?' shot John.

'Yes! Now go!'

As they ran out, Becky smiled. 'They're adorable. I'm sorry to hear about Arnie.'

'Thanks. I'm just glad they're getting time together again. It was pretty hard when Arnie was in hospital, and even when he was at home, he was often too weak to really do anything. They missed each other so much.'

'What type of leukaemia did Arnie have?'

'Acute lymphoblastic.'

'How long ago?'

'That he got ill? We had the diagnosis 3 July last year.' She shuddered, remembering. 'But let's not talk about that. You want to hear about leaving London for life in the countryside.' A buzzer went off and Grace pulled the scones out of the oven and put them on the side to cool. As she picked them off the baking tray, she wrinkled her nose. 'They're hard. Again! I can never seem to get this right. Ah well, we'll just smother them with cream.' She turned to Becky. 'So . . . the way the air smells different, how I can just walk outside my back door and go for miles across footpaths without ever seeing a car, the hideous commute back to London . . . ?'

Becky smiled and pulled out her notepad. 'All of the above.'

She typed up her notes on the train journey home. They had nothing to do with living in the country. At some point she'd have to come clean, but she still had work to do. The evidence was there in abundance, she thought, but it wasn't anything new. Not yet. She still needed to uncover something no one had found yet – something watertight. It would make the article like dynamite. Becky shivered a little as she contemplated the potential repercussions. But wasn't that what the best investigative journalism was all about? Holding unsavoury people to account? If she could find what she wanted, Terence wouldn't be able to pick holes in her story, in fact he'd be dazzled by what she'd achieved. Then she'd be able to tell Grace and the others what she was writing about. And she'd be offered the job.

For a moment, Becky imagined telling her mum. She'd take her out for dinner, maybe somewhere quite posh – posh for them anyway – and she'd buy some proper champagne. She'd watch her mum's face as she told her the news; that she was going to be the new reporter at the *Herald*. *Mum, this is all because of you*, she'd say. *Because of everything you've done for me over the years.*

Becky pulled herself out of her reverie and read back over what she'd written. It all seemed complete, accurate, except for one thing. She'd deliberately changed the names.

'You're late again!' called through Kate from the kitchen as Becky shut the front door behind her.

'Working,' said Becky, going to join her mum.

'Did you get the porridge oats?'

Becky pulled a packet out of her backpack. 'Your text arrived just as I was passing the supermarket.'

'Flipping heck! Organic? How much did that cost you?'

'It's better for you.'

'Not for my purse.'

'My treat,' said Becky wryly. 'It's actually only thirteen pence more for the same-sized bag.'

'Well, I hope they taste thirteen pence better.' Kate put them in the cupboard and turned to her daughter. 'So, you not gonna ask?'

Becky realized her mum had a big grin on her face. 'What? You've won the lottery?'

'If only.'

'Pay rise?'

'Guess again.'

'I give up.'

'I have . . .' Kate paused and took a breath for dramatic effect, '. . . a date.'

Becky stopped still. 'A *date*?' she said, as though she'd never heard the word before. 'With a . . . man?'

'What else?' Kate waited for a response, her nerves

kicking in the longer Becky took to congratulate her. It had been a long time since she'd last been asked out – nearly two years – and that hadn't gone well. In fact, she'd considered turning this one down as her history with dating wasn't in the least bit successful, but something had made her throw caution to the wind and say 'yes'. Then Becky engulfed her in a hug.

'Whoo! Who is he?'

'His name is Tim. I met him at work.'

'Colleague or customer?'

'Customer. New one. That is, I'd never seen him in the shop before. He asked me for my advice on fitting window flashings. Several times.'

'How do you mean?'

'He came in on Monday and I talked him through it, gave him a leaflet. He ends the conversation by asking if I fancy a drink, but I told him I don't date customers. So, he's back in Tuesday saying he doesn't understand the leaflet. I end up drawing him a diagram. He asks me out again. I still say no. Next thing, he's back at the help desk this morning. With a bunch of flowers.'

It was at this point Becky noticed the yellow roses in a vase on the kitchen counter. 'Blimey. He's persistent.'

'Yes. I'm not sure what made me change my mind.' Kate's eyes wandered to the blooms. 'Hmm. Anyway, he wasn't wearing a ring. Got all his own hair. And he seems nice. At the very least, we can talk DIY.'

'How old is he?'

'I didn't ask for his birth certificate. Mid-thirties?'

'And still single? Something wrong with him?'

'Something wrong with me?'

Becky looked chastised. 'Sorry. Course there's not. You're a catch.'

Kate raised an eyebrow.

'So, when are you seeing him?'

'Saturday. He's taking me to dinner. That OK?'

'Mum, of course it's OK,' said Becky. 'I don't need a babysitter anymore, you are free to live your life now that you are released of the burden of bringing me up.'

'Never a burden.'

'You know what I mean. I'll probably be working late again, anyway.'

'What *is* making your hours so long?'

Becky paused. She didn't like lying to her mum.

'Just got a tough boss. Big story. Got to prove myself, you know how it is.'

'I do. What's the story?'

'I'm sworn to secrecy.'

'No one will know if you tell me.'

'Mum, stop it.'

'A clue?'

'No. Now, why don't you tell me more about this Tim instead.' Becky went to the fridge, pulled out a half-drunk bottle of wine and poured two glasses in a determined effort to change the subject.

She couldn't tell her mum what she was investigating yet, there was still too much that could go wrong.

THIRTEEN

2018

'Pinch me!'

Tim did.

'Not there!' Kate laughed, slapping his hand away from her bum.

'You're most definitely not dreaming. You are one bona fide, deal-making, share-holding, arse-kicking hot lady.'

'Salt and vinegar?' asked Donny, from across the counter. His fish and chips were legendary, and Kate and Tim were out to celebrate her victory.

'Yes, please,' said Tim. 'Tell me again how he looked when you gave him a bollocking.'

Kate pulled a face, what she thought was part-surprise, part-bemusement, part-alarm.

Donny frowned. 'Was he constipated?'

Kate snorted and indicated the two plates of food. 'How much?'

Donny brushed her away. 'On the house.'

'No . . .'

'Don't argue. That's a fine thing you did today, and Becky

would've been proud.' He smiled. 'We're all proud, eh?' and with a nod of respect he went to serve his next customer.

They sat at a table in the window, the early-evening high-street bustle unfolding in front of them. The first workers to escape; mothers of young children herding their offspring home to bed; the older college kids with their lanyards around their necks, congregating in packs at the bus stop and outside the corner shop.

Tim lifted a chip. 'To safer trucks,' he toasted, and Kate tapped his chip with one of hers.

'Safer trucks,' she echoed. The pain of losing Becky was ever present, but what she'd achieved was no mean feat and maybe it would go some way to making her heartbreak more bearable. She could tell Tim knew what she was thinking. She still marvelled at how he'd come into her life and at such a difficult time, too. Some men would have found it too much – understandably, in many ways – but he'd stuck it out. She'd sometimes wondered if there had been another reason he'd stayed around, but then chided herself for being ungracious.

'Thanks, Tim.'

'What for?'

She took his hand. 'I'm incredibly lucky. I couldn't have done it without you.'

'You know what I think? I think that's bollocks because you're strong and you know what you want.' He winked at her and made his voice sultry. 'You're my kinda gal, Caitriona Ellis.'

She laughed. 'Really, you've got to work on that accent.'

'I'll have you know I was offered a place at Prada.'

'RADA, you buffoon,' she said, caressing his stubbled cheek.

He held her hand against his face and, leaning across the table, kissed her long and hard.

Kate still woke early the next morning, even though it was her day off. Force of habit after all those extra early shifts. But she didn't just have the day off; she had the rest of the week. Imagine! She stretched in bed. Tim had left at five to go to work, and the whole day lay ahead as hers and hers alone. She decided she'd have the luxury of reading in bed and, plumping up the pillows, she settled back with a romance book she'd started several months earlier but never had time to finish. Oh, this was the life! But after a few pages, she looked around the room, twitchy. Maybe she'd just get up instead, sort out the garden or something.

After a shower, she went downstairs to see a large note taped to the fridge: 'ENJOY YOURSELF!' She smiled and made breakfast, then went outside with the secateurs with the intention of cutting back some of the previous year's growth, but not even the cathartic job of tidying the bedraggled roses could settle her. She felt strangely at a loss, nothing to work towards, nothing to strive for. This wasn't what she'd been expecting at all. She was meant to feel settled, gratified with what she'd achieved, not have ants in her pants.

Company. That was what she needed.

Even though Kate allowed an extra five minutes for Iris

to get out of her chair and make it to the front door, it still didn't open. The windowsill was clear which meant that Iris had put Constanza away, so she'd clearly got up OK. She must have gone out. Maybe playing dominoes with one of her friends. Kate looked back across the street. She didn't want to go home, back to her empty house. She stood, indecisive for a moment, and then suddenly knew she needed to get rid of some of her excess energy and headed for the bus stop.

After a vigorous walk around the lake, Kate wandered amongst the trees, instinctively heading for 'Becky's'. She stopped and looked up. Yep, it was still there. Now what? She contemplated a walk the opposite way around the park, but it didn't appeal. She looked up at the tree again and then put her hands on the lowest branch and heaved herself up. Her feet came too and, before she knew it, she was surveying the park from a metre off the ground. The impulsiveness helped ease her unsettled feeling and she had a little giggle and carried on climbing, higher and higher still, giddy on the madness, the recklessness of it, until she was a good four metres up.

She sat on a horizontal bough and caught her breath. Looked towards the ground but felt dizzy and so quickly lifted her head. She'd figure out how to get down in a minute. Up here, where the warm spring breeze tickled the new leaves, she felt a release, free from the restlessness that had been binding her earlier. She clutched the trunk, smelt its earthy reassurance. There was a hollow just below her waist and she realized she was at the spot that Becky used to call the fairy home. She instinctively looked for the knife and fork, then remembered they were no longer there – Becky had brought them down when she'd changed it to a parking spot for alien ships. She glanced in again, wishing some part of her daughter was still there, and it was then she saw a bit of clear plastic. A bag tucked in the hollow. For a moment she just looked at it, puzzled, then reached in and pulled it out. It was sealed, a small clear bag that could be used for sandwiches, only in this one there was a memory stick.

She suddenly wanted to get down. Pocketing the bag, she slowly descended, finding it much harder than going up. Retrieving her jacket from the foot of the tree, she headed back across the park.

The bag sat by the kettle while she made tea, something to stall the opening of it; a bracing tactic. She wondered whose it was. It might not be Becky's, probably wasn't, she told herself sternly. The memory stick probably didn't even work – had been damaged by months, maybe even years, of cold and wet.

She took it into the living room and plugged it into the drive of her ancient beast of a computer. The memory stick appeared as an icon on her screen. It had no name. She double-clicked and the computer chattered and whirled and then a box popped up. In it was a single file, entitled 'R'. She clicked again. A document opened up and on it was a list of names, addresses and phone numbers. A glance told her she knew none of them, but the patterns of their post-codes looked familiar. They all started with TN – in fact they were all in the same place: Ramsbourne in East Sussex. She scrolled further down but the document stubbornly stopped moving. There was nothing else there.

What was it? Was it Becky's? Who were all these people? She didn't know the answers to any of these questions and, frankly, probably never would. *Unless* . . . No, that was a mad idea. A few more clicks on the computer and she discovered that a train ran to Ramsbourne every thirty minutes from London Victoria. The journey took an hour. *Only an hour!* But it was silly, pointless really. What was she going to do when she got there? But what was she going to do *here* . . . It was the country. Be nice to get out of London, enjoy the sunshine. Fresh air! It could be a day trip. A nice little excursion to the countryside. Before she changed her mind again, she took a single slurp of the tea, grabbed her bag and headed out.

FOURTEEN

The train-door button flashed and beeped as it opened. Kate was the only person to get off in her carriage and as she looked each way down the platform, trying to locate the exit, she saw only three other people: a sprightly-looking retired couple kitted out in rambling gear, maps in plastic pouches around their necks, and a girl in her late teens, long dark hair swinging as she ran down some steps to what Kate saw was the car park. The girl leapt into a small silver Mini that was driven by a woman who looked like she could be her mother and they were off. When Kate looked round again, she saw the ramblers had gone too, swallowed up into the green. A public-footpath sign, down the side of the station, was the only indication of where they might have vanished.

It was quiet. Deathly quiet. As she walked through the ticket office, she saw the station was unmanned – off-peak hours most likely didn't warrant the expense of a salary – and it unnerved her that there was no one to talk to, no one to help her find her way on this wild goose chase she'd embarked on. Looking around, it was apparent the station was not in the village centre. It seemed to be miles from anything. An empty road passed in front of her, disappearing into trees and more countryside. She got out her ancient, cracked phone to locate herself in the maps app – but there was no signal. What should she do? Walk? Which direction? For a moment, she contemplated going over to the opposite platform and taking the next train back home. Then a ladybird landed on her arm and Kate was buoyed by its arrival. Two tiny blue butterflies skitted across the heads of some cow parsley growing by the perimeter fence. A blue tit watched her from the ticket office windowsill. This place was beautiful.

'Oh!' she exclaimed as the ladybird flew off but, as she followed its direction, she saw up ahead a small railway outbuilding with a sign outside that lifted her heart: 'Taxis'.

As she walked towards it, she saw that it, too, looked ominously quiet. The door was shut tight. Then she heard a toilet flush, a whistling and the hut door flew open.

'Whoa!' said a man, clutching his chest. 'You'll give me a heart attack.'

Kate wasn't sure if he was joking or not. He'd said it lightly enough, but he was grey and tired-looking, appearing to be in his fifties but she suspected he was younger.

'Sorry. No harm intended . . .'

'None done.'

'Oh, good.' She paused, wondering if he was the right person to ask. 'Can I get a taxi?'

'Sure thing.'

'I need to get to Hawthorne Lane.'

This seemed to make him even more tired. 'Minimum fare five pounds,' he said pointedly.

Kate smiled. 'Fine.' She followed him to his car, a care-worn, middle-of-the-road estate, and got into the back, opening the window to waft away the overpowering smell of the cheap cardboard air freshener. She caught snatches of birdsong as they drove down narrow country roads. It was beguiling, idyllic, but she couldn't fully enjoy the journey as her mind was on her destination. She'd picked the first address on the list for no other reason than it was the first, but she still had no idea what she was going to do or say when she got there. Nor if she'd be welcome. She half hoped the residents would be out, then she could just enjoy the scenery and head back.

'What number?' asked the cab driver.

She needed time to compose herself. 'Could you just drop me at the end, please?'

He glanced at her in the mirror but said nothing, and two minutes later she was stepping out of the car. She handed a fiver through the window. 'Thanks.'

'No problem. Here.' He gave her a business card with 'Rob's Cabs' on it. 'In case you need to come back.'

She nodded, and then he was gone. She listened to the car speed away from the distant junction, then listened again. Nothing. Nothing except a persistent bird chirruping. Somewhere far off she thought she could hear a lawn-mower, but it suddenly stopped, and she wondered if she'd imagined it.

A sign – dusty with green mildew – a few metres from

where she stood told her she was in Hawthorne Lane. Large oaks gripped the verge, their still-small leaves dicing up the weak sunlight as it hit the road. Kate pulled her old leather jacket tighter and started to walk. The houses were tucked back from the edge of the road down daffodil-lined driveways; the happy yellow tops of the flowers head-banged in the breeze. She could smell the warm pleasant scent of an open fire from a nearby home. The first house was number five – something that struck her as odd. Where were numbers one to four? She carried on further; each house she passed was different from the previous one, each individual and characterful. But they were all old with a solidity that exuded comfort and security. They seemed wise, if houses could be considered as such, having laid their sturdy mortared arms around centuries of families.

Number twelve was particularly charming – a reddish-bricked detached house at the end of a gravel drive. A bright-green front lawn was the backdrop for a tree bursting with delicate pink-and-white blossom. Yellow painted shutters lay flat against the brickwork. This was it. Kate instinctively sighed. It was a place anyone would want to live in. As did Grace and Nick Stamp – or at least it was their names on the document she'd found. Were they still there? Did they know Becky? It was now or never, Kate decided, and she walked up to the glossy black front door. Rang the bell. There was no turning back now. Not unless she made a run for it. The silliness of this made her smile and it was still on her face as the door was opened by a woman in her mid-thirties with short, pixie-like blonde hair.

Kate instantly knew her visit was unwelcome, an inconvenience. The woman looked harassed.

'Yes?' she said brusquely.

'Hi. I'm . . . I was wondering if you might be Grace Stamp?'

'Yes,' the woman said again, and then while Kate hesitated, 'what do you want?'

'Um . . . I was wondering . . .' started Kate again, 'do you by any chance know a young woman called Becky Ellis?'

Grace frowned, partly suspicious, partly just thinking, then said: 'The journalist?'

Kate smiled, a mix of joy, relief. A connection.

'Who are you? Are you from the same paper?'

Kate was about to correct Grace when a small boy appeared at her hip. He was bald. Her smiled slipped.

'Because if you are, you can forget it. Yes, I do know Becky, but I haven't seen her for over a year. I'm not in the mood for time-wasters, for being picked up and dropped whenever it suits you. In fact, you can leave right now,' she added wearily and started to close the door.

'No, wait—'

'I'm busy.'

The door shut in Kate's face. An unceremonious rebuff.

It was a moment before she recovered enough to walk back down the driveway. She stopped in the lane and glanced back at the house. Felt embarrassed. And that poor boy . . . was he ill?

But Becky had been here.

Why? This was a part of her daughter's life that she knew

nothing about. It might be something small, something random that had no bearing on anything else, but it was *something she didn't know*. She suddenly, desperately wanted to. She marched back up the drive and rang the bell. Twice. The door opened in an irritated flourish but before Grace could say anything, Kate declared: 'Becky was my daughter and the reason she hasn't been in touch for a year is that she was killed in a road cycle crash last February. I'm here . . . I'm here because I think she may have been investigating something and . . . because I miss her.'

This time the door stayed open.

FIFTEEN

'She asked us what it was like moving out to the country from London. So not really investigating anything, unless you count my horrendous baking skills. We came here when I was three months pregnant – that was nearly seven years ago now.' Grace smiled. 'We had this tiny little one-bedroom flat with no garden and there just wasn't enough room for babies as well, so we went from an expensive London box to this place. Still not massive but it has a garden that you can actually get up speed in!'

Grace led Kate to the patio doors, which were open to the warm sunshine, and Kate looked out onto a lawn with a children's goalpost at either end. The sense of space was intensified as beyond the chain-link fence stretched a field full of oilseed rape; tall green shoots about a metre high that were just starting to break into flower. It was the kind of garden that Kate had wished she could have afforded for Becky when she was little. After built-up London where you rarely saw further than the other side of the street, it was intoxicating to be on the precipice of so much space and such a vast blue sky.

'Isn't it wonderful? We feel very lucky. It's so green.'

From across the lush field, with its yellow haze of just-blossoming flowers, a tractor was approaching. As it got closer to the house, the noise became deafening. 'Spraying season,' said Grace as she closed the patio doors, but not before Kate got a faint whiff of something that wasn't particularly pleasant.

'Yes, we love it here. It's a bit harder now I've had to give up work but Nick – that's my husband – he commutes up to London when he's not at the hospital.' She glanced across at the little boy, playing with his Lego at the kitchen table. 'Arnie's not been too well the last year or so but now the weather's getting warmer, we hope to get out more. Just to the garden. He's got leukaemia.'

'Oh, I'm sorry.'

'He'd gone into remission last year. About the time we met Becky. But a couple of months ago he had a relapse. He's on another course of chemo.' Tears pricked at her eyes, but she fought them back. 'Sorry. I feel for him . . . stuck here at home or the hospital, missing chunks of school, when John's forging ahead. His brother,' she explained.

'Is he older or younger?'

'Younger. By three minutes. John is Arnie's twin. They're inseparable, which makes it even harder, on both of them really, especially when Arnie just doesn't have the energy to play. We're waiting to hear on a donor. John wasn't a good match; his genetic make-up is too similar. It can cause problems.' She looked at Kate. 'Sorry, I've been going on about us all the time. I'm so sorry to hear about Becky. She was fun, sparky. I liked her. So did the others.'

'Who's that?'

'She got in contact with some other people in the village. Ian and Hazel Compton – they live a bit further down the lane, been here for donkey's years. And Ben and Sunita. They're down in Mallard's Road. I think there might have been a couple more, too.'

Kate recognized the names from the list on the file she'd found but she said nothing. 'Was this all for the article?'

'Yes. Last I heard from Becky was late February. She called, said there was something important she wanted to talk to Nick and me about. We arranged for her to come down the following Monday. But . . .'

'She died on Friday, the twenty-fourth of February.'

'I'm really sorry.' Grace studied her. 'You know, you look like her. Or rather, she looked like you. Your hair.'

Kate nodded.

'Sorry, I hope you don't mind . . .'

Kate shook her head. 'It's fine. It's nice to talk about her.'

'You didn't ever see it, did you? The article about how I traded accounting for baking? Becky said it was almost finished.'

'No, she didn't show me that one.'

'Oh, well. Fame and fortune will have to wait.'

Kate smiled. Saw the clock – she'd been there for over an hour. 'I'd better be going.' She stood. 'Thanks so much for talking to me. It's been a comfort to know a little more about Becky's life.'

'No problem. I just wish I'd had a copy you could've read.'

Me too, thought Kate as she walked back down the drive, hiding her unsettled feeling as she waved to Arnie and Grace through the window. She thought back to the last article Becky was working on just before she died, the one she refused to talk about with her. If it was just an innocuous piece about the pleasures of living in the country, why had Becky kept it so secret?

'It wasn't just her,' she said to Tim, later that evening. They were sitting at either end of the sofa, legs stretched out, Kate's resting over Tim's. 'I went to see another couple, Ian and Hazel. They live in this flint cottage at the end of the lane, next to the church, just them, no kids, ever, just a cat. I kind of got the impression they'd tried for children but had been unlucky. Anyway, same thing. Becky had contacted them about her story, interviewed them, and they'd talked to her about the joys of growing their own veg. And there was the Bolton family. Bit of a shock when I knocked on the door – guy who opened it was the taxi driver.' She giggled. 'Think that was the second fright I'd given him that day,' she said, recalling him starting as he saw her on the doorstop. 'I explained to all of them why Becky had seemingly vanished.' She paused. 'Her reputation was important to her. I didn't want them getting the wrong end of the stick, thinking she'd just abandoned her story.'

Tim massaged her leg. 'Don't blame you.'

Kate rubbed at her temples, trying to ease away the pain that wasn't shifting. 'I've got a stinking headache.'

'That's not like you.'

'I know. Any chance of a foot massage?'

'I was going to ask you the same thing.'

'I'll do yours if you do mine.'

'Deal.'

'But only if you've moisturized.'

'At my pedicure today.'

Kate sat up, amazed. 'You've been for a pedicure?'

'Have I heck,' said Tim. 'I've been on the 196.' He started to stroke the soles of her feet.

'Ah, bliss . . .' She relaxed fully for the first time that day. 'Do you know, there was one weird thing. About today.'

'Go on.'

'At each house I went to, there was someone ill in the family – or who had been ill. And I'm not talking just a cold. Arnie, the six-year-old twin, has leukaemia. Abby, the taxi driver's daughter, has had another type of cancer – soft-tissue sarcoma – but is in remission now. His wife has ME. Ian, the retired guy, he's got prostate cancer.'

'I thought living in the country was supposed to be healthy.'

'Yes . . . it made me wonder . . . about the other two on the list. I thought I might go tomorrow . . . see if I can talk to them. Especially as they might also feel that Becky has let them down. I'd like them to know.'

Her phone rang, and she reached for it.

'Hello? Gregory!' Kate sat up. 'No, it's not too late. Yes, I think so. Let me just check.' She covered the mouthpiece. 'It's Gregory,' she said to Tim. 'From Fresh Foods, you know. He's wondering if we'd like to go for dinner with him tomorrow night. He'd like to update me on the results of the risk assessment.'

'What's he want me there for?'

'I don't know. Because you're my boyfriend? And he's nice and making an effort?'

Tim shrugged. 'OK.'

'Thanks, Gregory,' said Kate. 'We'd love to. OK, *Greg*.' She laughed. 'See you then.' She hung up.

Tim raised an eyebrow. '*Greg?*' he repeated.

'He insists, apparently.'

Tim moved his hand sensuously up the back of her leg.

Kate groaned. 'I can't tonight . . . sorry.'

'What's up? Head still hurting?'

She rubbed her temples. 'I think I need an early night.'

He got up. Held out his hand. 'Come on, I'll tuck you in.'

She gratefully let him lead her up the stairs and got into bed. She tried to read but it hurt too much so she turned off the light. Her head really was pounding, and she didn't often get headaches. Must be all the emotions running high – being on Becky's patch, hearing about her. By uncovering part of Becky's life that she'd known nothing about, it felt as if it was new. As if it had just happened. As if she was still alive.

SIXTEEN

2001

Kate's hands were locked onto the steering wheel, her palms sweating, as they had been ever since she'd got this tiny box of a car onto the motorway. She'd only passed her test two weeks before, a miracle seeing as she'd just had a crash course of lessons, the minimum she could get away with, as she wanted to keep as much hard-saved cash as possible for her first-ever holiday with Becky.

After six years of working flat out to keep their tiny house, she'd also managed to put away a couple of hundred pounds every year, and when she'd told Becky they were going away, her eyes had lit up with so much excitement, Kate had felt bad she'd never been able to do it before. But then the excitement had become infectious and the two of them were now looking forward to it with such intensity, there was a lot of pressure on the holiday to deliver. She'd booked a mobile home by the beach in Devon and hired a car and now she was attempting to get to the former without dissolving into a sweaty nervous puddle and without Becky being sick all over the seats.

'Are you OK?' she called out, risking a glance in the rear-view mirror at her daughter's grey-green pallor.

'No,' came back the pathetic reply. 'It still smells.'

'I know, Becky. It's because the car is new,' said Kate. 'I'll open the window again.' She wiped her hand on her jeans, then quickly touched the window button. 'Fresh' air and traffic-roar entered the car.

'Are we nearly there?' asked Becky, hopefully.

'Yes,' replied Kate, thinking it would help neither of them if she told the truth. 'Try and get some sleep, eh?'

Becky picked her blue toy puppy up off her lap and held it close and, mercifully, in another few minutes, was asleep.

The mobile home was a little tired, but it had bright-yellow curtains and, from one window, you could glimpse the sea. Becky delightedly bounded around, opening each door, discovering 'the toilet!' and 'the cupboard!' as if she'd never seen one before.

The weather was glorious and so they quickly got changed into their swimming costumes and shorts. Taking Becky's hand, Kate followed the signs down the gravelly paths to the site's swimming pool. It was every bit as good as the picture in the brochure, with a pirate-ship slide and a large fixed plastic dolphin that shot water out of its mouth, and after dumping their bag and towels on a couple of miraculously still-empty sun loungers, they got straight into the water, laughing and splashing.

By two o'clock, they were starving, so Kate wrapped Becky in a towel, and pulled on her shorts and T-shirt, then they hurried over to the cafe at the side of the pool. They ordered their lunch and two milkshakes at the counter, then took the drinks to a table.

'I saw you in the pool,' said a lady sitting at the table next to them. She smiled at Becky. 'You were having such a good time.'

She looked to be in her fifties and was large and bosomy, with a towelling strapless sundress covering her swimming costume. The sundress was light blue and two large dark-blue breast-shaped patches had formed where her wet costume had seeped through.

'I'm Audrey,' she said, 'and this is my husband, Phil.'

Phil was also large, a hillock of a belly stretching through his T-shirt, and the only thing that adorned his bald head was a pair of sunglasses, the string attached to the arms making two black lines down behind his ears. Both he and Audrey were tucking into a burger on a flaccid bun with a mountain of chips, washed down by cans of beer. He raised a hand in greeting.

'Hi,' said Kate. 'I'm Kate and this is Becky.'

'Very nice to meet you both,' said Audrey. She looked up as two other people approached their table. 'Here they are! The terrible twosome.' She waved a hand at a late middle-aged couple in shorts, T-shirts, hats and sunglasses. 'Steve and Debbie, this is Kate and Becky. On holiday.' She turned to Kate. 'When did you arrive, love?'

'Today.'

'We come every year, don't we, Debs?' said Audrey as Debbie heaved her enormous stuffed-full beach bag onto a chair at the next table, before plonking herself down beside it. 'That's right. Well, last couple of years anyhow.'

Steve squeezed Audrey's fleshy shoulder before joining his wife. 'Always try and leave you behind on the motorway, never quite manage it,' he joked.

'Is it your first time?' asked Debbie, as she lifted her bleached-blonde hair off the back of her neck and flapped it to let in some air.

'Yes,' said Kate.

'It's all right, actually. Better than some. You gotta keep an eye on the pool. Gets a bit manky sometimes. Have to say, you never got that at our hotel in Marbella.'

Audrey groaned. 'Oh, don't bring that up again, Debs, you'll only get him started.' She looked at her husband and, sure enough, Phil was disgruntled.

'I told you we should've gone back to Spain.'

'Phil, you know we can only afford it every other year,' said Audrey.

'Yeah, but next year we *won't* be able to afford it because the bloody euro will be in and the thieving bastards will all be racking up their prices.'

Kate glanced anxiously at Becky, but she seemed oblivious, tucking into her cheese sandwich that had just arrived. Audrey flicked a hand on Phil's arm. 'Oi, watch your language. There's kiddies about.' She turned to Kate. 'Sorry about him.'

Kate smiled politely, realizing that, once again, she seemed to be mixing with people two or three times her age, and she wistfully wondered if other twenty-one-year-olds came to campsites like this, almost immediately knowing the answer. She suddenly had a slump of energy, felt old before her time.

Audrey glanced about. 'Are your mum and dad here?'

Becky, thinking she was the one being addressed, looked puzzledly at Kate, as if to check, then said, pointing: 'Mummy's there. And I don't have a daddy.'

Silence reigned. Audrey's eyes widened, then her features settled into barely concealed disapproval. 'Oh, right,' she said, and Kate saw Debbie was pretending not to look but was staring at her through her dark glasses. Audrey, too, was peering at her again, trying to do some maths.

'I had Becky when I was fifteen,' said Kate defiantly, partly to shock them further, partly because being constantly stuck with the wrong generation made her want to scream.

Phil stopped eating, but didn't look up. A moment passed then his jaw began moving again.

Becky looked at the plates of food that had been brought out to Steve and Debbie and their mountains of chips. 'Mummy, can I have some chips, please?'

'No, not for lunch,' Kate said gently. 'We're going out for chips later, remember?'

'That must've been hard,' said Debbie, with an overly sympathetic tone to her voice, 'what with your exams and all that.'

Kate knew she was fishing for gossip, nuggets of Kate's life that she could take away with her and regurgitate and judge when they were all four together later that evening. 'It was.'

'Did you manage . . . ? You know, to get your GCSEs?'

Kate bristled. Audrey's line of questioning was too personal; she suspected that Audrey was waiting for her to fail, *wanting* her to. By some miracle she'd managed to get English and Geography, but she'd failed the obligatory Maths and her only other respectable pass was in RE. 'A few,' she said evasively, hating being on the spot. She would have got up and left there and then, but Becky was still eating.

'Well, I think exams are overrated anyway,' said Steve. 'Look at that Richard Branson, he's done all right, hasn't he, and I don't think he even finished school. Now he's rich as Midas and hangs out with all sorts. Celebrities, politicians. He's even mates with Tony Blair, isn't he?'

'Another good man,' said Debbie. 'I'm so glad he won again. Proves he's the one the country wants.'

Kate didn't particularly follow politics, but she had an aversion to Tony Blair and his fake promises and fake smiles. She thought Debbie's proclamation was short-sighted. 'I don't think he really was the one the country wants. Loads of people didn't even bother voting. It was the lowest turnout in voting history.'

Debbie frowned, perhaps not used to being challenged by someone so young. 'What?'

Kate blushed, but continued. 'Well, it was only 59.4 per cent. That's quite a few short. Um . . . 40.6 per cent.'

It was a moment before anyone spoke. Then Phil looked up from his burger. 'I'm not being funny, love, but you don't seem like the type to know much about this kind of stuff.'

Her insides started to quiver with humiliation, but she forced herself to confront him. 'What do you mean?'

'Well, you're—' He stopped abruptly, having been sharply nudged in the ribs by Audrey. 'What I mean is, school was overtaken by something else, wa'n't it?' He laughed, pretending to make light of his comment. 'And it's not like you must get a lot of thinking time. Not now you have your hands full.'

'I can still have an opinion.'

He looked at her dismissively, then irritatedly, as if she'd completely failed to get his point.

'I think it's a bit different, don't you?' And he didn't wait for an answer, but instead got up and challenged Steve with a hearty slap on the back to a game of pool at the table that was under the shade at the back of the seating area.

'Well, if you'll excuse us, we're heading for the spa pool,' said Audrey. She got up and Debbie followed suit. Kate had already seen the sign for the spa pool. It was for over-18s only. With a polite nod, they left and, despite disliking both women intensely and not wanting for a nanosecond to join them, Kate felt like the outsider yet again.

Kate couldn't afford to eat out much at all, but she'd promised Becky that she'd take her to a restaurant on their first night. They drove into the small town, parked up and wandered along the high street until they came to a gourmet burger restaurant. It looked hip, fun – both things that Kate craved on a regular basis – and the clientele she could see in the window were all young. It seemed like a haven, a place where she could get a taste of what she frequently missed out on.

They walked in the door and were immediately seated by a cute-looking man of a similar age to Kate. He smiled at her as he held out her chair and she found herself blushing uncontrollably. She watched him as he walked away, wondering who he was and slipping into a fantasy of how, maybe, she might just meet the man of her dreams *on this very holiday*!

Becky was looking around the room, beaming.

'Do you like it here?' asked Kate.

'Mummy, please can I be a cafe slave when I grow up? *Please?*'

'A what?'

'A cafe slave.'

Kate looked around, bemused. 'Do you mean the waiters?'

'Who are they?'

'The people serving the food?'

'Yes, the servants. Please, Mummy?'

Kate laughed, despite the tightness in her chest. Disappointment. Panic. *Please, God*, she thought, *don't let her screw up her life like I have.* She knew better than to burst Becky's bubble. 'If you really want to. But I think you'll probably want to do something else really exciting instead.'

'This *is* really exciting,' said Becky, in awe, as a waitress approached their table.

'So, what's it to be?' Kate said to Becky. 'Fuzzy juice? Burger? Chips?'

Becky nodded, unable to fully process the myriad of

treats all at once. 'I love you, Mummy,' she declared earnestly, 'and not just because of the chips.'

They gave their order while Becky gazed reverently at the waitress taking it, then, just as their drinks arrived, Kate heard a voice say her name. She turned and recognized a face, at least it had hints of its past, but was now framed by a sophisticated, sleek white-blonde bob. Lara Tomlinson. Behind Lara was a very attractive man, full of self-importance, with a windswept boy-band hair style. He looked at Kate with a vague interest, which was extinguished when he saw Becky.

'It *is* you,' exclaimed Lara, surprised.

'Hi,' said Kate, self-consciously. She hadn't seen Lara for years. Lara had gone on to the well-respected grammar school, and then, Kate had heard, to university.

'What are you doing here?' asked Lara.

Kate shrugged. 'Eating,' she joked. Then, when it fell flat: 'We're here on holiday.'

'Nice,' said Lara. She stared across at the other side of the table, as if she were examining a strange creature in a zoo. 'Is that Becky?'

Kate felt a twinge of annoyance. 'Yes.'

'She's grown.'

'Babies do.' She paused. 'So, what about you?'

Lara tilted her head quizzically as if she didn't understand.

Her question seemed perfectly simple to Kate and she resented Lara's egotistical response, her fake lack of understanding just so she could be asked more about herself. 'What are you doing here?' Kate elaborated.

'Staying over at Barney's parents' place. They've got a

house right on the estuary. Awesome view from the bedroom.' She turned and glanced at Barney and they shared a smug, private smile. Kate had to wait for them to stop, for Lara to revert her attention back to her. While she was waiting, she saw the guy who'd seated them, the potential 'love of her life', flirt with two suntanned girls in short skirts. They looked carefree. Childless.

'They're not there at the moment so we're taking a long weekend. Bit of a celebration.' Lara paused for effect. 'I'm moving out to New York next week. Got a new job with the bank. Don't know if you heard? I went into banking after graduation.'

'Yeah?'

'Anyways,' continued Lara, 'they've given me a position in their New York office.'

A stab of envy. Lara had the sort of freedom she couldn't begin to imagine.

'It's in the World Trade Centre,' continued Lara, 'you know, the twin tow—'

'I know what it is,' interrupted Kate, two red spots appearing at the tops of her cheeks. *I'm not stupid.*

'Course,' said Lara. 'So, how about you? Still at the garden centre?'

'No.' She was, in fact, working in a supermarket, but had no intention of saying this to Lara.

'Oh, right. Did you end up going back to school then?'

Kate's face burned. She could see Becky looking at her, troubled that her mother was clearly upset. Kate forced a smile. 'Didn't find the time.'

'Oh,' said Lara. 'Shame.'

Kate willed her to go away, couldn't stand the sight of her a moment longer. There was an awkward silence. Lara looked around for inspiration, and her eyes settled on her boyfriend. 'Barney's heading to New York, too. We met at work,' she explained. 'He's joining me in October.' She turned to him and said teasingly: 'We'll be the British version of Carrie Bradshaw and Mr Big.'

'Are you a cafe slave?' asked Becky, hopefully.

Lara turned, surprised, as if she'd forgotten Becky was there. 'What?' But her perplexed frown froze Becky into silence. Lara looked at Kate, suddenly keen to go. 'Right, well, have a great holiday.'

Kate spoke through clenched teeth. 'Thanks. Good luck with the job.'

Lara nodded and then she and Barney turned away.

'Who's that lady?' asked Becky, as Lara led her boyfriend to the bar area, not the section by the restaurant tables, but around the back, out of sight. In twenty minutes' time Kate would see her slip past again, out the door, without even looking back at her old friend.

'Someone I used to know,' said Kate, suddenly feeling a sense of loss for a life she'd never had.

'Oh.'

Becky was watching her carefully, a look of consternation on her face, and Kate forced a smile. 'Come on, shall we eat our chips?'

*

As Kate drove Becky back to the campsite, the dreaded new-car smell began to inveigle its way into Becky's system again.

'I feel sickie, Mummy,' she said.

Kate glanced anxiously backwards. 'It's only two minutes, Becky. Can you hold on?'

Becky nodded bravely, and Kate continued driving but, just as she turned off the main road into the campsite, she heard the sound of retching. Quickly, she pulled over to the side of the road. She leapt out of the car and went to Becky's door, opening it to help her daughter, dreading the mess in the hire car she was responsible for. To her amazement, the car was clean, and Becky was looking at her wide-eyed, her mouth open and chin pushed forward. Kate quickly unbuckled her and led her out of the car to the verge, whereby Becky tipped her mouth forward and the vomit fell onto the grass at the side of the path.

'Well done!' said Kate, rubbing her back. 'You're so good. I can't believe it didn't go in the car!'

Becky looked proud. 'I made a cup, Mummy, like this,' she said and demonstrated the way she'd pushed her jaw forward. 'And now,' she said delightedly, looking at the sick she'd tipped onto the ground, 'it's a teapot!'

Kate felt a rush of love for her and she burst out laughing, until tears were streaming down her face.

'You're the best, Becky.' She enveloped her in a hug, burying her face in her hair and smelling its summer scent. 'So clever.'

'You're clever too, Mummy,' said Becky, nodding earnestly,

scouring Kate's eyes to make sure her mum understood the reassurance she was pressing on her. 'I didn't like that lady in the cafe.'

Kate felt her heart pinch. It was amazing what children picked up on. She held Becky tighter and for a split second all she could think about was what a failure she was, how her daughter deserved better. She pushed the thoughts away and looked Becky in the eye. 'I'm having the best holiday ever.'

'Me too, Mum!'

A week after they returned, Kate got back from work to find a letter lying on the doormat. With a mix of terror and excitement she recognized the handwriting on the envelope as her mother's. Her heart beat furiously in a moment of terrible optimism. With trembling hands, she opened it. Inside was a pamphlet. Frowning, she couldn't work out what it was at first and then, in horror, she dropped it. It fell onto the floor with a soft *pap*.

Her mother had sent her a funeral service. And on the front was her father's name.

Kate was trying to breathe but the pain in her chest was constricting her lungs.

She was completely on her own now. She'd always secretly hoped she'd see her dad again. That one day, there might be a family reconciliation, her mother would mellow as she, Kate, became an adult. She realized all that had been a fantasy.

Later, when she'd picked Becky up from Iris's and

was putting her in the bath, she looked at her daughter's soft hands, the baby fat almost disappeared, as she poured water from an old plastic cup over her head to 'make a waterfall' and knew she'd never ever desert her, no matter what she did. She didn't need her parents, nor a useless boyfriend – all she needed was Becky.

SEVENTEEN

2018

Tim met her at Victoria station and they walked hand in hand towards Belgravia.

'I got to both the other houses on the list,' said Kate. 'Met with Sunita and Ben Jones, who have two small children. She's had breast cancer but is clear now. Then at the last address I met another lady – Beryl Hart.'

'She OK?' asked Tim.

'Perfectly fine.'

'Thank God!'

'But her husband died last year. Yes,' she said, before he could ask, 'from cancer.'

'Flipping heck! All those people in one village? Seems a bit excessive, don't you think?'

'I know. I looked up the population. It's only just a thousand.'

'So, what . . . is the water poisoned or something?'

Kate shook her head, flummoxed. 'Can't be.'

'And do they all know? About each other?'

'I don't think so, not the full picture, anyway. Some are

aware of one or two ill people but seem to think it's a coincidence. They're just caught up in their own lives, trying to get well. Trying to keep things juggling. More than one have had to give up jobs because of illness, or because they need to look after their sick children. I just have this feeling . . . I don't think Becky was doing an article on what it was like to move from the big smoke to the country. Or at least, not the idyllic version of rural life as we were led to believe.' She looked up. 'We're here.'

They'd made it to the restaurant Greg had picked out. It was quietly expensive: waves of smooth taupe linen, soft lighting, exquisite wooden picture carvings of rice paddies on the walls.

'Oh, God, you didn't tell me it was oriental,' said Tim quietly as they followed the maître d' to the table.

'Is that a problem?' whispered Kate. 'Do you not like the food?'

'It's not the food, it's the chopsticks. I can't use them.'

'So? Ask for a fork.'

'I'll look like a right wally.'

'No one will mind.'

'I'm not showing you up.'

'Kate!' exclaimed Greg, getting up from his chair as they approached. He clasped her hand warmly and then turned to Tim. Kate introduced them.

'Delighted to meet you,' said Greg, shaking Tim's hand.

As they sat down, Greg tapped the wine menu. 'Do both of you like champagne? I thought it would be nice to have a toast, a moment to mark what Kate has achieved.'

Kate had never actually tried champagne, not the real stuff, and she suspected this restaurant only did the real stuff. She thought it probably wasn't something Tim would drink often either but they both nodded, and Greg leaned back and raised a finger towards the bartender, who seemed to automatically know exactly what he wanted as, very soon afterwards, a silver ice bucket on a stand was brought over and a cork was popped.

'To Kate,' said Greg simply, and they all three touched glasses.

Next was the business of food, and Kate opened the menu and blinked at the prices. She could sense Tim doing the same. Her lifelong thrifty guilt kicked in and she found herself ordering the cheapest thing listed.

Maybe Greg could sense her unsettled mood as, straight after they'd ordered, he picked up a black file that was on the seat next to him and extracted some papers. 'There's something I want you to see.'

He laid an artist's impression of the inside of a lorry carefully on the table in front of her.

'This is the passenger door of a lorry as standard, and this –' he placed another drawing over the top – 'is the passenger door with a vision panel fitted to the lower section. You can see the cyclist. Each of our lorries is going to be refitted. The first few will be done next month.'

Kate looked at the drawings. The extra window lower down on the passenger door was so simple and yet so effective. It gave a complete view of anything alongside the lorry.

If only it had been done just over a year ago. 'Thank you, Greg. I didn't expect it to be so quick . . . I expected a battle.'

He smiled. 'No battle. There was one other thing I wanted to ask you.' He paused nervously. 'I was thinking about whether you would like us to set up a bursary. In Becky's name. We'd like to support one aspiring journalist every year, perhaps to help them through university or other training or even just give someone the means to live in London as they get their foot on the ladder. I know a lot of internships these days barely pay anything; in fact, some-times, I think you have to pay the newspaper! I was wondering if you would like to help run it. Decide who the recipient should be every year.'

Kate kept silent.

'If I've overstepped the mark—'

'No, it's not that. I think it's a great idea. I just didn't expect it, that's all.' Overwhelmed, Kate turned to Tim who squeezed her hand under the table.

'She – we – always struggled for her to stay on her uni-versity course. Money was tight. It would mean a lot to Becky that someone else was getting a chance.' Kate smiled. 'She would have written it up: an underdog story.'

'Was that the kind of journalism she was interested in?' asked Greg, as their food arrived.

'Yes. Investigative, really. She hated any kind of unfair-ness. Injustice.'

'Investigative. That's good. So, did she work on local stories? National? I hope you don't mind talking about this,' he added quickly.

'No, it's fine. She did both, really. Well, I think she did. She was working on something big—'

Kate was interrupted by a loud exclamation from Tim, who had a pile of noodles in his lap and his chopsticks attacking his fingers.

'I'm a bit of a novice.' He shrugged, embarrassed, picking his dinner off his crotch.

Greg nodded at the waitress and a fork was subtly delivered in seconds. Tim looked at it for a moment and then picked it up. 'Never seen the point of the twigs, as you can't stab –' he speared a piece of beef – 'your food.'

He looked at Kate, who had deftly manoeuvred up a mouthful of rice. She shrugged. 'I used to work in a Thai restaurant.'

'So, what do you do, Tim?' asked Greg.

'I'm a bus driver.'

'I've always wondered about you bus drivers. Whether you're secret petrol heads. What do you drive?'

'A bus,' said Tim, flatly.

Greg's friendly smile faltered.

Tim got a pang of guilt and added: 'How about you? What do you drive?'

'Black Jaguar XJ saloon.'

'Ever take the bus?'

'Afraid not.'

'Didn't think so.'

Tim was smiling but Kate could sense his irritation. She nudged his foot under the table.

'Bet you get a lot of driver training for a job like that,' said Greg.

'Yes.'

'If you ever want a change, I could do with people like you on our crew.'

A minuscule silence.

'I'm fine as I am, thanks,' said Tim.

'Well, you know where to find me if you change your mind. Here, let me give you this.' Greg fished in his jacket pocket and put a business card on the table. Kate noticed that Tim took it about three seconds later than would be polite.

'OK,' said Greg, picking up the menu. 'Anyone for dessert?'

'He was just being nice. Friendly,' said Kate as they lay in bed that night. She frowned – the lamplight seemed so bright – and closed her eyes to block it out.

'He was being patronizing. "I could do with people like you,"' Tim mimicked. 'He doesn't even know me. I could be a kamikaze racing driver for all he knows. Turning my wheel with a pair of chopsticks.'

Kate opened an eye and smiled. 'OK, maybe a bit patronizing. But perhaps he was trying to make conversation.'

'I'm sorry.' Tim turned and put an arm around her. 'I didn't mean to spoil it for you.'

'You didn't.'

'There's just something about the way he was trying to buy me off. Like he could throw money at everything.'

'Do you mean the bursary?'

'No! Sorry. I think that's an amazing thing. Something for Becky's memory.' He leaned up on his elbow, looked sheepish. 'Maybe I'm just a bit jealous. Me in my scruffs and him all suited and booted.'

'Hmm, you were overdressed in my view.' She ran a hand over his bare chest. 'I prefer this look.'

Kate closed her eyes again and he stroked her forehead. 'Another headache?'

'Yeah. And I only had one glass of champagne.'

'That's two days in a row now.' Tim leaned over and switched off the bedside lamp. 'Too much country air!'

EIGHTEEN

'Are you sure you're OK?' said Iris the next morning. She was holding onto the side of the shopping trolley as Kate pushed it around the supermarket.

'I'm fine,' insisted Kate. The headache had left her a bit listless. She kicked herself for mentioning it, as it was nothing compared to Iris's fall. She'd tripped on the rug in her living room that morning and had been unable to get up, instead dragging herself to the phone over the course of what must have been about half an hour (Iris only knew this because her Mediterranean property programme had played through to the credits) and had called Kate, downplaying it as usual.

'It's nothing much, I just think I've bumped my elbow. I was wondering if you could pop over, love?'

'Sure, I'll come now,' Kate had said.

'Just one thing. If you could bring your key . . . I don't think I can get to the door.'

Kate had hurried over immediately, let herself in and helped Iris get up into her chair. She was more apologetic than anything and, having swallowed some paracetamol, had insisted on walking again after a bit of a rest.

Kate looked down at the list. 'Which coffee would you like? I don't know why you didn't just let me do the shopping and bring it to you.'

'Then I wouldn't have got out of the house,' said Iris. 'And believe me, when you get to my age, you take any opportunity to get out. Anyway, I have my stick. And you. The decaf, please, love. I'm going to try a new health and fitness regime.'

Kate put a jar into the trolley. 'Just as long as you don't forget to use me. No being a martyr and trying to manage when you genuinely need help.'

'Yes, love,' said Iris automatically.

'I mean it. It's our pledge, remember?'

'Oh yes, I do. Twenty-first of September, 1995. You had to go back to work, bless you, and I took care of Becky.'

'Yes, and in return, because you'd hardly take any money—'

'You didn't have any, love.'

'I promised to take care of you when you—'

'Became an old codger.'

'Didn't say that.'

'Didn't need to. We both know it's true.' She put a hand on Kate's. 'And you do know I appreciate it, don't you?'

Kate nodded and looked at the list. 'Sushi? Really?'

'Like I said. Clean living. Oh, I do think it's great how that man is setting up that bursary. When does it start?'

'This year. He wants to advertise next month and then we'll be going through the applications together. He wants

me to do the interviews with him too. *Me!* I've never interviewed anyone in my life.'

'Think you'll be good at it?'

Kate thought for a moment. 'I know what a passionate
journalist looks like.'

'There you are then. So, you'll be spending a lot of time
with him.'

'Who? Greg? I guess so.'

Iris pulled a face.

'What?'

'You know men. How they can read something into
nothing.'

'How did you know? Tim was a little . . . wobbly last
night.'

Iris smiled knowingly. 'They're all the same. My Geoff
was never keen on me working at the dispatch centre. Specially as I was mostly on nightshifts. All those male drivers
hanging about waiting for a job.'

'Yeah, but you didn't—'

'I did my crosswords. And entered competitions. Won us
a washing machine. Still going, it is, too. You know, as
much as I wasn't keen on his jealous streak, it was nice to
feel loved. He was never possessive, never stifling. The irony
was he always wanted me home of an evening and then the
minute I retired – early mind, so we could spend some time
together – he went and took up with the angels. Never been
so lonely as that first night at home without him. I suppose
I was getting a taste of what he'd had all those years.'

Kate squeezed her arm.

'And I've never really said this, but it was only you turning up with your Becky that stopped me from sinking low. Gave me someone else to look after.'

'Let's just say we saved each other's bacon,' said Kate.

They'd stopped at the chilled aisle.

'What's that?' asked Iris, pointing at some plastic filled trays.

'Sushi.'

'It looks like fish.'

'That's right.'

'Is it raw?'

'Yes.'

Iris pulled a face. 'Stick it in the trolley. Maybe you could do with some as well.'

'Whatever for?'

'Those headaches.'

'There haven't been that many.'

'Two in a row? Funny how it's been both times after you've come back from that place. Ramsbourne, did you say it was?'

'That's right. Yes, I suppose it has.'

'Maybe it's an ill place.'

Kate snorted. 'Don't be daft. Not the whole village is ill.'

'Isn't it?'

'No!'

'Well, must be just that part of the village then.'

Kate pondered. 'I think you just hold a deep suspicion for the countryside.'

'Never lived anywhere but south London and never seen

the need to. Except maybe Spain,' she said wistfully. 'Always fancied trying that flamenco. Had a good pair of legs in my time.' She looked into the trolley. 'Are we done? I could do with a cup of decaffeinated and an organic rice cake.'

After Kate had escorted Iris back on the bus and put her shopping away for her, she headed home. She felt at a loose end. In truth she wasn't used to having so much time off. An email pinged in her inbox and she saw it was from Greg, inviting her to check over the wording for the press release for the bursary. He'd suggested it might be called the Becky Ellis Foundation and she agreed and emailed him to say so. He answered back straight away, saying how glad he was that she approved. Then the computer went silent. There didn't seem to be anything to do and she was distracted, unsettled. *All those ill people* . . . she couldn't get it out of her head.

She idly googled Ramsbourne and clicked on a map of the village. She found her way around the lanes, going from house to house, looking at all the ones she had visited, and realized that they *were* all in the same part of the village, to the south. She zoomed in. What else was around there? Nothing. Only a farm and a small river that ran further south. She wasn't even sure what she was looking for and sighed; it was silly, really. She'd let Iris's words get to her.

Realizing she was wasting a day inside when the sun was gently warming everything, she decided to make the most of it. Changing into an old bikini she'd bought when she'd taken Becky on her first holiday, she dragged the moth-eaten sun-lounger cushion from under the stairs, and took her sunglasses, a lemonade and her still-unfinished book out into the tiny garden.

The weather was glorious and after a few minutes she put the book down and closed her eyes. Her skin felt warm and caressed. She could feel herself dozing, the sounds from the world outside fading as she drifted off: distant traffic, shouts and laughter from some young people from the college, a grass-cutting machine in the local park at the end of the road. She listened to the thrum of the engine as it got closer and then faded away again as it turned and headed in the opposite direction. She was almost asleep when it returned for its next loop and she found herself getting irritated at it for preventing her from napping. Such an incessant noise. It was getting louder and louder as it approached. Familiar. The noise mentally poking her: *you remember me*. Round and round, up and down. *Grace's back garden. A tractor looping the field again and again.* She suddenly opened her eyes. A weird thought.

The farm.

The tractor.

The crop-spraying. The *smell*. The headaches.

Kate sat up. It couldn't be. Could it?

She went back inside to her computer and typed 'crop-spraying in the countryside' into the search engine. Boom – there it was. Article upon article staring her in the face:

Crop Sprays Damage Health

Pesticides Campaign

Links Between Herbicides and Cancer

It went on and on. There were pages of them.

'I know it's quite late,' said Kate as Grace opened the front door, surprised to see her.

'The boys are outside,' said Grace, and Kate waved through to Arnie and John playing football in the garden. 'Time for a coffee?'

'Love one.' As Kate waited, she was drawn towards the open patio doors, and watched the twins play in the garden. On the other side of the chain-link fence was the field. There was no buffer, nothing to protect them. The spray would come right into the garden, most likely up to the house, carried on any breeze. This would happen again and again, every time the tractor did a loop of the field. And how many times a year? Fifteen? Twenty? And that wasn't the only field – there were acres of them.

'Thanks,' she said as a mug was handed to her.

'It's especially beautiful at this time,' said Grace, looking outside. 'Evenings growing lighter and the crops still new.' She smiled. 'So, what brings you here? Did you find Becky's article? Double-page spread on how I swapped a career in accounting for making dodgy Swiss rolls?'

Kate didn't answer straight away. She didn't know how to, what to say. She was beginning to wonder if she had made a mistake coming, but then . . . if what she thought was true, how could she not say anything? Grace was looking at her expectantly.

'Yes. About that article. I think it might have been about something else.'

'Something else?' repeated Grace.

Kate paused. 'I . . . you may not know this, but Becky always wanted to be an investigative journalist. Someone who would root out the truth. She liked stories that exposed corruption or wrongdoing.'

Grace smiled.

Kate ploughed on. 'I went to see all the other families here in the village that Becky had been visiting. Not just the ones you mentioned, there were others, too.'

'Right. I'm still not following.'

'Did you know that there are five cases of cancer just in the few streets in the south of Ramsbourne?'

Grace frowned. 'Five?'

'Yes.'

'I don't understand. What has this got to do with us?'

'I think the reason Becky was here is that she was investigating something serious. I think she was trying to prove a link between the illnesses in the village and –' Kate turned her eyes to the field of glowing yellow – 'that.'

Grace followed her gaze. Could see nothing. 'What?'

'The crops. Or rather, what's sprayed on the crops. The pesticides and herbicides.'

'What?' Grace laughed. 'No. I mean, I know it doesn't smell too good, but it can't be dangerous. It's right outside. Near our home. I mean, it's a metre or so from the garden. It's going on our *food*. No, this is all wrong.'

'Have you ever heard of something called glyphosate?'

'Er . . . yes . . . vaguely. Isn't it some sort of weedkiller?'

'It's a chemical used in a large number of pesticides and herbicides. It's classified by the World Health Organization as "probably carcinogenic to humans". There are other chemicals too. Sometimes – quite often – they're mixed up. Various combinations are sprayed.'

'I don't understand what you're telling me. We're being poisoned by what's going on the crops? You do realize how mad that sounds?' challenged Grace.

'I know it sounds far-fetched. But there's scientific evidence that exposure to pesticides can cause cancer and other diseases, too. Parkinson's, birth defects, damage to the nervous system.'

Grace shook her head stubbornly. 'But . . . this can't be right. Not here. You must be talking about somewhere overseas. Where the regulations aren't as tight. No one would allow something like that to happen here.'

'I know it's hard to take in,' said Kate anxiously. 'But I think they have – they do. I've been looking into it.'

'Hang on, but what about the doctors? Why haven't they picked this up? No one's once said that Arnie is ill because of what they're putting on the crops at the end of our garden.' Grace was struggling. 'And the children play outside all the time.' She suddenly became triumphant. 'No, no, you see, they *both* do, so why is one ill and not the other?'

'I don't know. I'm sorry, Grace, I wasn't sure what was best to do but I really do believe this is what Becky was investigating. I thought you ought to know.'

There was a pause.

'Have you told the others?' asked Grace, and Kate sensed a defensive tone in her voice.

'No. I just came to you. I haven't . . .' Kate suddenly deflated. Then, a rumbling sound in the distance. It grew steadily louder: it was mechanical, an engine. A tractor appeared on the brow of the hill, making its way across the field towards them. Behind it was a large boom that stretched out several metres over the crops, and from the entire length of that boom emanated a light mist. It drenched the crops and rolled across the air, a continuous hissing discharge, and as the tractor grew closer, a distinct chemical smell began to filter through to the garden.

Grace stared, apprehension contorting her face. She shot an agitated look at Kate, unsure of what to say, what to do. Kate could begin to taste something foul in her mouth and she involuntarily recoiled. The shouts from the boys as they played their game of football were still audible above the tractor – just. The machinery continued to approach, getting louder and ever closer.

'Get in, get in!' shouted Grace suddenly, running towards her children in panic. They stopped kicking the ball, bewildered by the look on their mother's face. She grabbed each of them by the hand and pulled them back into the house, Kate bringing up the rear.

The patio door slammed shut, and Kate saw that Grace was shaking. They watched as the tractor drove past the perimeter of the field and the spray meandered gently across the garden. Then, a few minutes later, as quickly as it had appeared, the tractor vanished, back down the hill in another loop around the field. It would only be a matter of minutes before it returned.

'Ah, Mum, I was about to score!' complained John.

'It's bath time,' said Grace quickly. She looked up at Kate. 'So, I'm afraid I'm going to have to ask you to leave.'

Kate started. 'Of course.'

It was a swift goodbye and Kate took the train straight back to London. As it raced past the innocent-looking, glorious yellow fields, she thought about Grace, her twins. She thought about the terrible thing she had just imparted and felt guilty. But she knew she hadn't read all those reports wrongly. She also had the sense that she had only touched on the tip of the iceberg.

'I don't understand,' said Tim, pouring Kate a cold beer as she sat at her computer. 'How can farmers be allowed to spray this stuff? Surely it's illegal?'

'You'd think, eh? But look – it's here,' she said, pointing at the screen. 'There's this rule the regulators use – is it safe according to the "Bystander risk assessment"? In other words, they assume that there'll only be occasional, short-term exposure to these chemicals, just a few minutes, say. They don't take into account if you live next door to a farm where it's being sprayed regularly. Sometimes more than twenty times in a season.'

'This is *here*? In this country?'

'I know it's hard to believe.' She came away from the computer and sat down next to him on the sofa, sinking into the worn cushions in the middle. 'But think about it.

What's gonna happen if suddenly someone owns up to the fact that this is a national scandal? Think about the pay-outs.' Kate took a sip of her drink. 'I read this story. About this retired guy who was in his driveway that backed onto a field when the sprayers came past. He was sorting some-thing under his car, couldn't get out in time. His mouth and chest were burned by the chemicals. His vocal cords col-lapsed and now he can hardly speak.'

Tim's mouth dropped open. 'That's . . . *horrific*. And the industry and the government know about this but still do nothing?'

'Yep. There's loads more, too. I've found story after story of people who've suffered – kids, old people – some of them fatally.'

'But . . .' Tim shook his head, bewildered. 'They can't do that.'

'Except they do.' Kate exhaled. 'It's awful. What d'you do?'

'What can you do? Apart from don't buy a house next to a farm.'

'But that's so wrong. What about all those people who didn't know about this when they bought their homes? Who still don't know about it? Whose children, families, are getting ill. It's not just houses you know, some schools back onto the fields. Imagine your kid playing outside at breaktime every summer for twelve years, breathing this stuff in. Getting it on their skin. There's been reports of sickness, rashes on children—' Kate was interrupted by her phone. She looked at the cracked screen, bit her lip. 'It's

Grace. I think I really upset her today. I shouldn't have just gone down there, wading in with this.'

'I don't think it's the sort of thing you can water down.'

Kate picked up the phone. 'Hello?'

'Hi, it's Grace.'

'I should apologize—'

'No. No, it's OK. There's something I've remembered. When the twins were babies, John was the sleeper. He'd go for at least two hours every morning and afternoon. Arnie would only nap for an hour at most. He'd wake his brother and I'd have a grumpy baby on my hands for the rest of the day. So, I changed their routine. I'd put John to bed in the cot upstairs and Arnie –' she caught her breath – 'Arnie, I would put in the pram. Outside. So he didn't wake his brother. He'd sleep in the garden. He'd be there when all those sprayers went past.'

Kate swallowed. 'It's not your fault, Grace.'

Grace started to cry, small controlled sobs. 'I didn't know. I didn't know.'

Kate couldn't sleep. She listened to the sound of Tim snuffling beside her and felt the tiredness in her bones, but her mind wouldn't switch off. Every time she thought about Grace and Arnie, she was enveloped by a wave of outrage and helplessness. It was so unfair. Big companies, big corporations, they could do what they wanted. Nobody listened. Nobody cared as long as they were making money. Her fists were clenched and, sighing, she tried for the umpteenth time to relax. It was like what had happened with

Becky, all over again. How many people had to die before someone did something? She felt Tim stir beside her. Her restlessness was disturbing him. She suddenly sat up. *Someone has to do something.* She nudged Tim. He groaned.

'Tim,' she hissed.

'Wha' is it?'

'It's the rules again. The rules are wrong. Bystander, my arse.'

'Huh?'

'Someone has to change the rules.'

He rubbed his eyes. 'I thought you already did that?'

She switched the light on and he winced. 'No, listen. These crop-spraying rules. Maybe that's what Becky was trying to do. Expose the insanity of the "bystander" method. Let people know what was really happening. How ill people were getting.' She sat up suddenly, proud. 'My daughter. She wanted to tell everyone what was going on.'

'She was amazing.'

'She was. But she never got to tell her story. What if . . .'

'Hmm?'

'Well, Becky can't tell her story anymore. What if someone did it for her?' She paused. 'Me.'

'You?'

'Don't sound so surprised.'

'I'm not! I think it's a brilliant idea.'

It was a ludicrous idea. She didn't have the first clue about journalism. She slumped back down on the bed.

'I didn't even finish school. Let alone go and get a degree.'

'So?'

'So, I work in a DIY store. It's not exactly high-flying stuff.'

'Who cares.'

'No one will take me seriously.'

'Greg did.'

'That was different.'

'How?'

'Well, I was personally involved.'

'And you're not this time?'

'Not really . . .'

Tim held up a hand. 'Just stop right there, young lady. Your brilliant daughter was taken away in her prime and didn't get to finish one of the most important stories of her burgeoning career. *Your daughter*.'

'But I can't write!'

'You're pretty persuasive. Need I say it again? Greg. Can't believe I'm quoting this man's name so much and in my own bed,' he added, grumbling.

'But that was just me talking. Gobbing off.'

'Write down what comes out of your gob. Simple pimple.'

Kate lay back on the pillows. Thought for a moment. 'But what about spelling, grammar, sophisticated words? All that stuff?'

'I do believe there is a magic button on the keyboard for all that guff.'

'Sophisticated words?'

'Maybe not that bit. But there's a – what's it called – thesaurus.'

Kate was quiet for a moment. 'You really think . . . ?'

'Yes.'

'Even with my crappy education?'

'Yes.'

'Even though—'

'*Yes*.'

She snuggled in next to him. 'Well, I suppose I can give it a try.'

'Good. Now, can we go to sleep? I've got to be up at five.'

She kissed him. 'Yes. I love you.'

'Elephant juice too. Now, lights out.'

She flicked the switch. Lay there. Still buzzing. Maybe . . . just maybe she could. She owed it to Becky to try. She was pretty sure no one else at Becky's paper had picked up the story – if they had, Grace and the others would've been contacted, they'd have known about it. She heard Tim's breathing soften as he fell back to sleep.

She'd have to regain Grace's trust. Try and get her to talk, confide in her. The others, too. She'd have to do more research. There was science stuff to figure out as well. Chemicals. Reactions. She had been pretty good at science before she got pregnant. She'd taken chemistry and biology at GCSE, passed neither but the potential had been there. She might have to find experts to talk to, interview. This was going to take a while. Months maybe. She suddenly thought of Arnie and wondered how ill he was. Whether time was on his side. And Rob, working all hours as a cab driver for Abby and his wife, Helen.

She nudged Tim again.

'Uh . . . ?'

'Sorry. But it's not just the story.'

'No?' he said in a muffled voice.

'It's money. They need money.' She sat up straight. 'In fact, that's the most important thing.'

'Eh?'

'They need money, Tim.'

'Espect they do.'

'Someone needs to help them get it.'

'That's great, Kate. You're a wonder. I know you can do it.'

He rolled over and she let him sleep. Flipping heck, she'd just gone from not being sure whether or not she could write a few words to deciding to help them get compensation. She was mad! She lay there for a moment, her heart still racing.

There was something else. A warm thought spread throughout her body. *Becky, this is how I make it up to you. I have no idea what I'm doing but I'm going to try. For you.*

NINETEEN

Becky shivered in the large farmhouse kitchen and decided against taking her coat off. She'd taken advantage of the fact Terence was out of the office all morning and snuck out to Ashdown Farm in Ramsbourne. She hadn't bothered to make an appointment, preferring to surprise Justin Holmes, the farmer.

He'd been unintimidated when she'd introduced herself as a journalist (it was only a small exaggeration) from the *Herald* and she suspected her youthful looks were what had got her through the door. He wasn't bad-looking himself: late twenties with a definite wholesome vibe going on.

Justin noticed her pinched face. 'Sorry,' he said, 'heating's not on. Doesn't seem any point when I'm out on the farm all day.'

'No problem,' said Becky breezily and watched as the kettle came to the boil, sending billows of steam into the cold room. As Justin made them both a mug of coffee, she looked around. It was as far from a cosy farmhouse kitchen as you could get. It had an unloved air about it – the Aga was cold, and Becky wondered if it was ever used. A microwave had centre stage on the worktop and when Justin opened the fridge to get milk, she saw a few ready meals and that was about it. Several pairs of boots stood haphazardly at the back door in some mad dance formation and a single series of muddy prints had at some time traipsed across the room. Perhaps he'd been in a rush – forgotten to take them off. A lone breakfast bowl, the cornflakes drying out and sticking to the china, sat by the sink. *He's obviously single*, thought Becky, and then he handed her the burning-hot coffee and the scalding mug demanded her attention.

He took a sip of his drink and watched her, a smile on his face that was almost flirtatious. It was clearly down to her to start the conversation, which was fair enough as she'd doorstepped him.

'Thanks. For the coffee.'

'Pleasure.'

She looked around the kitchen. 'Nice place you've got here.'

'Now I know you're just being polite.'

'Been here long?'

'A couple of years.'

'And before that?'

'I managed a farm for the National Trust. In Kent.'

Becky nodded. There was a momentary lapse in the conversation as she mentally tried to finesse her approach.

'As flattering as it is to be cross-examined like this –'

Justin smiled and waved a hand towards the window – 'I do have work to get on with. Perhaps we could get to the point?'

Becky straightened up. The point it would be. 'I wanted to ask you about your farm – specifically the crop-growing process.'

'What about it?'

'I know all farms – most farms – spray their crops regularly. I'm interested in finding out more about this – what you use and when.'

'Why would that be of interest to you?'

'Are you aware of links between illnesses and the chemicals used to spray crops?'

'Hypothetical.'

'Maybe. Not everyone says so, though.'

'Nothing's been proven.'

Becky smiled. 'Not yet. Could you tell me what you use on this farm?'

'No.'

'Why not?'

'It's none of your business.'

'Could you tell me how often you spray?'

He didn't answer her this time.

'Are you aware of several cases of cancer in residents in the houses surrounding your farm's land?'

He paused. 'What's your point?'

'Ever think there might be a connection?'

He took the coffee out of her hands, which was a shame as it had finally reached a pleasantly warm temperature.

'Are you throwing me out?' said Becky.

'Only if you refuse to leave.'

'Those families – they'd love to know what was actually in those bottles of pesticides. What chemicals were going on their gardens, their pets, their children.'

'It's time for you to go.' Justin opened the back door and the wind gusted into the room, freezing it further.

'Whose products do you use? Which manufacturer?'

'Out.'

He came over to her and put a firm hand between her shoulder blades. Pushed her towards the back door.

'OK, OK!' said Becky, hands up in surrender. 'I'm going.' Her bike was leaning against the wall and she put on her helmet and straddled the seat. She looked back at him. 'It's gonna catch up with you all, you know. At some point, this is all going to come out in the open.'

He gave a wry smile, and she cycled away, wincing against the cold. The track was frozen solid, and her bike weaved and bumped across the ruts of mud. She knew he was watching her. A glance back confirmed this. So, no rooting around then. As she went through the yard, she saw the pesticide store – marked by the obligatory 'hazardous' warnings on the outside. If only she could go over, but he'd be on her in seconds.

She still cycled surreptitiously closer, looking longingly at the grey steel box, wishing she knew what was inside. And then she noticed something. One of the stickers on the container's exterior had a small corporate logo at the bottom. *Senerix*. This, Becky knew, was an agrochemical company, who made numerous products for farm-crop management. It was a small victory, but nonetheless, joyous. She turned and pedalled for the track that led to the road.

She slunk into the office around noon, knowing Terence wouldn't be in for another half an hour. She looked around to see if anyone had noticed her late arrival, but it was quiet – people were out working or grabbing some lunch before the team meeting. Darcy, one of the PAs, glanced up but just gave her a friendly wave. Becky had some work to urgently catch up on but couldn't help first firing up her computer. A couple of minutes on Google, just to satisfy her curiosity.

Senerix's website came up. It was sleek and professional, with bright colours and pictures of smiling personnel in sunny fields; the epitome of the healthy outdoors. Snapshots of lush green crops with the company slogan emblazoned over: 'Your Food is Our Future: Crops in our Care'. Becky clicked onto the 'Products' tab and then hovered, unsure. There was a whole range available – did Justin use their pesticides or herbicides, or any one of the other six products Senerix produced? She chose herbicides and a list of eight came up, all with powerful, gladiatorial-sounding names.

She picked the first one: Crixus. It was a herbicide that killed broadleaf weeds and grasses in a number of crop fields including wheat and oilseed rape. She went to click on the product data sheet.

'What's that?' said a voice behind her. Flustered, she immediately closed the tab, hoping, praying, Piers hadn't seen anything.

'Do you have to go round creeping up on people?' she said crossly, as she pulled out the notes she was supposed to be working on.

'I've missed you.'

Becky felt herself tense. Saw Darcy looking over at them from the other side of the office.

'Where have you been all morning?' asked Piers.

'Your admirer's watching.'

'Huh?' Piers looked up, saw Darcy and gave her a wave. She smiled but the frown on her face didn't entirely disappear.

'There's nothing going on between us,' said Piers.

'Don't have to explain yourself to me.'

'I know that. But me and Darce – we're just mates.' He leaned in further and Becky pulled away, conscious of Darcy's gaze.

'She likes you. She's of the belief you like her. Have a bit of decency.'

'Not sure why she should think that.'

Becky rolled her eyes.

'Anyway,' continued Piers, 'you've not told me.'

'What?'

'Where you've been.'

'Following up on a call from the news desk. Cat up a tree.'

'Think you're funny?'

She turned round on her chair and faced him. 'Think you're subtle? I know you want the reporter job.'

'So do you, Ellis,' replied Piers.

'What is it with you and surnames? Some hang-up from your days at your oppressive boarding school? My name is Becky.'

'Anything you say, Ellis.'

Irritated, Becky turned back to her screen.

'Are you trying to trump me with some story?' asked Piers.

'Don't know what you're talking about.'

'Hand to hair!' said Piers, victoriously. 'Now I know you're lying.'

Damn! She had to work on her poker face. Becky checked the clock. Twenty-five past twelve. She stood. 'Daily conference. Last trainee there has to make the tea.'

'Since when?'

'New initiative. Terence announced it this morning. Did you not get the email?'

She waltzed off, leaving him stymied. *A minor triumph*, she thought. It wasn't true, but it was satisfying to see Piers's reaction, nonetheless.

The moment Becky came home that night she threw her bike helmet and bag down and ran up the stairs two at a time. She had the house to herself – her mum was on her date with that guy Tim who'd stalked her at B&Q. Becky mentally sent her a good luck wish as she opened up her laptop and began searching Senerix's website. She double-clicked the product data sheet for Crixus. At the top were pictorial warning signs: a lifeless tree and overturned dead fish, and the outline of a human head and chest, with the heart ripped out. Underneath the visual warnings, there were several statements in bold type: **'Suspected of causing cancer if inhaled.' 'Suspected of damaging the unborn child.' 'May cause damage to the nervous system through prolonged exposure or repeated exposure.'**

This stuff is going onto our foods, she thought. She knew it would be scientifically tested – vigorously tested – and there would be evidence that the weeks and months from application to harvest, the rain, the time passing, would neutralize the harm to humans. Personally, she'd still rather not take the risk.

But the massive oversight was that when these chemicals were applied, when they were undiluted by time and weather, there were people, families in their gardens just metres from the edges of the fields. And because of the current rules, it was legal.

Becky sat back in her chair. As sobering as it was, deep down she knew all this was still speculation. Not the piece of damning evidence she craved, evidence that would prove the chemicals caused Arnie's and the others' illnesses.

She pulled up the file with all the personal information she had on the families in Ramsbourne – names, addresses, telephone numbers – and downloaded it onto a memory stick. Then she deleted the original document. She tucked the stick into her jacket pocket – she would hide it tomorrow, somewhere out of the house. Something made her want to protect these people, from what exactly she didn't quite know, but a growing sense of unease was making her extra vigilant with her information.

Becky glanced at her watch. It was getting late. Her mum might be home soon, and Becky was looking forward to getting caught up in the fun of the post-date conversation. She was about to leave her room and go downstairs when an email notification popped up. One new message: a Facebook friend request. She grimaced when she saw the name: Adam Langley. She hadn't seen him since graduation day. He'd been at UCL too – had a room in the same house share as her best friend Maria on her journalism course. He'd taken a shine to her, in a bit of a cringy way, she'd thought. He was always a little too close for comfort, tried too hard. She remembered one occasion when she'd been over to see her friend and he'd made 'too much' shepherd's pie for himself and wondered if she – and Maria – would join him. They'd sat in the cramped kitchen eating lumpy mashed potato, his sports kit drying on a rack near her elbow as he had some sort of squash match to go to later that evening – she hadn't paid much attention to what it was.

It had taken him a long time to accept the hint that, sweet as he was, she just wasn't interested. He'd got a first-class honours in chemical engineering and had asked if he could take her number at the ceremony afterwards. Becky was ashamed to say, she'd given him a false one.

Nosiness – that natural journalist's instinct – made her click on the email. She opened up Facebook. There he was, bespectacled, with floppy reddish-blond hair, a dimple in his chin. *So, he's managed to track me down*, she thought ruefully. She didn't have the heart to reject the request, so she just ignored it. *Bye bye, Adam*. About to close the site, her eye suddenly landed on something and her heart leapt. That logo. It was the second time she'd seen it that day. Goosebumps rose on her arms as she scanned the page. Oh my God, he was a Research and Development assistant at Senerix Agrochemicals. *Oh happy, happy lucky day!* This was one of those rare pieces of luck that Terence called 'journalist's gold'. Should she accept? What would Terence do? He'd go for the story, obviously. And then there was Piers – she had to beat Piers.

Becky clicked on 'accept friend request' and then started to write a friendly 'It's been so long' message.

TWENTY

In the farmhouse kitchen, Justin turned up the thermostat then went back to his laptop. He was almost done with his monthly management report. It had been a long, drawn-out day, starting with that girl who'd ambushed him first thing in the morning. *Becky*, he thought, letting the name become familiar in his head. His mouth twitched into a smile: he'd liked her sparkiness, had fancied her if he was honest. Could've chatted her up if she hadn't gone banging on about that eco-warrior stuff. Maybe she'd come back. He rather hoped she would. She'd said she worked for a decent paper. It was unlikely to turn into anything, but he'd better mention it. He went back to the keyboard and typed in a short sentence and then sent the report.

It was still dark when he got up the next morning, and cold enough that his breath came in clouds in the bedroom. He threw a fleece over his pyjamas and knew he'd need coffee to start the day.

As he jogged down the stairs, he thought he heard a sound below him and slowed up, listening carefully, muscles tense. Then, from the hallway, he saw a light on in the kitchen. He stopped in his tracks, braced himself for an intruder. Whoever was in there started to whistle. Something bright and jolly.

Justin stepped into the room and was greeted by the sight of a tall, thick-set man with a horseshoe moustache.

'Good morning!' said the man, speaking with a strong eastern-European accent. 'Coffee?'

Astounded, Justin looked around and saw that the man had boiled the kettle and was pouring water into two steaming mugs. There was something very discombobulating about a bulky man in black leathers stirring the contents of a mug as if for all the world he were working in a tea shop.

'Who the hell are you?' asked Justin.

The man put down the kettle and held out his hand. 'Janković.' Despite being in his early sixties, Janković had the solid build and height of a younger man, with an impressive amount of brown still present in his close-cropped hair. The grey in his moustache was the only thing that hinted at his true age.

'Justin,' he replied automatically, while at the same time wondering why he was adhering to polite formalities.

'Yes,' said Janković. An affirmation, as if he already knew.

Justin pulled his hand away. 'Are you going to tell me why you are in my kitchen?'

'We have the same boss.'

'What?'

'He sent me.'

'I don't understand – you have a key?'

Janković waved at the phone charging on the counter as he pulled out a chair and sat at the wooden table. 'Call him if you like.'

Justin cast his eyes towards his phone. Then, without turning his back on Janković, he picked it up and dialled.

'Hey, it's Justin. Can you call me?' He hung up. 'It's his answerphone,' he said to Janković.

'I will make sure he listens to your message.'

Justin could feel his anger rising. 'I want you to get out. Now.'

'Not possible, my friend.'

'You what? You break in here, start fucking around with the coffee like you're in charge of a breakfast buffet. You can take your sorry Polish arse out my kitch—'

'No, no, no!' thundered Janković, as he slammed his fists on the table. He stared at Justin, eyes cold, his bulk leaning towards him threateningly. Justin could feel his heart hammering. This man was a lunatic. He rapidly thought of something with which to defend himself, mentally calculated the distance to the knife block.

Janković suddenly burst into loud guffaws. 'Not Polish. Serbian.' He sat back down. Took a genial sip from his coffee mug.

Justin was silenced.

Janković watched him. 'You sent your report.'

'Yes.'

'You will let me know if she comes back.'

'Who?' asked Justin, even as he knew the answer.

Janković placed a card on the table. On it was printed a number. Then, without any rush, he got up and left.

Justin waited a full five minutes before he moved – only when he'd heard the sound of a motorbike start up and then drive off down the lane.

He picked up the card. He crushed it in his hand, went to throw it away, but at the last second, something stopped him. What was it Janković had said? *They had the same boss.*

Maybe he'd wait.

Why would his boss need the services of someone like Janković?

Troubled, Justin recalled his hope the night before that Becky would come back to the farm. Now something made him hope that she wouldn't.

TWENTY-ONE

2018

Kate walked through the open door of the unfamiliar room and looked around, sick with nerves.

She was back in a classroom.

There was only one other person there so far; a thirty-something woman sat in the second row of desks. If the woman hadn't been there, if she hadn't looked up and smiled a friendly smile, then Kate would have walked out again. Instead, she croaked a 'hello' and self-consciously made her way over to a desk a couple of rows behind.

She sat down and wondered what to do next. Should she get out her notebook? A pen? Should she wait? She tried to see what the woman had done but couldn't see past her shoulder. *Oh God, please don't let me show myself up*, she prayed inwardly, getting a flashback to her nightmare from the previous night where she failed to answer the (very simple) questions the tutor was asking and suffered the scornful stares of the rest of the class.

She wondered what her high-school teachers would say if they could see her now, Caitriona, the disappointment, the girl who threw her life away for a night of foolishness, now sitting here at Croydon College, on the night-school course for Civil Litigation. She imagined a few raised eyebrows, perhaps condescending expressions. She wondered what her mother would say.

Other people started to come in, giving her a nod or smile as they took their seats. All in all, there were about twelve of them, all ages, all colours.

Then a small, bird-like woman entered, walking quickly, precisely, glasses perched on her tightly curled auburn head. She reached the front of the class, pushed the glasses to the top of her nose and examined everybody in front of her.

'Marvellous. A full house. Let it still be as such by week fifteen.'

The group shuffled. *It's amazing how quickly you can feel you're a schoolgirl again*, thought Kate.

'Anyone got anything to say about attendance?' asked the tutor.

Maybe it was the nerves, and the fact she'd almost bolted, but Kate couldn't help feeling defensive: why had this woman waltzed in without knowing anyone and suddenly assumed they were all going to turn into a bunch of skivers?

'Better make it interesting then,' Kate mumbled.

The teacher swivelled. Beady-eyed her.

Oh bollocks, thought Kate. She had not intended to be heard but, cheeks pink, she forced herself to hold the teacher's gaze.

'Very good. A challenge. An understanding of what is

rightfully yours, what you have paid for, what you expect. And what if it isn't . . . interesting?'

'Then I want my money back,' piped up an old black guy at the back. The class laughed.

'Excellent! I can see we're all going to get along famously. I'm Gloria Chapman, your tutor. Solicitor for thirty-five years, now retired. From the back – name; why you're here.'

The class began to introduce themselves. The old black guy was Clifford. He had a number of properties that he rented out and wanted to be 'well equipped' when it came to knowing what he could hold his less-reputable tenants liable for. There was a young mum – a professional – looking to go back to work but with a career change and so considering signing up for a degree; the course was a taster. A couple of solicitors were looking to expand their knowledge base. Then it was Kate's turn.

'Hi, I'm Kate Ellis. I signed up to this course because there's someone I know who I think deserves compensation.'

Gloria stopped, intrigued. 'Care to elaborate?'

Kate hesitated, squirming, hating the spotlight. She was sharply aware of how woefully unqualified she was, how she really had no idea what she was talking about.

'Um . . . it's a young boy who lives in a village in Sussex. His house is right next to a farm. I have reason to believe that the chemicals that are continually sprayed on the crops next to his house have made him really ill.' She cleared her throat nervously. 'And he's not the only one. There are several people, all in the same area.'

Gloria nodded. 'Is it illegal?'

'Is what illegal?'

'What the farmer's doing.'

'Actually . . . no.'

Gloria looked around at the rest of the class, eyebrows raised. 'So how do you intend to sue him?'

'Um . . . I just think it's wrong. What he's doing. Surely it's against the boy's human rights or something?'

'Or something?' echoed Gloria.

Kate felt herself getting hot. 'That's why I'm here. To figure out what's possible.'

Gloria appraised her. 'Tort law. That's what's possible. Your farmer has a duty of care to his or her neighbouring residents to make sure they don't come into contact with pesticides that could cause them harm. If they do, through his actions, he has a duty to compensate.'

Kate was scribbling furiously.

Gloria continued. 'Can you prove a causal link between what the farmer has done and this boy's illness?'

'Um . . .' Kate looked up, bit her lip. Gloria's eyebrows went up again.

'So, who owns your farm?' asked Gloria.

'I don't know.'

'How are you going to find out?'

Kate was silent. She had no idea.

'Anyone?' said Gloria, casting her eyes around the room.

'Land registry,' called out Clifford, the property owner.

Gloria smiled. 'Correct! And if a company is listed as the owner?'

'Companies House,' added Clifford.

Kate wrote it all down in her notepad.

'Of course, your farmer will have public liability insurance,' said Gloria.

'Would that cover any claim that might be made against him?'

Gloria smiled. 'Depends. Might cover up to ten million. You going for more?'

Kate had no idea at that moment. All this information was swimming in her head; in fact, she was finding the whole process hard to pin down.

'Any experience as a lawyer?' asked Gloria.

Kate looked up from her notepad. 'No.'

Was that a look of scepticism? Or curiosity? She felt herself wobble.

'So, you're acting as a litigation friend.'

A what?

Gloria saw her face. 'You've got a lot to learn.'

Kate didn't answer. That was obvious.

'Big project,' said Gloria.

'Yes.'

'Better grow some balls.'

Kate staggered back home just after ten that night, shutting the door against the rain. She hung up her wet coat in the hallway and went to collapse on the sofa.

'How's the student?' said Tim, as he hastily tidied up some papers on the coffee table.

'I know nothing. *Nothing.*'

'Come on, it wasn't that bad, was it?'

'I honestly don't know if I'm going to be able to do this. There's some smart people on the course. People with degrees. Years of experience. I'm definitely the novice.'

'And your point is?'

'It's hard, Tim. Really hard. Everyone else seemed to "get" stuff a lot quicker than me.'

'You'll speed up. It's just new, that's all. You figure out what you need to do?'

'Find out who owns the farm – to start with anyway.' As Kate put her feet up on the table, she accidentally knocked off one of Tim's documents. She picked it up, just as he also went for it. He held out his hand.

She noticed the pile on the table for the first time. They looked official. Financial papers, legal documents. 'You have a busy night?'

'Just doing a bit of filing. You know.' He opened and closed his hand for the document she was holding.

As Kate passed it over, her eyes caught the top of it.

'But this is addressed to you in Northampton,' she said, surprised.

'Where I used to live. You know that.'

She did: it was where he'd grown up and his parents were still there, in the same house they'd been in for forty years. They'd Skyped once or twice, not having managed to meet yet. Kate had been caught up in her own life and they couldn't bring themselves to visit for a weekend, as it would disrupt their routine of Friday night bingo.

'But . . .' She blushed, feeling as if she was prying.

'What?'

'The date on the top of the letter. It's January last year.'

'And?'

'Well, that's only a couple of weeks before we met.'

'And?'

'I thought . . . well, you didn't ever say that you'd only just moved down south.'

'You never asked,' he said briskly. 'Is it important?'

No, thought Kate, she supposed not.

TWENTY-TWO

Kate had risen early and taken the train to Ramsbourne, nervous about the task ahead. She walked down the dirt track that ran adjacent to Hawthorne Lane. It was muddy and large, squelchy ruts ambushed her supermarket trainers, however hard she tried to avoid them. She made a mental note to look in the second-hand shop for a pair of wellies. Then, after about half a mile, she came into a large yard, flanked by seven or eight big outbuildings: Ashdown Farm.

Kate looked around at the barns and the massive steel silos, wondering where the farm manager might be. Or perhaps he was in one of the two thousand acres he managed.

One of the barns had its doors wide open. She tentatively made her way across, looked into the cavernous space. Bales of hay were stacked at one end, reaching far up to the ceiling – several times her height. The room had a sweet, earthy smell and, other than the hay, it was empty.

'Can I help you?'

She jumped. Flustered, she turned on her full-beam smile at the man who stood in the vast doorway, his arms folded.

She tried to make out his features, but he was in silhouette. Best to speak.

'Hello. I'm looking for Justin Holmes.'

He stepped forward into the light cast from a window and she recognized his face from the farm website.

'You've found him. And you are?'

'Caitriona,' she said automatically, not wanting to give her familiar name. She held out a hand. He didn't take it and she nervously dropped her hand by her side.

'What can I do for you?'

There was no warmth to his eyes, and his rolled-up shirt-sleeves exposed the wiry muscles on his forearms. He was blocking her exit.

'I've been looking around the area . . . thinking of moving here. And I was curious . . . about your farm. Crops, is it? As opposed to . . . cattle . . . or sheep?'

He didn't answer.

'I love the country, green fields,' she said, echoing Grace. 'Then it goes all golden when it ripens. Wheat, anyway. Do you have wheat?'

'We do.' He spoke cautiously.

'Ah, OK. Interesting. Yes . . . I was also wondering about how you grow it. You know . . . when you dig the field, plant the seeds. What kind of stuff you spray on the crops.'

'Why?'

'Sorry?'

'I said, why? Why do you want to know that?'

She smiled disarmingly. 'Just interested. If it's going to be in my back yard.'

He studied her a moment. 'They're all standard, all approved.'

'Herbicides?'

'Naturally.'

There's nothing natural about them, thought Kate. 'What's in them?'

'Like I say, they're all licensed.'

'Can you tell me what the chemicals are? Just curious, you understand.'

'Where did you say you were looking to move?'

'Oh, in Ramsbourne.'

'Yes, I got that. Where exactly?'

Flustered, she answered quickly. 'Hawthorne Lane.'

'Didn't think there were any houses for sale there.'

Stupid, stupid, thought Kate. Why hadn't she been more vague? 'It's only just come on the market. Not yet advertised.'

A pause and then he nodded, and she was unsure whether he believed her. 'Good luck. I'm quite busy . . . if you don't mind.' He stood to one side, allowing her to walk out of the barn.

'Sure. Nice talking to you, Justin. Great farm you've got. Who's the owner here, by the way? Someone local?' In fact, she knew it wasn't. Her online investigation had told her the farm and the land were owned by a nondescript company that was registered in Cyprus, a place notorious for hiding the true individuals behind companies.

'If you have anything you need to speak about, you can talk to me. Now, as I said . . .' He smiled coolly. 'Lots to do.'

'Course.'

She walked back out into the sunshine, sensing him right behind her. Once on the track, she looked back to see that he was watching her, making sure she left. A few metres down, the track took a turn to the left, near some oak trees. She stopped. Checked behind again and saw she was out of view of the farm. *Damn*. That hadn't gone how she'd wanted it to. She'd hoped to have more of a look around. But now Justin was about, she couldn't check anything out. Unless . . . maybe he *did* have lots to do. Maybe he would be off in one of the fields in a minute. She looked up. Dare she?

Dropping her bag on the ground, she hoisted herself up one of the oaks. Carefully and slowly, she climbed until she could see back to the farm. There he was. Talking to someone else, another worker it looked like. Then he headed back up to the farmhouse, got into a Land Rover and started it up. In a panic, Kate realized he was heading for the track and that in a few seconds he'd drive right past her. She cursed as she saw her bag at the foot of the trunk. There was no time to rescue it now. It was partially hidden by some long grass and she prayed it would be enough. Holding her breath as he drew closer and closer, she shrank back into the tree, grateful for its new-leaf coverage.

Then he was gone. She waited a moment until her heart calmed, then looked back up to the farm. The other worker had changed into a suit of some sort: white, from head to toe. He turned, and she saw he wore a respirator mask. He headed to a small building set aside from the others, a corrugated-steel container outside the barn she'd just been in. He went inside and reappeared with a plastic container, the contents of which he started to pour into a vessel at the back of a piece of machinery attached to a tractor. Once it was empty, he took the plastic container back to the steel box. He attached a pump to the vessel, and waited for a while. Then, after removing it, he got in the cab and began to drive away from the yard, the machinery dragging behind. It was then she realized what he was doing. He was going out to spray the fields.

It was a sobering sight. Despite the sunshine, she shivered. She couldn't quite believe what she'd just witnessed. How could an operator be kitted out like that and still no one did anything about the residents, just metres from the spray?

Kate made her way back down the tree and retrieved her bag. Scurrying back up the track, she kept her eyes open for any other workers but, to her relief, no one else seemed to be around.

She tentatively headed for the steel container emblazoned with 'hazardous' stickers but the door was closed. She tried the handle and her heart leapt as it turned – he hadn't relocked it. She stepped inside. There were shelves from floor to ceiling, stacked with a wall of plastic containers. The labels thrust themselves in her face: bright-orange 'hazardous' warnings, skull and crossbones, '*Toxic!*' written again and again. The majority of them were a product called Crixus, manufactured by a company called Senerix. Knowing Justin could come back at any moment, she quickly got out her phone and took photo after photo. Then she heard a Land Rover drive through the yard and she froze.

Kate risked a peek out of the container and saw Justin park outside the farmhouse. *Please don't come into the yard*, she urged silently. Instead, he went into the house and she took her chances. She ran across the yard and back down the track as fast as she could. She didn't stop until she'd got all the way to the train station. Thankfully, there was a train due in three minutes and it was only once she'd jumped on, breath heaving, and the doors had been locked shut behind her that she could sink into her seat with relief.

TWENTY-THREE

2005

Kate sat down on the metal-legged plastic chair in the head-teacher's office, Becky taking the seat next to her, swinging her legs quietly back and forth. With a pang, Kate noticed how Becky's feet just touched the floor now, another marker of how she was growing up.

'Thank you for coming in,' said Mrs Parker ('Call me Mrs P'), going to sit opposite them. Over Mrs P's shoulder, out of the window, Kate could see the playground teeming with kids and parents – a swathe of blue uniforms ready to go home. She had no idea why she'd been summoned to this private meeting with the headteacher but had been told by the office staff that it was 'nothing bad'.

'So, as you're obviously aware, it's Becky's last year of primary school,' said Mrs P. 'Have you had any thoughts on where next?'

Kate looked at Becky, nonplussed. 'Well . . . it would be Priory . . .' It was the local state school, part of a large Academy chain that hoovered up most of the kids in the area.

Mrs P smiled. 'Hmm. And I wouldn't be one to knock Priory, but I wondered if you were aware of Hillcrest?'

Kate was, vaguely, in the same way she was aware of skiing holidays and branded trainers. Things other people did. People with money. She wondered why Mrs P was talking to her about it; surely it was obvious they could never afford a private school – for that's what it was. She had added to the money her dad had given her at Becky's birth, a carefully put away ten pounds a month, for that was all she could afford. It was intended to help with Becky's university costs, so she couldn't think about blowing it on school fees. Kate inwardly snorted. It would barely cover half a term, anyway. She felt a rosy glow appear at the top of her cheeks.

'It's not really an option,' she said, thinking, *you might as well ask me to fund a trip to the moon.*

'I think it could be.'

Kate opened her mouth to speak but Mrs P gently held up a hand.

'Allow me to finish. Once a year, they take in a child from a local primary school and offer them a full scholarship. As you're aware, Becky is extremely bright, and she works hard.'

Kate felt Becky bloom next to her.

'I think she has a good chance,' continued Mrs P, 'and I would certainly write her a glowing reference.'

Kate didn't know what to say. Her daughter at a fancy private school? It was so far from the realm of possibility she couldn't quite imagine it. And anyway, would she fit in with all those hoity-toity posh kids? Would she be happy?

'At least go and see,' said Mrs P. 'They have an open evening next Thursday.' She turned to Becky. 'You'd like to see it, wouldn't you, Becky? If you got in . . . well, I believe they have horse riding.'

Kate gave Mrs P a hard look – *seriously?* – but the wily head just smiled back at her. Becky, of course, was fidgeting in her seat with excitement. 'Can we, Mummy? *Please?*'

Kate mentally thought through her shift pattern at the restaurant for the following week. Thursday was her night off. Looked like they'd be going to this school, then.

She'd been rendered silent by what she'd just seen: the 200 acres of grounds (actually, she hadn't seen all of these, just a swathe of green); the new 25-metre pool; the huge, well-equipped gym; the climbing wall; the photos of the trips to Mexico, Silicon Valley, China; the modern classrooms which she'd been told were filled with just a handful of bright-eyed children; the energetic teachers; the peacocks that wandered through the grounds, the kids passing them as if it was the most normal thing in the world.

All this had been presented to her by a girl a mere three years older than Becky, who had more poise and confidence than Kate had ever possessed in her life. In fact, right now, she felt deeply uncomfortable, as if someone had let her look around this place by mistake. She'd looked for fault but found none and, to her shame, had even wanted to dislike this young tour guide but she could criticize nothing, and the girl was warm and funny and had taken Becky under her wing.

They were back in the main hall, a large space with a stage and enough equipment for a West End production, in time for the headmistress's speech. Small round tables were spread around the room, covered with linen cloths, and as Kate drew nearer, she was astounded to see they were loaded with bottles of wine and sparkling water and tiered trays of canapés and petit fours. With the theatrical lighting set to something soft and inviting, the overall look was like some kind of high-end restaurant.

Kate took a seat, and Becky, wide-eyed, asked her mother's permission to help herself to cakes. As her daughter got stuck in, Kate looked around the room. The tables were beginning to fill up with prospective parents and pupils, teachers assisting on the sidelines. A couple of people approached her table, nodding a friendly hello as they took their places, while talking with confidence and enthusiasm about what they'd just seen. A woman offered to pour Kate a glass of wine and she got an unexpected surge of bravery. Why shouldn't she have some wine like these other people were so casually doing? As if it were the most ordinary thing in the world to turn up to a school open day where free food and alcohol were offered. Food that was way more upmarket than she could ever serve at home.

She took a sip and sat up in surprise. It was nice, felt smooth on her tongue. For the first time that evening, she started to relax.

A woman passed by, heading for the next table along, her daughter by her side. Kate's eyes were drawn to her – or rather, the woman's coat. It was a subtle pink in what looked like the most luxurious soft wool Kate had ever seen. As the woman sat, the coat undulated in waves and folds around her tall, neat frame. She'd pinned a brooch onto one of the lapels, something creamy and pearl-like, and the whole effect was truly a thing of beauty.

Kate couldn't help staring; its impracticality was something alien to her. This coat did not look like it would tolerate rain or mud or public transport and would positively baulk at a practical backpack clinging to its back like a crusty, aged limpet. The coat's owner did not notice Kate, didn't seem to be aware of much but her own self and her offspring. So distracted was she by this woman and her outer garments, Kate reached for her glass of wine without looking and accidentally knocked it over. A large red pool spread across the white tablecloth and dripped onto the floor.

Mortified, Kate inwardly cursed – *so clumsy!* – but a quick glance up reassured her no one had really noticed.

'Are you OK, Mummy?' asked Becky and Kate nodded. She saw a pile of paper napkins on one of the tables on the edges of the room, a table full of spares: several extra bottles of wine stood sentry-like, should their services be required. Kate went over and grabbed a handful of napkins and then got on her hands and knees and started to mop up the wine on the floor.

'Excuse me,' a crisp voice cut over to her. Kate looked up.

'Yes, you.' It was the woman in the pink coat.

'I'm afraid we have a little spillage here, too,' she said, pointing at a spot on the floor with her foot.

Kate's gaze rested on the puddle of liquid, her face the same level as the pointing shoe. For a moment, she didn't understand.

The woman was looking at her expectantly, with a hint of impatience. Kate suddenly realized the woman was waiting for her to act so she could go back to her conversation undisturbed. The woman obviously thought Kate was some sort of staff member. A cleaner-upper. Someone below herself in status.

Becky was frowning, and Kate felt the heat rise in her cheeks. She ignored the woman and slowly got up and sat back at her table. One or two people next to her glanced around, maybe even rolled their eyes, but no one said anything.

The woman realized her faux pas. Then she laughed at her silliness and turned her pink-clad back. No apology. No acknowledgement of her rudeness. No embarrassment.

Just dismissal.

During the headmistress's speech, Kate's humiliation blossomed into anger and she cut the woman (who she would later learn was called Julia Cromwell, as her daughter, Violet, would be in Becky's class) several daggerlike looks. Not one of which Julia Cromwell noticed.

It was only when Becky began to outshine Violet in her lessons that Julia began to take any notice of either of them.

TWENTY-FOUR

2018

'Two hundred and forty-seven? Seriously?' said Kate, wide-eyed.

'Just goes to show how many budding journalists out there need help.' Greg put a large tower of paper on the table in front of them. 'You still up for it?'

'Course. How many are we narrowing it down to?'

'Depends on how many you want to interview – and, of course, how many great applicants there are. But I would suggest around fifteen max.'

Kate reached over to take the top CV off the pile.

'Wrong bit of paper,' said Greg, wagging his finger, and he handed her the gin-tasting menu instead. 'If we're going to get through these, we need sustenance.'

She smiled. They were in a quiet bar just around the corner from the Vietnamese he'd taken her to and their visit had coincided with gin-tasting night.

'Leather and raspberry?' Kate marvelled. 'Are they having a laugh?'

As Greg ordered two leather gins from a young waistcoat-clad bartender, Kate took in her surroundings. The bar had the feel of an atrium, with floor-to-ceiling windows and skylights. Moroccan-patterned tiles in shades of chocolate and orange covered the floor and the room was awash with green palms in copper pots. It was unlike anywhere she'd ever been before. The cocktails arrived in elegant martini glasses carried on a silver tray by the waistcoated bartender.

She took a sip. It was sublime. Kate got a sense of her world opening up. Who knew leather could taste so awesome? Who knew people made drinks like this? For that matter, who knew bars like this existed?

'Wow.'

'I'll second that,' said Greg, placing his glass down. 'Before we start, I just wanted to apologize. If I offended Tim the other week, I certainly didn't mean to.'

Embarrassed, Kate brushed it off. 'It's fine. He's fine.' She could sense him checking her, making sure he hadn't caused any harm.

'Nice guy,' he said.

'He is. You married?'

'Divorced.'

'Oh, sorry.'

'Don't be. She found someone who works less. I now get to work more without worrying about leaving her. Win-win.' He handed her half the papers. 'Let's go through a pile each and highlight the ones we think shine. Just to recap, what are we looking for?'

'A passion for journalism,' said Kate. 'Dedication and genuine need.'

'OK.'

She looked down at the first sheet. 'Blimey . . .'

'What?'

'This person . . . Andrew . . . has written, "I am bilingual in three languages."'

'No . . .' Greg said, laughing.

'"Current salary: thirty-four thousand. Salary desired: two hundred and fifty thousand." It's not a job! Have they not read the ad properly?'

'It appears not.' Greg cleared a space on the table. 'Reject pile?'

She nodded and picked up another CV. '"I think I will make a good journalist as I am quick with typing. Thirty wpm or fifty wpm with an espresso."' She flicked further down the page. '"I am drawn to investigative journalism by my love of finding out what the latest fashion trends are worn by celebrities." No. No, no, no!'

'My turn,' said Greg. '"My dream is to be an astronaut but as I have absolutely no chance of this happening, I'm seeking a career as a journalist instead."'

Kate groaned. 'Who are all these people?'

'Don't worry, it'll improve. Go on. Turn the next one over.'

She picked up the next application. 'Gillian Harris, aged twenty-one. Graduating from Sheffield University this year. On target for a first-class honours degree in Journalism.'

'Impressive.'

'Worked part-time on a local newspaper throughout university. Hold on, it says here she's been offered an internship with the *Guardian* – beat twelve hundred other applicants. But she can't afford to take it up.'

'One for the interview pile?'

'Definitely.' She smiled. 'This is a good thing we're – you're – doing,' she said. 'Becky would have approved.'

'It's all inspired by her.'

'Thanks, Greg,' she said.

'What for?'

'Helping keep her memory alive. It's been hard, the last year. Some people talk about her; some think it makes it too painful. But I'd rather talk. If I don't, it's as if she was never there.'

'It'll never be like that.'

'Last Christmas, I got my first card addressed just to me, without her name in. It was from a girl from work. She thought she was being sensitive, but it had me weeping on the floor. It was as if Becky had been erased. And that's my greatest fear. That she'll be forgotten.' Kate felt herself get emotional and quickly picked up another paper. 'Look at this one. Three spelling mistakes in the opening sentence! Becky would've had her red pen out. She was a stickler for spelling. Grammar too. Only person I knew who could use a semi-colon properly. Or at least I think she could. I wouldn't know the difference.'

'What was her writing like?'

'What do you mean?'

'Well . . . you said before she liked to work on investigative stories.'

'That's right.'

'Anything in particular?'

'Her first piece at the paper was on corruption in the Premier League – bribes and so on. Not her story but she supported her boss.'

'Impressive. What else?'

'There was something she was working on just before she died. Something big.'

'Oh, yeah? What was it?'

Kate paused. She suddenly realized she didn't want to say anything about Becky's unfinished story – not yet. She had a lead she was hoping to follow up in the morning but until anything was concrete, she didn't want to discuss it with anyone. She shrugged. 'She never told me. I'd ask but it was too top secret.' *That wasn't a lie.* She looked at him and got the sense he didn't believe her, but he smiled.

'If you do find anything, it would be great to know. We could incorporate it as part of Becky's legacy. Something inspirational to put on the bursary website.'

'That would be good.'

'Did she have a computer? There might be something there that would give you an insight into what she was doing.'

'Some kids broke in. Trashed the house. They took it.'

'Oh, I'm sorry.'

'It's OK.'

'Notebooks?'

Kate brightened. 'It's possible. I haven't actually cleared her room out.' Her face fell again. 'Actually, we didn't find any when we put it back together again after the break-in.' She sighed inwardly. *If only I still had the laptop, it might have given me more information*, she thought. *Like who owns Ashdown Farm.*

'So, where did she get it from? You in journalism too?'

Kate let out a bark of laughter. 'Me? No. I work in B&Q. She's the one with the brains.'

'You have brains.'

'Seriously. You have to stop it. It's embarrassing.' She paused. 'I didn't even finish school.' Kate picked up the next application and showed it to Greg. Attached to the front was a picture, not of the applicant but of a cat dressed in a blazer and balanced behind its ear was a pen.

When she got back, Tim was in bed, reading, his glasses perched on the end of his nose. He pushed them onto his forehead as she walked into the bedroom.

'I was about to call,' he said.

'Sorry. Got carried away, lost track of time.' She snuggled up to him.

'Did it go well?'

'We found a few good candidates in amongst the crazies.'

'Good.'

She leaned over and kissed him, and Tim cracked a smile. 'You stink of booze. He take you anywhere nice?'

'Some ridiculously fancy cocktail bar.'

'Did he.'

'Don't be jealous. It was rubbish.'

'I know you're lying. By the way, something I need to tell you.'

'What?'

'It's Iris. She's been in hospital.'

Alarmed, Kate sat up. 'What?'

'She had another fall. Bashed her face. She's fine now,' he quickly reassured her. 'I called the ambulance, she was checked out, a couple of strips put on, and then I brought her home in a cab.'

'Thank goodness. Why didn't you call me?'

'I didn't want to disturb you . . . knew you were busy,' he said, and she frowned. 'It wasn't like I couldn't take care of it myself. She's *fine*,' he reiterated.

'Did she call? Here?'

'No, she couldn't get to the phone. I saw the sign,' he explained. 'The flamenco lady hadn't been put back on the windowsill.'

Kate bit her lip. 'Maybe I should cancel my plans tomorrow.'

'That doctor? It's taken you ages to track him down.'

He was right. Kate would go and see Iris in the morning and then decide what to do for the best.

TWENTY-FIVE

Kate was horrified to see that Iris was sporting a black eye to go with the cut on her cheek, when she went round the next day. 'It's the sideboard's fault,' said Iris. 'Attacked me on my way down.'

'Are you OK?'

'Fine. Bit bruised. Ego too.'

She pointed to the handrail she'd reluctantly decided on putting next to the toilet. 'I feel like an invalid,' she grumbled to Kate. 'Never get old.'

'I think that might be out of my power.' Kate had come over with her toolkit and was marking the place on the wall where she was about to screw the rail in.

'Good God, to think it comes to this. Still, if I'm going to have one, it should be there. The last thing I want is to fall with my knickers around my ankles.' She clutched her bosom. 'The shame of it!'

'Sorry I wasn't around yesterday.'

Iris flapped her away. 'Tim was there, don't worry. Good night with Greg?'

'Yeah. Some great CVs,' said Kate.

'And how's it going with this detective work?'

'You mean Becky's story?'

Iris nodded.

'Well, I still don't know who owns Ashdown Farm. It's virtually impossible to find out the real individual behind these offshore companies.'

'Scheming tax dodgers?'

'And the rest. I've had to throw myself at the mercy of a forensic accountant.'

'Never heard of them.'

'Me neither, until in class the other day. They specialize in digging up dirt. Investigate what's really going on behind the scenes.'

'Sounds expensive.'

'It is. Four hundred.'

'To do the job? I suppose that's not too bad.'

Kate grimaced. 'An hour.'

Iris's mouth dropped. 'Good God. How on earth . . . ?'

'Like I say, I begged for mercy. Managed to persuade the trainee to take pity on me. Still costing a bit but I've got a couple of discounted hours out of her. Might not be enough but it's worth a try.'

'So, what are you going to do when you find out who it is?'

'Sue him. Or her. On my course, I've found out that I can pursue them under "tort law".'

'Sounds painful.'

'I'm slowly building up the case about the poisons that these people have had sprayed on or near them and what it's done to them. And –' she took a deep breath – 'I've found a doctor!'

'To make them better?'

'If only that were possible. No, who also believes that herbicides are bad news. This doctor has had several children in his rural village become ill with cancer. He's written a report stating that there is a link between herbicides and leukaemia – and in that report he mentioned Senerix, the agrochemical company who make the stuff that's put on the fields at the farm in Sussex. I want him to look at Arnie's case, and the others, and put his claims on record.'

'Will he?'

'Not yet. I emailed him last week, but he fobbed me off.'

'He scared?'

'Probably. He doesn't know me. It's a big thing to put your name to for a complete stranger.' Kate started to drill, and the conversation paused. Iris, sitting on the loo lid, picked up her TV-listings magazine.

'So, what next?' she said when the drilling abated.

'I thought I'd go and see him. Try and persuade him . . .' said Kate, tentatively.

Iris beamed. 'Good for you. Where is he? Local?'

'France.'

'Oh my Lordy Lord.' Iris wafted her face with her magazine.

'It's not that bad.'

'It's positively foreign!'

'I know. Exciting, isn't it? I've never been abroad before. I've got my flight booked . . .'

'When for?'

Kate's eyes shone. 'This afternoon.'

'What?!'

'After getting his email, well, I wasn't going to take no for an answer, so I rang his surgery and asked for an appointment to see him. The earliest they could fit me in was tomorrow morning.'

'But I thought he fobbed you off?'

'He did.'

Iris was puzzled. 'Go on.'

'He thinks I'm a patient. I phoned up for a medical appointment. Gave the receptionist another name so he didn't refuse to see me. Pretended I was on holiday there but have unfortunately contracted a virus that needs professional attention.'

Iris laughed. 'Sneaky!'

'There, that's done now,' said Kate, patting the handrail. 'Why don't you give it a whirl?'

Iris eyed it with a mixture of suspicion and disdain. 'Oh, all right.' She grabbed the rail and pulled herself up.

'Ta da!' said Kate. 'You will be all right while I'm away, won't you? I was going to ask Tim to look in on you.'

'I'll be as right as rain.' Iris looked at the rail. Sighed. 'I suppose I could always hang a towel on it. Disguise it. Right, time for some Rooibos tea. Stops the signs of aging apparently.' She made her way towards the kitchen. 'Just make sure you don't come back until he's made a statement. Signed!'

TWENTY-SIX

Her first trip overseas. She was actually in *Bordeaux*! *In France!* Kate was slightly amazed that she'd made it as she gazed across the river at a stunning bridge, lit up in the gathering dusk. Flying had not been without its challenges. It had never occurred to her that she might not know what to do. The check-in man had looked at her in puzzlement when she'd asked what happened after she'd handed over her new passport. After being directed through security, there were yet more *Krypton Factor*-like challenges to navigate. Where did she go next? She couldn't call Tim as he was navigating a 196 bus through the rush-hour traffic. She was about to ask a friendly-looking fellow passenger when Greg had rung her to double-check the shortlist of CVs for the bursary. She'd kept him on the line a minute longer.

'Could I ask a favour?'

'Sure.'

'It's a bit embarrassing but . . . I'm at an airport. Where do I find the plane?'

He'd been stunned into silence and then burst out laughing. She indulged him. *Yes, yes, very funny. Whenever you're ready.*

The laughter died. 'You're not joking, are you?'

'That's why I asked.'

'Have you never flown before?' He sounded amazed.

'Now, let me think. Yes, there was that time I flew first-class to the Bahamas and lay on a beach for two weeks having someone massage my toes and spray me with mists of pure mineral water.'

He laughed again.

'I could really use a hand here – I kind of need to not miss this.'

'Sorry. You go to the gate.'

'Gate? What gate?'

'You see a bank of screens?'

Kate looked around. Saw some a few metres away and headed over. 'Yes?'

'Your flight will be listed. And when they're ready, they'll put the gate number up. As soon as they do, you follow the signs and go sit in a small holding pen until the airline crew direct you onto the plane.'

'Thank you.'

'It's a little less luxurious than your previous trip.'

'That's it. I'm going home again.'

'Where are you off to?'

'Short break. France.'

'Nice. Any particular reason?'

'Just fancied it. Never been.'

'Clearly.'

There was a moment of silence, where it was evident she wasn't telling the whole story, but he didn't pry.

'Sorry to bother you,' she said. 'I'm pathetic.'

'No, no,' he reassured her. 'You're normal.'

She wasn't really, she was a stunted adult with less life experience than most, due to a teenage pregnancy and a lack of education. *Not that I'd change having had Becky for the world*, she quickly thought.

Now, as she looked around the pedestrianized streets of Bordeaux, Kate felt herself slow and relax as she moved with the ebb and flow of the evening crowd. She took the time to take in her surroundings: wrought-iron curls above heavy wooden doors, white stone buildings oozing grace and majesty – and the lights! Lights everywhere: on the buildings, in the squares, turning the trees into clusters of glowing emeralds. This was a city that came alive at night. And walking around it was free.

Kate was worried about how much this impromptu trip had cost – with the expense of paying the forensic accountant, every penny of her savings had long gone, and she'd had to sell a good chunk of her shares. *It's important, it's important*, she told herself firmly, quelling the rising anxiety. The doctor's testimony was crucial to her case. She had to get Dr Zayan on side tomorrow – how, she still had no idea, but it would be an expensive failure if she didn't.

Kate was hungry but had already decided to avoid the restaurants. Street food was cheaper. She found a deli and bought a baguette filled with Brie and tomato for a few euros and went to sit on a bench in the centre of a square. It was lively; cafes lined the wide pavements and the outside tables were filling up, garlanded by groups of people with their glasses of wine and plates of charcuterie. There were a lot of smokers, Kate noticed. And dogs, the French seemed to like their dogs, many hunkered under chairs and tables, chins settled on paws for the long night. It wasn't a loud, frenzied crowd as it might have been in London, where drinkers stood in crowds, talking at high volume, blocking the pavements. No one stood here. They sat in civilized groups.

It was a shame she couldn't join them, she thought, find herself a table for one and order a drink and watch the people go by. She looked longingly at the cafe nearest to her. An empty table beckoned. *Oh, what the heck, why not?* It would cost less than ten euros and seeing as this was her first-ever trip abroad and something she'd been yearning for all her adult life, she could allow herself an hour of escapism.

She walked over and took a seat, the iron chair scraping on the cobblestones. No one else took any notice of her, no one looked at her strangely, wondering why she was alone. She picked up the menu. A waitress appeared and Kate scanned the wine list. Understanding very little of it, her eyes settled on one word. *Well, when in Bordeaux . . .* She pointed to it on the menu. 'A glass of this one, *s'il vous plaît.*'

As she sipped the wine, enjoying its smooth warmth, she thought about what she was going to say to Dr Zayan tomorrow. Wondered how he was going to react when he learned that she didn't have a virus after all.

*

189

The following morning Kate ordered a taxi to St Couraque, a small village fifty kilometres north of Bordeaux, as it had no train station and that was the only way she could see to get there. It cost eighty-five euros, which made her wince – she could ill afford it. The car picked her up at eleven from her hotel and wound its way through the city, crossing the river with St Michel cathedral behind her, the sun on the water lighting her way ahead. Once they'd left the main road, the car looped through the countryside that had made the region so famous. Rows upon rows of neat ordered vines marked dark-green grids across the landscape. Occasionally, they would pass a grand chateau standing sentry over the burgeoning crops below. It was serenely beautiful, a landscape that had inspired artists for decades.

As they came into St Couraque, with its cobbled square, the church bells were striking noon and the dozen or so shops were bringing in their goods from the front, ready to close for lunch. Kate paid the driver and he drove off, the engine noise fading fast. The last of the shutters went down and then it was quiet. She saw a few people turning into side streets, presumably to their homes, then noticed she was the only person left in the square. Feeling disconcerted, she looked around for Rue Albert, which she knew was one of the roads leading off the square, and headed down it.

A very neat, very clean front door with a buzzer, and a gold nameplate with the name Dr Bernhard Zayan embossed across it, told her she'd reached the right place. Kate pressed the buzzer and the door clicked open. Inside, a middle-aged receptionist with her hair in a bun looked up.

'*Bonjour*. You must be Madame Thomas.'

'Yes, that's right,' said Kate. It had been necessary to concoct a fake name, so Dr Zayan didn't automatically dismiss her.

'The doctor is free now,' said the receptionist and indicated another door to the side of her desk.

Kate knocked tentatively.

'You can just go in,' the receptionist instructed.

She opened the door. Dr Zayan sat at a large modern desk, a computer in front of him, books lining the pale-olive painted walls. A small box of children's toys stood in the corner and, projecting out from behind a blue curtain, Kate could make out the end of an examination table.

He looked up and rolled his wheeled chair back from the desk. 'Take a seat.'

She did, noticing a photo of a vibrant brunette hugging two small boys Blu-tacked to the wall in front of him. *His wife and children*, she thought.

'So, I understand you are here on holiday?' he said with a thick accent.

'Yes . . .' said Kate. He had striking blue eyes, made even more noticeable by the fact he had incredibly short hair, shaven almost to his tanned scalp.

'And you have some virus, no?' he prompted.

'Not exactly.'

He frowned and checked his computer. 'I must apologize . . . this is what we have . . .'

Kate took a breath. Smiled. 'I'm actually here because . . . I wanted to talk to you.'

He raised a bemused eyebrow.

'A while back, a woman wrote to you. A woman from the UK, asking if you would talk to her on record about your experiences of – and beliefs on – the use of herbicides in agriculture. Specifically, the beautiful vineyards,' she waved a hand towards the window, 'around here.'

He stiffened, and the welcoming smile had gone.

'And I know you refused,' she hurried on, 'but—'

'You can tell her no. And you can also tell her to stop sending her . . . friend?' He raised an eyebrow. 'You can tell her to stop sending you to come out and harass me.'

'There's no need.'

'Pardon?'

Kate said nothing, just smiled hopefully.

He sighed. 'It's you.'

'Guilty as charged. Listen, before you kick off,' she said quickly, 'please just hear me out.'

He said nothing, and she was encouraged. 'As I said in my email, a little boy I know is ill – really ill, because he has leukaemia. I believe he got this disease from the crop-spraying that goes on right outside his house and I want to help him, his family.' She paused. 'I'm a lawyer . . .'

He looked at her sceptically.

'. . . in training –' she kept on talking despite his look of disbelief – 'and I'm planning to sue the people responsible for spraying these poisons metres from where he – Arnie – lives. I'm building my case and you . . . you are a brick.'

He stood. 'I am not,' he said softly.

'Please don't throw me out. I've come all this way

specially . . . I know you're an expert on this. Those children, in your article – you've ascertained before that herbicides have caused cancer. Twelve children in this village alone, whose school backs onto vineyards – twelve children in eight years have had cancer—'

He cut her off. 'I know my patients.'

'You wrote about it, said how you believed it was because of the herbicides, sprayed right up to the edge of their playground, spray that drifted through the open windows of their classrooms—'

'I'm sorry but I can't help you.'

Kate dug into her bag. Pulled out the photos she'd printed off from her phone, the containers of Senerix products that she'd taken at the farm. 'Are these the same chemicals?'

He looked at them for a moment. 'Put those away, please.'

She didn't. 'Please, Dr Zayan, I need you.'

'You should ask your own British doctors.'

'They don't know what you do. You have the proof.'

'I have no proof,' he said with finality. 'That is the problem.' He walked to the door and held it open.

Burning with disappointment, Kate refused to move at first. 'Why won't you help?'

'I'm sorry you've had a wasted trip.'

He was hiding something, she knew it. 'Why won't you help?' she repeated.

He hesitated, and for a moment she thought he was going to buckle.

'My next patient is here.' He indicated the way out. 'If you please.'

Kate saw a young girl, about nine or ten, in the waiting room with her mother. 'Is she one of them?'

He didn't answer at first, and she had the feeling he wasn't going to tell her, then: 'Yes. She is doing really well. She's been in remission for a year now.'

'Well, Arnie isn't. He's still waiting for a donor match.'

Dr Zayan put his hand on her arm and firmly pulled her aside, away from the open door. 'Do not try to tell me how horrific cancer is, how devastating it is for these children,' he said with a quiet fury. 'I have seen more than I care to, remember?'

He let go of her arm and she left the room.

Dr Zayan smiled as the woman and her daughter went in. The door closed behind them.

Stupid, stupid, Kate thought. Why had she let herself get emotional? She'd completely messed it up and now her chance had gone. Heavy-hearted, she made her way towards the exit.

'*Excusez-moi?*' Kate turned and saw the receptionist was looking at her sharply. 'You need to pay, please.'

TWENTY-SEVEN

Tuesday, 31 January 2017
– twenty-four days before the accident

Becky could see him sitting at the table in the window, studying the menu with great concentration. She hesitated; if she was going to bail, now was the time, but then he looked up and the delighted smile of recognition made her blush and her heart sink in equal measure. *You've made your bed, now lie in it,* she told herself and pushed open the door of the bistro.

He stood and was about to take her coat when a waiter beat him to it, and then there was a bit of a delay while they got in their seats, Adam chivalrously not sitting until she had done so, which turned into an awkward display of a badly timed Bavarian knee dance.

'It's really good to see you,' he said, and she brushed aside the niggling uncomfortable feeling she got at the way he didn't take his eyes off her. 'You look just the same.'

'Not older? Wiser?' she said lightly.

'It was only six months ago! I'm so glad you got in touch. I tried to call you, after graduation. Got a different person.'

Oh shit, she thought, keeping the smile fixed on her face. 'I lost my phone,' she said, and the lame excuse hung mockingly in the air.

There was a faltering silence and then he said, 'Well, here we are.' He gestured around the bistro. 'Lunch!'

'Yes!' agreed Becky. 'Is your office near here?' They'd met in a place only a five-minute walk from the paper – he'd insisted on it being in this part of town because it was close to where she worked.

'Not really. I'm based in Surrey – just outside Walton-on-Thames.'

'Blimey, you didn't . . . That is, have you come in all this way just for lunch?' It was a two-hour round trip. Already feeling slightly suffocated, she was dreading his answer.

He laughed. 'No. Don't think I'd get away with taking a lunch break that long. I'm the most junior member of the team. A few of us are up here for a conference. In Granary Square.'

It was a few minutes from her office. She was relieved the venue suited him just as much as her.

'So, congratulations,' he said. 'On the hotshot reporter gig.'

Becky laughed. 'Thanks. But I'm only a trainee.'

'Me too.'

'Where is it you're at again?'

'Senerix,' said Adam.

She deliberately looked blank.

'It's an agrochemical company. But dull stuff compared to you,' he added quickly, changing the focus back onto her, much to Becky's frustration. She'd have to go with it for a bit and if she opened up, then he'd feel duty-bound to recip-rocate. 'It's the *Herald* you work for, then? Very grown up. Actually, one of the few decent papers around.'

That little puff of pride; she got it every time she walked through the front doors of the huge glass building. Had to pinch herself that she actually worked there. For a news-paper that had a reputation for honest, fearless journalism.

'Which department?' he asked.

'News.'

'Investigative?'

'Uh huh.'

He whistled softly. 'Must be exciting. Working on any-thing good at the moment?'

She smiled coyly.

'Let me guess, you're not allowed to say.'

'Not yet.'

'But you're going to change the world?'

Becky looked at him to see if he was mocking her, but his eyes were all sincerity.

'I always knew you would,' he said.

'So, how about you? Out changing the world too?'

She felt a little flutter of journalistic instinct: he had hesi-tated, she was sure of it; his eyes had momentarily clouded over.

He recovered. Smiled. 'That's right. Making our food industry safer right at ground level – no pun intended.'

'Sounds impressive. What exactly is it you do?' She knew but she wanted to hear him say.

'I work in R&D. Developing new – and improving existing

– crop-care products. You know – herbicides, pesticides, fungicides.'

Her heart did a quiet leap. 'What are you working on at the moment?'

He laughed. 'Can't say. Especially to a journalist!'

Becky laughed along with him, glad he wasn't aware of her original motives for this lunch. 'Only trainee, remember. Although, I have applied for a reporter's job.'

'Think you'll get it?'

'Dunno. Stiff competition. My fellow trainee,' she said drily.

'Is she good?'

'He. And yes . . . he's highly thought of. I'm trying to trounce him with a story I'm investigating.'

'And we're back to embargoed conversation.'

She smiled. 'What are we going to talk about then?'

'What we're having for lunch? I'm ordering the chicken burger and chips,' said Adam, looking at the menu. 'Lucky I'm playing squash tonight.'

'You still play?' said Becky.

'Love it.' He hesitated, then: 'You don't fancy joining me sometime, do you?'

Her face fell – she didn't even consider squash a real sport, it was just hitting a tiny ball against the wall of a small room.

The waiter interrupted to take their order. 'What's it to be?'

Becky glanced up at Adam and saw an opportunity. Maybe a game of squash wouldn't be such a bad idea after all. How hard could it be? They'd do the namby-pamby game and then maybe they could go out for dinner, talk some more.

She looked Adam in the eye. '*Two* chicken burgers and chips, please.'

He grinned. 'So, is that a yes? You going to burn off the calories with me?'

'Why not? I can't do tonight . . . but soon?'

'OK,' said Adam. 'So, are you going to give me your number? So we can arrange the game?'

'Sure.' Becky scribbled down her number on a paper napkin and handed it to him.

'Should I check it before you leave?'

Becky inwardly squirmed. Feigned nonchalance. 'No need. No mistakes this time.'

'I thought you said the reason it didn't work before was because you'd lost your phone?'

The blush flooded up her face. *Rumbled*. But she wasn't going to admit it. 'Oh, yes. How silly of me to forget!'

'Yesterday's ten stories that got the most readership,' said Terence, flicking up a slide on the drop-down projector screen behind him. 'Nice one, Lizzie, top of the charts again.'

A low chorus of whistles and cheers went around the room, where twenty or so of the *Herald*'s staff were gathered round a large table for the daily conference. Lizzie, one of the senior reporters, acknowledged this with a wry arch of an eyebrow above her blue-rimmed glasses.

Terence clicked on his laptop and the slide behind him changed. 'Tomorrow's front page. Is this the best photo to tell the story of our headliner?' An unimpressive picture of an erupting volcano illuminated the wall behind him. 'We can do better. I want to see lava.' The picture editor was scribbling in her notepad. 'A new lead's come in from the news desk,' continued Terence, 'premiership football player has been accused of sexual assault by his children's nanny. The nanny has been on the phone. Lizzie?'

'On the university-places scandal.'

Terence's eyes roved around the room and Becky suddenly realized he was looking between her and Piers, who was sitting two chairs along. She felt herself straighten up. She'd absolutely love this assignment, kill for the chance to run with her first story solo.

'Piers, can you follow up?' said Terence.

Becky slumped in disappointment. Then a thought suddenly struck her. She spoke up. 'Wouldn't it be better if I went? Female perspective? More likely to confide?'

Piers instantly began to protest but Terence held up his hand for quiet while he contemplated. It didn't take long.

'All right. Next time, Piers.'

Becky glowed with delight. Out of the corner of her eye, she could see Piers was silently seething.

As they filed out of the room, he fell into step beside her. 'Uncool, Ellis. Totally uncool,' he said coldly.

'Oh, come on, Piers. You'd have done the same if you had a pair of boobs. It makes sense anyway and you know it. She's hardly likely to open up to—'

She stopped abruptly as Piers had stepped right in front of her. 'To what?'

She faltered.

'Go on, say it. Posh boy like me? You think you can play that working-class card?'

'Hey, I'm working cl—'

'You went to a private school just like I did.'

'*Scholarship*, rich boy. And my mum held down all sorts of low-paid jobs to keep us going. What about your parents? I hear your dad has a number of companies, one of the wealthiest men in Britain. What are they, anyway?'

'None of your business.'

'No, hold on, if we're wheeling out our backgrounds, where is it your dad holds these companies of his? Sure there's nothing that would be a conflict of interest with you working here? Wasn't that long ago the Panama Papers scandal broke.'

'You don't know what you're talking about. But if you want to go down the road of dirty tricks, then bring it on.'

'That's not what . . .'

But he'd gone, striding off down the corridor, and Becky realized with a sigh that what had been a little feisty competition had now developed into all-out war. She had made herself an enemy. She caught Darcy looking over, having witnessed their altercation. Darcy followed after Piers, and Becky watched as she draped an arm over his shoulders.

Cycling home that night, Becky's mind was even more preoccupied than usual. She'd been in touch with the nanny and had persuaded her to do an interview, an exclusive. It had taken some delicate coaxing, and she'd worked hard to win the girl's trust. Bollocks to Piers; she knew she'd been the right person for the assignment. She kept thinking about Adam too, that moment where he'd hesitated at lunch. He'd been uncomfortable for some reason, she was sure of it, and she was convinced there was something he knew, something interesting, and she was going to find out what. She pushed her legs harder through the dark streets, the buzz coursing through her body. She felt infallible.

She didn't see someone following her. Didn't notice the motorcyclist, face covered by a black-tinted visor, stay a short distance behind her. Neither had she noticed him the day before, nor the week before that. She always took the same route, taking the back streets to get away from the traffic of Gray's Inn Road, down Red Lion Street and then cutting south-west at High Holborn until she got to Victoria station, and when she pulled in and headed for her train, the motor-cyclist always continued straight past her into the night.

TWENTY-EIGHT

2018

'I totally screwed up,' said Kate, as she followed Tim under the railway bridge, heading for the South Bank. 'Wasted an unbelievable opportunity.'

'You did your best.'

'I let my emotions get the better of me. I went and got all Erin Brockovich. Started getting on my high horse.'

'That's a good thing!'

'Well, yes, it would have been if I was Erin. But I'm not. I'm me.' Kate had been kicking herself ever since she arrived back the night before, her whistle-stop trip to Bordeaux a pricey disaster, and she'd been saying as much ever since Tim had met her at the airport.

'I need to wise up. I need to get this right.' *For Becky as well*, she added in her head.

'And you will.' Tim took her hand, turned her to face him. 'Can we talk about something else, just for this evening?'

Kate sighed. He was right: she was being a bit of a broken record. The sound of steel drums warming up drew her gaze to a small stage near the river bank.

'I thought it would be fun,' said Tim. He paused. 'I thought it would cheer you up.' He took Kate's other hand and she was compelled to look up into his blue eyes. Eyes that radiated good intention, that urged her to break into a smile. She did.

'That's better,' said Tim.

'Sorry. Have I been very difficult?'

'Nah. Well, actually, yes but I get it. I know how much you needed that doctor on side, but you'll find another.'

She didn't think it was anywhere near as easy as he made it sound. She'd approached a couple of other medical professionals who'd voiced concerns about the links between herbicides and cancer but had heard nothing back.

He saw her look of despondency. 'You *will*. Now, come on.'

Tim led her to where a small crowd was gathering meaningfully near the band and handed over two tickets to a tall Rasta man.

'What's that for?' said Kate warily, eyeing the crowd, who were standing expectantly. She noticed everyone was paired off.

The Rasta guy joined a girl in skin-tight snake-green shimmering hot pants and a crop top, on a small stage. The girl was holding a mike.

'Everybody ready?' said the girl in hot pants, gyrating her hips in anticipation.

'Ready for what?' said Kate.

Tim was looking very pleased with himself. The steel-drum

players started up, the sound of sunshine and the Caribbean cheering the nippy London spring evening.

'It's ballroom,' said Tim.

'In those clothes?' said Kate, nodding at the hot pants.

'With a twist. Come on, shake your tush.'

'Tush?'

'You've just gotta follow them.' He nodded at the black couple on stage: fluid, sexy, perfectly matched.

She laughed. 'No pressure, then.' But she tentatively mimicked their easy counting and instructions.

Tim held her tight and whispered in her ear. 'This is nice, eh? Spending time together.'

It was, she realized. It had been too long. 'Great date,' she murmured into his ear.

'Glad you like it.'

'How many have we had?'

'Seven. This is the eighth.'

'In a year and a half?'

He spun her around. 'Pretty rubbish, eh?'

It was. But so much had happened. So much in her life had been ripped away or turned upside down.

'We should have more,' said Tim.

'I agree.'

'While we can,' he said meaningfully.

'What do you mean?'

He smiled. 'I've got something to ask you.'

Her heart froze in terror – or was it excitement? Excitement! The way he was looking at her, the way that always made her heart melt.

'Is it a big thing or a small thing?' she asked.

'Very definitely a big thing.'

'For us? Me and you?' she asked pointedly.

He nodded, and her heart leapt again. This was one of those life-changing moments, she could tell. How did she feel about getting married? It wasn't something that had ever occurred to her, her life being set on its untraditional path since that fateful night back when she was a schoolgirl. Now she was on the verge of being proposed to, she felt herself swelling with a new kind of joy.

'I've been thinking . . . for a while now,' said Tim, 'about you and me. I love you—'

Kate melted. 'Aw . . .'

He smiled. 'Stop interrupting. I do. And I'd like to think we were permanent. You're certainly the person I want to spend the rest of my life with.'

Kate prepared herself. She smiled and gave him the space to say the momentous thing.

'And I'd like to make a future with you.' He took a breath. 'One that maybe isn't limited to just us?'

She frowned, confused. Was he suggesting that they see other people?

'I've been thinking . . . maybe we could talk about start-ing a family?'

She stopped still. Gobsmacked. 'A baby?'

'Yes.' He took in her reaction. Smiled tentatively. 'Is that so bad?'

'No . . . I mean . . . it just took me by surprise, that's all.'

'Why?'

Now he said it like that, calmly, rationally, she didn't really know. 'Well, you're the same age as me . . . more or less.'

'I'm thirty-six. About time I started a family.'

Kate squeezed her eyes shut for a moment, tried to make her brain catch up, to get past the shock. She felt as if she'd been caught napping. Why wouldn't Tim want children? She'd always thought she'd had hers and had been too wrapped up in everything to even think about his situation.

'It's been difficult, knowing when to bring it up,' said Tim. 'When we were first going out, it's not the sort of thing you do. "Fancy going to the cinema, and by the way, do you want kids with your popcorn?" And then, after Becky, you and me got waylaid a bit.' He held a hand up. 'Completely understandable. But my feelings haven't changed, and it would be wrong to go on keeping this to myself. I thought you'd rumbled me actually, the other day. When you came back from your first night at college.' She was staring at him blankly. 'I was checking my finances. In case you were worried. I can cover us both if you wanted to take a bit of time off.'

Kate didn't know what to say. A baby. Good God, a *baby* . . .

'It's a big thing.'

'Yep. I know.'

'Children are . . . they're all consuming. Take over your whole life.'

'And?'

'Well, I'm quite full on right now.'

He was quiet for a moment. 'You mean Becky's story.'

'It's important to me.'

'And a child is important to me.'

But why now? she thought, and immediately knew the answer. She was only just the right side of forty. 'Can I have some time?'

'Course!' Sensing her reluctance to continue the conversation, he was quick to reassure her.

They looked at each other, not sure what to say next. The dance teachers were calling out some instructions and they both made a show of paying attention.

'It's just a surprise, that's all,' said Kate in his ear as they started dancing again.

'It's OK. I should have given you more warning.'

He held her, and they were both grateful that the tension had eased. It was a temporary reprieve, that much they were both aware of as they spun around.

A baby, thought Kate again. She couldn't help wondering what would happen if she said no.

TWENTY-NINE

2008

Kate was avoiding her boss. She kept to the back of the restaurant where she found endless small jobs to make herself look busy: tidying the shelf of napkins, wiping down the china dishes that held the selection of Thai dipping sauces that they served with the complimentary appetizers.

Rick knew she was avoiding him, and Kate could tell this irritated him by the way he kept glancing over, with his sunburnt face from the weekend's unexpected heatwave, wanting to interrupt, but unable to while she was so busily employed. Actually, what was really annoying him was the fact that at work the day before she had asked to speak to him privately. He'd smiled knowingly and taken her to his office, a tiny room downstairs, crammed with files, industrial-sized boxes of Thai crackers and a desk behind which he had a swivel chair.

As he'd closed the door, his hand had run across her shoulder blades and down her back. She'd stiffened and stepped aside, turning to face him. Then she'd explained that she no longer wanted to have sex with him; that a relationship wasn't what she was really looking for at that moment. In truth, it was less a relationship, more a quick, heated fumble across the desk, followed by a can of warm Coke while he talked at her for the last ten minutes of her break about the difficulties of running a restaurant. At thirty, he was only three years older than her, but acted as if he'd already hit late middle age and would moan and gripe in a way that drained her.

Rick had not taken the news well. Not wanting to jeopardize her employment, she avoided telling him the sex and the rare male company was not worth the flat, depressing feeling she was left with afterwards. Instead, she reassured him it was her, not him, and said hadn't they had fun over the last month, hadn't it been naughty and weren't they risqué.

Rick was now behaving like a child whose sweeties had been taken away. He'd called her a tease and then followed her around with his dark, brooding eyebrows and his peeling nose, and Kate was deeply regretting ever getting involved with him in the first place. In fact, she wasn't really sure why she had, except it had been nice to be flattered for once, to have a man take an interest in her. It had also been a practical arrangement, as it had not impacted on her home life at all.

She stood up from putting all the clean dishes away in the cupboard and looked out across the restaurant. It was a reasonably nice place, set in an exclusive village just five miles from where she lived. Her three full tables were still eating lunch and her colleague, Kannika, had just taken an order for drinks from another group. She saw Rick clock her lack of activity and was about to find herself another job when the front door opened and in came two women. Kate's heart sank as she recognized one of them as Julia Cromwell. Becky had mentioned she lived in the village.

Kate had seen Julia briefly at various school events: assemblies where Julia had sat tight-lipped as Becky had been awarded certificates for exceptional grades in her end-of-term exams or had a solo in the Christmas concert. Kate had also noticed how Julia had refused to clap as Becky crossed the finishing line on sports day, two places ahead of Violet, Julia's daughter.

Kate moved over to Kannika and asked if she wouldn't mind waiting on Julia's table. Sympathetic to what was clearly something personal, Kannika was just agreeing when Ricky sidled up to them.

'Kate, I think you should do it. You've spent long enough scuttling around at the back here.'

Kate reminded herself he was wounded. 'I'd rather not,' she said calmly. 'If it's all the same to you.'

'We can't pick and choose our customers.'

'I'm not. I just don't particularly get on with that lady, that's all.'

'Why?'

'Pardon?'

'Why don't you get on with her?' Arms folded across his mini-paunch, Rick was enjoying her discomfort.

She wasn't going to explain to him how Julia had treated

her like a skivvy, had taken a deep and personal dislike to both her and Becky. It was none of his business.

'This is a restaurant, Kate. You are a waitress. It is your job to wait on the people who come in here, whether you like it or not.'

'I really don't mind—' started up Kannika.

'Kate's got it,' said Rick sharply.

Kate glared at him. Whatever had possessed her to fall for this small-minded, power-hungry lobster. She half considered telling him where to stick it but she couldn't afford to get fired. Roll on the end of her shift. It was Becky's thirteenth birthday and she was going shopping to get her a present.

Picking up a serving pad, Kate made her way over to the table where Julia was sitting with her friend.

She plastered on a smile. 'Good afternoon. Would you like something to drink?'

Julia looked around and a curl formed at the edge of her lips. 'Well, well.'

Kate stood as Julia looked her up and down, taking in her red-and-gold Thai-style outfit. For the first time, Kate felt as if she was in fancy dress.

'I had no idea,' said Julia.

'Do you two know each other?' asked Julia's friend.

'We do . . .' said Julia. 'Our daughters go to the same school.'

Kate caught the surprised flicker in the other woman's eyes and did her best to ignore it.

'In fact, they're in the same class,' declared Julia.

'Oh, how nice,' exclaimed her companion. 'Friends?'

'Besties,' said Julia, smiling at Kate. Her companion lifted an eyebrow as she caught the subtle sarcasm.

'Drinks, ladies?' repeated Kate.

'I'll have a sparkling mineral water,' said Julia's friend.

'Me too,' said Julia.

Kate went to walk away when—

'Oh, actually, make that a Diet Coke,' said Julia.

'Sure,' said Kate, going to the fridge.

'Changed my mind. I'll stick with the water.'

Kate froze. Was Julia winding her up? She glanced back over her shoulder but there was no smirk on Julia's face, in fact she wasn't even looking her way, she was deep in conversation with her friend. As Kate moved off, she heard Julia speak again, her voice lowered.

'Her child's on a scholarship. Probably felt sorry for her. She'll be some quota-filler, bound to be. They need to show they're helping out the lower end of society but really the whole thing is tokenistic. I mean, look at the mother. Daughter's not got much hope of a future, not with that sort of millstone around her neck.'

Kate froze, her face burning. She daren't look around; tears were pricking at her eyes, and that woman . . . she couldn't let Julia see her face. She felt mown down, sliced in half by Julia's words, and the worst bit was Kate found herself questioning the truth in them. She felt a sudden urge to run, and thought about leaving her shift there and then, but she saw Rick watching her from across the restaurant and remembered she was going shopping for a gift later, a gift she wouldn't be able to afford if she lost her job. She stumbled on, willing the lunch shift to be over.

At the end, when she went to clear the table, she found the final insult. Julia had left no tip.

Kate was still subdued when she got to the shopping centre. Julia's words had reverberated round and round in her head the entire bus trip. She hurried to the phone shop, hoping that shopping for Becky's present would distract her. As she went in, she was faced with a display, right in the middle of the shop floor, of the new Apple iPhone. It had become a phenomenon since it had been released at the end of last year, but was laughably expensive.

Kate walked past the display to some cheaper phones, near the back. She picked one up. It was all right; it made calls. She glanced back over her shoulder at the shining touchscreen of the iPhone. *It could actually connect to the Internet!* She remembered her careful savings; the ten pounds a month she'd put away for Becky's university fees had grown a bit over the years. There were some girls there in the shop, dressed in the uniform from Becky's school. They were picking up the phones and playing with them. A salesman was hovering attentively, as one of the girls negotiated a purchase. Then Kate saw who it was: Julia's daughter, Violet. She watched as Violet got her purse out of her bag and pulled out several twenty-pound notes. The phone was put into a plastic bag while Violet's friends gathered round, a captive audience. Then Kate watched as they left the shop, arms linked, heads held high, oblivious to anything other than their own self-absorbed amusement.

Kate sighed. She looked again at the iPhone stand, but it was impossible. The university money was untouchable, that was what she'd always promised herself. It represented Becky's future, a future that was going to be very different to her own.

No, she just couldn't afford an iPhone. *If some people tipped when they were given good service then maybe things might be different*, she thought darkly, but pushed those thoughts aside and bought a simpler model.

'Oh, Mum, I love it!' exclaimed Becky, throwing her arms around Kate's neck.

'Happy Birthday, Becky,' said Kate, her voice muffled under the hug.

She'd watched carefully for a shadow of disappointment in Becky's eyes as she opened her gift, and had found none, but still couldn't help thinking Julia Cromwell had ruined her daughter's birthday. A ridiculous thought, she knew, but ever since lunchtime, a cloud had settled over Kate that she just couldn't shift.

She served up the tea – Becky's favourite. Her daughter grinned as the plate was set in front of her.

'I love you, Mum. And not just because of the chips.'

Kate smiled as they got stuck into their burgers and fries. 'Good day at school?'

'Yeah. Got a bit of homework though. Algebra. I'm a bit stuck . . .' Becky looked up at her mother and Kate felt herself tense.

'Not sure I'll be any good to you.'

In fact, Becky was learning stuff that Kate found was way beyond her own ability. Not just in maths, but in other subjects too. It embarrassed her that she couldn't keep up, couldn't help her daughter. Kate saw Becky's crestfallen face and her stomach twisted. She forced a bright tone. 'What about one of your friends at school? Claire?' Kate glanced across at the box on the table. 'You can phone her!'

Even as she said it, she felt as if she was fobbing Becky off, but her daughter knew better than to push and so she nodded and said she'd call Claire after tea.

Later that night, after Becky had gone to bed, Kate snuck a look in Becky's schoolbag. She pulled out the maths exercise book, feeling herself getting more despondent and fuller of self-loathing as she flicked through. The homework had been done but she didn't understand any of it.

Julia was right, thought Kate.

She'd never better herself.

Never amount to much.

What was she?

She was a millstone.

THIRTY

2018

Kate could hear the murmuring and chattering of voices coming from Grace's living room. 'How many have come?' she whispered.

'Everyone,' said Grace.

Kate's eyes widened. 'Seriously?'

'Yes. They've all got your letter and are intrigued. They want to hear what you have to say.' Grace handed her the mug of tea she'd been making. 'Are you ready?'

Not really, thought Kate, and then mentally kicked herself. If she was going to do this, there was no point in whimpering her way through it. She stood up straight. 'Lead the way.'

Grace looked at her. She opened a kitchen cupboard, grabbed a bottle of rum, and put a slug in Kate's tea.

'Whoa!' said Kate, but she picked up the mug and took a sip. She pulled a face, for it tasted disgusting, although a slow warmth was already cascading through her body. 'How's Arnie, by the way?'

'We've had some good news. A donor's been found and it's a nine-out-of-ten match.'

'Wow. Wow?' checked Kate. It sounded good, but she was no expert.

'It's good,' affirmed Grace. 'Just one more session of chemo and then we'll be looking at a transplant around July.'

'That's great!'

'It is. But it's a long road still. I know it's a good thing – hopefully –' Grace automatically touched the top of the wooden table – 'but part of me's dreading it. The normal chemo's bad enough but this one will really take it out of him.' She took a deep breath. 'They've warned me what to expect.'

'But when the transplant works . . .'

'Yes, I know. It'll all be over-ish. Imagine! You know, the thing that means the most to me,' said Grace, 'isn't winning some court case against the farm – although it's important that this gets out there for everyone to hear – it's finding out the truth. Arnie's so ill. And we're not out of the woods yet.' Her voice caught, but she carried on. 'Everything he's been through and, so far, no one's interested in why. We know what we suspect – why he's ill – but I feel like no one's being honest with me. Not only that, there's a deliberate desire to keep the truth away from me. And that's all I really want, Kate. I want to know the truth.'

Kate thought of Becky. How she didn't fully understand her accident. It was a terrible thing, not knowing exactly what had been done to your child.

Grace took her arm. 'Come on, let's not keep them waiting any longer.' She led the way and as they entered, the room hushed. All eyes were on Kate and she noticed every seat was taken. A space had been left in front of the fireplace. The space was for her.

She went to face the gathering.

'Thank you everyone,' she started, 'for taking the time to come to this meeting.' She paused. Expectant faces. She took another mouthful of rum tea. Somehow this was harder than when she'd stood up at the AGM. Then, it had just been about her and Becky. Now, she was in the midst of a whole group of people who were suffering in one way or another, and she was mindful of their personal anguish. Sunita, the young mum who'd had breast cancer, was directly in front of her on Grace's blue armchair. She had had a mastectomy and was, so far, in the clear. Sunita gave her an encouraging smile.

'You know who I am,' continued Kate, 'and how I got to know you through my daughter. You also know why I'm here and why I've asked you to come tonight. And I know you've also talked amongst yourselves about the reason I believe there's so much illness in this community. In my letter, I said that I think each of you deserves financial compensation for the trauma and everything that's gone with that, and I am here to ask if you would like me to help you get it.'

'Sorry to state the obvious, love, but you don't look like no lawyer.'

It was Ian who had spoken. He was a retired farm worker who'd been diagnosed with prostate cancer four years ago – almost immediately after he'd stopped working.

He'd lived in his cottage with his wife Hazel for four decades. They'd originally wanted to sell up and spend their retirement in Italy, but the illness had prevented the move at first and now they were too anxious to go in case anything else happened and they needed urgent medical care.

Kate smoothed the fabric of her jeans self-consciously. 'I'm not, not officially . . . but I'm training. At night school. It's a Civil Litigation course. And I've been researching . . .' She pulled a thick pile of files out of her bag and held them up. 'I think we can build a case.'

She was met with silence and got a strong sense they were humouring her.

'Has anyone done anything like this before?' asked Sunita.

'Yes. There was a recent landmark case in California. A school-grounds worker who has been diagnosed with Non-Hodgkin lymphoma took a major agrochemical company to court, saying their herbicide product, which contains glyphosate, caused his terminal illness. He was awarded several million dollars in compensation.'

'Wow, so he actually beat them?' asked Sunita.

Kate could hardly lie to her. 'The company is appealing.'

'Anyone else?' asked Ian. 'What about in this country?'

'No . . . but that doesn't mean to say we can't be the first,' she added quickly. Look, I've prepared a pack for each of you documenting evidence, cases around the world linking pesticide and herbicide use with cancers and other illnesses. The rise of Parkinson's in rural Lincolnshire amongst people who live near potato farms. People who live near a cranberry-growing area near Cape Cod who have been found to have twice the risk for all brain cancers. Farm workers with prostate cancer, even livestock. The farm here heavily uses a product called Crixus which has been cited in other reports where cancers have been found.' She held out the folders she'd got out of her bag earlier, but no one reached for one. 'The bottom line is, do you believe the chemicals sprayed on a regular basis just metres from your home are the cause of your families' illnesses? If so, are you prepared to fight those who've done this and demand their acknowledgement, an apology and compensation?'

'But surely you need proof? Or at least very strong evidence that shows that there's a direct link between this Crixus and cancer?' Ian's wife, Hazel, had spoken. 'You see, the thing is, a lot of us are aware of some of these incidents and events but there's one thing that's not been said here tonight. It's all legal.' She waved a hand towards the window. 'That farmer out there is not breaking any laws.'

'Yes, surely you need scientific evidence,' said Sunita. 'Professional statements, academic papers. Have you got anything like that?'

Kate kept the optimistic smile on her face. 'Not yet . . .'

'And what are the chances of us winning, if we even get this to court?' asked Ian.

'Well, it's hard to know for sure. But that's not a reason not to bother, is it?'

The taxi driver, Rob, had remained silent until now. When Kate had gone to his house, she'd kept her eyes from the weed-entangled garden, the piles of washing stacked in the kitchen. His wife, Helen, who had ME, had been in bed and his daughter, Abby, had had soft-tissue sarcoma but was now in remission. Kate knew he was responsible for the care of them both, plus he paid all the bills. 'Just because we're ill and we live next to this farm . . . . it doesn't actually prove anything,' he said.

'I'm working hard to—'

'You're wasting your time. They're never going to pay up. Even if you do manage to pull together some sort of case, you're going to be locked into a legal battle like this American fella that will be delayed for years. Not everyone here has that sort of time.'

Kate refused to buckle. She gave a hopeful smile as she looked around the room.

'It's very nice of you,' said Sunita kindly, 'to think of us like this, but in all honesty, for a lot of us it's too much effort when it's so likely to fail. We've got enough on our plates just dealing with the day to day.'

'I'll do all the work.'

'Why?' said Ian. 'What's in it for you?'

'I don't want a cut. If that's what you're thinking,' said Kate quickly. She paused; she'd never really considered this question fully before, but she knew the answer as if it were ingrained in her brain. 'Like my daughter before me, I cannot stand an injustice. I'm helping because I'm sick of seeing the small guy, the ordinary person, get shafted, while the rich and the powerful continue to get richer and more powerful. We are not second-class citizens. They need to know we're not going to put up with it,' she insisted, 'and they need to change. And the only way they'll do that is if we hit them where it hurts most – in their pockets.' She looked around the room; everyone was listening, but it was impossible to tell if she was getting through. No one spoke. Kate took a deep breath. 'I feel I need to do it to make sense of my daughter's death.'

'I'm in,' said Grace and Kate threw her a grateful look. She looked around the room again, waiting for others to follow, but some glanced away, some smiled apologetically.

'In order for it to work, it really needs to be all of you. A united front. It makes the case much stronger,' she added, but her words fell to the ground. The silence grew awkward and suddenly Kate felt foolish.

'OK . . . well, thanks for coming anyway and I'm sorry for wasting your time.' She suddenly had to get out of there. She gathered together the files and hurriedly stuffed them back into her bag and then, clutching it all tightly, made an embarrassed exit.

Grace ran after her. 'I'm sorry.'

'It's OK,' said Kate quickly. In truth she was deeply upset.

'They're just so preoccupied. Take it from me, I know.'

Kate's phone beeped, and she dug it out, expecting it to be a text message from Tim, seeing when she might be home, but it was an email. From the office of Dr Zayan.

She opened it and read it through. Eyes shining, she looked at Grace then walked back into the living room and resumed her place.

'Listen up, please, everyone. I know you want to go home but I've something else to say.' She held up her phone. 'I've just had an email from a Dr Bernhard Zayan in France. I went to see him recently as he believes that herbicides have caused cancer in a number of school children in his village whose school backs onto vineyards. In particular, products made by the same company that makes those used here.' She started to read the email aloud.

'Dear Kate,

I have been thinking about your visit a lot since you left. I have also been thinking about the people you told me about in your English village. They remind me of the people here in my French village and I know what it is like to want to help, to seek justice for them. I admire you wanting to do this.

This will be a complex journey, full of shocks and outrage. Did you know that the president of the main cancer charity in France was previously the chief executive officer of a major agrochemical company? How is that, you ask yourself? Because this is a tightly controlled industry, where big money is at stake. Millions – billions – of dollars.

Some say these corporations will never admit it. But that is also what they said about the tobacco industry. So maybe there is hope.

Against my better judgement, I will help. I will write up whatever reports and evidence you need. I will tell you what I know about Crixus and will let you have access to my research. Your friends in England deserve more people on their side and if I can be one of them, I will.'

Kate looked up. She knew at once that something had been ignited. It wasn't just *her* anymore; there were other people on board. A doctor, a professional, had offered to back them.

She took a punt. 'I need all the details: when you moved here, how often the spraying took place, when you or your family members became ill. We'll need to do medical reports, determine the costs of your future care needs. I'm sorry, it will be hard, but we need to be thorough. I'd like to visit each of you in turn, starting as soon as possible. I have my day job too, but I'm going to fit this case in around work and night school using every spare minute I have.'

Nobody objected. A smile bubbled up inside her. She was in. *She was in!*

The rest of the email, she'd keep to herself for now:

You will need more, though. More support, much more evidence. It is a huge battle and they will try to crush you like an ant.

You may have read my article, but did you bother to read the responses? The scathing counter-articles written by Senerix's in-house 'scientists' questioning my training, my medical knowledge, even my motivation? They said my claims were 'fake science', made me seem like a deluded fool, a man out of touch.

The resistance from these companies is so strong. And yet it is like fog. Impossible to grasp, to move aside. Impossible to see a clear way through. This is how the chemical companies like it. They will do anything to keep it that way. They will lobby governments and fund their 'research' programmes. They will fight. And they will deny, deny, deny.

Yours,

Bernhard

That part, she would think about later.

THIRTY-ONE

Kate put every spare waking second into her campaign. She interviewed the villagers, family by family, learning how peoples' windows were regularly covered with a thin film of chemicals after spraying, the same film that rested on children's bike handles, garden-swing ropes, the clean washing on the line and the surface of ponds that pets would drink from.

The more she spoke to them, the angrier she got, but she had to contain it, to keep focused and calm. More than one family had had to leave their houses when spraying took place, although this was hard when they were woken at five in the morning by the fumes that came through their open bedroom windows. She also contacted doctors and research scientists around the world, asking for their professional support. She would work late into the night, typing away on her ancient computer, trying to organize her notes into a coherent case. She would anxiously back everything up – twice.

Kate had been nervous when she'd started interviewing the families in earnest. She was aware she was asking them to talk about some of the most painful events in their lives. But the person she was most nervous of was Rob, the taxi driver.

He was sitting opposite her now at a small table, tucked away in a corner of Ramsbourne's local cafe. It was late afternoon in the middle of the week on an unseasonably cold day and several people were huddled over steaming coffees. A large glass of orange juice, which Kate had bought, was on the table in front of Rob. Kate watched as he drew patterns in the condensation on the glass, knowing he was uncomfortable, knowing she was too.

'How's Helen?' she asked.

'She's OK. Having a good week, actually. She's been up and about a bit. Did the food shop yesterday.'

'That's great!' Kate exclaimed, then immediately regretted her showy burst of enthusiasm as Rob had closed up again. 'Um . . . well, if it's OK with you, I'd like to go over a few of the facts.' She paused. He said nothing. 'When did you move to Ramsbourne?'

'Helen and I came here when Abby was five . . . seven years ago.'

'And you've lived in the same house the entire time?'

'That's right.'

Kate wrote it down in her notepad.

'And . . . when did Abby get ill?'

He flinched. 'It was Helen first. She got ME four years ago. Had to give up her job as a dental nurse.'

'How bad is her illness?'

'She's not making it up, if that's what you mean. It's a proper disease you know, not just some excuse for being lazy or anything.'

Kate held out a placating hand. 'I know, I know. What I meant is, is she able to help with the running of the house?'

'Not often.'

'Are you able to get anyone in?'

He stared at her coldly. 'Who's going to pay for that, then?'

Kate nodded. 'The reason I'm asking is that I have to assess costs – as part of figuring out what compensation you should be entitled to.' She took a breath. 'Back to Abby . . . when was she diagnosed with sarcoma?'

'Two years ago.'

'And now . . . ?'

'In the clear.'

'That's great,' said Kate.

'So, you really think you can have a go at whoever owns this farm then?'

'Yes, I do.'

He frowned at her, eyes hostile with scepticism. 'How much?'

She was taken aback by his bluntness.

'In compensation? Well, it would depend on everyone's types and levels of illness, loss and hardship. But something in the region of two to five million.'

'So, what's that work out at each?'

Kate shook her head. 'No, that would be just for you. And Helen and Abby. I did a bit of checking – a carer costs approximately fifteen pounds an hour. If you had help for only two hours a day, assuming Helen needed help for the next forty years, that's nearly half a million. And her care needs could well go up. And there's Helen's loss of earnings, your loss of earnings while you're caring for them both. And Abby . . . hopefully she's going to be fine now but if . . . in the future . . .'

He stared at her for a moment, then started laughing. It was loud and hard, and people were looking round. She got embarrassed and was about to ask him to stop, when he suddenly ceased.

'You seriously think whoever owns this farm is going to pay two million for each of us?'

'Well, each case will be different, but potentially, yes.'

Kate could see Rob was angry. He took a sip of his drink, seemingly to try and calm himself down before he spoke.

'I've been doing a bit of research myself since you came along. Once you'd persuaded us all to come with you down this road, I thought maybe there's a chance – Kate seems to think so. I came across this article from a few years ago. A case in New Zealand. An organic farmer had his entire crop contaminated by his neighbouring farmer's genetically modified seed, which blew over during harvesting. His whole livelihood gone. So, he decides to sue. Quite right too, you'd think. And he's got all the evidence, all the proof. A no-brainer, right? Except what happens next is that this other farmer, the GM one, he gets a call from some top fancy lawyer offering to help him out. Represent him. Oh no, he says, I can't afford the likes of you. You don't have to, says this lawyer, cos someone else is gonna pay my humungous fees. The GM-seed manufacturer heard about your little dilemma and has offered to cover all costs. And, seeing as they have very deep pockets, they could just go on paying and paying –' Rob waved his arm around – 'ad infinitum. Or at least for as long as it took to stop the other guy, the organic guy, from winning. All the GM farmer had to do was promise to keep this little arrangement a secret.'

'I—' started Kate.

Rob held up a hand. 'I'm not finished. It would've been cheaper to just compensate the organic farmer, but they couldn't do that as that would mean they'd have to *admit to being in the wrong*. And that GM-seed manufacturer, well, guess what? They also make herbicides. If they're going to those lengths to protect their seed business, what do you think they – or any other similar company – is going to do about their herbicide business?' He paused. 'So, what happens when Ashdown Farm's herbicide supplier gets wind of what you're up to? Realizes you're planning on making this public – and apportioning blame on their very lucrative product?' He leaned across the table. 'What's gonna happen then?'

Kate was silent. She'd seen the same article and had been as outraged as Rob was now. But she wasn't going to give up. Hell, they'd hardly started.

Rob stood. 'I'll give it a couple of months. Don't let us down, Kate. No fannying about, it's not a game.' He took his coat from the back of his chair and turned to leave. Kate watched as he crossed to the door then, drawing up his hood against the rain, he left without a backward glance.

She sighed. Already the weight of this undertaking was resting heavily on her shoulders. She'd learned quite a bit on her evening course, but it wasn't anywhere near enough. She was completely out of her depth. As she started to pack up her notebook, a new truth stared her in the face: she needed help.

Kate gathered her jacket and bag and left the cafe. As she made her way down the road, a man crossed a little way in front of her. For a brief moment she caught his face and thought it looked familiar. But then he turned away and headed into the pub. Where had she seen him before? Tall, with a horseshoe moustache. She shook her head, couldn't remember. Not wanting to miss her train, she hurried on.

Janković walked slowly through the pub, looking around methodically, not finding what he was looking for until he came into the snug. He stopped in the doorway. A fire was lit against the cold and Justin Holmes was holed up at a table, alone, working on some paperwork.

Justin looked up as Janković unzipped a pocket on the front of his damp leather jacket and pulled out a sheet of paper. He unfolded it and laid it over the paperwork on the table.

'What are you doing here?' said Justin, taken aback.

Janković tapped the sheet of paper and Justin looked down, even while knowing what it was. There, printed out, was his resignation letter. His second resignation letter.

'I thought we'd been through this,' said Janković.

'I quit.'

'Not possible. You are a highly valued member of the company.'

'What if I just left?'

'We'd find you.' Janković smiled. 'Why the sudden change of heart? Has something happened? Someone been in touch? A new visit from a newspaper?'

Justin tried to keep his voice steady. 'No.'

'Only, you know you are supposed to let us know. If there are any.'

'There hasn't been.'

Janković sat back languidly in his chair, arms out-stretched so his fingertips reached the table. 'You were not meant to find out. And as you did, you will have to stay in employment. You've had a pay rise, a significant one.'

'It's not—'

Justin stopped talking as Janković suddenly stood. He moved away from his chair, walking around the table until he was behind Justin. Justin made himself sit still, not turn around. Suddenly an excruciating pain seared the back of his neck, accompanied by a sickly burning smell. Justin leapt up, clutching his neck in agony. 'What the fuck!'

Janković was standing behind him, a red-hot ember pinched in some tongs. Justin backed away as Janković replaced the ember on the fire.

'Job for life!' said Janković. Then he turned and left the pub.

THIRTY-TWO

It had been several days since Becky had had her lunch with Adam and he still hadn't called. At first, she'd been amused, it served her right if he was making a point after she'd given him a fake number all those months ago. She deserved pay-back. But after the first weekend had been and gone, her amusement gave way to a mild indignation that steadily grew as the days passed. Why hadn't he called? Was he playing hard to get? Had he lost her number? She *knew* she should've typed it straight into his phone.

She took one end of the sideboard in Iris's house as her mum lifted the other, and they shifted it across the room.

'Bit further,' instructed Iris as she watched. 'Bit more, little bit more. There!'

Kate and Becky put it down and they all stood back and appraised their efforts. Iris had wanted to move her furniture around so her armchairs were in the sun. The warmth helped with her arthritis.

'Looks good,' said Becky. The sun was streaming through

where the sideboard had been. 'Look at all that toasty space, right by the window. It'll be like living in the tropics.'

'I'll probably spend most of the day asleep now,' said Iris.

'Right, now for the chairs,' said Kate. 'And that table needs moving too.'

'We could do with a man,' said Iris. 'A strong one.'

Becky giggled. 'Mum's found one.'

'Oh yes, I've heard about this Tim. Bit of all right, is he?'

'Don't know,' said Becky. 'Mum hasn't introduced me yet.'

'I've only known him three weeks,' said Kate.

'Well, I'm relying on you to make a full assessment,' Iris said to Becky, 'when you do meet him. I want his entire backstory.'

'What!' said Kate.

'I'll check him out, don't you worry,' said Becky to Iris. 'And I'll let you know.'

'Hello, I am here. In the room,' said Kate, waving her arms about.

Iris continued to speak to Becky. 'Good. Your mum's told me a few nice things, but, well, they can be real charmers these DIY types. I just hope he's everything he's seeming to be.'

'Unbelievable,' said Kate, to herself really as no one else was listening.

Iris finally looked at Kate and beamed. 'Anyone for a cuppa? How's about I go and put the kettle on?'

She went into the kitchen and flicked the switch on the kettle, just as her phone began to ring on the table. She picked it up but didn't recognize the number. *Could be one of those cold-callers telling you you've had a car accident*, she thought. She contemplated not answering but caved in. It might be important.

'Hello?' said the caller.

'Hello,' said Iris coolly.

'I know, I know, it's been a few days. Sorry . . . things have just been totally manic, and I had to go back home for a bit – my mum fractured her wrist at Zumba – long story but, well, I know it's short notice but what are you doing tonight? Fancy a game of squash and some dinner?'

'I'd love to, dearie, but I don't think my hips are up to it.'

'What?'

'Pardon?'

'I thought . . . You were supposed to be someone else.'

'Charmed, I'm sure.'

'Sorry . . . it's just . . . never mind.' The caller, a man, sighed. 'Seems I've been fobbed off again.'

'Iris, who are you talking to?' called Kate from the living room.

'Wrong number,' called back Iris. 'No need to explain,' she said into the phone. 'I think I get the gist. Whoever she is, she's not worth it.'

The man on the phone gave a low laugh. 'You know, I think you're right. Sorry to disturb you.'

'No problem at all.'

Iris hung up and went back out into the living room, pocketing her phone as she did so. One of the armchairs was now in the window, bathed in sunlight. She went to try it out, and within minutes was basking in the winter sun.

'OK?' said Becky, smiling.

'Oh, it's like being one of those lizards in the heat lamps. You know, like you get in the zoo,' said Iris.

From the kitchen they heard the click of the kettle switching itself off.

'Tea,' said Iris, going to get up.

'You stay right there,' said Becky. She went into the kitchen and poured the hot water onto teabags in mugs. While she was waiting, she thought she might just check her phone again. Maybe there would be a text. Actually, she might as well admit it: he wasn't interested. But she'd still look. For the last time, she told herself. Her phone wasn't on the table where she'd left it. Becky looked around – had she put it back in her bag? Coat pocket? It was in neither place. But there was Iris's phone on the counter.

She picked it up, took it into the living room. 'Iris?'

Iris opened one eye.

'Whose phone have you just picked up?'

She pulled it out of her pocket, looking at it, bemused. 'Well, mine, isn't it?'

Becky yelped. 'That's mine!'

She quickly scrolled through the call history and saw a number she didn't recognize. 'Who was that person you just spoke to?'

'Didn't get his name.'

Becky's heart leapt. 'It was a man?'

'Yes. Asked me out to dinner.'

Becky groaned. Immediately called back. 'Hello? Adam?

It's Becky. You just called? My phone was answered by my daft—'

'Who are you calling daft?' Iris piped up.

'. . . but adorable surrogate grandmother.' Becky held her breath. 'She said something about going out for dinner?'

Totally and utterly humiliated. That was the only way to describe how she felt. She'd decided early on not to throw in the towel because she thought . . . it seemed a long time ago now . . . but she'd thought it would get better or *she'd* get better. Instead, she was a panting, sweating mess on the wrong side of a 10–1 score – for the third time. And she suspected he'd actually let her win her solitary point as the ball had seemed to be heading for his racquet, but he'd mysteriously missed it. She'd started this match thinking she'd hold a conversation at the same time, perhaps find out more about what Adam did in his work, probe him about the stuff he *could* talk about in order to try and read between the lines about the stuff he couldn't, but she'd barely been able to draw breath – and she considered herself fit. More than once she'd caught herself admiring a shot from Adam or the way he seemed to move from one side of the court to the other like a demented ping-pong ball.

A bit like now. He whacked the ball against the wall and, for the umpteenth time, it flew by her faster than the speed of light.

He'd won. Thank God. They could stop.

'I think that's it,' he said modestly.

'Oh, really? Shame. Let's have another match.'

He looked surprised, but game. 'OK. You serve first,' he said, kindly.

She looked at him as if he'd lost his mind. 'I will never play this game again as long as I live. Which might only be another four minutes.' She opened the door and gulped in the air of the corridor: it was slightly stale and vaguely chlorinated but mercifully less sweaty (much of it her sweat) and cooler than the air in the squash court.

She was vaguely aware of her dishevelled appearance but the time to care, or be able to do anything about it, had long passed. 'I just couldn't keep up. What have you got on the sides of your trainers – wings?'

He laughed. 'I enjoyed that.'

'You would. You won. And without breaking a sweat. What was that squash club you used to play for back at university?'

'Ah . . . that was the national team,' he said sheepishly.

She stared at his grinning face and realized she'd been had.

'But I did play for the uni club too. Just forgot to tell you the other bit.'

Becky started to laugh until tears ran down her face, mixing with the rivers of sweat, and she thought she probably looked even more unattractive.

'Right. Now you've made me run fifty-seven miles in a small box like a deranged hamster, I'm starving. Where are we going?'

They were in his neighbourhood this time, partly to take advantage of his gym membership. After showering and changing, Adam took her to a Lebanese restaurant on the high street. They ran in from the needle-sharp sleet to a smell of warm spices. It was packed, being a Saturday night in Clapham, and they were immediately asked if they could vacate their table by nine as the restaurant ran two sittings.

'Nothing like being made to feel welcome,' said Adam after the waiter also suggested they ordered within the next five minutes 'before the table of ten, otherwise you'll be waiting for your food'.

'Here's the welcome,' said Becky as a belly dancer shimmied towards their table, her dark-rooted blonde hair and false pink nails incongruous against her authentic costume. Being seated meant naked flesh at eye level. Neither knew where to look and, embarrassed, Becky ended up burying her nose in her wine and Adam stared at the picture on the wall behind her head. Then, to their relief, the belly dancer moved on.

'She was quite good,' said Adam politely and Becky couldn't help giggling.

'Are you a dancer?' she asked.

'Good God, no. Actually, funny story: I used to do Morris dancing.' He smiled expectantly, and Becky wondered if she'd missed the punchline.

'Actually . . . maybe more of an embarrassing story,' he amended.

'No, funny too. Very. Did you get wooden sticks?'

'Yes. Another funny story. Girl opposite whacked my arm by mistake. Broke my radius.'

Becky was horrified. 'That's awful!'

'At the time, yes. I remember crying. But then I got a plaster cast. Was the cool kid at Chipping Camden Primary for a few weeks. Made a change from being the nerdy one with carrot hair,' he said, running his hand through the golden red flop on top of his head. 'Best of all, I got a present from my parents to cheer me up.' He spread his hands wide, eyes lighting up. 'A chemistry set.'

'Oh my God, I always wanted one of them,' said Becky. 'Thought I'd be able to do magic.'

He looked bemused. 'I was more interested in making compounds. Did you get one? A set?'

'Mum had no spare cash. Had to make do with vinegar and bicarb of soda to make a volcano.'

'Wow. There's something about the way it just fizzes up, it has a life of its own, exploding there right in front of you—' He checked his enthusiasm. 'Sorry. Anyway, that's what got me into chemistry.' He paused, wistful. 'I'll never forget that set. What about you? How did you know you wanted to be a journalist?'

Becky thought back. She'd always known really, even if she hadn't recognized what it was when she was very young. As a seven-year-old she'd seen another classmate bullied by a horrible girl – Karen Jenkins. Karen had taunted a plump girl with a bowl haircut, calling her fat and saying she stank because she was always eating cheesy-puff crisps. She was, and she did, but Becky had felt angry on her behalf – and angry at herself because she didn't stick up for her.

Then Karen had turned her attention to Becky, picking

on her because of her second-hand uniform; she wore a mix of garments that were often too big or slightly on the small side depending what was available at the school sale. Her grey pinafores were shiny with age and over-ironing and her white shirts had long ago lost their bright sparkle. The bullying happened frequently and when Karen had deliberately flicked paint over her skirt, it just got too much, and Becky had begun to cry. Karen had put her face up against Becky's and warned her that if she told, she'd 'be dead'.

At seven, it was a risk too big to take and so instead, Becky had written a story in her creative-writing session in class later that afternoon, only in order to save herself from an early demise, she'd decided to cleverly disguise the names. A code that only she, Becky, would understand. The bully would be known as Jaren Kenkins.

Empowered, she wrote up the story, relishing the details, vindicated that the facts were on the page. She remembered feeling sad that no one would actually know who it really was, and true justice would never be served. The next day, Karen was mysteriously absent for part of the lesson and reappeared with red eyes. Rumour had it she'd been to see the formidable head, Mrs Parker. Becky's teacher had taken her aside and quietly said that if Karen ever bullied her again, Becky was to come and speak to her immediately. And the plump classmate suddenly started sharing her cheesy puffs with her. Becky had spent a number of years wondering how the teachers had found out.

As she relayed all this to Adam, it spawned further childhood stories. Adam had grown up in the beautiful rural

Cotswolds, an only child with professional parents. He'd lived in a large, comfortable house, his mum taking a career break from her job as a GP when he was young and only returning part-time during his school years. Becky told him of how Iris had brought her up during the day while her mum worked, and she'd never met her father. Adam had played in the woods that were a part of their garden, his father building him a treehouse over several weekends. Becky had gone to the local park just around the corner from her home and had loved going so high on the swings she felt as if she were flying, her feet seeming to lift above the horizon, as she pushed herself so she could see only sky.

Once or twice, she had turned the conversation to his work, but it had been difficult to engage him on it and he always ended up changing the subject.

They ate their way through lamb kebabs and flatbreads and finished the bottle of wine that Becky had persuaded Adam to drink with her. A little part of her thought that if he drank, he might open up a bit about his work.

By the time the waiter was hovering with the bill, they'd also polished off yet more wine to accompany the baklava and both were feeling quite tipsy.

'I'm paying,' said Adam but Becky insisted on splitting the bill. They headed towards the exit looking warily out of the window, where small particles of icy water hit the glass and dribbled downwards.

'Right,' said Adam, 'I'm going to get you a cab.' He rang a local company whilst they huddled under the eaves, but all their drivers were fully booked for at least two hours.

'Another company?' said Becky.

He tried two others, but they had no drivers available until eleven either.

'It's cold,' said Becky, shivering.

'I'm really sorry. I should have booked this when we first got to the restaurant.'

'It's OK. I'll get the train.'

'It'll take as long as the wait. Engineering works, remember.' He wondered for a moment whether to say it. 'I only live five minutes away. If you want to wait there. It's warm . . .'

'Have you got coffee?'

'A cafetière.'

'Get you!'

He laughed but didn't make a move.

'Well, come on then,' said Becky. 'It's freezing!'

They hurried down the brightly lit high street, Becky huddled against the cold, her hood pulled up over her head, the sleet stinging her skin through the thin denier of her tights. They turned down another street, then another, and then they were soon in a residential road with solid-looking Victorian properties. Halfway down, Adam dug in his pocket for some keys and then pushed open a pillar-box red front door, indicating for her to go first. She stepped into a communal hallway and there was something rather intimate about the small pile of mail addressed to Adam on the side table, a window into his private life, his domesticity. A door opened, and a young woman started to speak.

'Adam! I've finished . . .'

She tailed off when she saw Becky, and the DVD she held aloft in her hand sunk to her side. 'Didn't realize you had company,' she said.

'This is Becky,' said Adam, gesturing. 'And this is Trixie.'

Trixie was pretty and plump with purplish-black tousled hair and enormous brown eyes. She was wearing – inappropriately, considering the weather outside, thought Becky – a pink-cotton vest pyjama top and shorts. On her feet were large fluffy bootee slippers.

She looked Becky up and down, hiding her hostility badly. Becky, in her inebriated state, was torn between feeling annoyed – wondering exactly who Trixie was – and a perverse superior sensation of being the one going up to Adam's flat. She knew this irked Trixie, which was ridiculous, as Becky didn't think of him in that way at all.

'Good night?' asked Trixie.

'Yes. At Shiraz. Becky is a friend from uni. Waiting until her cab arrives.'

Trixie nodded and appraised Becky again. 'Nice to meet you,' she said insincerely. She turned to Adam and smiled. 'We still on for the movies tomorrow night?' she said, which Becky thought was more for her benefit than anything else.

'Course,' said Adam. 'I'll come and knock for you.'

'Great!' Trixie beamed, and Becky felt her watching as she followed Adam up the stairs, her smile no doubt morphing into a scowl.

His flat was immaculate. Fresh white walls, wooden floors and expensive plantation shutters. Furniture that was well made, comfortable, sturdy. Lamps were deftly placed, rugs had been chosen in subtle shades of neutral and well-controlled colour. The whole effect was like something out of a John Lewis catalogue. He flicked a switch near the fireplace and the coals began to flicker and glow in the most realistic way. It was a flat for a grown-up, with a grown-up lifestyle. It spoke of career success and a new independence. Becky was surprised. He hadn't shown much interior-design aptitude at the house he'd shared with her friend and, in fact, she distinctly remembered passing his open bedroom door once and seeing a stack of science magazines passing as a bedside table and a plastic supermarket bag masquerading as a bin.

'Wow,' she said.

'Not me. Mum made it nice.' He looked embarrassed. 'Makes me sound inept – which I am. But it's not like she's here all the time. Never, in fact, well obviously she came to organize the place and she pops in every now and then to say hello . . .' He trailed off, realizing he was digging a hole. 'Coffee?' he said brightly, leading her to the equally well-thought-out kitchen.

He wrestled with the cafetière and then poured them both extremely strong coffees.

'Sugar?' he asked, and Becky shook her head. He then added some for himself.

'Three spoons?!' exclaimed Becky.

He blushed. 'It's a prop. For, er . . . extreme situations,' he said and then blushed some more.

There was a self-conscious moment between them, and Becky found herself going a little red too.

They took their drinks back into the living room and Becky felt herself sinking blissfully into the new sofa. She stretched her socked feet out towards the flames, enjoying the sensation of playing at grown-up houses.

'Nice sofa,' she said, stoking the soft cover.

He was looking at her strangely, almost with a sense of unease.

'What's up? Have I taken your seat or something?'

'No! It's fine,' said Adam quickly, sitting next to her. 'It's woven chenille.'

Becky giggled. 'What's that?'

'I don't know.'

'Well, I like it. Your mum has good taste.'

The coffee, on the other hand, was disgusting.

'Actually, I've got something in the fridge,' remembered Adam, once they'd both politely coughed after the caffeine-attack in their throats. 'It was a house-warming from Trixie. I've never wanted to drink it alone . . . Shall we?'

Becky knew she'd had enough already and that he should probably save it to drink with Trixie, but what the hell. The coffee abandoned, the cork was popped, and the bubbles overflowed. Adam went to a CD player on the teak book-shelf. 'What's your thing?' he asked, holding up half a dozen CDs.

'Extensive collection,' teased Becky.

He peered at them. 'I hate to say this, but I think Mum may have bought these too. Fancy any?'

'Lucky dip?'

He slotted in a CD and the opening bars to Fun's 'We Are

Young' started up. 'Oh my God,' said Becky, sitting up. 'Spring 2012. Revising for my mock A Levels. This got me through.' She started to sing, softly at first, feeling self-conscious. '*Tonight. We are young . . .*'

And then he joined in: '*We can burn brighter than the suuuuunnnn.*'

They fell about laughing. 'All I wanted in life back then was to be cool enough to live in a teen movie and this was the perfect soundtrack,' said Adam. 'Listening to it made me feel like I could speak to girls.'

'You're doing all right,' said Becky and he smiled bashfully. She watched as he took a drink. He held the glass between his fingers as if it were something incredibly fragile and his spectacles seemed to get in the way of the rim as he tipped it towards his face. She felt a pang of fondness.

'You've got a great place. How long have you been here?'

'Last September. Moved in when I got the job.'

'So, what are your plans in this fabulous new job?'

'Oh, you know, the usual. Work hard, get promoted.'

It was off pat, almost dismissive.

'Are you going to invent a ground-breaking new pesticide?'

'Maybe . . . How about you? Going to break some big story?'

'I hope so.'

'Well, good luck to you,' said Adam and he joined her again on the sofa and chinked her glass.

'And you,' pressed Becky, but he was sitting upright, looking at his fizz. She turned sideways to face him, tucking her feet under her legs. 'We're the lucky ones. Employed graduates. In industries we love.'

Adam didn't answer at first, just looked straight ahead. Then he turned to her. 'Ever wonder if you made a mistake?'

She looked at him in surprise.

'You have all these big ideas,' he said, 'these ambitions. But the reality isn't quite the same.'

'What is it? The company?'

'Yeah.'

'Leave?'

'Bit difficult. This flat. It's got a big mortgage.'

Becky was wide-eyed. 'You *own* it?'

'Well, no, the bank does. But, yes, I bought. Lucky, eh? How many twenty-one-year-olds can afford their own home?'

'Not many.'

'Exactly . . . My parents advised me to get on the property ladder. They put down the deposit but now I'm paying twelve hundred a month. I can't leave my job, I need the money. And I don't want to let them down.'

He looked so downhearted that she leaned over and put her arm around his shoulders.

'Hey, don't listen to me,' he said. 'I'm just whinging. Like you say, I'm one of the lucky ones.'

It would've been the moment to take her arm away, but it felt nice there, so she didn't. 'I know what you mean,' she said, 'about not letting them down. Mum brought me up alone. Went without so I could have stuff. This job I'm going for . . . I feel like I really need to get it. Show her it's all been worthwhile.'

'You will,' said Adam firmly and he was looking at her with such intensity, such belief, that she leaned in and kissed him.

He was so surprised, she began to think it had been a bad idea, but then he put both their glasses on the walnut side table cum magazine rack and kissed her back. Before long, they were pulling at each other's clothes on the mocha rug and, for a brief moment, Becky worried it was still new (and not what his mother had intended) and was she *really* doing this, and wouldn't it complicate things, but she didn't stop.

Afterwards they lay there in each other's arms, the light from the fire flickering on their bodies, and she listened to his heart beating.

'Adam?'

'Yes?'

'Why do you want to leave?'

He was quiet for so long she thought she'd annoyed him with her question.

'I'm not so keen on their ethics.'

She spoke softly. 'In what way?'

Another long pause. 'I can't say.'

They were jolted apart by a loud buzzer sound. 'Your taxi,' said Adam and he went to the intercom and spoke to the driver. 'She'll be down in a minute.'

Becky considered cancelling, continuing with the conversation, but the mood had been broken and she suddenly felt awkward in her nakedness. They both hastily pulled on clothes, and then it was time to say goodbye.

'I had a great night,' said Becky.

'Me too.'

They stood there, smiling self-consciously at each other, then the buzzer went again, making them jump.

'Want to do it again?' said Adam quickly.

'That would be great.'

He held her hand down the stairs and kissed her before she ran out into the sleet.

She waved as the car began its journey through the icy black night. Then, as they turned the corner, she stared out of the window, not seeing anything, her mind full. One question burned away at her: what was Adam afraid of?

THIRTY-THREE

2018

The heat from the day had lingered and the classroom was stuffy. Kate stifled a yawn as she took her seat. The long hours were taking their toll and more than once she'd lain on the sofa, reading through legal papers, only to have them slap her in the face as they jolted her awake. The more she read, the more she realized just how out of her depth she was but had got no further in figuring out how to keep her promises to Grace and the others.

'Right,' said Gloria, as she took her position at the head of the class. 'A change to this evening's lesson. We are not going to evaluate a range of contractual disputes, but instead I've managed to persuade Jill Pattinson to come and talk to you. Jill doesn't normally do talks to students as she simply doesn't have the time but let's just say she owes me one, and I have, as a gift to you all, pulled a favour.'

Kate appraised the new arrival. She was tall with cropped grey hair and as skinny as a beanpole. Her outfit was equally formidable: a tailored grey jacket and pencil skirt, and an incongruous pair of patent purple heels, which gave her a sense of fun – or attitude. Kate couldn't quite decide which.

'Jill is a solicitor who's worked in civil litigation for over thirty years. She's going to outline a couple of her more significant cases, notably those in the area of negligence. Please listen and take notes as there will be questions on them next week.'

Kate sat up, her tiredness abating. These cases may well have aspects that were relevant to what she was trying to achieve. As she listened to Jill speak about what had happened to her clients and the passion with which she fought to win them compensation, she became inspired by her sense of natural justice, and her determination to fight until the end. As Jill brought her talk to a close, Kate suddenly got an idea. It was mad, presumptuous, but she didn't stop to question it.

As soon as class was over, Kate clutched her things in her arms and ran out into the corridor, but Jill had already left and was outside, walking back to her car.

'Excuse me?' Kate called, dropping her notepad, but Jill turned, so she didn't stop and pick it up, just ran up to her. 'My name's Kate Ellis. I'm a student . . .'

'Yes, I saw,' said Jill, a touch impatiently, thought Kate.

She got to the point. 'I hope you don't mind me approaching you like this, but I was wondering if I could ask you for some advice.'

Jill checked her watch. 'I really do have to be somewhere . . .'

'I'll be quick. I'm trying to put together a case on behalf

of a group of people, as their litigation friend, only, I think I may have bitten off more than I can chew, and I could, to put it simply, use some help. They could use some help.'

The expression on Jill's face was not a welcoming one.

'It's a big case. The fee . . . they couldn't pay now but I think as claimants they could win a lot of money . . .'

'And you are qualified to know this how?'

Kate was taken aback. This was not the passionate, charming woman who'd just been speaking to them all in class.

'If you had a moment – not now, I realize you're busy,' said Kate quickly, 'but at some point, perhaps I could come and see you, explain more.'

Jill was getting in her car, a low silver Mercedes. 'I'm sorry, I really do have to go.'

'But wait—'

'Let me give you a piece of advice. They always tell you it's a big case, a no-brainer, and that they're entitled to thousands . . .'

'No, they're not saying—'

'But very rarely is that the case.'

'There's a young boy, he's seriously ill—'

Jill shut the door and drove off. Kate stared as she accelerated out of the car park and then, in a couple of seconds, she'd gone.

'Old bat,' she said, under her breath.

'Charming,' came a voice from behind her.

Kate spun around to see Gloria holding her dropped notebook. 'Not you.' She took the book. 'Thanks.'

'I couldn't help hearing a bit of that,' said Gloria. 'Firstly, as you know, the agreement we have in place is that no student is to collar any of our guests. No asking for jobs, ways in the back door, putting them in an awkward position—'

'I wasn't—' started Kate.

'So, did you find out who owns your farm?' interrupted Gloria.

She shook her head. 'Not yet. Trail has gone as far as Cyprus.'

Gloria nodded. 'So, what are you going to do?'

'Keep looking.'

'And the evidence? Causal link?'

'I'm still looking for that as well.'

'You need something indisputable,' said Gloria. 'Lawyer-speak for smoking gun.'

'Right.'

'One other thing. I can tell you care a lot about this compensation case of yours. Word of advice . . .'

Another one, thought Kate.

'Don't let yourself get emotionally involved.'

Kate finally saw red. She thought of Arnie, enduring painful and difficult treatment; his parents, having to watch their son go through it; and the others too. And there was Becky. This was her way of making amends. 'Don't get emotionally involved? Is that really how you lot operate?'

'Well, yes,' said Gloria, to Kate's departing back. 'That's how you win.'

Kate carried on walking. 'I can't be doing with this,' she muttered under her breath.

'Is that it then?' called Gloria. 'You're quitting the course?'

Kate could hear the smile in Gloria's voice. 'No,' she yelled back. 'I'm not going to self-sabotage my education. Not twice in one lifetime. And anyway, I bloody well paid for it!'

THIRTY-FOUR

Sunday, 12 February 2017
– twelve days before the accident

Becky had woken in the night more than once, partly due to the excessive thirst from the alcohol. But after a glass of water, what had stopped her from dropping off again was the guilty, uncomfortable feeling. Adam had sent her a text – four, in fact, since she'd left his flat. She'd enjoyed his company and just a few hours ago had wanted to see him again but now she wasn't sure. And the fact he was so keen made her feel even less sure. The first message had arrived when she was in the cab: 'Had a really great night. Text me when you get home safe. X'

It was a lovely sentiment so why did it make her heart fall a little? She felt a flicker of panic, of wanting to create distance. She'd waited to reply until she'd got in the door: 'Me too. Home now. Pretty knackered so bed for me.'

Almost immediately he'd sent the next text: 'I'm going to hit the sack too. Wishing you some sweet dreams 😘'

To which she'd responded: 'Night. X'. The addition of the kiss had been something of a dilemma. Without had seemed too abrupt, but its inclusion was undeniably borne out of a sense of guilt.

He'd then added: 'Night to you too. Don't let the bed bugs bite! XX'

At which, she had to admit, she'd cringed. He must have done the same, as another came pinging in: 'Sorry! Bit naff.'

Her heart sank again, and she thought that she could safely let him assume she'd fallen asleep, hence justifying her lack of response. His texts betrayed just how much he liked her. She liked him too, just wasn't sure her feelings for him were as strong, and whether her desire to see him was based on her journalistic hunger to find out what he knew. He was a nice guy and she didn't want to lead him on.

Now it was the morning after, and Becky lay in bed, her head throbbing, pinned to the mattress by a nausea that intensified if she moved too fast or too upright. She could tell it was morning by the laser beam of sunlight doing its best to slice her head in two as it pierced its way through the crack in the curtains. *Need more sleep*, her body intoned, and she slowly turned over, pulling the duvet up higher to block out the light and wishing she hadn't drunk Trixie's champagne.

She fumbled for her phone on the bedside table, tentatively curious to see if the cold light of day had adjusted Adam's enthusiasm. There was an unopened text from him. She eyed it warily and was about to read it when her bedroom door opened a crack. Becky quickly pulled the phone under the covers and shut her eyes. It was barely ten, far too early to get up on a Sunday.

'So, you're awake,' said her mother, coming into the room with confidence now.

'No, definitely asleep,' mumbled Becky, thinking, *how did she know?*

'I could always tell when you were pretending,' said Kate brightly. 'Your eyelids flicker. Same as when I had to get you up for school when you hated Miss Hanbury.'

'She was a witch,' said Becky. 'Expected me to know my twelve times table and I was only nine.'

'You can't stay in bed all day, it's gone ten! And I have a surprise for you!'

'Can it wait?'

'Most definitely not!' Kate flung the curtains open triumphantly on 'not'.

Becky cried out and buried her head deeper under the duvet. 'Mum, that is not funny.'

'Don't you want to see your surprise?'

'It's outside?'

'Yep.'

'Therefore, it requires me to leave the bed.'

'Well, you wouldn't want it in here. Come on,' Kate urged. 'I take it that's a hangover,' she said, disapprovingly. 'This, I promise, will cure it.'

Knowing she'd get no peace unless she did as she was bid, Becky slowly sat up and put both feet on the carpet. Then, holding onto the side table, she hoisted herself up as if she were an invalid, and shuffled over to the window.

The once-grey world had turned into blinding white and vibrant blue, and she half expected a celestial chorus to cascade down from the heavens. At some point in the night the sleet had turned to snow and the street was covered with a very commendable layer of the stuff. This wasn't a vague flurry that was already melting, this was a deep, 'I mean business' chunk.

'We're making a snowman!' said Kate. 'And a snowdog!'

'I don't have any gloves,' said Becky hastily, heading back to bed. She wasn't quick enough. Kate had darted in front of her.

'We're not wasting this day. I have a spare pair. Spring sale 2007 from the garden centre, remember?'

Becky looked at her mum's earnest, excited face and couldn't help smiling. Maybe some breakfast would help.

The miracle of porridge didn't fail and forty-five minutes later, Becky was at the front of the house following her exuberant mother's new footprints in the snow.

'Snow angel?' said Kate.

'Come on, that's just some cheesy thing they do in the movies. The reality is cold, wet stuff seeping up the back of your jacket and a freezing arse.'

'Someone's a bit grumpy this morning.'

'Not at all. I am enraptured by this Dickensian vision of perfection.' A snowball landed on the side of her head. 'Oi!' Becky pounded together a handful of snow and threw it back at her mother, who squealed. It missed.

'OK, truce!' shouted Kate, arms in the air. So, Becky started on a snowman, rolling a ball of snow around on the ground so it grew bigger and bigger.

'How was your night?' asked Kate.

'Great. Good food. Weather atrocious and no cabs so we had to wait at his place for a bit. He's got a really nice flat in Clapham. Right opposite the Picturehouse. Lots of fancy furniture. He's even got bamboo flooring.'

'His own place, is it?'

'Yes. All grown up.'

'You know . . . if you ever get the urge to do the same . . .'

'Get some bamboo flooring?'

'You know what I mean. Move out of home. Get your own space. I wouldn't mind.'

'Are you kicking me out?'

'Saw right through me.'

Becky glanced over at her mum, to see if this was a subtle hint. Despite the fact Kate was deliberately keeping her face low as she moulded the snowdog, Becky could tell she didn't want her to leave at all. She smiled; she had no intention of going anywhere.

'I'm quite happy here,' she said, 'otherwise, who else is there to drag me out of bed at an unsociable hour to make snowmen? There, that's the head,' and she plonked a large ball of snow on top of her earlier, larger ball. Next to it, Kate's snowdog had acquired an impressively upright tail. 'Anyway, maybe it's *me* cramping *your* style,' Becky continued, 'now you've got this hot new man, Tim. Only, I notice you haven't invited him over yet . . . is that because of me? Because I'm here taking up the other half of the sofa?'

'You weren't here last night. After midnight I heard you come in.'

'I didn't wake you?' said Becky, concerned.

'Not at all. Trust me, once you have children of your own, you'll know it's one of the perils of being a parent. You can never settle until they're home safe. Doesn't matter how old they are.'

'Really? What about when I'm thirty?'

'Probably still be awake.'

Becky imagined herself at thirty. 'Maybe you'll have grandchildren by then. They'll be keeping you awake at night.'

'You'll still be living here when you have kids? Not with your other half?'

'We'll drop them off with you – while we go out on the town.'

Kate laughed. 'I see.' But there was something about the idea of looking after Becky's children that filled her with warmth.

'You can stay,' she said graciously. 'In fact, it might make it easier.'

'For what?'

'Dinner Friday week.' Kate paused. 'I'd like you to meet Tim.'

Becky stood up straight. 'Wow.'

'I know we've only been on a few dates, but I'd like to introduce him to you.'

'He's *serious*.'

'I don't know, like I say we've only been on a few dates—'

'But introducing him to the family!'

'Well, there's only me and you . . .'

Becky and Mum, Mum and Becky. It had always been the two of them. She smiled. 'Sounds good.'

'You're free?'

'I'll make sure I am,' said Becky and her mum looked pleased.

'So, what about you? Are you going to see this Adam again?'

There it was again. The fidgety feeling. She'd checked the text he'd sent that morning and he'd asked her out. Wanted to know if she was free on Tuesday after work to go to an evening event at the Science Museum.

'He wants to. Tuesday.'

'But you don't?'

'It's not as simple as that.'

Kate waited for Becky to continue, knowing she would.

'He could be a source,' she said, cautiously.

'So, he's helping you with a story?'

'Except he doesn't know it.'

'Ooh. So you're infiltrating his mind . . .' Kate suddenly realized something. 'Does this have anything to do with your big story? The secret one?'

Becky refused to meet her eye. 'Might do,' she mumbled. She sighed. 'Am I using him?'

'I don't know, are you?' said Kate carefully. She watched her daughter wrestle with her conscience from the corner of her eye, while she added the face on the snowman. 'Ta da!' she said, as she stuck in stones for eyes. She stood back and admired him. 'He's very handsome. Go on, take a pic. Send it to Adam.'

Becky smiled at her mum, propping her arm around the snowman's neck as Kate got on the other side.

'Say snowball,' said Becky as she held out her phone to take a selfie.

'Snowball!' they both chorused, grinning, and Becky took the picture. She sent it off and a reply pinged back almost instantly, which she read aloud.

'"Is that your mum? She looks like your sister!"' Becky groaned.

'He's got a way with words. I like him,' said Kate. 'Go on, go out with him.'

'You think?'

'Yes. Otherwise you'll only be moping at home on your own.'

Becky looked up, surprised. 'Why? Where will you be?'

Kate said it as casually as she could. 'I'll probably stay over at Tim's. We're going to the movies and it finishes quite late and I don't want to be paying for a cab.'

Becky's first thought, for which she was later ashamed, was a sensation of being abandoned; her mum not being the constant, at home every night regardless of what she, Becky, was up to.

'Only, I can come back if—' started Kate.

Becky was mortified at her earlier selfishness. 'No, you go. I've decided to go out with Adam, anyway.'

'Not just because . . .'

Becky was quick to reassure her. 'No.' The truth was, she could hardly just ignore him. They'd had sex together. If things weren't to get awkward, they needed to meet up again. Something lighthearted and friendly. What could be the harm in one more meeting?

'Great! So, we both have hot dates.'

Her mother's face was so illuminated with happiness that Becky was once again reminded of how important this man, Tim, must be to her. She smiled, and her thoughts turned to Adam. It was a good idea to see him. Maybe he would even talk more about his company.

Becky's massive oversight was highlighted early on Tuesday morning. The doorbell rang at 7.30 a.m. and Becky got there first, with Kate hot on her heels. Standing on the step was a woman dressed in a fleece and comfortable shoes, brandishing a large bouquet of red roses.

'Nice snowman,' said the woman, nodding back over her shoulder. 'Are you Miss Ellis?'

Becky, baffled by the bunch of flowers, was about to confirm she was when—

'I think they might be for me,' said Kate and, sure enough, the card was for a Miss K. Ellis and they were from Tim.

'"From your bus driver",' Kate read aloud. '"I hope this is the beginning of a very long journey for us. XX"'

'Wow, what prompted that, then?' said Becky. 'He taking you out on the 196 tonight?'

Kate cocked her head. 'It's Valentine's Day.'

'Oh, right.' Then it sunk in. 'Oh, right!' She'd only gone and agreed to a date with Adam on the corniest day of the year. A day that was full of unspoken expectations, and where the capacity for embarrassment was limitless. She groaned inwardly before reminding herself it was all just meaningless commercial rubbish and she would ignore it. Maybe he hadn't noticed it either.

'Happy Valentine's Day!' said Adam, as she walked up to him in the foyer of the Science Museum. He leaned over to kiss her softly on the cheek.

'You too,' she said, a fraudulent smile on her face.

The airy, pristine-white foyer was populated with numerous couples and a few people on their own, trying not to look too desperately at the front doors.

'You look nice,' he said as she shrugged off her coat and handed it in at the cloakroom.

'So do you.' And it was true, he did. His deep-turquoise flowered shirt picked out the sunset tones of his hair.

They had tickets for that night's special event – *Robots Through the Ages* – and made their way to Room 25, which held about thirty people. Towering above them, right in the middle of the room, was a huge dull-silver robot, with a neon-green grill mouth, cone-shaped green ears and a single green antenna sticking out of his head. His large silver-framed eyes took up half of his head and suddenly they lit up and he began to march/slide across the floor. To Becky, it seemed as if he was coming straight for her, and she couldn't help but be intimidated by his eight-foot lumbering frame and those eyes that were looking right at her and she instinctively grabbed Adam's arm, laughing nervously.

'Say hello to Cygan,' said a woman cheerfully, her head mike amplifying her voice, and Cygan lifted his arm in greeting to the crowd's tentative giggles and nervously raised fingers.

The woman, Sally, then introduced herself as the museum's robotics expert, and after a short background on the Italian-designed Cygan, an example of the most advanced technology in the world back in the 1950s, she invited groups to take a closer look, as the rest wandered around the other exhibits.

'It's quite terrifying really,' said Becky, looking back over her shoulder in wonder.

'He's over fifty years old,' said Adam. 'They're much more sophisticated now.'

'That's even more terrifying,' said Becky. 'Did you ever think of getting into robotics?'

'Chemistry was always my thing. Matter, reactions, forming new substances.'

'And how are those new substances going?'

He was studying a display showing one of the earliest robots from the sixteenth century. 'You mean work? It's OK.'

'Tell me more.'

'Not much to say.'

'You don't talk about it much.'

'Just a bit boring, that's all.'

'Trust me, I'm interested.'

He stopped looking at the sixteenth-century mechanical monk and turned to her. 'Why?'

'Because I'm interested in what you're interested in.'

He smiled, pleased. 'It's going well. It's good. We're testing a new product.'

'What does it do?'

'Kills the cereal aphid in barley.'

'Sounds impressive. Is it dangerous?'

'Well, you wouldn't want to put it on your cornflakes,' he joked. 'But no, of course it's not dangerous.'

'But isn't that exactly what you're expecting farmers to do? Spray it on our cornflakes?'

He frowned. 'Well, not like that, no.'

'You're right. Ignore me, I'm being silly.'

He smiled at her, unsure.

'Ethics improved?' asked Becky, gently.

A flicker across his face. 'You should forget about that. I was talking rubbish.'

'You sure? Only, it didn't sound like it at the time. It sounded like you were being put in a very difficult position.'

'No, honestly . . .'

'Are they asking you to do something you don't agree with?'

'I don't want to talk about it—'

'Something to do with one of their products? Something that isn't strictly safe?'

'I said, I don't want to talk about it,' he snapped, voice raised.

A silence. The people around them looked up, nudged each other – *a tiff on Valentine's Day!* – then gradually lost interest and picked up their own conversations again.

'Sorry. I didn't mean to be rude,' said Adam. 'Hey, look!'

Becky turned to see another robot come into the room. This one was modern, eerily lifelike, white supple 'skin' covering its body from head to toe and, as Sally explained, eyes that moved in response to sounds, to people entering its peripheral vision as it rotated its head. *It doesn't have vision*, thought Becky, *it's a robot*, but it certainly looked as if it did when its head stopped at her and the dull grey-black of its pupils seemed to bore right into her. Then it turned away and walked up to another woman.

'Do you want to dance?' it said charmingly, its voice smooth and digitally pure.

The woman looked taken aback but was blushing – *actually blushing*, thought Becky.

'Why don't you say yes?' said Sally. 'Don't hurt Charlie's feelings!'

'OK, yes!' said the woman and Charlie held up his arms and she tentatively touched his hands and they started to move across the floor.

'I like you,' said Charlie. 'Will you be my Valentine?'

Laughs from the crowd. The woman gazed up at Charlie as if it were a real person, flattered by the attention. 'Um . . .'

'She's spoken for!' called out a man. He moved closer, pretending to raise his fist in jealousy.

More laughs. It was mesmerizing, and Becky was struck by how humans could be moved by a sophisticated piece of robotics and yet be inured to the plight of real people. *Half of us probably walked straight past at least one homeless person on the way in*, she thought. It was easy to ignore the unfortunate if you weren't directly affected. It was easy to forget, to walk on by. Her job was to redirect the public's attention, tell the story, *expose* the story. *I need to pursue this.*

'Adam, I think there's something I should say.'

'Sounds serious,' he said, smiling.

She took his hand and led him to the edge of the room, away from the crowd.

'You're really a robot?' he joked, and she smiled weakly. 'No . . .'

'*You're* the one dating Charlie and I should go over and punch him.'

'No . . .' she said again, ignoring the uncomfortable realization that Adam seemed to think that she and him were dating and he had reason to be jealous. 'I'm researching something for work. It's about herbicides.'

His joviality stalled, and a wary look crossed his face. 'Go on.'

'I've been talking to a number of families who live near a farm. Each of these families has someone ill in their household. With serious diseases. Cancers, ME, Parkinson's. I firmly believe it's because of their proximity to the chemicals sprayed on the fields. And these products . . . they're made by Senerix.'

A flicker of horror, then confusion, hurt. 'Hang on . . . Is this why . . . ?'

She shifted her eyes from him, knowing what was coming, unable to hide the guilt.

'Is this why we're here tonight? Why you agreed to come out?'

'No . . .' she began lamely.

His eyes opened wide. 'Is this why . . . Saturday night happened?'

She blushed. 'It's not exactly like that . . .'

He was shaking his head now, incredulous. 'You slept with me to get information about the company where I work?'

Becky bristled. 'No!' But her brain was scrabbling around, checking this denial was true. Had she?

'I thought this had all come a bit out of the blue. Contacting me like that. It surprised me – I always had the impression I irritated you at uni.'

Becky twisted her face away and looked at the floor.

'It's OK. I get it,' said Adam.

'Anyone else want to have a romantic dance with Charlie?' called Sally. Sally caught Becky's eye and proffered the robot invitingly. Becky turned her back.

'Shall we go and get a drink? Talk this over?' she said to Adam.

He was silent for a moment and she saw he was conflicted. She smiled hopefully, expecting him to say 'yes'.

'I'll be honest, I think I should be getting back.'

Her heart sank.

'See you around, eh?' He shifted from one foot to the other, not sure what the protocol was for abandoning a date mid-way through, then started to walk off.

'Please don't go,' called out Charlie, sensing someone leaving the room.

'Wait . . .' said Becky and Adam stopped. She knew she'd called him back then because she saw her story disappearing. And when he looked back, he knew it too.

'I liked you,' said Becky. 'I *still* like you. The reason I'm coming clean is because I don't want to deceive you.'

'I know,' he said and then he turned and left.

It had been an emotional reaction. Granted, his ego had been pricked and it had been hurtful to know why she was interested in his work but that wasn't all that was going on here, Becky thought as she travelled home. She'd caught Adam's look of horror when she'd told him about the herbicides and what they were doing to people. It hadn't been one of surprise, it had been a look of recognition, of understanding. *He had known she was right.*

And that meant only one thing. He hadn't just left because his feelings were hurt. There was another reason, too. He was scared.

As Becky walked up the front path to the dark, empty house, she felt a pang of regret. She hadn't lied when she'd told Adam she liked him. She'd enjoyed his company more than she thought she would. As she got out her keys, she noticed the slumped, half-formed, grey boulder that was the remains of the snowman. Sighing, she let herself in and closed the door.

THIRTY-FIVE

2018

'Are you sure you want to do this?' asked Greg.

Kate nodded. She followed him around the back of the Fresh Foods depot to where half a dozen identical lorries were parked up. Her first thought was one of panicked terror – what if *the* truck was here – but a quick glance at the registration plates reassured her.

'You OK?' Greg asked gently. 'Because we can stop any time you want to.'

'No, it's fine.'

He led her to the first truck, the one nearest to them, and they approached it on the driver's side. He took out the keys and clicked the button. A beep and a flash of lights. He opened the door for her and indicated the steps so that she could climb in.

She swung herself up and into the cab. It was high and, at first, she only looked directly ahead. Then she made herself look to the left. It was extraordinary – practically the entire passenger door had been converted into a window. She could see the wheels on the truck parked next to her.

And if she could see its wheels . . . she thought about the height of a cyclist.

'Do you want to see what it's actually like for a driver to see a cyclist?' asked Greg.

She nodded.

He beckoned to a worker across the yard who pushed a bike over then got on it, edging backwards between the two trucks. It was amazing – he was completely visible. She looked at where the top of his head came – and with a shiver saw it didn't reach anywhere near the bottom of the original window, he was simply too low down. Becky wouldn't have been seen at all. So maybe it had simply been an accident. Maybe Becky hadn't been as vigilant as she usually was, and it had been a brutal accident that – as Greg was now demonstrating – could have been avoided.

'These are the first vehicles to be completed,' said Greg. 'The second phase will be done next week.'

'It's good,' said Kate. The worker looked up at her through the window and respectfully nodded. 'Really, really good.' Her voice cracked. She suddenly wanted to get down. Greg held out a hand, which she gratefully took as she climbed out the cab. *It's done*, she thought, *what I set out to do, to protect other cyclists*. But being here was painful and made the memories of that day too close and she wanted to leave now.

Greg understood. 'Do you have time for a coffee? There's this nice little place just down the road. We can discuss the interviews for the bursary if you like, go over our questions.'

'A coffee would be great,' said Kate and Greg took her

to a small Italian coffee house with scarlet geraniums spilling out of the window boxes. They ordered two cappuccinos and sat at a small wooden table outside.

'I've drafted up a few questions,' said Greg, 'but if you want to ditch or change any, that's fine. Also, of course, add your own.'

'I've never interviewed anyone in my life,' said Kate, smiling self-consciously.

'You're going to be just fine,' said Greg. 'I was looking at dates. Would you be free to interview on the tenth of August?'

'I'm not sure,' said Kate. 'It's my birthday. I think Tim might be planning something.'

'OK . . .' Greg pulled out his phone, tapped on the screen. 'The following Tuesday?'

'Works for me.'

'Good. Then, assuming we find someone successful, I've been speaking to our HR manager and she's suggested starting the scheme early September. I was thinking of doing a small event, at the office. Get a photo of you and the winning candidate. I think it would be good to publicize the scheme for next year.'

'Sounds great.'

Greg took a sip of his coffee. 'So . . . it's been a while. What have you been up to?'

'Oh, you know, work, the usual.'

'How did your trip go?'

'Trip?'

'France.'

'Oh, yes!' *Damn*, she thought. She didn't really want to talk about it. 'Fine. Short.'

'Short?'

'It was only a day.'

'Oh. I thought you said it was a break?'

'It was. A short one.'

'Sounds very mysterious.'

'Not really. Just fancied a change from my routine. You know.' He was looking at her and she knew he didn't believe what she was saying. There was a momentary awkwardness as she braced herself for more questions, then Greg smiled, breaking the tension.

'I'm going myself in a couple of months. Lille.'

'Oh, yes?'

'My son lives there.'

'You have a son?' said Kate, surprised.

'Yes. He's just got a job for a French transport company. Graduated in French and computing. It'll be my first visit.'

'What's his name?'

'Matthew.'

'Do you get on?'

Greg laughed. 'Mostly. Now he's left his teenage years behind.'

Kate winced sympathetically. 'They're hard, aren't they?'

'Always trying to defy you.'

'Never tell you anything.'

'Or if they do, fifty per cent of it isn't true. I'll never forget when I found cigarettes in Matthew's school bag. Confronted him about it, and he tells me they're his mates.

He's "looking after them" so his friend "doesn't get into trouble with his mum."'

Kate laughed. 'It's like they think we were born yesterday. I remember Becky coming home from school once with her skirt hitched up to mid-thigh. Tells me there'd been an announcement in assembly that morning. If you walked to school rather than have your parents drive you, you were allowed to shorten your skirt, as it was less restrictive for moving around.'

She smiled at the memory. Recalled Becky's wide-eyed fourteen-year-old practised look of innocence, her green-and-black checked skirt revealing her lovely long legs, her not really having a clue what it meant, what it might invite.

'Roll it back down,' Kate had instructed.

Her daughter's face had reddened in indignation. 'But it's true!'

'I think we both know it's not.'

'It is, Mum.'

'Really? Shall we call the school office now?' Kate picked up the phone, held it aloft.

Realizing she'd been rumbled, Becky exploded in teen-aged fury. 'You never let me do anything!' she said, stomping up the stairs, and Kate pulled a face as she saw her daughter's knickers on display at every stamp.

'We had a big row,' she told Greg, 'and she said she wanted to go to Paris where they were "free and bohemian". Somehow I convinced her to stay in south London.'

Greg laughed. 'She sounds spirited. Strong opinions. I would've liked to have met her.'

'Fortunately, the angst period didn't last long. Only a few months, then she miraculously metamorphosed into a pretty cool young woman. One that I could recognize as my daughter.'

Kate's phone began to ring. She looked at the screen – it was Tim.

Greg glanced down, saw the glass was cracked. 'Wow, you can see through that?'

Kate shrugged. New phones weren't high on her agenda at the moment.

'You want a top-up?' asked Greg, indicating her cup as she answered her phone. She nodded, and he went to the counter.

'Hey, you,' Kate said into her mobile.

'Hey, you, yourself,' said Tim. 'Everything OK?'

'The trucks are transformed,' said Kate.

'I'm glad. You still there?'

'No, I've come for a quick coffee with Greg. We're going over the questions for the interviews.'

'When do you think you'll be home?' asked Tim.

'Not sure. Is there something going on?'

'No, no. Just wanted to make sure I was back for you, that's all.'

She felt a burst of affection. 'When do you finish work?'

'Last route is at four. Should be home by six-ish.'

'OK. I'll be back by then.'

'Great. Love you.'

'You too,' said Kate, as Greg returned with two fresh coffees.

It took less time than she thought to go through the questions and, realizing she was only a bus ride from Elephant and Castle, where Tim's route started, Kate decided to head there and ride home with him on his last journey of the day.

She arrived early at Tim's stop and two 196s left before she knew Tim would even have started work. But he wasn't driving the 4 p.m. or the 4.08 p.m., or even the next two buses. At half past, she wondered if she'd got the time right, but was certain that was what he'd said. So, where was he? She tried ringing but got his voicemail. Another 196 turned up and she dithered for a moment – should she still wait?

'You getting on, love?' asked the driver and she did, wondering all the way home what had happened to Tim.

She got off at her stop and walked the short distance back to the house. Letting herself in, she called out but was met with silence. He wasn't home. Puzzled, she went to the kitchen to make herself a cup of tea. She dumped her bag on the table and filled the kettle. Flicked it on. Then she turned to open the fridge and stopped dead. The side door that led out into the garden was ajar. Was Tim in the garden? She stepped out, walked around to the back of the house.

The garden was empty. With a chill, Kate stood on the small lawn and looked up at the house. The windows stared back at her as a heart-stopping thought formed in her mind. Was anyone inside? *Don't be silly*, she told herself. Tim had been on a later shift that morning, he'd probably come outside for breakfast, then forgotten to lock the door before he left for work.

She returned to the house and, standing in the middle of the kitchen, listened carefully. There was no sound from upstairs. Taking a large knife from the drawer, and feeling rather foolish, she walked slowly through the house. Ground floor first, then she crept quietly up the stairs to the two bedrooms and the bathroom.

There was no one there.

She lowered her hand and let out a small laugh. She'd have to remind Tim to lock up – anyone could've got in. She heard the front door open and Tim's voice shout out.

'Kate?'

'I'm here.' She came running down, forgetting she still had the knife in her hand.

'What the . . . ?'

'Oh. Sorry!' Kate explained about the open side door, but Tim was puzzled. 'I didn't go out there this morning,' he said.

'Are you sure?'

'Positive.' He frowned. Looked around. 'Has anything been moved? Taken?'

The relief she'd felt a mere five minutes ago was rapidly evaporating. 'I don't think so,' she said, moving into the living room. The crappy TV was still there, as was her ancient PC. But there was something wrong.

'Did you use my computer this morning?' she asked.

'What? No. Why would I use your computer?' It was true, he never did. He had his own tablet – much faster and newer than her PC.

She went over to the tiny desk in the corner of the room.

Touched the pull-out tray for the keyboard. When she'd left it this morning, she'd slid it back under the desk. She distinctly remembered. Panicked, she checked the tower – it was still there. She switched it on and had to wait for the agonizingly slow old beast to start up. She scrabbled through her papers, college textbooks, research printouts, notebooks.

'Some of my stuff has gone,' she said. 'To do with the case.'

The computer had finally resurrected itself and she clicked urgently, cursing when it didn't respond quickly enough.

She opened up her latest file, the one into which she'd typed her case so far. It was still there. Stymied, she looked at it, until suddenly, she understood. She checked the file statistics. The file had last been opened that day, at 16.09 hours. *Somebody had been in her house at just after four o'clock that afternoon.*

'What's happened?' asked Tim nervously.

'Someone's been here. Taken things. Copied my files.' She pointed at the screen. 'This one, it's got everything I'm building into the case. All the stats, the interviews, the evidence. It's been opened, while we were out. Someone's read it, copied it.'

The screen pinged. Now the computer had had time to warm up, it was informing her of a new email.

Kate turned back to her computer. She opened up her email account. At the top of her inbox was the new message.

She clicked.

STOP OR WE WILL KILL YOU.

She recoiled.

'Who sent this?' said Tim, his jaw dropping.

Kate was shaking. 'I don't know.'

'What is it, some sort of joke?'

'Not very funny,' said Kate.

Tim looked at the address. 'It's come from a nondescript free account.'

She nodded. Tucked her shaking hands under her arms.

'How did they even know you were involved in this?'

'I don't know.' Then, in a sudden realization, she gasped, and the floor spun beneath her. 'Oh my God,' she said.

'What?'

She pointed at the screen. 'This . . .'

'What about it?'

'They're threatening to . . . to *kill* me. If I don't stop looking into the story that Becky was writing.'

He frowned. 'Yes?'

'Do you suppose . . . what if Becky got one of these?' She took a deep breath. 'What if . . . her death wasn't an accident?'

It was dawning on Tim. 'Oh my God.' He put his arm around her. 'No . . . no, it can't be.'

Stricken, she looked at him. Wanted to believe him but the worm of mistrust was burrowing itself deep inside her mind. 'I think I'm going to be sick.' Kate jumped up, hand over her mouth, and ran into the kitchen, retching into the sink.

THIRTY-SIX

The police were making signs to leave. The male officer put his mug down on the coffee table, cleared his throat.

'We'll be doing a door-to-door over the next day or so,' he said. 'And, as my colleague says, we'll pass on our report to the cyber-crime team.' The female officer, who sat next to him on the sofa, nodded. 'Obviously, if you get any more disturbances or you see anything suspicious, anyone hanging around, please let us know.' He paused. 'You might want to reconsider your campaign. If you think it's causing someone to target you.'

Kate bit her lip, felt Tim looking at her. 'Yes,' she said, non-committally. Of course, they were right. But the truth was, it wasn't as simple as that.

After she let them out, she went into the kitchen where Tim was tidying away the mugs. She sank onto a chair in exhaustion.

'I still can't believe it,' said Tim. 'Isn't it a bit extreme to . . . do away with someone because of a newspaper exposé?'

'Is it? What if Becky's report had led to compensation? Millions of pounds. Enough to ruin someone.'

'But you heard what the police said. There's no proof, no direct link to anyone. And we couldn't tell them of anyone we suspected.'

Kate groaned. 'If only we still had Becky's laptop . . .' She suddenly banged her forehead with her fist. 'I can't believe I've been so stupid.'

'What?'

'The break-in. Last year. It wasn't those scally kids we thought it was. It was *them*. They took Becky's laptop. That's all they wanted. To know what she was working on.'

'I guess it's possible . . .'

'He knows,' said Kate, fiercely.

'What?'

'Justin Holmes. The farm manager. He knows who owns the farm he works on, but he won't tell me.'

Tim put his arms on her shoulders. 'I know but—'

'Oh my God!' Kate pushed his hands away. 'I've just remembered.'

'What?'

'That man. The one with the moustache that I saw in Ramsbourne. I'd seen him before, remember? Only I couldn't recall where.' She took a deep breath. 'It was outside the court. The day of Becky's inquest. He was there, Tim, right there, talking to the driver's solicitor.'

'I don't understand.'

'They're connected. They must be. He has something to do with this.'

'Do with this, how?'

'I don't know. I just *don't know*, Tim.' Kate suddenly

found herself crumpling, sucker punched by these new revelations. 'Maybe we should tell the police.'

'Tell them what? A bad man we don't know is up to something, but we don't know what?' Tim sat beside her. 'You
need to get rid of all your evidence,' he said, gently. 'I can help
you. You need to tell those people in Ramsbourne, too.'

Kate frowned. 'Tell them what?'

'That you're quitting.'

'What?'

'Well, you're not going to carry on, are you?'

'I don't know. I mean, it's not just about me.'

'Hold on. You suspect Becky was deliberately got out of
the way because she was trying to expose a story and now
they *know* you're working on the *same* story – worse, you
want to *sue* them – and you want to carry on? Are you
mad?' Frustrated, Tim rubbed his eyes. 'They're not joking,
these people. They're dangerous. And now they know
exactly what you're doing. They've read your files – they
know *everything.*'

'Not everything. I didn't keep the names of the villagers
on there.' In fact, like Becky, she'd kept them on a separate
memory stick and hidden it in a plastic bag in the bird box
in the garden instead. She'd bought it when Becky was five
but, to their disappointment, not one bird had ever nested
in it. Now it held treasure of another sort.

'They know plenty.'

Kate suddenly leapt up and went into the living room,
frantically searching the message on her computer screen.
'There's got to be a clue on here. Something.'

Tim was right behind her. 'There's nothing.'

'Here!' said Kate. 'It was sent at twenty past four this afternoon.'

'What does that tell you?'

It was when she'd been standing at the bus stop waiting for Tim. It reminded her that she'd missed him.

'Where were you this afternoon?'

He looked bemused by her question. 'What? At work.' He frowned. 'What are you insinuating?'

'I went to meet you. Your last bus.'

A flicker of something in his eyes. Nerves? She watched as Tim blinked rapidly. 'I clocked off early. Soon after I rang you. Had a bit of a dizzy spell. Bosses don't like you behind the wheel if you're not up to it. Health and safety rules.'

'Are you OK?'

He quickly reassured her. 'Oh, yes. Fine now.'

Kate appraised him. 'Why are you so against me doing this?'

'I don't know, because I don't want you to die?'

It was sarcasm but gently done; the look on his face was one of disquiet.

She put her hand on his. 'I understand why you're so worried, but it feels wrong to just throw away everything I've done.'

'You've done enough,' said Tim. 'Look at everything you've achieved, those trucks today. You're amazing. What you've done is amazing—'

'So, let me finish,' said Kate. 'I can't abandon her, Tim. I might not be smart, or have a string of qualifications, but that much I do know. And I'm struggling, God dammit. Half the time I'm just winging it, scared to death, but I can't let her down. Another couple of months, then I'm sure all this will be over.'

'And if it's not?'

'I can't stop, Tim. If I did, I'd become a part of it.'

'No—'

'She's my daughter. How can I live with myself if I don't carry on?'

THIRTY-SEVEN

2010

'It's a new initiative,' said Becky. 'We voted it in. The whole school. Ninety-seven per cent of us said "yes". Come on, Mum, it'll be fun.'

Kate secretly thought it would probably be one of the worst days of her life. The school had dreamed up 'Family Woman Day', where the mothers of the pupils got to go in with their children and take part in the school day.

'Is Claire's mum going?'

'No.'

'There we are then.'

'But only because Claire's mum is in Zurich for her work. If your mum's not around, you're allowed to bring someone else. Your aunt. Or grandmother.'

Of which Becky had neither. Kate was an only child and she hadn't spoken to her mother for over fifteen years. Dervla would be turning sixty this month – still a relatively young woman. Kate hadn't told Becky, but she'd sent her mother a birthday card and a photo of Becky, taken on her fifteenth birthday. Kate wasn't expecting her mother to suddenly become a doting grandmother, first in the queue at events like this Family Woman Day, but such a lot of time had passed, she was quietly hopeful that they might re-establish contact.

Kate looked at her daughter's pleading face. It would be cruel to say no. If she kept her head down on the day, maybe she'd get away with it.

'OK.'

Becky beamed. 'Thanks, Mum. And don't worry about the quiz. We'll be together for that bit.' Then, knowing what her mum's response would be, she pegged it out of the kitchen, grabbed her bag and, calling out a goodbye, slammed the front door shut.

Quiz? What quiz? Jesus, what had she just agreed to? A cold lump of dread started to make itself comfortable in Kate's stomach.

Two weeks later, as Kate lay in bed after the alarm, she briefly considered feigning illness, before dismissing the thought. Becky was so excited about this Family Woman Day and the clue to survival was in the name: it was a single day. Even if it wasn't much fun for her personally, she could get through it. There just wasn't the time for it to get that bad. This practical thinking gave her a little boost and she ran down the stairs, stopping as she saw the post on the mat. She could hear Becky getting the breakfast ready in the kitchen, singing along to the radio.

Kate bent down to pick up the mail, her heart stalling as she saw a weather-beaten pink envelope tucked amongst the others. Her address, which she'd carefully written in the bottom right-hand corner, had been ringed and someone had scribbled 'Return to sender' next to it. She recognized the handwriting. It was her mother's.

Kate turned the envelope over – it hadn't even been opened. Even after all these years, it hurt.

'Breakfast's ready,' said Becky, appearing in the kitchen doorway. 'Hey, what's up?'

'Nothing,' said Kate, brightly. She tucked the pink envelope back in amongst the others and walked past Becky into the kitchen.

So far, it hadn't been too bad. In fact, Kate had even enjoyed the school assembly, listening to the headmistress talk about various pupils' achievements, seeing their faces light up as they went to the front to collect their certificates for an inter-school sports match or Duke of Edinburgh scheme. And Becky had won something, too. Seeing her go up on stage to collect her prize for leading a politics debate made Kate glow with pride.

Assembly had been followed by time in the classrooms, something Kate had been dreading in case she was asked a question, but she needn't have worried. The lessons had been deliberately designed to be inclusive and Kate had found herself taking part in a science experiment where Becky took the lead.

Kate was aware of Julia Cromwell, on the other side of the classroom, but she appeared to be engrossed in the same experiment with Violet and hadn't even glanced her way.

Lunch was surprisingly tasty, and Kate had struck up conversation with some of the other female relatives. Claire's grandmother, Sue, was a retired nurse who was currently fitting in as many foreign trips a year with her also-retired husband as they could, while they still 'had all their marbles'.

The quiz was scheduled for after lunch and as everyone filed into the main hall, there was a competitive buzz in the air. To Kate's dismay, she found that she and Becky had been put on a table with Julia and Violet. Claire and Sue made up their team. Kate felt her earlier confidence evaporate as the questions started coming and Julia nominated herself as team captain and therefore the one who would write down all the answers. Julia also monopolized the debates over the answers and Kate grew quieter as the afternoon wore on. She could sense Julia growing more scornful, and was just wishing the whole thing could be over when Julia suddenly addressed her.

'What do you think, Kate?'

Kate hadn't even heard the question, in part because she'd tuned out a while ago, finding many of them too difficult to answer. She gave Julia a blank look.

'Come on, keep up,' said Julia. 'Don't let the side down.' Her tone was light, but Kate had caught the disdainful glint in her eye and she flushed.

'We're on the general knowledge round. Means everyone gets a chance of getting something right, whatever their background,' said Julia. Kate glanced up sharply, but Julia was smiling around the table. 'So, to recap: who won the British Grand Prix earlier this year?'

'Lewis Hamilton,' said Kate.

'Well done, Mum,' said Becky.

'Yes, thank God,' said Sue. 'I know nothing about sport.'

Neither do I, thought Kate, but she'd heard her boss Martin talk about it a couple of days ago at lunch. She looked across the table, but Julia wasn't writing the answer down.

'Are you sure?' asked Julia. 'Only, I thought it was Mark Webber.'

Was it? Kate stumbled in her thoughts. Come to think of it, Martin had mentioned him too. Or had he won the Monaco Grand Prix? Julia was looking at her expectantly.

'Lewis Hamilton,' said Kate, firmly. She was sure that was right.

'Well, we know who to blame if we lose,' said Julia airily as she wrote down the answer.

Kate bristled, her jaw set tight as doubt once again took hold. She looked across at the answer sheet, at Julia's swirling handwriting, Lewis Hamilton's name burning itself on her retinas. Maybe she should say something – she wasn't sure after all – but then the answer sheets were being handed over to the neighbouring tables for marking.

The headmistress began to read out the answers, Julia giving a little nod of confirmation at each right answer they'd got, clocking up the points with a one hundred per cent success rate so far, until, finally, they were on the last question.

'Question twenty,' said the headmistress. 'Who won the British Grand Prix earlier this year?'

Kate's stomach churned. *Oh God, please be Lewis Hamilton*, she thought.

'The answer is Mark Webber!'

Kate flushed.

'Never mind,' said Sue. 'None of us were sure.'

But Kate didn't hear her kind words. All she could feel were the waves of disdain emanating from Julia.

'Seems like we'll have to settle for second,' said Julia as the roll call of winners was read out. Kate felt Becky give her hand a squeeze under the table, but she wouldn't be comforted. She considered leaving at that point, but there was still one event left – the Year 11 charity auction. As much as she wanted to go home and put her pyjamas on and curl up in front of the TV, she wouldn't give Julia the satisfaction of thinking she'd driven her away.

Kate gritted her teeth; she'd see out the last part of this Family Woman Day. She may not know the answer to a quiz question but there were two things she absolutely did know for sure. The first was that she wished she was a better mother for Becky, one she could be proud of. The second was that she hated Julia Cromwell.

THIRTY-EIGHT

2018

Kate stepped off the train, her bag weighing heavily on her shoulder, and she shifted it to stop it cutting into her skin. Her discomfort was intensified by the heat. It was a corker of a summer's day and the air smelt green, of plants and their perfumes in the warmth of the sun. She passed the start of the public footpath with its thigh-high nettles, where countless bees hummed greedily, dipping in and out of a gnarled, woody buddleia. As she exited the station, Kate paused for a moment before going to Rob's taxi 'office'. He'd sent her a message, short and to the point, asking if he could see her and had refused to elaborate further until they were together.

He'd heard the train and stepped out, seeing her on the pavement. She waved and made her way over. Her eyebrows went up as she came closer – he had a purplish-black eye.

'Thanks for coming,' he said, gruffly.

'No problem.'

She waited for him to suggest somewhere they could talk but he just stood there awkwardly.

'Shall we go for a drink? Lemonade in The Wheatsheaf?' suggested Kate.

Rob was embarrassed. 'Um . . . maybe not there.'

'Don't tell me you got that –' Kate pointed at his eye – 'in the pub?'

'Been barred for a week.'

'Right.' She looked behind him at the office. 'You got anything cold in there?'

''Fraid not. There's a vending machine on the platform though.'

He bought two chilled fizzy drinks from the machine and they sat on a bench facing the railway tracks, the heat warping off the gleaming metal. It was quiet: no cars, no people. The pop of the ring-pulls cut across the sounds of nature: birdsong, a hoverfly. They each took a welcome drink and Kate was beginning to wonder how long it might take for Rob to let her know why he'd asked to see her. She glanced across at him and he was staring into the middle distance.

He sensed her looking and turned his head. 'There's been a development,' he said abruptly.

Kate was wary. 'Oh, yes?'

'Cancer's come back.'

'*What?* You mean . . . Abby?'

He nodded. 'Different one, though. Brain cancer.'

It was a moment before she could speak. 'I'm so sorry, Rob.'

'She's got to have an operation to cut it out. Because of the nature of the tumour, it has to be this special consultant. He's in a hospital up in London.'

'But he'll see her, right?'

Rob nodded. 'Surgery, then depending on how much he can get out, might be radiotherapy as well. We're going to need to find a place right near the hospital. It's gonna take a few weeks.'

'When?'

'In the next couple of months.' He cleared his throat. 'It's gonna cost. Rent up in London, no wages for a few weeks. More than I've got.' He paused. 'I've had an offer of some cash.'

'That's good . . . ?' said Kate, questioningly.

'Yes. *I* think so.' Rob was defiant. 'It's from Justin Holmes.'

She tensed. 'Why's he offering you cash?' she asked, although the answer was already forming in her head.

'We had a bit of an argument, me and him.' Rob pointed to his eye. 'I kinda lost it, seeing him in the pub on Saturday night, drinking without a care in the world. And me, with Abby and Helen . . . I told him what I thought of him.' He paused. 'I told him we was – me and a few others – planning on suing his boss.'

She blinked. 'You did what?'

He saw the look on her face. 'You would've done, too, if you'd seen him sitting as smug as you like.'

'No, I wouldn't.' *Jesus*, thought Kate, *what had he said?*

'Anyway, next morning, he comes knocking with an offer. Enough to pay for all our expenses.' He took a deep breath. 'But it would mean I'd have to drop the case.'

Kate's mouth dropped. Then, somewhere in the distance,

a noise. The track started humming. The far-off sound of a train approaching, at speed. *Oh my God, had Rob told Justin that she was the one behind this campaign?* Is that why her house had been broken into, her private documents searched? Is that why she'd been sent an email threatening her life?

'Rob?'

'Yes?'

The train was getting louder.

'Did you tell Justin how all this started? Did you tell him about Becky? About me, and how I offered to pull this case together?'

He looked at her impassively. Behind him, over his shoulder, she saw the train come hurtling around the corner, straight at the station. Rob opened his mouth, spoke, but she was buffeted by the thundering noise and the sucking wind of the train and heard nothing.

Then it passed. She saw he was irritated.

'What do you take me for? I didn't mention you. Or the others – not any names,' he said tersely. 'Just said there was a few of us in the village.'

Kate nodded. 'If you need to pull out, Rob, I totally understand.'

'But it's not just me. It's all of us or I get nothing.'

'What? This is bribery.'

Rob spoke brusquely. 'The way Justin was talking, there's money for the others, too, but we all have to drop it. Every single one of us. Now. Or I don't get anything.'

'The bastard. Have you told any of the others? About your offer?'

He shifted on the bench. 'A couple. Not all. Actually, I thought . . .'

'What?' Then it clicked. 'You want *me* to do it?'

'I just thought – they listen to you.'

Kate exhaled. 'I can't do that, Rob, you know I can't.'

'I told you: he'll give them money too.'

'Maybe it's not about the money, Rob.' And then she felt awful. She'd spoken without thinking. 'Sorry. I know this is important. For Abby.'

'Way I see it, it's been over a month since you said you was gonna do this. I've gone along with your plan long enough.'

Kate shook her head. 'Oh, Rob . . . it's going to take longer than that,' she said, her voice catching.

'So, what are you waiting for?'

'It's the owner of the farm. The anonymous director. I still need to find out who he or she is.'

'And how long's that gonna take?'

'I don't know.'

'Well, weeks? Months?'

'I'm sorry, Rob.'

'Cos we haven't got months, if you know what I'm saying.'

'Can't you get the money from somewhere else? Friends? The bank?'

'Bank and me don't exactly see eye to eye at the moment. Bit of a falling-out over the mortgage payments. I guess that's why the credit-card applications failed.'

They both sat in silence.

'Rob, can I ask you something?'

He nodded.

'Have you accepted?'

'That's not the point. He needs to know we're all backing off. Not just me. Or I get nothing.'

Kate thought for a moment – something wasn't quite right.

'What was Justin like? When you told him about the plan to sue his boss?'

'Like you'd expect. Not happy.'

'Yes, but was he worried? Anxious? Panicky?'

'Well, I don't know. He was quite insistent about it being dropped. Made sure I understood fully what the deal was.'

Kate nodded.

'Why do you ask?'

'Do you mind telling me how much he offered?'

'Ten.'

'Ten? Ten what? *Grand?*' Try as she might, she couldn't keep the incredulity out of her voice.

Rob flashed her a look. 'It's a lot of money.'

'I know, it is. But is it enough? What if Abby needs further treatment? What about Helen? My estimate for her home-care help was eleven thousand a *year*, remember? And that was *very* conservative.'

'But you ain't got *nothing* yet.'

'Rob, you may not realize this but that farm will have insurance – public liability insurance. If we win against them, the insurance company will pay out much of the claim.'

'So?'

'Well, don't you wonder why he's so desperate to shut this down?'

Rob shrugged. 'Dunno. Save his boss the headache?'

'You reckon? I think there's more to this. Why's his boss got him doing the dirty work for a start. He's just the farm manager. Maybe he knows something about those chemicals being sprayed on those fields. Something his boss wants to keep very quiet. And if we all go away, there's a good chance it *will* be kept quiet.'

'Like what?'

'I don't know.'

'See, that's the problem, Kate. You've got good intentions, I'll give you that, but at the moment, it seems like it's just wishful thinking—'

'It's more than that,' she jumped in.

'Remind me again, how close are you to taking this to a court?'

She didn't answer.

'See.' He took another sip of his drink. 'Some of the others have already agreed.'

'Who?'

'Ian.'

'Who else?'

He set his lips hard.

'Have some refused?'

His eyes blazed, refusing to admit defeat. 'They'd change their minds if you told them to.'

'Oh, Rob, I don't think they would. Some of them

maybe, but some just want to know the truth. They want the truth out there. And they want justice.' She sighed. 'Look, there's only one way to resolve this. We need everyone to take a vote. If you want to back out, then I wish you the best.'

'He won't pay me unless we all back out.'

'Well, let's see what the rest want to do.'

'You're going to persuade them to stay in.'

'What kind of person do you take me for? I'm just going to lay out the facts, Rob. Everyone has to make their own decision.'

'You look warm,' said Grace drily as Kate followed her friend into her kitchen. It was a massive understatement; half an hour sitting in the blazing sun with Rob then a two-mile walk to Hawthorne Lane had left her frazzled. She took the glass of iced water Grace offered her and gulped it down.

'Better?'

'Much. Thank you.'

'I'm surprised you didn't get a lift with Rob. Was he out on another job?'

Kate grimaced. 'He was there.' She filled Grace in on their conversation – and the promise to hold a vote.

'God, this is a sorry, shitty state of affairs,' said Grace. 'I feel for him, I really do. And that poor girl.'

'Me too. I just wish I could promise him something more.'

Grace nodded. 'When are you going to hold the vote?'

'As soon as possible. I know you're not around much . . .'

'No. Chemo starts again next week. Part of me's dreading it. It's so intense this time. But part of me wants to think it's the last ever time, then he'll be given the transplant, then, well . . . we just have to hope it takes.' Grace's eyes briefly lit up: cautious hope mixed in amongst the pain. 'I'll talk to Nick but I'm certain he'll think the same way as me.' Grace looked at her. 'You have to carry on, Kate.'

Kate felt the full force of her friend's belief in her, the trust she'd do a good job. It gave her strength. 'I'm going to a trade conference next week, there's going to be a lot of people there from the agrochemical industry. I'm hoping to corner a few.' She suddenly remembered what she'd been carrying in her bag – she pulled out two large wrapped boxes. 'For the boys.'

'Arnie! John!' called Grace and they came running in. 'Look what Kate's got for you.'

Identical looks of ecstatic anticipation. The paper was ripped off in 3.4 seconds, then there were exclaims of delight.

'A dog!'

'Mine's got a green collar, what's yours got?'

'Red!'

They flung their arms around Kate and she hugged their warm, small bodies, flooded by a rush of affection. She helped get the toy dogs out of the limpet-tight plastic packaging and the boys immediately pushed the buttons on the leads so the dogs started walking. John pushed another button and his dog barked.

'Look, she's saying, "Thank you, Kate, you're the best!"'
He fed her with the food that was included in the pack, then
made her poo it out. 'I'm going to call mine Kate,' he
declared, and she laughed as she watched her namesake
defecate plastic bones on the kitchen floor.

'Mine's called Lucky,' said Arnie, spontaneously hugging
it. 'Like me,' he added, 'because I've got my own pet!' He
held out his hand. 'Here, Lucky!'

Kate looked at the small six-year-old boy who'd be going
into hospital again in a few days' time and wished with all
her heart that he would indeed be lucky.

THIRTY-NINE

Wednesday, 22 February 2017
– two days before the accident

Try as she might, she just couldn't focus on her work.
Which was bad, because her interview was in only a couple
of days' time, but Becky found her gaze wandered around
the office, her mind distracted by the fact she'd called Adam
to apologize three times and not once had she got through,
nor had he called back.

The first time had been later on Valentine's night itself.
She'd come home to an empty house and called Adam while
she made cheese on toast in the kitchen, her mum's enormous
bunch of roses in a large vase on the table in front of her.

She fingered the soft petals as she waited for him to pick
up, feeling her stomach twist when he didn't.

'Hi, Adam, it's me, Becky. I haven't behaved brilliantly
and I'm sorry. I don't want it to end like this so . . . please
will you give me a call?'

She'd checked her phone all the next day but there had
been nothing. No call, no text. She'd come home from work
to find her mum completely loved up, she and Tim sending

and receiving text messages like teenagers, her mum guf-
fawing at some joke, which she'd shared with Becky. 'Look!
He thinks I look like a Hawaiian lady,' she'd said, then held
out her phone with a photo of the two of them both mysteriously garlanded with flowers over their winter coats and
Becky had smiled indulgently.

When Kate had asked about Becky's own date, Becky
had been matter-of-fact: 'Think I might have blown it,
Mum.' Kate had been so sympathetic and *sorry* that Becky
had had to make out it was more of a mutual thing and
both were fine about it. But she wasn't fine. She wanted
to see Adam again, as she really enjoyed his easy friend-
liness.

She tried him again the following evening and then at the
weekend, when her mum was out with Tim – and staying
over at his house (but only if Becky was OK with it). Becky
had sent her off and contemplated a Saturday night alone,
made all the more poignant by remembering she'd been
having dinner with Adam only the week before.

Three messages were enough. He clearly wasn't going to
contact her again, and she would only humiliate herself by
pursuing it. Instead she *had* to concentrate on her interview.
She desperately wanted the job, but she knew that Piers was
going to be very hard to beat.

Terence was conducting the interviews and Becky had
agonized over whether or not to tell him about the herbicide
story. Stories about illnesses and herbicides had appeared
before but this one was different, she could sense it. She
knew she was onto something, but a crucial element was

missing, this she sensed too, and she wished with all her heart she'd not been so stupid with Adam.

More than anything, she wanted to be able to tell her mum she'd got the job. She wanted to pay her back for all the sacrifices she'd made.

Becky made herself focus. There was work to do. She needed to get back in touch with Grace, the mother of the twin boys in Ramsbourne. Grace had, quite naturally, been chasing her on the status of the story and Becky knew she had to come clean. It was also only fair that she let Grace – and the others – know what she'd discovered as she'd researched her story. She needed to go and see her.

Becky called Grace's number and, getting her voicemail, left a message asking if she might be free late the following Monday afternoon – it would be a good time to go to Ramsbourne as Terence was out at a budget meeting.

Turning back to her computer, she tidied up the interview she'd done with the nanny who'd accused the footballer of assaulting her and then sent it to print so she could proofread it. She saw Piers get up from his desk and head towards the printer station on the other side of the office. He gave her a wink as he passed, and she glared at him in return. She wondered how confident he was about his interview – he'd made sure she knew he was up first, 'always means you make the best, most lasting impression,' he'd said, which she knew was hardly a scientifically proven fact but nevertheless still rattled her already grated nerves.

'Printer's chewed up your docs,' said Piers as he appeared

back at her desk. He flapped around the first page of her article as if in proof.

Becky went to take it from him, but he flicked it out of her reach and glanced down at the text.

'"She said she didn't think she'd get the job. There were much better candidates than me",' he quoted, laughing, delighted with his wit.

'Give it here.'

'But, Ellis, it's so interesting. So *accurate*.'

'Don't be a dick.'

He grinned, knowing he'd got to her, and dropped the paper, letting it waft slowly down where it skimmed the desk and fell on the floor.

She glared at him, not wanted to grovel around on the carpet.

'Sorry,' he said, unexpectedly. 'Here, I'll get it, you go and check the jammed doc.' He bent down and retrieved the paper, glanced at it. Shrugged. 'Actually, it's really well written.' He looked her in the eye. 'You know why I give you a hard time. You're the competition. And you're good.'

Don't be flattered, don't be! thought Becky, annoyed. *He's playing you.*

'I know,' she said imperiously and, head in the air, walked past him, over to the printers, looking for the one with a jam. They all seemed to be working fine. She scouted around the worktops, looking for her article, but couldn't see it. Darcy, the PA, was standing by the post-out tray, engrossed in something she was reading, and then Becky recognized it. Her article.

'Not for publication yet,' she said sharply.

Darcy jumped guiltily. 'Oh, sorry.' She quickly smiled. 'Couldn't help it. It's good.'

'So everyone keeps saying,' murmured Becky and, taking the document back, she looked it over. It all seemed to be fine, no scrunched-up or half-printed sheets. Puzzled, she turned and looked back towards her desk.

In her seat was Piers, on her computer.

The little shit! She marched over, furious. 'What the hell do you think you're doing?'

Damn it, she hadn't locked her screen before she'd left, and now he was searching through – what?

'Get off that,' she said angrily, pulling the laptop away from him. She quickly checked the screen and saw he'd been scanning through her search history. 'Are you really that desperate?'

'It's your own fault,' said Piers pleasantly. 'If you weren't so secretive all the time . . .'

Becky fumed, biting her tongue to stop herself from shouting at him.

He seemed amused by her anger. 'Oh, come on, you'd have done the same.'

His lack of shame only served to infuriate her further and she was about to explode when her phone started ringing. That would be Grace, calling her back. She slammed her laptop screen shut, took the phone from her bag – hiding the screen from Piers's inquisitive eyes – and then headed off quickly to the only place she knew she'd get some privacy. Bolting the door behind her, she sat on the loo seat and answered.

'Hello?'

'Becky, it's Adam.'

Her heart leapt. 'Adam! Hi . . . how are you?'

'I'm fine. I got your messages.'

'I'm sorry,' said Becky quickly. 'I behaved abominably. But it wasn't just about—'

'It's OK,' interrupted Adam. He stopped, quiet for a moment, and Becky waited, wondering why he was calling her.

'No need to apologize, OK? No hard feelings. I'd like to meet. There's something I need to tell you.'

Becky's heart began to race. 'Is this to do with your work?' she asked tentatively.

He paused. 'Yes.'

A wave of excitement gripped her. 'Is it about the thing you couldn't talk about?'

'Yes.' It was so quiet, it was almost a whisper.

'When?'

'Huh?'

'When do you want to meet?'

'Oh . . . can we do Friday? After work?'

'Yes . . . oh, shit, no. I can't, sorry. I've said I'd meet my mum's new boyfriend. Sorry. Big thing.' *Damn*, she thought, but quickly offered up an alternative. 'But I can do Saturday?' She waited, on tenterhooks.

'Fine,' he said. 'That's fine. But I don't want anyone to know.'

'I won't say anything.'

'No, you don't understand. I don't want anyone to see us together.'

Becky was surprised. 'What . . . you think you might be being . . . *followed*?'

'Yes . . . no . . . I don't know. I just don't want it. OK?' He was getting agitated.

'It's OK, we can do it any way you want.' She thought quickly. 'Premier Inn. Holborn. I'll text you the room number. Say 10 a.m.?'

'OK.'

'I didn't recognize your number.'

'No. This is a new phone. Temporary.'

He sounded afraid then, and she got a shiver up the back of her neck.

'I'll see you Saturday, OK?' she said.

'Yeah. See you then.'

He hung up and Becky clutched her phone, heart thumping. He was going to tell her something. Something big, she could sense it. She stood up, smoothed down her skirt, composed herself, then opened the cubicle door.

'*Jesus!*'

Piers was standing by the sinks, leaning against the wall. Becky stared at him in fury and dismay. *What had he heard?* She thought back frantically. Nothing – except where she'd agreed to meet Adam. Shit. She'd have to re-arrange. Think of somewhere else.

Piers watched her. 'Who was that, Ellis?'

'Just fuck off, Piers,' said Becky, angrily. 'Just FUCK OFF!' She barged past him and stormed out, the door slamming behind her.

FORTY

2018

Justin pulled the tractor up in the yard and jumped down from the cab. He was hot and grimy; the sun had turned the ground to dust. He headed towards the farmhouse, slowing as he neared the building: leaning against his motorbike, with his face cast up to the sun, was Janković. As Janković turned, Justin quickly resumed his normal step. He walked on and into his house, without even acknowledging his visitor.

Of course Janković followed, as Justin knew he would, letting himself into the kitchen. Justin felt Janković's eyes follow him, watching as he got a glass of water from the tap. In anger, he spun around.

'What?'

'Nice to see you, too.'

It grated on Justin that Janković was so calm. 'Cut the bullshit. Why are you here?'

'Just checking up on our little arrangement.'

'I offered Rob Bolton the money. Like you said.'

'He's in?'

'Yes.'

'And the others?'

'I don't know yet.'

Janković frowned. 'Don't take too long with that. We want to get this tidied up as soon as possible.' He paused. 'For all our sakes,' he said pointedly.

Justin didn't trust himself to speak; he took a sip of water.

'You know a Caitriona Ellis?' Janković asked.

The question took Justin by surprise. Did he? *Jesus, yes.* That woman who came to the farm a couple of months ago. Asking questions. Wasn't she a Caitriona?

'No.'

'You're lying.' Janković walked over to the knife block and extracted one. He took it to the table and sat down, all the while holding the blade up, inspecting it. 'You've broken our trust.'

'I won't be a part of this.'

'You already are. You're the one who gave us all the information. Told us about the journalist busybody.'

'Yes, but I didn't know you were going to . . .'

'Go on. You can say it.'

Justin gritted his teeth. *Don't let him rattle you.* 'You still haven't told me. Why did she die? It's only spraying. Happens everywhere.'

'Nothing you need to know about.'

'No? If I'm such a *valued member of the company*, I want to know.' Justin, bolstered by a rush of bravado, took a step forward. Folded his arms.

Janković looked him up and down. Then suddenly he placed his left hand on the table and, gripping the knife, stabbed the wood between his splayed fingers at a rapid speed. A quick-fire *bang! Bang! Bang!* He left the blade sticking up in the table and gave a triumphant laugh. 'Pretty good, no?' he said, flexing his unscathed fingers.

Justin stared. The man was off his head.

'Serbian army,' said Janković. 'Little trick I learned. In the boring bits. When we had no surveillance to do. Of course, now it's all different. Not possible to hide. Technology changes everything. Now I can find out anything I like about anyone. Where they go. Who they speak to. If they run.'

Justin swallowed. *I will not be intimidated by this thug.* 'What if I tell you and your paymaster to stick your threats up your own arses? What if I tell everyone what you did?'

Janković picked his helmet up off the table and smiled. 'Now you know not to do that. It's not a good idea. Not a good idea at all.'

He turned and left, and Justin sank into a chair. He had a desperate urge to just pick up the phone and call the police. Pray for some salvation. But he couldn't do that. He would be dead.

He had to get himself out of this situation. Only trouble was, he didn't know how.

FORTY-ONE

The machine beeped as it scanned Kate's ticket and she pinned it onto her suit jacket – the one she'd bought earlier in the year for the AGM – then she was into one of the cavernous halls of the London Excel conference centre.

She looked at the floorplan that had been thrust into her hand, a detailed layout of this year's 'Agrochemical Britain' conference. Some of the larger companies and organizations had booked stands. Mini pop-up representations of their multi-million-pound corporate successes. The place was awash with delegates strolling, striding, back-slapping and hand-shake pumping. There were hardly any women.

Kate found the section for Senerix's stand. The person she wanted to talk to was Dr Roger Harris, a man in his fifties who had been with the company for over a decade and was a senior scientist in the R&D department. She'd tried contacting him numerous times, via email and phone, each missive requesting an interview.

Not once had she got a reply.

Kate prowled surreptitiously around the periphery of the stand with its green-and-yellow logo present at every opportunity. She pretended to read leaflets and study the displays flanked by bottles of their products but was actually gauging who Roger was. At one point another Senerix employee, a younger man with red hair, asked if he could help with anything, and when she politely refused, he looked at her strangely before eventually moving off. She caught him glancing her way once or twice again from across the stand and it began to unnerve her – what was his problem?

After a couple more minutes, Roger bade farewell to the man he'd been deep in conversation with and, with much mutual shoulder-squeezing and hearty laughing, the man finally left, and Roger was alone.

Now's your chance, Kate told herself and, stuffing the leaflet she'd been idly reading back into its slot, she headed for Roger with the directness and swiftness of a torpedo.

'Hi,' she said, arm out, offering a handshake.

From behind his wire-framed glasses, he looked bemused at her appearing from nowhere but gave a professional smile.

'Hello. Roger Harris,' he said, taking her hand.

'I know who you are,' said Kate.

He looked taken aback.

'It's on your name badge,' she indicated.

He laughed loudly, and she caught a whiff of garlic from the night before. He looked at her badge. 'Caitriona Ellis.' He frowned, stroked his beard, sensing familiarity but unable to place it. 'Have we met before?'

'We haven't. But I have emailed you. Three times, in fact.'

He tried to make a joke out of it. 'Did I reply?'

'No.'

The one-word answer and her challenging stare made him begin to look around at his colleagues. Seek out reinforcements.

Enough of this, thought Kate. *You'll throw your chance away.* She tucked a long, loose curl behind her ear. 'Which sort of made me feel a little neglected,' she said with a smile.

Roger smiled back. Glad – and flattered – to be back on friendly terms. 'I'm sure I wasn't neglecting you.'

'I didn't think you were that kind of man. So, anyway, as I was here, and I knew you were here . . . I thought maybe you'd have a minute to chat.' She saw him glance around at his colleagues again. This time, instead of seeing if anyone was aware of his conversation, he checked to make sure they weren't.

'I'm sure we could manage something,' said Roger. 'In fact, I don't have any appointments for half an hour.' He indicated one of the pop-up booths, placed around the pop-up stand. 'Shall we?'

She led the way he indicated. As she slid into the booth opposite him, she shrugged off her jacket.

He put his elbows on the table, hands clasped. 'So, what can I do you for?'

'Well, I was hoping to learn more about what you do here.'

He puffed himself up with importance, then chuckled at the enormity of his company's – and therefore by way of association, his own – professional achievements. 'Can you stay all day?'

She forced a smile. 'I was particularly interested in your products. The chemicals you make to protect our crops.'

'There's a few. We are able to manage and control the vast majority of threats to our crops, whether fungal, herbal or insect-based.'

'Amazing. I'm sure I read somewhere that there had been a study that showed that organic farming could produce the same yields with crops rotated more freely?'

He shook his head dismissively. 'Don't think so.'

'Oh, really? Must've got mixed up with something else. Silly me.' Kate saw Roger's gaze had wandered. 'Stop looking at my tits.'

His eyes sprang up. 'I beg your pardon?'

She smiled. 'So, are they all perfectly safe then, these chemicals?'

'Safe as houses.'

'Even glyphosate? Only, I'm sure that one was classified as – oh, what was it? – "probably carcinogenic to humans". You have any glyphosate in your products? In Crixus?'

'Sure. But I promise you, it's nothing to worry about.'

'*How* safe is it?'

'Eh?'

'How safe?'

'Perfectly. It's used in agriculture all over the world.'

'Sprayed on crops?'

'Certainly.'

'What if there are people living nearby? When it's sprayed?'

He hesitated. 'Yeah, fine. Course it is. Where did you say you were from again?'

She ignored the question. 'Has Senerix done any long-term studies on human exposure to glyphosate and the other chemicals you use to manufacture Crixus?'

He cooled in front of her eyes. 'It's safe,' he reiterated. 'They're all safe.'

'But have you *tested* what happens with long-term exposure, such as that experienced by residents near farms?'

He refused to answer.

'I'll take that as a no. Or maybe it's a yes, and you didn't like the results. So how can you claim they're safe? Because I, and several other people, believe that they cause a number of life-threatening diseases.'

He laughed, patronizingly this time. 'Darling, you could drink any of our products as if they were orange juice.'

'That's your claim?'

'They're not going to harm anyone.'

'That's good to hear. Perhaps I could film you?'

'What?'

She reached over to the shelf at the side of the booth. Retrieved a small plastic bottle of Crixus from the display. 'Drinking a glass of this. As if it were orange juice.'

He stared at her, eyes glinting. 'Don't be ridiculous.'

'It's not me who suggested it as a possibility.'

Roger stood up. 'I think this meeting is over.'

'Ah, come on, Roger, there's loads I'd still like to talk to you about.'

He gave her one last look and walked away. Kate

watched him and then picked up her bag and jacket and left the stand.

She'd barely gone fifty metres when a hand landed on her shoulder. 'Excuse me?'

She jumped, whipped round. 'You!' she said angrily.

'Sorry if I scared you,' said the red-headed man. He smiled, and Kate noticed he had a dimple in his chin. He was looking at her strangely, as if he was trying to place her. 'I'm sorry to bother you but –' he suddenly looked unsure of himself – 'are you, by any chance, Kate Ellis?'

Who was this man? Kate scanned her memory bank but didn't recognize him. Was he a customer from work?

He seemed to notice her discomfort. 'Sorry. I'm Adam Langley. I think I might have been friends with your daughter, Becky?'

It took a second, and then it came flooding back. The guy from Becky's university. The one she'd been dating, albeit briefly.

'Am I right?' he said. 'Are you her mum?'

She nodded. 'I am.'

'Phew. Thought I was about to totally humiliate myself there. How is Becky?'

She looked at his face, earnest and curious. *He doesn't know.*

She lightly touched her fingers on his arm and said, her voice catching slightly: 'She . . . died. Last year.'

He staggered backwards, and she immediately thought she should have broken it to him in another way. But what other way was there?

'I'm so sorry,' he stammered. 'I didn't realize.'

They were standing outside the cafe area, which was quiet as it was still a way off lunchtime.

'Would you like a coffee?' asked Kate.

They sat at a table and didn't speak for a bit. Adam spent a lot of time stirring his drink, adding a large amount of sugar, Kate noticed. He took a sip and then stopped looking down at his drink and met her eyes.

'When did she die?'

'Twenty-fourth of February.'

His eyes flashed with recognition, horror. 'That was the day before . . .' He pulled himself up, got a grip. 'We'd arranged to meet,' he explained. 'On the Saturday. The next day.' He paused, shamefaced. 'I thought she'd stood me up. I was annoyed with her. She never answered her phone or Facebook. Just went offline.' He blushed. 'It had happened before,' he explained.

'I'm sorry I didn't contact you to let you know,' said Kate. 'Your number wasn't on her phone.'

'That's OK. I was so sure she was going to show. I even googled her name, found noth—' he quickly checked himself, stopped talking.

'How did you recognize me?' asked Kate.

'She – Becky – sent me a photo. You were in it.'

Kate cocked her head quizzically, but he was already clicking on his phone. He turned the screen to face her. Her hand flew to her mouth. There she was with Becky, the day they made the snowman.

'I remember that day,' she said. 'She had a massive hang-over. Just spent the evening with you, I think?'

He blushed bright red and she realized they'd slept together. She hadn't meant to embarrass him, but it felt strange to learn he'd been intimate with her daughter. She sharpened her interest in him, wondered what their relationship had been like – whether he'd treated Becky well.

'We went out to dinner,' he said. 'I took her to a Lebanese restaurant near my place in Clapham.'

'Can I have a copy of the photo?' Kate asked.

'Of course. What's your number?' He sent it over and when the beep arrived on her phone, Kate touched her bag lightly.

It seemed strange that there had been no record of Becky's original message on her phone, nor Adam's reply. Nothing to or from Adam at all. Which was odd – why would Becky have gone to the trouble of deleting them all? She'd been uncomfortable about dating Adam but that had been because she'd considered him a source, hadn't wanted to cross the moral line.

Her eyes caught the green-and-yellow in the distance. She looked over Adam's shoulder at the Senerix stand. So, he worked there. And Becky had considered him a source for her story. The story she, Kate, was now following. Had Becky deleted his details to erase any trail between them?

Why? What did he know?

'Why were you and Becky meeting on the Saturday?'

'What were you talking to Roger about?'

They'd spoken simultaneously and there was a nervous pause in the conversation.

'Becky said that you were helping her with a story,' said Kate quietly, watching his face.

He affected puzzlement. 'Really?'

'About herbicides.'

'What about them?'

'She was researching the health effects on families who lived near regularly sprayed fields.'

'We didn't ever speak about it,' he said casually, but she could hear the strain in his voice.

She nodded. Took a sip of her coffee. 'But is that what you were supposed to be meeting about? The day after she died?'

He didn't know what to do with his hands, was fiddling with his teaspoon, and she placed her hand over his to still it.

'Please tell me, Adam. It would help me to understand the loss.'

He looked up sharply. 'Why?'

Damn, she hadn't meant to say that, to alert his suspicion.

Adam seemed to be wrestling with something. 'Kate, how did Becky die?'

She spoke slowly, carefully, watching him. 'She was knocked off her bike. Just a few streets from her office. A lorry turned into her path.'

His eyes widened as he took this in. 'I'm so sorry,' he repeated, but behind his eyes unease was looming, she could sense it. Her own heart beat quicker as her sickening suspicions were brought to the surface again.

'What happened to the driver?' asked Adam.

'Nothing. It was recorded as an accidental death.' She paused. 'Something that I still don't understand on many levels. Not least because she was such a careful cyclist.'

Adam had sat back in his seat, his arms looped over the back of his chair, but he looked anything but relaxed.

'Is there something wrong?' asked Kate. She saw him glance back towards his company's stand. 'Is everything OK? You look nervous about something. Or someone.'

'Not at all.'

'Why did you google her? When she didn't turn up?'

'What?'

'You just said – you googled her name.'

Tiny beads of sweat were forming at his hairline and Kate felt goosebumps rise up on her skin.

'I should get back, actually,' said Adam. 'It was nice to meet you.' He quickly stood and held out his hand but didn't wait for her to shake it, instead he grabbed his jacket. 'Great. Right, well enjoy the rest of the conference.'

And then he was gone, swallowed up in the crowd.

FORTY-TWO

Kate had gone to the library to print out the photo of Becky in the snow then taken it home and placed it carefully on the fridge. It had been taken twelve days before she'd died. She would stare at it, looking deep into Becky's eyes, wondering how much her daughter had known of whatever it was that Adam was keeping from them.

He and Becky had planned to meet up on the day after she'd died. Had she already had a sense of what the meeting was about? Kate would stare so hard she began to imagine she could read something in Becky's expression, a crease in her forehead, a sharpness to her eyes or maybe something in the way she was carrying herself. She stared until her eyes blurred and then she would bang her head against the fridge in frustration and despair; no matter how hard she tried, she couldn't read her dead daughter's mind.

Kate came home from her early shift with just enough time to stop at Iris's before heading to Ramsbourne. It was the day of the vote. Kate had emailed everyone explaining that one person wanted to withdraw, and they needed to get together to decide what they were going to do next.

She quickly grabbed some juice out of the fridge and,

seeing Becky in her woolly hat, decided to call Adam again. It would be the third time since the day of the conference.

One ring, two . . . four . . . seven . . . She held her breath.

'Hi, this is Adam. If you leave me a nice message, I'll call you back.'

'No, you bloody won't,' she muttered, hanging up. She gulped down the juice and headed out.

Kate was feeling guilty as she walked up Iris's path. It had been a while since she'd spent any time with her and today, she only had half an hour before she had to go and catch her train.

There was no answer when she rang the doorbell. She tried again, but nothing. Kate stepped back a moment to check the window – yes, Constanza had been put away. She got her phone from her bag and rang Iris's number. She could hear another phone ringing and pulled her mobile from her ear – it was Iris's phone in the house, responding to her call. Then she heard something else. A faint cry. 'Help!'

Kate quickly got out her bunch of keys, found Iris's Yale and put it in the lock.

'Are you OK?' she called out, as she hurried inside.

'In here,' said Iris.

Her voice had come from the living room. Kate ran in and found Iris lying on her side on the floor. She flew over to her. 'What happened?'

'Hips. Or was it knees?'

'Oh my God. Here, I'll lift you under the arms.'

She put her hands under Iris's armpits and could just

about get her upright. With her help, Iris managed to shuffle over to the armchair.

'Thank goodness we had a date,' said Iris. 'Didn't think I could stand it for much longer.'

'How long had you been there?'

'Just after lunch. I was coming in here with my Rooibos.' Iris pointed to the carpet near the window where a mug lay on its side, its contents long cold and now staining the cream carpet.

Kate looked at Iris in dismay. 'That was hours ago! Are you OK?'

'I am now.'

'Is there anything hurt?'

'Just my pride.'

'I'll have to come over more often.'

'You'll do no such thing.'

'But—'

'Doesn't matter if you come over every hour, I could fall the minute you left. Only way to stay upright is to have you live here with me.'

Kate went to speak but Iris held up a shaky hand. 'And that, quite frankly, wouldn't work.' She smiled. 'Can't stand the way you slurp your tea.'

Kate gaped, open-mouthed. It was the first she'd heard of it; anyway, she didn't.

But Iris wasn't looking. She rested her hands on the frilly arm covers on her chair. 'No, I'm going to have to think of something else.'

Kate was wary. 'Like what?'

'Oh, I don't know. There's these very nice homes . . .'

'I'm not having it. I said I'd look after you—'

'Don't be ridiculous,' said Iris sharply. Then seeing Kate's face, she softened her voice. 'Sorry. Didn't mean to snap. It's just not practical. You have a life, a very busy one with a very important task ahead, and I need to face up to knowing when the time is right to seek help.'

Kate went to open her mouth again.

'*Professional* help.'

They sat in silence for a moment. 'Would you at least talk it over with me? See if we can find another solution so you can stay in your own home? It's what you said you always wanted to do.'

'Changed my mind.'

'Seriously?'

'Yes. They have non-stop dominoes at Sunrise Royal Oaks. And bingo.'

Kate raised an eyebrow.

'OK, we can talk,' relented Iris and patted the chair next to her. 'Why don't you make us both a fresh tea and get comfy?'

Kate's face fell. In an instant, Iris had clocked it.

'You have to be somewhere.'

'I'm sorry . . . I'm meant to be in Ramsbourne. I'll cancel,' said Kate rashly, wondering how she was going to explain to all the families who were gathering on her behalf.

'Don't be daft.' Iris was staring out of the window. Kate followed her gaze but there was nothing there. Just the tree growing out of the pavement that had been there ever since she remembered.

'Look at them, chasing each other,' said Iris and Kate saw two squirrels leaping around the tree. 'They've always entertained me. Ever since I moved in. Generations of the little blighters. We can talk tomorrow. It's fine.'

Kate knew it wasn't. Not really. But there wasn't much she could do. 'I'll bring cake.'

Iris smiled. 'Whatever you like.'

Her eyelids started to droop, and Kate realized she couldn't have had her post-lunch nap.

'Can I get you anything?'

'I'm fine here, love. You go on.'

'I don't have to go yet! Got another ten minutes.'

'It's OK. Bit tired if I'm honest.'

'Well, if you're sure,' said Kate, reluctantly. She gathered up the fallen mug and took it into the kitchen. When she came back, it looked like Iris was asleep. She gave the carpet a quick scrub, then realized she'd need to get a move on if she wasn't going to miss her train.

She crept out of the room but as her hand went to pull the door to, Iris spoke, her eyes still closed.

'By the way, any news with your break-in?'

'Nothing. Police haven't had any leads.'

'Funny how you've had two in the same number of years. Makes me nervous.'

'Just unlucky,' lied Kate.

Iris nodded and was quiet.

Kate waited a moment, then left the room and closed the front door softly behind her.

FORTY-THREE

They were all crammed into Rob's front room until Abby, his daughter, suggested they go into the garden. Outside on the overgrown lawn was a bench-and-table set, like the sort found in pubs, and the villagers sat or perched with a couple spilling onto folding garden chairs. Everyone was there with the exception of Nick and Grace, who were in hospital with Arnie.

Kate tried to speak to everyone in turn, small snippets of catch-up conversation. Sunita was next to Ian and Hazel. Helen, Rob's wife, had managed to come to the meeting and was sitting in a garden chair, with Abby at her feet. The evening was warm, and the sun was just beginning to dip in the sky, bathing everyone in a golden light. Behind them, in the fields, the oilseed rape was aglow. A blackbird was singing his heart out, his melodious call amplified on the still, warm air.

Rob came into the garden looking harried. 'Does anyone want a coffee or a tea?' he asked feebly and everyone, perhaps sensing his exhaustion, declined. He turned to Kate: the floor was hers.

She stood and faced everyone. Some faces were more

trusting than others, but all of them had the battle-hardened look of people who had experienced more heartache in their lives than was fair. Right at the front was Abby, who was looking at her intently. Kate had been surprised, and a little uncomfortable, to see that she was there. The outcome of this meeting had a direct impact on her, but that, Rob had insisted, was exactly the reason she *was* there.

Kate cleared her throat. 'Thank you, everyone, for coming here today. As you know from my email, the reason we've met is that one of you has been approached by—'

'They know who it is,' interrupted Rob.

She looked at him and he shrugged.

'OK . . . so, Rob has been approached by Justin Holmes and has been made a financial offer, a compensatory offer. However, the stipulation is that he – and the rest of you – would need to withdraw from any legal action in order for this payment to be made. If only one, or a few of you agree to pull out, the offer is off the table. It would have to be everyone.'

A low murmur started up and Kate held up her hand, so she could continue. 'Rob has also said that Justin indicated further payments would be available to other families who decided not to sue, although this hasn't been confirmed.'

'He seemed pretty certain,' said Rob.

The murmur started up again and Kate spoke louder. 'This is one route to explore. The alternative is that we continue, and we take this case to court. I have to be honest, I do believe the rewards would be greater – and just as importantly, this scandal would be out in the public.'

'And how long,' said Hazel, 'until we take this to court?'

It was the question Kate knew would come but dreaded answering. 'I don't know. I'm not going to lie to you people. There's work I still need to do but I'm doing my damnedest to get all the pieces in place.'

'And in the meantime, what happens to us?' asked Ian.

'I appreciate that this is hard, the waiting, the frustration, but I need a little more time.'

'Time's up, lady,' said Rob.

Her heart sank but how could she, in all honesty, argue with him? Maybe she should just walk away, tell them all to ask Justin for payouts. Maybe that was the fairest, most decent thing she could do. Let him pay them, God knows they deserved something. She was about to voice these thoughts when Sunita stood.

'The way I see it, we had nothing before Kate came to us. She's the one who started all this, who put the idea into our heads. She's the one who's been working her socks off. I think we need to follow this through. It's too important not to.'

'That's easy for you to say,' said Rob, 'you're in remission.'

Sunita looked stung. 'It's not about that.'

'You going to stop my daughter from getting what she needs?'

Helen put a hand on Rob's arm and, still bristling, he stopped talking.

'I think we should put it to a vote,' said Kate. 'Those who want to withdraw from the case, raise your hands.'

Rob's hand shot up instantly, followed by Helen's. Ian's too.

'Those who want to continue?' said Kate.

Sunita and Hazel. They already knew that Grace and Nick had voted in favour.

She didn't need to spell out who had won. Rob's face was dark and desperate.

'You lot,' he said, pointing, 'you're playing with a little girl's life.' His voice was cracking. 'What gives you the right to decide what happens to her?'

'It's not like that, Rob,' said Hazel gently, trying to placate him, but he flung her hand away.

'I just hope you're satisfied. Whatever happens, this is on you.'

'Now, hold on a minute,' said Ian. 'That's my wife you're speaking to like that.'

'I don't give a shit,' said Rob. Then everyone was talking, shouting; months of worry and desperation exploding.

'Everyone, please stop arguing!'

The voices quieted. Stopped to see who had spoken. Abby was standing in front of them.

'It'll be OK, Dad, it'll be OK. We'll find the money for London. And Kate's gonna win for us. Right, Kate?' And she turned and looked at Kate with such an expression of belief, it was like a punch to her gut.

Kate didn't dare speak, just nodded.

The meeting broke up soon afterwards and Kate made her excuses and left. Rob wouldn't even look at her, so she saw herself out and started the walk back down the lane towards the station.

Dusk had fallen now and under the trees, the fading light barely got through. The street lamps were sporadic, and she wished she'd brought a torch. As Kate passed Grace's house, she sent a silent wish to Arnie, even though she knew he wasn't there.

It had been an emotional evening and she was tired. It felt nice to be walking, although by the time she got a train back to London, it would be late. She wondered how Iris was, and whether Tim had managed to spend any time with her, and decided to call him to find out.

She stopped to open her bag but as her footsteps fell silent, she thought she heard another set behind her. She turned, but saw no one, just the dark, empty lane. The hairs went up on the back of her neck. It was strange; she could have sworn she'd heard something. She suddenly didn't want to be standing there in the middle of the lane and hurried onwards.

She heard it again. The rhythmic tread of someone walking, the weight of the footsteps indicating it was a man. He must be behind her, following her. She quickened her pace but then all was silent. She risked another stop. Listened. Didn't hear anything but her own pulse pumping in her ears. Perhaps she had imagined it.

A hand landed on her shoulder. She screamed, and a second hand covered her mouth.

'Shush,' said a voice in her ear. It was a voice she recognized, although she couldn't place it. She went rigid with fear, knowing she wouldn't be able to escape, to outrun him, even if she tried. His grip on her lessened, then he removed his hand, and it was Justin Holmes who stepped into her view.

'What the—' she started but he spoke over her.

'You need to stop this thing. Who are you, anyway? Some sort of reporter?'

'Stop what?' she said tremulously.

'Don't mess about. You don't know what you're getting in to.'

Suddenly something snapped inside her. An animalistic anger and pain that boiled over, and she knew no fear. 'Oh, I know,' she said. 'I know exactly. I know what you're doing in those fields. And I know what your bosses did to my daughter.'

He frowned. 'What?'

'They killed her! Got that man to mow her down on her bike. Eighteen months ago. An innocent girl, my girl.'

He staggered backwards. 'You're her *mother*?'

She felt all the air go out of her. *He hadn't denied it, it was true.*

It was all she could do not to collapse. She made herself breathe. 'I'm not going to be bullied by you. Or Rob. You've both become very pally. And you're short-changing him. Ten thousand? It's insulting. His daughter's brain is worth a mere ten thousand to you?'

Justin didn't answer, he was just staring at her and it was then she noticed something odd. He was hyper, wired. There was something frantic about the look in his eyes, a deep, long-suffering fear.

'You need to stop, you *need* to.' He'd grabbed her arms in his urgency and she tried to back away, but he was gripping her too hard. 'Trust me, pack it in, while you still can.'

'Get off! Get off me!' He was frightening her, and she tried again to pull away. Eventually she shoved him off and then turned and ran.

FORTY-FOUR

The storm that had been threatening all day was finally coming, Kate could smell it. The metallic tang to the air, the sudden drop in temperature – like a monster's cold breath warning of its imminent arrival.

Then, in the distance, the faint roll of thunder.

Oh God, please don't rain, thought Kate, pulling her jacket closer. She'd forgotten her umbrella and didn't know how long she'd have to wait, partially hidden by the perimeter hedge, outside this steel-and-glass building just off a roundabout in Surrey. It wasn't her first visit that day – she'd also spent a fruitless two hours watching and waiting early that morning. And now she was back again, just making it for – she checked her watch – five forty-five, having bunked off work early, claiming to have a migraine.

It had seemed like a good idea the night before. She'd got home late and Tim had been waiting up. By the look on her face, his immediate thought was that the vote hadn't gone well.

'Does everyone want to quit?' he'd asked as he made her a cup of tea.

'No, only Rob, Helen and Ian. The others want to carry

on. I saw Justin,' she said, sinking down onto the kitchen chair. 'I told him I knew Becky had been killed.'

'Oh my God. What did he say?'

'He didn't deny it. He had every opportunity.'

Tim came and put his arms around her and she rested her head against his chest.

'He also told me to stop.'

'The campaign?'

'Yes.'

'So, he knows you're behind it.'

She nodded.

'Was he threatening?'

'Not in so many words. Not like that email.'

'Was that from him?'

'I don't know. I didn't ask. At first, I was just terrified – he jumped me in the lane. Then I saw red, I was fuming at him.' She shook her head. 'I still don't have enough for a watertight case . . . and they're all so trusting. That girl . . . Rob's girl. She looked me in the eye and said I could do it. But I don't have *enough*. I still don't even know who owns the farm.'

She rested her head in her hands, despondency seeping in. 'I'm running out of money, Tim. I can't keep this up. I can't keep paying this forensic accountant.'

'So, don't.'

'But then what? It'll all be wasted. And I can't do what I promised those people.'

'But you can't go bankrupt for them. They'd understand that.' He paused. 'Maybe it's time . . .' he started tentatively.

Her head shot up. 'What?'

He shrugged. 'There's got to be a point when you have to call it a day. Practically, if nothing else. And the threats worry me . . .'

'Threat,' she corrected. 'Only one so far.'

'How many emails saying you'll be killed do you want?' said Tim, unable to hide his exasperation.

'Are you saying I should stop?'

'Don't you *want* to?' said Tim.

He was right. She knew he was right, but his instinct to give up the fight bothered her. Lately, he was always trying to subtly persuade her to chuck in the towel. Why should she be bullied into submission? *Because you've had a death threat*, said her inner voice, but this just made her more mutinous.

'I've found my voice, Tim. For the first time in years – ever, in fact. I'm not the stupid girl from school any more who people pity. I'm listened to.'

If only that Adam would call her back. If only she could speak to him – and then she had a brainwave so obvious, she kicked herself for not thinking of it before.

'I'll go to his work,' she said.

Tim frowned, frustrated by what he saw as another of her impulsive gambits.

'Adam. I'll go to his office, wait outside and I'll catch him sooner or later. I'm going to *make* him talk to me.'

And that declaration, Kate remembered, had made for a coolish remainder of the night between her and Tim. A light kiss on the lips as they went to bed, and a brief goodnight, before they both turned over and lay back to back.

The thunder clapped again, louder this time. People were exiting via the revolving door at the front of the building, its wheel turning under the green-and-yellow brand logo that they'd all signed up to. Most of them headed to the car park at the side of the building.

A fat drop of rain landed on Kate's hand. Then another. The anonymous workers were walking faster now, putting up umbrellas and hoods, which would make it harder to spot Adam amongst them.

Splat. Splat. Splat, splat, splat. Kate groaned. Why had she left her umbrella in the staff room? She could see it now, on the table where she'd had a tea break and eaten her pre-packed sandwiches.

The trickle of workers was growing to a steady stream and she had to concentrate, which was hard when the rain was pelting her eyeballs. Then she thought she saw him. He'd come through the door and was taking an umbrella out of its cover. A quick press of a button and it unfurled like a great black crow spreading its wings, shielding his red hair – which had thankfully made him stand out a little.

Kate moved from her position and quickly headed over to him. He was standing outside the building, looking around for someone.

'Adam!' she called as she approached.

He turned and then, recognizing her, his face fell.

She stood in front of him, drenched now, and saw him looking to escape. 'Please, I need to talk to you.'

'What are you doing here?' he hissed, stepping away from her.

'I believe you know something. About what's going on in there,' she said, nodding towards the building behind them. People were still leaving and giving her quizzical looks as they hurried to their cars. She must look a sight, standing there, hair plastered to her face, clothes sodden.

'Please go away,' Adam said, under his breath, pretending to act as if all was normal, as his colleagues nodded goodnights.

'No. I won't.'

He surreptitiously grabbed her arm and pulled her to one side. His outward demeanour was one of normality, but his voice was tense. 'You've no idea what you're doing,' he seethed, 'no idea at all.'

'You're hurting me,' said Kate.

He seemed surprised at how hard he was holding her arm and let go apologetically. Then he looked over his shoulder towards the office. Kate followed his gaze. Was the security officer watching them or looking at the storm lighting up the sky?

A car drove in off the roundabout and pulled up outside the main entrance. She saw Adam's look of relief, and realized this was his lift he'd been waiting for. Her time was up. She had to get through to him.

'Please,' she begged. 'If you won't do it for me, do it for Becky.'

He stiffened, but then the driver's window slid down and a young woman cocked her head. 'Hiya,' she said to Adam, but she was looking questioningly at Kate.

'Er . . . this is Kate,' he said.

'Hello,' said the girl, then she frowned, though not in an unfriendly way. 'You look familiar. Have we met before?'

'I don't think so . . .' said Kate, turning to Adam for a pointer.

'This is my girlfriend,' he said, 'Trixie.' And then he quickly went round to the other side of the car and got in, making it clear to Trixie that she should wind up her window. Kate ducked her head down so she could see into the car.

'Please, Adam. Please think about this!'

Trixie looked bemused, but Adam stared straight ahead out of the windscreen. 'It's been nice seeing you again,' he said, affecting a pleasant tone for appearances' sake, and then he nudged Trixie and they drove off.

Kate thought about chasing them down the street but that would achieve nothing – it wasn't as if she'd be able to keep up. A horn beeped impatiently behind her and she realized she was in the middle of the road. She moved out of the way, then began the long, wet walk back to the station.

FORTY-FIVE

'But he's obviously hiding something,' said Kate, sitting at the kitchen table. She buttered some toast for her and Tim. 'He was tense from the moment he saw me, more so because I doorstepped him at his work. And he didn't want anyone to see us talking.'

'I don't disagree with you. But if he won't talk to you, I can't see how you're going to make him,' said Tim. He handed her a mug of tea and sat opposite her. 'Have you had any more threatening messages? Phone calls?'

'No, nothing.'

'The silence makes me more nervous . . .' said Tim. He looked at her for a response and she stopped eating.

'I can't give it up.'

Tim bit his tongue, but she knew he was exasperated. It was becoming a real sticking point between them and had the heat to boil over into a full-blown argument. Her phone beeped, alleviating the tension.

She got up from the table and looked at the screen of her phone. Her heart leapt.

'It's an email from the forensic accountant.' She quickly opened it up. Maybe there would finally be some good news. As she read, her excitement grew. 'She's managed to find out that the Cypriot company – you know, the anonymous one that owns the farm – paid a huge invoice three years ago, transferring all the profits to another company. Based in Anguilla in the Caribbean.'

'So, she's found out who's behind it?'

Kate's shoulders slumped as she read on. 'No . . . "Unfortunately the Anguilla commercial registry does not disclose director details. I've written to the relevant clerks but it's unlikely – impossible, I should say – that they will be able to give me any names. I'm afraid that this would be the last task that I could complete without issuing further invoices."' Kate sank into her chair and dropped the phone on the table. 'A dead end.'

'I'm guessing you can't ask her to do any more . . .' said Tim.

'I'm completely broke. Doesn't matter how much overtime I do, I still can't keep up with these payments.'

Every way she turned, she seemed to hit a brick wall. She was exhausted and running out of ideas. A movement outside caught her eye.

'What the . . . ?'

There was a man in Iris's front garden hammering a 'For Sale' sign into the grass. Kate leapt up and rushed out the house.

'What's going on?' she demanded.

'On the market,' said the man, unfazed.

Kate went up to Iris's front door and rang the bell,

urgently. After a while, she could see Iris through the glass, ambling towards the door, less urgently.

'Is there a fire?' said Iris lightly, then saw the man over Kate's shoulder. 'Oh. They weren't supposed to put that up until later. I wanted to speak to you first.'

'You're *moving*?'

'Well, yes.'

'*Why?*'

'Oh, Kate, I can't stay here forever. Not as I'm getting older. It's harder every day. Who'd have thought we revert back to toddlers, always on our backsides,' she mused.

'I told you, I can help.'

'And I told you, that's not practical,' said Iris in a firm voice. 'And I don't want to be a burden,' she added.

The postman called up the path. 'Package for you, darlin'.' He handed over a large envelope to Iris.

'It's my welcome pack,' said Iris, smiling brightly. She indicated the logo on the envelope. 'I've found a lovely place. Not far from here. That Sunshine Royal Oaks, you know, I mentioned it? It's not for the completely infirm, I'm not there yet, but they've got a warden on duty. So, if I fall, I just click my tag and – hey presto! – he appears! Just like a genie.'

'I wish you'd talked this over with me first.'

'Well, I was going to . . .' said Iris and Kate was reminded of how she hadn't been able to stay the other day. 'And then I knew you'd just try and persuade me not to go. And I had to make my own decision. So, I got myself a taxi there yesterday, got the grand tour. And you'll never guess what?'

'What?'

'My old friend, Christine Sturley, is there. You know, the one who worked at the taxi office for a bit, then when she and her husband retired, they moved to Spain? Well, she's recently widowed and back. Missed the seasons.'

'Sounds like you've made your mind up.'

'I have.'

'Well, at least I have a few months while you find a buyer.'

Iris looked awkward. 'Actually . . . they've got a room for me now. Someone else was lined up to have it but they ended up moving closer to their family. You have to take them when they come up or the wait could be endless.'

'So, when are you going?' asked Kate in trepidation.

'The thirteenth.'

'Of what? *August?* That's only a couple of weeks away!'

Iris gave an apologetic smile. Then she sniffed, and her eyes began to well up. 'Don't think it's not difficult to leave,' she said. 'I'm going to miss this place, and you. Mostly you.'

Kate's own chin began to wobble, and she threw her arms around Iris. The two women held each other for a while.

'Life changes,' said Iris. 'Things move on.'

FORTY-SIX

Friday, 24 February 2017 – the day of the accident

Terence was sitting across from Becky, scribbling on a piece of paper. A summary of her answer to the interview question: 'How do you deal with conflict?' She'd outlined how she would manoeuvre her way around a tricky personality, diffusing friction where she could and getting the subject on side, mentally brushing aside her increasingly impatient responses to Piers.

He looked up. 'Is there anything you would like to ask me?'

'Yes,' said Becky. 'When will you be making your decision?'

'By the middle of next week.'

Becky's stomach fluttered in equal amounts of extreme nervousness and extreme excitement. She still had time to get her story to Terence before he picked his candidate for the job. But what if, when she met Adam tomorrow, he didn't tell her anything of any real consequence? What if he *did*? She felt her whole future rested on this one meeting. Becky had booked another nondescript hotel, texting Adam on his 'temporary' number to rearrange.

'Anything else?'

Becky shook her head and went to get up.

Terence held up a hand. 'Just a minute.'

She was surprised. Sat back down again, a flicker of apprehension running through her as Terence came from behind his desk and perched on the edge of it next to her.

'I'll get to the point,' he said, matter-of-factly. 'It's been noticed you've spent quite a bit of time out of the office the last few weeks.' He raised an eyebrow, watched her. 'Most of that time seemingly to coincide with when I've not been here.'

Becky felt a hot flush rise up in her cheeks. *Piers.*

'I . . .' began Becky. How was she going to explain this away? She decided to come clean. 'That's right.' There was a hint of defiance in her voice.

He nodded, and she detected – what? He was subtly impressed? He was waiting for her to continue, but she didn't want to say any more. Not yet. Damn Piers for putting her in this position.

'Want to explain why?' said Terence.

'Not really.'

Terence's tea paused halfway to his lips.

'What I mean is, I *will*,' said Becky. She saw his frown and knew she had to concede a little. 'There's a story . . . I've been researching it for a while. And there's another part to the puzzle. I'm finding out tomorrow.'

'Care to tell me what you know so far?'

She felt frustration creep in. She didn't. She really wanted to get the full picture, the hidden grenade she knew Adam had. She looked at her boss.

'I take it that's a no,' said Terence. He paused, and she waited, wondering if she was about to get a massive bollocking.

'I'm fine with a bit of skiving,' said Terence. 'All the most resourceful investigative journalists go AWOL from time to time.' He paused. 'But don't do anything stupid.'

Becky looked up, hope in her heart. Was this his way of giving her permission to carry on?

'And most importantly, know when to speak up.'

She grinned, buoyant. 'I will. I mean, yes, I know. I'll be careful.'

Terence frowned, and for a moment, Becky thought he was going to change his mind.

'I'll tell you everything on Monday. First thing,' she promised and shifted forward on the sofa, poised to leave the room.

Terence thought for a moment, watching her, then nodded – *the most beautiful sign in the world*, thought Becky. The 'go do it' nod. She beamed and stood up.

'Thank you,' she said, her hand on the door handle, and before he could say another word, she left the room.

Her joy was short-lived. She saw Piers as soon as she stepped out of the office. She walked over to where he was making a tea in the kitchen area.

'Ellis!' he said as she approached. 'So nice to see you.'

'Really below the belt, Piers. What kind of journalist is a grass?'

He looked puzzled. 'What are you talking about?'

'You know *exactly* what I'm talking about.'

He frowned. 'You've really got to explain this one. Honestly, I'm in the dark.'

She poked a sharp finger into his muscly, white-shirted arm. 'You've been on my case ever since the job ad went out. Sneaking around, following me. Trying to sabotage me. Where do you draw the line, Piers? What lengths will you go to to ensure I don't get this job? Gonna do my legs in so I can't even get here?'

He was keeping up the pretence of being bemused, and she shook her head in disgust and turned away. Went back to her desk. She saw him return to his work area and glance over to her every so often. She didn't want to speak to him, so put on her headphones and opened up her laptop.

Becky soon became engrossed in her work and it was a few rings in before she heard her phone. She paused her music and went to answer it. It was a number she didn't recognize.

'Becky Ellis.'

'Hello, Becky. This is Justin Holmes.'

Becky immediately sat up. The farm manager. From Ramsbourne.

'Hi,' she said, questioningly.

'That story, the one you came to see me about.'

'Yes?'

'Have you written it yet?'

Becky didn't answer.

'If you have, delete it.'

Becky was silent for a moment. 'Is that you telling me or asking me?'

'Warning you. I have a bad feeling about it.'

'Well, you see, the thing is, I think it's a story that needs to be told.'

'You're wrong. Don't do it.' He paused. 'There are people who won't like it.'

'By people, you mean you?'

'No . . .'

'Who?'

'Look, despite the fact you came onto my property and ambushed me, I like you. So please listen to me. It's really not a good idea. And do not mention this call to anyone.'

'How do these people know I'm writing this story? I've only spoken to you.'

There was a silence down the phone.

'Who have you told?' demanded Becky.

Silence.

'Can I speak to them?'

'You need to stop. Now.'

Becky twisted in her seat. She thought of Grace and Arnie and Abby and found herself getting riled. 'Who are you to tell me what or what not to write?' she said. 'There is a story here that neither you nor anyone else has the right to stop.'

'But there is no story. Nothing that anyone hasn't heard already. Speculated about before. You have no proof.'

Becky smiled to herself. *Adam.*

'Well, that's where I think you're wrong,' she said emphatically, and she hung up. She sat watching the mobile on her desk, half expecting it to ring again. But it didn't. It stayed silent.

FORTY-SEVEN

2018

'Happy birthday to Kaaa-ate. Happy birthday to you!' Tim and Iris (with a little bit of Donny thrown in between wrapping pieces of haddock in paper) finished singing to her.

Kate beamed. 'Thank you.' She blew out the candle that was stuck into a separate chip that Donny had put on a small plate. Tim had originally planned to take her and Iris to the new Mediterranean 'fusion' restaurant on the high street. But she hadn't wanted him to. Truth was, she was still feeling guilty about how much more he'd taken on financially at home as she'd been so strapped for cash. And anyway, Iris thought 'fusion' sounded like something you did with a soldering iron.

'Make a wish,' insisted Iris.

Kate closed her eyes. *I need a miracle*, she thought. 'All done,' she declared.

'Then let's get stuck in,' said Iris, picking up a piece of fish with her wooden fork.

Tim reached under the table for the large, wrapped box they'd all been pretending wasn't there and slid it across the floor to Kate. 'This is for you.'

Kate smiled and ripped off the paper.

'I love it!' she said of the top-of-the-range bread machine.

'It's so you can make your own. Organic. Because, you know . . .'

'Thank you,' said Kate, beaming.

'And now,' said Tim with a deep sigh, 'I can finally come clean.'

'About what?'

'Do you remember, the day of the break-in, you came to meet me for my last shift?'

Kate nodded.

'That's why I wasn't there. I was shopping.' He looked at her. 'I always got the feeling you were suspicious.'

She had been, a little. Kate blushed. 'Not really.'

'So, as you can see, it wasn't me breaking into the house and sending dodgy emails,' he said, smiling, although Kate could detect an edge to his voice. She flicked her eyes in warning towards Iris who had been ping-ponging her gaze between them.

Iris pushed a small box across the table. 'And this is from me,' she said.

Kate delicately unwrapped it. Inside was a jewellery box. She looked up at Iris before opening it, and Iris waved her on. Kate lifted the lid of the box and gasped. Lying on a bed of black velvet was a pair of 1950s Hollywood-style dia-manté drop earrings, each with five strings of glass stones cut to look like diamonds.

'They were given to me for my twenty-first,' said Iris.

Kate snapped the box shut and held it back over the table. 'I can't take them,' she said, immediately.

'Now, don't talk nonsense. Who else am I going to give them to? You're the closest I've ever had to a daughter. I want you to have them.'

'Really?'

'Yes. Now put them on.'

Kate lifted them out of the box, the stones brazenly dazzling, their capacity for capturing and catapulting light undiminished in the sixty years of their existence. She put them in her ears.

'Wow,' said Tim, eyes agog.

'Feels a bit daft wearing something so stunning in a fish-and-chip shop,' said Kate.

'No reason to,' said Iris.

'Thank you,' said Kate, clasping Iris's hand. She loved them, but the gift was tinged with sadness for her. Iris passing on heirlooms had something reminiscent of inheritance, something she couldn't bear thinking about. She didn't want Iris to be tidying up her life. It was bad enough she was moving to sheltered housing.

'Did you have any other nice birthday treats? Anything from work?' asked Iris.

'A twenty-pound store voucher.'

Iris frowned. 'Get away. Really?'

'From my boss. My colleagues did a whip round and bought me some flowers.'

'Thank goodness. Or all you'd be getting from them is a new screwdriver for your birthday. A sign of being truly middle-aged.' She patted Kate's hand. 'Happens to us all. Mind you, what I'd give to be middle-aged again, I'm now geriatric-aged.'

Kate's phone beeped.

'Maybe that's your boss now, sending you details of a large delivery of chocolates to make up for his paltry present.'

'It's the forensic accountant,' said Kate, surprised. 'She's the one who's been helping me find out who owns the farm,' she explained to Iris. Kate scanned through the email. 'Oh,' she suddenly said, her face contorting in confusion.

'What?' asked Tim.

'She says she's been sent an email in error. From the Anguillan registry clerk.'

Iris and Tim exchanged a look. 'So, what does it say?' asked Iris. 'Has she found out any names?'

'Not exactly.'

'What do you mean?'

'She's discovered that the farm's parent company is owned by yet another holding company. But the name of the director has been kept anonymous.' Kate bit her lip as she kept on reading.

'And?' prompted Tim.

'And that holding company owns not just the farm but other things too.' She shook her head in disbelief. 'Including the agrochemical company Senerix and . . .'

'What? Come on, I can't bear the suspense,' said Iris.

'Fresh Foods.'

'Fresh Foods,' repeated Iris, 'haven't I heard that name before?'

'It's Greg Hollander's business,' said Tim slowly. 'You know, the man who's doing the bursary with Kate.'

Kate couldn't figure it out. Dazed, she looked back at the email. There it was in black and white. Foxgold Ltd, registered in the tax haven of Anguilla, owned Ashdown Farm in Ramsbourne, and Senerix, the chemical company that supplied the farm, and Fresh Foods where Greg worked.

Tim was the first to break the silence. 'There has to be some connection,' he said slowly, 'with Greg.'

'Does there? Why?' Kate tried to form some clear thoughts. 'Just because Greg works there – at Fresh Foods – it doesn't mean anything. It's the main holding company we're interested in.'

'It's too much of a coincidence.'

'But . . . big companies gobble up smaller ones all the time – have loads of separate brands under their umbrella. Unilever for example. What is it, Ben and Jerry's, Surf washing powder . . . loads more.'

Neither Iris nor Tim said anything. Kate thought of Greg, of everything he'd done. The way he'd pushed to change the trucks, the bursary he'd so generously set up.

'And Greg wouldn't be behind, you know . . . all the stuff that's been happening.'

'What stuff?' asked Iris.

Kate shook her head. 'No. If he was bad news, then why's he been so helpful, been spending so much time on these projects?'

'To keep you close?' said Tim.

She laughed. 'You make it sound like I'm the enemy.'

'Well, maybe you are – to him,' said Tim.

'What stuff?' repeated Iris.

Tim spoke to Kate. 'Did you ever tell him about the case?'

'No. No, I'm sure I didn't.'

'Is anyone going to tell me what's going on?' asked Iris.

'The break-in . . .' said Kate. 'We think it might have been something to do with this case I'm working on.'

'Oh my giddy aunt.'

The three of them sat in silence. No one was eating, and Kate had completely lost her appetite. *Greg couldn't be involved in this, could he?*

FORTY-EIGHT

Later that night, Kate lay in bed, subdued. She was dimly aware Tim was rubbing her back, trying to buoy her up, take her mind off the evening's revelations. Were they revelations? Because they didn't reveal anything, not exactly. Tim's hand moved around to the side of her breast and she could sense him getting amorous. She pushed him away.

He nuzzled the back of her neck. 'You sure I can't persuade you?'

'Sorry.'

'Only, I was hoping . . .'

'Not tonight.' She rolled over to face him. 'Too much on my mind.'

Tim watched her for a moment, wrestling with something. 'I've got something on my mind too.'

She felt guilty. She hardly ever paid any attention to what might be troubling him. Perhaps something was going on at work. 'What's up?'

'Same as we've discussed before.'

She frowned. 'Sorry . . . you're going to have to remind me.'

He was silent for a moment. 'A baby, Kate. I would like to talk about having a baby. With you.'

Her heart sank. 'It's just not the right time – not with everything else that's going on.'

'But . . .'

'What?'

'Well, look where we are. What we've been celebrating tonight. The fact is, in another year or so it may not even be an option. It could be difficult now, even . . .'

Kate tensed.

'I'm sorry,' he said. 'It's just really important to me.'

'I said I needed some time.'

'I know. But it's months since I first brought this up. And realistically – is your case anywhere near over?'

She didn't answer; they both knew it wasn't.

Tim took a deep breath. 'I guess I've got to accept that what you're doing is bigger than me or you.'

She opened her mouth to deny it, but no words came. Having a baby right now felt like completely the wrong thing to do.

He held up a conciliatory hand. 'It's OK. I'm not saying that to throw my toys out of the pram. It's just the way it is. So, what do you think you're going to do?' he asked.

'About what?'

'Greg.'

Kate shrugged. 'Not sure yet. I'm seeing him in a few days.'

'You're not still going . . .'

'We're interviewing candidates for the bursary. It would look strange if I suddenly cancelled.'

'But—'

'I honestly don't know what to do for the best. You see, there's something else we've overlooked here. Something important.'

He waited for her to continue.

'If there's an ounce of truth to what we've been hypothesizing tonight, that Greg's involved somehow, then I've been working with the man who had my daughter killed.'

Tim placed his hand on hers. 'I know, but we don't know for sure. It might just be a coincidence, like you said earlier.'

'There's something else.'

He looked at her, puzzled. 'What?'

'If it's true . . . then I didn't persuade him to improve his fleet of trucks at all. I persuaded sweet bugger all. He was pretending . . . playing me the whole time.'

Tim sat up. 'Now, I don't think—'

'Which makes me just the same dumb arse girl as always.' Kate took a deep breath. And now . . . well, she was just kidding herself, right? Deluding herself she was some sort of amateur lawyer, when actually she was just a school dropout, who would amount to nothing out of the ordinary.

FORTY-NINE

2010

They were still in the main hall, but Julia and Violet had moved to another table. It smarted, even though Kate had no desire to sit anywhere near them. She glanced across: Julia was laughing and joking with another mother, someone she seemed to know well. *Oh, how I detest her.*

The headmistress had been furnished with a gavel and was tapping it on the podium in front of her and calling for quiet so they could begin. The first lot was a bottle of sparkling wine that a pupil was holding aloft.

'I can vouch for it!' called out Julia. 'I made it!'

Confused, Kate looked at Becky.

'She owns the vineyard,' whispered Becky. 'Along with several acres of farmland.'

Kate watched as the bottle went for fifty pounds. *On a single bottle of wine!* she thought, not quite believing anything could taste that good. She sat drinking her tea, clapping politely as each item got sold off. Mothers were bidding for gifts for their children, prompting squeals of delight when they won. A set of horse-riding lessons. A generous voucher for a fashionable clothing store. They were all part of a club, one that excluded her and Becky.

The headmistress was announcing the next prize: two tickets for the Grand Prix at Silverstone in 2011. Kate's mouth dropped, of all the . . . The heat rose up in her again as Julia looked over to her table with a mocking smile and then started to bid.

Oh, stuff you, thought Kate, turning away. She bit back her tears and kept her gaze towards the stage. She heard Julia's yelp of delight as she won, heard her daughter's exclamations of excitement.

'And now for our last item,' said the headmistress. 'A two-week break at Longueville Manor, the most highly rated hotel in Jersey.' A picture of a lovingly restored mansion with luxurious gardens flicked up on the screen behind the headmistress.

'Oh, look, that's where Uncle John stayed while he was house hunting,' exclaimed Julia to her daughter.

How her voice grates, thought Kate. *The self-satisfied smugness, the sense of entitlement.*

'It's lovely, everyone,' Julia called out jokingly and a bubble of laughter erupted in the hall.

Kate sat ram-rod straight, consumed with hostility.

'So, if I can start the bidding at one hundred pounds?' asked the headmistress.

Kate raised her hand.

'Mum?' asked Becky, startled. 'What are you doing?'

'Bidding,' said Kate through gritted teeth. If she did some overtime, she'd be able to pay for it. It was for Becky, anyway. She'd never taken her anywhere special before, maybe this was one way she could do it.

'But . . .'

'Two hundred,' called a voice.

'Thank you,' said the headmistress.

Kate's heart did a little shudder when she heard Julia speak but she wasn't going to give up that easily. 'Five hundred,' she called, firmly.

Becky looked in alarm at her mother. 'What?'

'Shush, Becky,' said Kate. 'I need to concentrate.'

'A thousand,' said Julia.

The room had caught wind of this tussle, the building tension, and eyes were roaming around in interest.

'Twelve hundred,' called out Kate, her stomach constricting as she realized that was a heck of a lot of overtime.

'Thank you,' acknowledged the headmistress, after a minuscule pause. *She knows my financial situation*, realized Kate, the added humiliation fuelling her anger further.

'Two thousand,' said Julia.

The room gave a collective intake of breath.

'Two thousand two hundred!' said Kate, aware that she was way out of the realms of overtime. There was only one place where she had this sort of money. A precious, untouchable sum that had taken her years to save. But some menace had caught hold of her and wouldn't let go.

'Two and a half,' called out Julia.

'Has your mum gone mental?' asked Claire, sotto voce, leaning into Becky.

'Mum, you have to stop,' urged Becky, her voice lowered.

The hall waited with bated breath.

'Three,' said Kate.

A murmur rippled across the room.

'Are you sure, love?' asked Sue, awkwardly.

Kate was dimly aware that her daughter was looking at her, stricken, and that Becky knew what money it was she'd just blown: her entire university savings. But now Kate had gone down this hole, there was no way out. For the first time since she'd started bidding, she looked across at Julia, saw the small taunting smile on her face.

Then she realized: Julia was just toying with her, as a cat might a mouse it had by the tail. Suddenly Kate felt her bravado crumble. *Oh, please God, let her bid more*, she thought.

The whole room was waiting. Julia turned her head towards the stage, her blonde layers fluttering as she did so. She smiled regretfully. 'I'm afraid I'm going to have to let my opponent win this one,' she said graciously.

All eyes swung to Kate. She had been caught in a trap. A trap of her own making.

'Any other bids?' asked the headmistress, holding it open longer than she should, Kate knew, a last act of redemption.

No one came forward to save her.

The headmistress still hesitated, not wanting to condemn Kate to her purchase. Kate's cheeks flamed. The entire hall was watching. Becky was sitting by her side, eyes pained, seeming small and curled up in herself.

Finally, the headmistress tapped her gavel. 'Sold,' she said.

There was utter silence. No one clapped. A few faces looked embarrassed, turned away for her sake, Kate knew.

The headmistress rallied. 'Congratulations! That concludes our day, ladies. Thank you all so much for coming.' People started to rise in their chairs, make their way out.

'You must send us a postcard,' said Julia, as she glided by.

As soon as they got in the house, Becky ran up to her room and closed the door.

Kate stood at the bottom of the stairs. Her heart sank as she thought she caught the sound of a sob.

Climbing the stairs after her daughter, she walked along the landing, stopping outside Becky's door. She knocked.

Silence.

'Can I come in?'

She got a muffled 'OK', so entered. Becky was lying on her bed staring up at the ceiling.

'I'm so sorry,' said Kate. 'I'll work overtime, every weekend. There'll be money for university. Maybe not as much, but . . .'

'I don't care about the money, Mum.'

Kate knew she was putting on a brave face, that she didn't want to be a burden. Becky had insisted she was going to get a part-time job anyway, but the savings were meant to give her more time to study.

What Kate also knew was that Becky would be the talk of the school in the morning, the butt of the jokes that already made Kate burn with shame. 'And I'm sorry if I've made it difficult with your friends,' she said.

Becky stayed silent.

'It's just that woman . . . she wound me up. I felt like I had to show her . . .'

'Show her what, Mum?'

'I don't know. I lost the quiz, I felt stupid. The poor dumb girl who didn't get a proper education. A decent job.'

Becky sighed. 'Mum, you're not dumb. The only dumb thing you've done is let people tell you that's what you are.'

Silence rang out across the room. After a moment, Kate took a step towards the bed. 'Room for one more?'

Becky shoved up and Kate went to lie down next to her, their shoulders touching, each feeling the warmth of the other.

'If she'd gone to four thousand, would you have done five?' asked Becky.

Kate thought. 'No.'

'Oh?'

'I would have jumped straight to ten. Wiped the smile off her face.'

Becky let out a small giggle. 'Why stop there?'

'You're right. Twenty.'

'Thirty.'

'Fifty.'

'A million!' said Becky. 'A million pounds for the swanky Jersey holiday just so you can't have it, Julia. Stick it up your bum.' They laughed so hard, tears started pouring down their faces. When the laughter subsided, Kate took Becky's hand.

'I'm sorry I let you down, Becky. One day I'll make it up to you. I promise.'

FIFTY

2018

'They're not like the photos of the fellas on the website,' said Iris as she watched three men in cargo shorts and T-shirts with the moving company's logo on the back, carry her remaining furniture out of her house and into a large van.

It was true, they were huffing and puffing, and the blue T-shirts had dark sweat patches stretching long under the armpits. But it was a hot day in August. And no one did house removals carrying a box in one hand and holding a thumb up on the other.

Kate had set out a garden chair on the front pavement, so Iris didn't have to stand while her house was unceremoniously emptied. After they were done, Iris wanted to check nothing was left behind and would then follow on in a cab. Kate was going with her to help get her settled and unpacked. Most of the big furniture had already been sold to a second-hand furniture man on the high street and Iris had just kept what would fit into her new flat.

'Do you have a buyer yet?' asked Kate.

'Oh, I meant to say. Had an offer this morning. Couple with a young family. I've accepted.'

'Congratulations.'

'They seem very nice. I'm sure you'll get on with them.'

'Won't be the same, though,' Kate couldn't help saying.

'Give over. We'll see each other all the time.'

'Can I get you ladies a cold drink?' called Tim from Kate's open kitchen window.

Iris raised her stick in acceptance. 'You've got a good man there,' she said.

Kate glanced across at her. Wondered if her neighbour had detected any of the growing tensions between herself and Tim, but Iris was waving her stick at the bearded removal man.

'Be careful!' she shouted as they lugged her sideboard across the front lawn, dodging the postman.

'Nothing for me, I hope,' said Iris.

'Nope. Seems Royal Mail haven't cocked up your re-direction,' said the postman, stopping to hand Kate a pile of envelopes. 'Bit for you though, darlin'.'

She took the stack and sifted through it as the postman moved on. A statement of her water account, a couple of pieces of junk. Then, at the bottom, a small padded envelope, the kind used to send something fragile. She turned it over. Her address had been printed out in bold, black type and stuck on the front.

Curious, she opened it and peered inside. There was something shiny and metallic at the bottom of the envelope. She frowned, not comprehending. Then recoiled as she saw what it was.

'Here we go. Two lemonades with ice,' said Tim, carrying a tray with two glasses over from Kate's house. He'd put a tea towel over his arm and held out the tray with a flourish. The ice chinked as it rolled and melted in the sun. Two cocktail umbrellas stuck out the tops, each speared into a strawberry. His smile fell when he saw Kate.

'What's wrong?'

Unable to speak, she handed over the envelope. Tim placed the tray down on the grass, took the envelope, put his hand inside and pulled out the contents.

'What the . . . ?'

'What is it?' asked Iris, shifting forward in her chair to get a better look. 'I can't see.'

Tim paused. 'It's a bullet.'

'A what? Bullet? What, you mean from a gun?'

'Yes.'

'A real one?'

'Yes.' Tim looked the envelope over. 'There's no note, no address, nothing.'

'Who the hell would send something like that?' asked Iris.

Kate looked at Tim. 'I . . . we don't know.' She rubbed her face with her hands. Then her head snapped up with an idea: 'What if it's Rob? He's got reason to stop me.'

'Stop you doing what?' asked Iris. 'Has this got something to do with your investigation?'

Kate hesitated.

'Yes,' said Tim.

'Someone wants to stop you so much they're sending death threats?' exclaimed Iris. 'What in the world . . . ?'

Kate pulled her phone from her bag and stabbed at the keys, searching for Rob's number.

'What are you doing?' asked Tim.

'Calling him. I'm not letting him get away with this.'

Rob answered immediately. 'Kate.'

'Where do you get off, sending me bloody bullets in the post?'

'What?'

'It's sick, that's what it is. You're a sick man, Rob Bolton. I'm not quitting this just so you can get your pay-off. There's other people affected here too, and I will not be bullied. He's not offering you enough anyway, it's paltry what he's trying to get away with.'

'He's not offering me anything because he's dead,' snapped Rob.

She reeled. 'What?'

'He had an accident. Fell into the grain silo. Would have been like quicksand.'

'Oh my God.'

'So, my "paltry" offer,' continued Rob, 'has vanished. Luckily, I've managed to borrow from Ian. And just for the record, I've not sent you *anything*. Bullets? You really think I'd be sending you bullets? I wouldn't even know where to get one, even if I had the time to do such a thing, what with caring for my sick wife and daughter.'

'I . . . I didn't . . .'

'Ever thought you're losing it, Kate?'

'I'm sorr—' she started, but he'd hung up. Upset, she looked at Tim.

'What's happened?' he asked.

'Justin's had an accident. At the farm. He's . . . he didn't make it.'

'What? *Another* accident? And you've been sent a bullet. Will you listen to me now? You have to quit this.'

'Tim . . .'

'What if it *is* Greg? You can't go and see him tomorrow.'

'Excuse me, Iris,' said Kate and she pulled Tim aside. Spoke under her breath. 'Will you stop?'

'I think it's good Iris knows about all this. Maybe you'll listen to her because you won't me,' said Tim, stubbornly.

'I've told you: I can't just not turn up. It's the interviews. It'll look weird. Suspicious.'

'Tell him you're sick.'

'I'd just have to reschedule.'

Tim exhaled, his frustration threatening to boil over.

'What's he going to do? In broad daylight?'

Tim took her hands. Pleaded. 'Look, Kate, this isn't about me wanting you to stop for my own sake. It's not about me wanting a family. I care about *you*.'

Kate looked across at Iris, who had tactfully turned away. 'This whole thing has been about Becky,' she said softly. 'Doing something for my daughter and being the mother I'm supposed to be. Keeping my promises. I'll take it to wherever it goes. I will not quit.' She looked up at him. 'And I'm not scared. I might have freaked out there, when I got that thing in the post, but I am not scared.'

FIFTY-ONE

Adam sat in the chair, his hands lightly clasped in his lap. His boss, Roger Harris, was sitting a few metres away, watching him. Roger's boss was in another wide leather chair on the right-hand side of the room, also watching him. Adam glanced over at her; she was younger than Roger and dressed in a severe grey suit, which she wore with a tie. He'd only met her twice since she'd joined the company and he didn't think she'd remembered who he was. And yet . . . here she was at this meeting. Neither of them said a word.

There was another man present, one he'd never seen before. He was the only person in the room who wasn't watching him; instead he was sitting at a desk, engrossed in some task with a mobile phone. The man's face was bent over, concentrating, and all Adam could see was that he had a long moustache. On the desk next to the phone was a knife, something Adam found odd and disconcerting.

He looked back to the silent Roger. Adam had been summoned to his office first thing that morning and he had no idea why. Despite the modern room's air-conditioning, he felt a bead of sweat break loose and run down the side of his face.

Roger suddenly spoke, making Adam jump. 'Thank you for coming up. We thought it was a good time to have a review of where we were with things. More specifically, our commitment to company confidentiality.'

All eyes were back on Adam again, scrutinizing him for a reaction. The silence was excruciating but Adam kept the pleasant and nonchalant expression on his face and waited.

'I just wanted to make sure that everybody here knew that confidentiality was something to be taken very seriously,' said Roger.

Adam crossed his legs. 'Of course.'

'Well, that's good to hear, but I think we need a little more reassurance. You see, we all hold a very privileged position working here and sometimes we may see documents that are not meant for us. And that can get the imagination going. And sometimes people from the outside world might like to know what's in those documents and might try and approach us. Wheedle it out of us.' Roger smiled.

Adam felt his stomach fall. They knew about Kate coming to see him. He kept his composure. 'You have nothing to worry about.'

They were still staring at him. The screech of a piece of Sellotape being pulled from a roll startled him and he looked over to the moustached man who had the tape between his teeth. The man's eyes were now also on Adam as he bit through the tape. Then he started to cover a mobile phone box with wrapping paper.

'That's good to hear, Adam,' said Roger. 'Because we take breaches of security very seriously. Very seriously indeed.'

Roger's boss suddenly got up out of her chair and left. Adam stared open-mouthed at the closing door.

'And we would have to act immediately and with great severity if we were to find any staff member had broken their NDA,' added Roger.

From the other side of the room, there was the sound of a piece of fabric being cut. Adam looked over to see the moustached man slice through a piece of blue ribbon with white polka dots, using the knife that had been on the desk. He then started to tie the ribbon around the gift-wrapped box.

'Do we understand one another?' asked Roger.

Adam swallowed down his anger and fear. 'Yes,' he said. 'We do.'

Roger stood. 'Well, that's terrific. Glad to hear it.' He went over to Adam, slapped him hard on the shoulder then left the room.

Adam stared after him. What the . . . ? Why had he been left alone? He heard the dull thud of a knife in wood and turned to see the moustached man sitting back in his chair with his feet on the desk. In front of his shoes was the knife, sticking upright from the desk. Adam's eyes flicked from the knife to the man.

'You can go,' said the man impatiently.

Adam turned and walked stiffly away.

Once he'd gone, Janković leaned back further in the chair, pulled his phone from his pocket and dialled.

'Yes, it is all done.' He surveyed his handiwork on the desk. 'I've put a pretty bow on it and everything.'

FIFTY-TWO

It had been back-to-back interviews ever since she'd arrived. Every so often Kate snuck a glance at Greg, who was sitting to her right in the large conference room, and still found it hard to believe he could be in any way involved in Becky's death. It seemed absurd, fantastical.

The last candidate, a young man from Wales, who had been offered a place at Exeter to read journalism, was just finishing up. As with all three of the bursary finalists, Kate had been struck by how passionate and determined each of them was, how each wanted to make their mark in the world.

Maddie, Greg's PA, led the candidate away. The conference room suddenly seemed too big for just Kate and Greg. She looked over and realized she was nervous.

'He was very impressive,' said Greg, referring to the student they'd just interviewed.

'He was.'

'Do you have a favourite?'

'I think I need more time,' said Kate.

'Sure. Do you want to email me? Maybe later this week?'

She nodded.

'And are you still on for our little celebration next month? We can take a picture of you and the winner and have our PR department write a piece for the press.'

'Sounds great,' said Kate.

'And talking of celebrations . . . I've got you a little present.' Greg had a boyish grin on his face as he opened up his briefcase, then paused for a moment, with the gift hidden behind the lid. Then he brandished an envelope. 'Happy birthday!'

It was totally unexpected. 'Thank you,' said Kate. 'You shouldn't have.'

He brushed away her embarrassment and waited for her to open it. She untucked the envelope flap and inside was a cardboard wallet emblazoned with the British Airways logo. Mystified, she lifted the flap and pulled out two first-class tickets to the Bahamas and details for a week's stay in a hotel tantalizingly called Turtle Bay.

Her mouth dropped. She let out a small, incredulous laugh. 'Oh my God . . .'

'So now you get to try the lounge where they absolutely won't let you get lost, although I can't guarantee they'll spray your feet with mineral water at the hotel,' said Greg.

She handed it back to him. 'Greg . . . this is too much. I can't accept this.'

He swept aside her protestations. 'Nonsense. You can pick your own dates by the way, you just need to call them, and they'll rearrange for you.'

'Seriously, I can't—'

'I'm not taking no for an answer.'

Kate was still staggered by the generosity of his gift – and how he'd remembered their conversation during her first experience of airports. *Was this what he did? Blindside you with kindness while all the while sending you death threats?*

'Have you ever been yourself?' she asked.

'Where? The Bahamas?'

She shrugged. 'The Caribbean.' *Anguilla.*

He laughed. 'More of a Seychelles man. At least, my ex-wife used to drag me there, but I'd only stay a week then leave her to it. I got itchy feet. But my excuse was always that something needed urgent attention at work. Which, to be fair, was often true. Still is. So, how are you going to fill your time now that the bursary is almost up and running? Other than our little ceremony, this is it now – at least until next year.'

Fill her time? My God, if only he knew. *Maybe he did.* She shrugged. 'Back to the day job.'

A sharp rap on the door made her jump. It was Maddie. 'Your lunch appointment's arrived,' she announced.

'I'll be there in a minute,' said Greg, dismissing her.

Kate started to gather her things.

'Just a minute,' said Greg. He reached back down into his briefcase.

Kate's eyes widened as be brought out another gift. 'No . . . no . . . enough now.'

'It's nothing.' He slid the present across the table to her.

She was adamant. 'I can't.'

'Go on. Don't make me return it.' He pushed it a little closer to her.

Kate looked at the gift, a small wrapped package tied with a blue bow with white polka dots.

Sighing, she pulled it closer and then unwrapped it. Inside was a brand-new mobile phone.

'No cracks,' he said.

'It's too much.'

'See it as a thank you. For bringing certain things to my attention.'

She looked at him.

'The trucks. We're a safer, better company because of you. I'll always be grateful.'

'He was normal,' she said to Tim when she got home.

She'd found him sitting in the living room watching daytime TV, which was unusual for him.

'Normal?' he asked.

'Well, he didn't do anything weird.'

'So, you trust him?'

'I don't know.' Kate sighed. 'I need a tea,' she said, heading for the kitchen. 'Fancy one?'

She stopped dead. Sitting on the kitchen floor was a large duffel bag, packed full. It was Tim's. She heard him switch off the TV and come up behind her.

'I think it's for the best,' he said quietly. 'For now, at least.'

She spun around. 'You're moving out?'

He nodded tightly.

'But . . .' What should she say? That she didn't want him to go? Yet, even as she tried to form the words, they sounded selfish. She'd kept him waiting for so long, kept him hanging, and, deep down, she didn't know if she'd ever be able to give him what he wanted – what he had a right to want.

'If anything happens, you call, right?' said Tim gruffly.

She could stop him, she *should* stop him, but somehow her arms and mouth weren't working. She watched as he picked up his bag. He hesitated for a moment, but still she said nothing, just remained in a sort of stunned, immobilized state. He leaned down and kissed her on the cheek. Then he walked out of the room.

A few seconds later she heard the front door shut.

FIFTY-THREE

Kate looked across the help desk at the bald, fat man in front of her and tried to remain patient.

'You need fifteen-millimetre compression olives,' she said.

He looked downright scornful. 'Are you sure, darlin'?'

'No. I just made it up because I wanted you to get drenched in water.'

'Really?'

She sighed. 'No.'

'I'd like to see you drenched in water,' he said, his eyes making a beeline for her breasts, clad in the company T-shirt.

'Oh, you're irresistible.'

He grinned.

'Not. Do you think that is even the remotest bit appealing? You making suggestive comments? Because it's not. It's sexist and rude and makes me want to puke up all over this desk,' she snapped.

'All right, keep your hair on,' he said, clearly annoyed and a little alarmed. 'You're a bit too thin for me, anyways.'

'That's lucky, because you're a bit too thick for me.'

His face puckered in indignation and then he walked

away, rolling his shoulders in an attempt to appear manly and unfazed.

Kate gritted her teeth and forced herself not to throw something at the back of his head. She didn't want to be at work today. In fact, she hadn't been herself ever since Tim had left. Her first boyfriend had come full circle and become her first break-up. And it bloody hurt. It was hard to get up in the mornings and stand at this desk talking to partially evolved human beings like the one she'd just encountered.

Tim had texted a couple of times since he'd moved out, to check she was OK, that no more unpleasant deliveries had arrived, that she was locking the door at night. But each of his messages had been to the point: practical, functional missives that were signed off simply with his name. She missed his warmth and easy humour. God, she missed *him*. She pulled her new phone from her trouser pocket again, to give it a sneaky check, just to see if he'd been in touch. They weren't allowed phones on the shop floor, but Kate had taken to breaking the rules. She was feeling mutinous.

Her heart leapt as she saw there was a message, but it was from Grace, not Tim. Kate had sent one to her a couple of days ago, asking how Arnie was doing. She quickly opened the reply.

'Not so great. He's got severe graft vs. host disease. Grafted cells attacking his liver. He's back in critical care.'

Kate stared at the screen, reeling. *Critical care?* When had that happened? Everything had been fine – *fine*. Surely, he'd be OK? Wouldn't he? Wasn't the match a nine out of ten or something? People didn't die from a transplant as good as a nine out of ten.

She checked the time of the message – it had been sent just over two hours ago. Kate dialled Grace's number – but it went straight to voicemail.

'Hi, Grace, it's me, Kate. I'm so sorry to get your news. I—' She paused, not knowing what to say. 'If I can do anything, anything at all, let me know.'

She hung up, still shaken. Everything Arnie had been through, and now this. It wasn't fair. Angry tears sprang to her eyes. He was just a child, six years old for God's sake, and other people, a chain of faceless politicians, corporations, scientists, had decided his fate for him.

She put her phone back in her pocket and pinched the bridge of her nose. She shouldn't cry on the shop floor. She quickly glanced around in case any customers were heading her way and saw a mother pushing her trolley down the aisle across from her desk, her young son sitting in the child's seat. He was clutching a brightly coloured child's watering can, something the shop had on as a promotion. The mother was browsing the garden products and Kate saw her pick up a bottle of weedkiller and read the front label with its reassuring claims of 'quick action' and 'targets roots', and how it would make your garden so beautiful, so *perfect* by killing the weeds. The mother placed a bottle in her trolley.

Kate stepped from behind the help desk and walked over to the woman. 'Excuse me?' she said as she plucked the bottle of weedkiller from the trolley and put it back on the shelf. 'I really wouldn't recommend this stuff.'

The woman looked bemused. 'But I need it,' she said and placed it back in again.

'No, honestly, you *don't*,' said Kate, putting the bottle back, more firmly this time.

'Yes, I *do*,' said the woman, plonking the bottle back in.

'Maybe you don't understand. This stuff kills people.' Kate turned the bottle over, indicating the back label. 'Glyphosate. There are numerous reports about it being carcinogenic to humans. I just worry . . . it's not great to chuck it all over the garden when you have little kids outside.'

The young boy, who'd been getting more alarmed at Kate's behaviour, began to cry. His mother picked him up, along with her bag, and started to walk away. 'You're bonkers,' she said. Kate didn't even watch her go. She ran her arms along the shelves, sweeping bottles of weedkiller off the shelf and into the woman's abandoned trolley with a crash.

'Kate?' said a smooth, corporate voice in her ear. She ignored it.

'Don't make me have to call security.' It was Martin, her manager. She stopped, out of breath.

'Shall we have a little chat?' said Martin.

'You can't let your personal issues affect your work,' said Martin in his 'calm voice', the one she suspected he learned on his 'staff management and morale' courses. She looked at him. He was only in his twenties, but already heading towards being overweight, and he liked to gel his thinning hair, which actually made it look even thinner. He was sitting on a low chair next to hers with an air of self-importance about him, of stoically bearing the extra responsibilities management brought.

She considered getting up and leaving his office, but that would probably just inflame matters.

'There should be a clear dividing line between what goes on at home and what we do here.'

'You are poisoning our customers and their children,' said Kate.

'I beg your pardon?'

She spoke clearly, as if he were having difficulty understanding. 'A large proportion of domestic weedkiller products contain glyphosate, a highly contentious ingredient that has been labelled by the World Health Organization as being probably carcinogenic.'

He looked uncomfortable, as if he had not received the latest memo from Head Office.

'We should not be selling it,' said Kate.

'I see.' Martin quickly turned to his computer, tickled a few keys. 'It's on our stock list,' he said, emphatically.

She stared at him, incredulous. 'Is that what you follow? Stock lists? Is that how you make your decisions?'

'But it's one of our biggest sellers,' he added, bemused by her tone.

'What about thinking for yourself? What about your *humanity*?'

Martin turned away from the screen, placed his hands on his knees. 'I'd like you to go home and cool off.'

She was already standing, grabbing her bag. 'Oh, I'm going—'

'And don't come back un—'

But she didn't hear the rest as she'd slammed the door behind her.

Kate let herself into her quiet, empty house, threw her bag on the kitchen table and slumped into a chair, head in hands. What a mess. What a goddamn awful mess she'd made of everything. She glanced up in futile hope at the kitchen window, but of course there was no longer any Iris across the close.

Oh God, what if Arnie died? What if he died and she, Kate, had done nothing about this whole sorry situation? She'd not found out who owned the farm, nor had she gathered enough evidence to be able to sue anyone. She'd failed Arnie, just as she'd failed all the others, including her own daughter.

Kate scraped back her chair, unable to sit still any longer. She opened the fridge door and grabbed a juice, drinking it straight from the bottle. The fridge closed shut again and right there, stuck on the front, was an envelope she'd put on it a few days before.

Her tickets.

To the Bahamas.

She suddenly grabbed them, dumped the juice on the drainer, picked up her phone and started to dial.

The communal lounge was warm with late-morning sunshine and the windows and doors to the garden were thrown open. Some of the residents had even escaped the high-backed chairs and were outside, strolling amongst the sunflowers and lavender or sitting on the wooden benches dotted around the gardens, sunhats and large sunglasses shielding very still faces, which may well have been asleep. A couple of women, dressed in Lycra, with sweatbands around their grey heads and small weights in their liver-spotted hands, power-walked purposefully across the extended lawn.

Kate brought her gaze back into the room and scanned it for Iris. She wasn't there. Outside the patio doors, a small group was gathered at the far end of the lawn and in amongst them, Kate spotted her. She hurried over, just as Iris, one hand on her stick, was throwing her boule with the other.

'Kate!' said Iris, turning. 'What a nice surprise.'

'Hiya,' said Kate, kissing her on the cheek. 'Are you free later?'

'Yes! What did you have in mind?'

'A little break.'

'Break? What, you mean an excursion? Like the garden centre?'

'Not exactly. We're going on holiday.'

'Holiday?' repeated Iris, puzzled.

One or two of the other residents, sensing excitement, stopped playing and looked across.

'You and me. In fact, maybe we should go and pack.'

'Really? Now? I'm in the middle of a game,' said Iris, indicating the boules.

'Yes, but . . . I have a cab booked to take us to the airport in a couple of hours.'

'Airport?' Iris clutched her bosom.

Kate lowered her voice. 'I need you. Please, Iris. Please say you'll come with me.'

Iris hesitated. 'How long for?'

'Only a few days.'

'So, you've already got the tickets,' said Iris, sternly.

Kate had the grace to look sheepish.

'Well, you were very sure of yourself, m'lady. How do you know I even have a passport?'

Kate blanched. She hadn't even stopped to think about that. 'Are you saying you don't?'

'I might have. Just in case I ever decided to go to Spain,' said Iris wistfully. 'Anyway, why the urgency to go on holiday?'

'Why not?' quipped a resident. A cheer went up as someone's boule hit the small target ball.

'I'll explain as we pack,' said Kate. 'So, is it a yes?'

Iris deliberated. 'OK then. Why not. Where are we going?'

'Greg gave me tickets to the Bahamas for my birthday.'

Iris's eyes popped. There were impressed murmurs from the group. 'We're going to the Bahamas?' said Iris.

'No, I've changed them,' said Kate. 'We're going to Anguilla.'

'Anguilla?'

'It's a lesser-known island just north-west of Antigua,' Kate whispered in her ear.

Iris smiled. 'I know where it is. It's also where that company is based, the one you got the email about.' She tapped the side of her nose. 'Say no more. Let us pack for our mission.' And she led the way back across the lawn, Kate at her heels.

FIFTY-FOUR

The monoplane flew low over the Caribbean Sea, and Kate peered out of the window at the palette of aquamarine and turquoise dotted with white yachts, giddy with excitement, nerves and a sense of utter disbelief at where she actually was.

They were flying from Antigua to neighbouring Anguilla. The two pilots had greeted each of the seven passengers with a handshake and a supporting arm and helped them climb aboard, and the same pilots were now keeping up a friendly commentary. Titbits about the island – its serenity, its notoriously beautiful beaches, its gracious and friendly people, and the thriving live music present at many of the island's eateries, including Anguilla's famous reggae musician, Bankie Banx – all of which built up the anticipation so that when they were coming to land, both Kate and Iris had a sense they were stepping into paradise.

The pilots gave a warm farewell and said they'd look out for the 'two English roses' at Sandy Ground, the island's 'entertainment capital', a bay with half a dozen or so bars and restaurants, mostly right on the beach.

Customs was more like a personal welcome, and a driver,

Magic, took them in his air-conditioned taxi to the hotel where they'd be staying the next seven nights. Magic was as gentle and gracious as the pilots, proudly pointing out sights along the way or indicating which direction on the sixteen-mile-long island held which piece of interesting history or the best beaches.

It was another world compared to their lives in south London. Kate stared out the window at the intense blue sky, the palm trees, the odd random goat grazing at the roadside. The scrubland was broken up every now and then by glimpses of the Caribbean Sea, the sunlight bouncing off it. Everything was bathed in a trance-like brightness. She'd been worried that Iris wouldn't enjoy the flight, but the first-class tickets had ensured they'd had everything they needed for a comfortable journey, and both had slept well in their bed pods.

Kate had used the refund from the Bahamas hotel to book their stay in Anguilla. There had been a small amount of money left over and this was going to fund the daily essentials of their week-long trip. That was all the time she had to get the information she needed before the money ran out.

As they stepped into the hotel reception with its fresh white-washed walls, they were greeted by a lady carrying two cool glasses of iced fruit juice on a carved wooden tray. Colour was everywhere, in the smiling lady's green dress, on the animal and flora prints on the walls. A man wearing an orange shirt offered them a warm, sweet-smelling, tightly rolled small towel.

'Oh, look, Kate, he's giving us a wash cloth!' exclaimed Iris, in delight. The journey, although comfortable, had still racked up considerable hours and refreshing face cloths were a small joy. They were checked in and then led to their quietly luxurious rooms, with an interlocking door between the two. Soft buttercup walls and honey-coloured floor tiles, with large, plump beds and mango-and-rattan furniture. A balcony led outside and looked directly over the beach with its white, powdery sand and turquoise water. There was also a view of the hotel's infinity pool.

Kate laughed, goggle-eyed. 'Isn't this ridiculously beautiful?'

'I've never seen anything like it in my life,' said Iris, breathless. 'It must have cost a fortune,' she added with a worried note to her voice.

'It did. But it's one of the cheaper ones, believe it or not. Anyway,' added Kate, going back in and testing out the bed, 'it's my birthday present, remember?'

Iris unzipped her case. 'I'll unpack later, there's just one thing . . .' She pulled out a Spanish figurine of a flamenco dancer and placed her on the dresser.

'You brought Constanza?' asked Kate.

'Of course. If I was ever going to get away, and it seems it's taken you to do it, she was always coming with me.'

The pool was the first stop. Long and oval, it ran parallel to the sea and was flanked by palm trees. No sooner had they found their sunbeds, than an orange-shirted man approached with two glass dishes.

'Homemade mango sorbet, madam?' he said to Iris.

'Oh, thank you, but I didn't order any,' said Iris.

'It's with our compliments,' said the friendly young man and Iris raised her eyebrows. 'Well, thank you very much,' she declared.

Amused, Kate ate hers then decided to swim. Iris declined, saying she'd just rest her eyes instead.

As Kate struck out in the water, she thought about what lay ahead. She was still acutely aware her plan had a high chance of failure and part of her was wondering if her impulsive decision to exchange her luxury holiday for another luxury holiday was a mistake. Despite the fact the airline tickets were non-refundable, she was aware she'd spent half a deposit on a flat on a whim. A highly ambitious whim, in the hope that she might be able to somehow persuade an official at Government House to give her confidential information about an offshore company called Foxgold Ltd. It was unlikely – highly unlikely – but without any other options, and emotional from the news about Arnie, she'd cashed in her chips and gone for it.

The office would be open tomorrow and she planned to go there first thing and – what? Beg? Cajole? Trick? At that moment, she had no idea. Kate flopped over on her back and the sound of the gentle waves just a few metres away momentarily disappeared as her ears submerged in the water. She floated, gazing up at the clear blue sky, feeling the warm island breeze brush over her in a muffled world. It felt surreal. People like her didn't come to places like this, and she'd somehow stumbled down this rabbit hole and was lost, out of her depth. She was in a dream, and in dreams you had very little control over your actions, your fate. Unexplained things happened, and reality was snatched away from you when you least expected it. Unsettled, she righted herself again, wanted to hear the relatively stabling sounds of her surroundings.

There was one clear, hard fact: this was the end of the line. If nothing came out of this trip, she'd have to quit. She had no other choice; she would have exhausted all her options. This cold dose of reality propelled her out of the pool and back to her sunbed. As she lay there, drying off in the sun, she sensed Iris waking next to her.

'Have I been asleep?' asked Iris, blinking. 'Or am I still dreaming? Oh, isn't this place magnificent! Warm, though,' she added, fanning herself, 'warm, but magnificent.'

Another orange-shirted man came up to her. 'A chilled towel, madam?'

Iris stared. 'Pardon?'

'To cool you off.' He handed her a folded rectangle of fluffy white cotton.

'It's cold!' she exclaimed, laughing, and draped it over her.

'Yes.'

'How are they chilled?'

'We refrigerate them, madam.'

'You put the towels in the fridge? Who'd have thought it? Well, it's very nice. Just what I needed.' She smiled as her towel-bearer moved on. 'What a lovely man,' she mused. 'How's the water?' she said to Kate.

'Fab.'

'Is it? Then I shall go for a dip!' Iris stood.

'Can you manage?' asked Kate but Iris flapped her away. She made her way to the shallow steps and waded into the warm water, the skirt from her swimming costume lifting and floating around her, and she turned and smiled at Kate with such vitality she looked about ten years younger.

They decided to go outside the hotel to eat that night and explore the pilots' recommendation of Sandy Ground. By chance, Magic was their taxi driver again and he greeted them like long-lost friends.

With the sun beginning to set behind them, they walked barefoot along the sand, Iris holding Kate's arm for support.

'Do you mind if we don't go far tonight?' asked Iris, looking wearily down the small beach. 'Only, I think it must be past my bedtime back home.'

'This must be what they call jet lag,' said Kate, yawning. She glanced up at the beach bar adjacent to them. 'I reckon this is the one tonight then, don't you?'

They sat at a table on a raised wooden veranda right by the beach and ordered whole grilled red snapper and a Sandy Sizzler cocktail. Iris sipped through her straw and her eyes nearly popped out of her head.

'That's bloody lovely,' she exclaimed, before taking another sip, then another. She placed a hand on Kate's. 'Oh, this is turning out to be such a lovely holiday, Kate. And the heat, it's helping with my arthritis. Thank you.'

'Glad you came?'

'I'm beginning to wonder why I've been such a stick in the mud. All those years telling myself I never wanted to go anywhere. I think I might have been very foolish. You see, Geoff was more of a caravan-in-Wales type of man. Sometimes we even ventured as far as the Cotswolds. He liked the open road, liked driving with his home pulled along behind him. You'd think with all that taxi-driving at work he would have had enough, but he loved it. It was his life. I just fell into the same routine.' She slurped the last of her drink, then held her glass and looked around hopefully. 'Can I get another one of these?'

A smiling face obliged, bringing over a fresh drink and their fish.

'So, are we all set for tomorrow?' asked Iris, tucking into dinner. 'Oh, my word, this is delicious. *Delicious!*' she called out to the bartender who'd brought it over.

He indicated another man sitting in a small group at the bar. 'George, here, caught it this morning,' the bartender called back, and Iris gave the fisherman an appreciative wave.

'As ready as I'll ever be,' said Kate. 'I think we're going to have to play it by ear a bit.'

Iris nodded. 'Have you had any more nasty threats?'

'No.'

'Good. And what about who was behind that bullet? You are being careful, aren't you, love? I worry now Tim's not there and with me gone as well. Can't you and Tim make up?'

Kate reluctantly shook her head. Truth was, she didn't know how. She was acutely aware of how sporadic her experience was in the art of relationships and had the uneasy feeling that this lack of experience was what had made her fail with Tim. Even Becky, at the tender age of seventeen, had recognized her mother's inadequacies. Becky had suffered her first real heartbreak – a three-month relationship with a boy from school had ended when he'd dumped her for another girl who had her own car. He'd broken up with Becky by text and she'd come down from her room where she'd been getting ready to go to the cinema with him, sobbing her heart out.

Kate had held her tight and eventually got the story out of her. She'd felt anger towards this boy she'd never met who'd caused her daughter so much pain and wished with all her heart she could wave a magic wand and make it better.

'What do I do, Mum?' Becky asked between tears.

Kate pondered the question. Got a flurry of nerves as she realized she didn't really know how to help. She wished she had a memory book of experiences to draw on, to share with her daughter. All she knew for sure was that if she saw this boy – Jake, Becky kept on calling him – she'd like to punch his lights out.

'Kick him in the goolies.'

Becky stopped crying. 'What?'

'That'll work, won't it?'

Her daughter started laughing. 'Oh, Mum . . .'

Kate was embarrassed. 'OK, I admit, I don't know. I don't know anything. I'm making it all up as I go along. I'm just an ordinary woman trying to muddle my way through. Sorry, your mother's failing you.'

'You're not, Mum,' said Becky. 'Just . . . maybe don't become a marriage guidance counsellor.'

'Really?' said Kate.

Of course, in a few months, Becky had realized just what a toad Jake was, but somehow, Kate felt that in Tim, she'd lost someone quite special. She shook herself; no point in getting maudlin.

Iris was sucking on her straw again and finding only air. A look up and the bartender understood. 'They're so wonderfully helpful here,' she said.

'Um . . .'

'What?'

'They're . . .' Kate indicated the drink.

'Yes?'

'There's probably quite a bit of rum in them.'

Iris picked up her fresh glass. Took a sip. 'Really? All I can taste is juice. So, have you? Got any new ideas on who sent that vile bullet?'

'Tim thinks it's Greg,' said Kate.

'What about you?'

Kate shrugged. 'There's no real evidence.'

'There might be tomorrow.'

There just might, thought Kate. If they managed to get any information. She watched as the bartender began to light the candles in carved-out pineapples – a Caribbean version of pumpkins at Halloween. Then the sound of a guitar tuning, a tambourine waking up. A gravelly voice across the sound system: 'Ladies and gentlemen, it is time for a few tunes.' The band of four launched into some jazz and a ripple of energy caught across the small crowd.

A gentleman with greying afro hair got up from the bar. He approached their table and gave a small bow. 'Good evening, ladies.' He beamed. 'Could I persuade you to join me in mashing some sand?'

Kate looked at where he was indicating: a group of locals and tourists were dancing. Some on the wooden veranda, some directly on the beach. He was a little old for her, perhaps, but what harm could come out of a bit of dancing on a warm evening in the Caribbean?

'I'd love to,' she said, standing.

There was a silence while she waited, expecting him to lead her to the beach, but the gentleman didn't move. Confused, she smiled at him and he smiled back.

'That would be wonderful,' said Iris, getting to her feet, and the gentleman crooked his arm and led her to the sand without so much as a backwards glance at Kate.

She stood at the table, feeling the blood rush to her face, and then looked up and saw the fisherman watching. She quickly sat down. Took a sip of her drink and then laughed at herself.

Seemed she had underestimated this island – and Iris. She watched the two of them dance, slower than the others but with no less enjoyment. Kate wondered how old the man was. He didn't look more than early sixties – but maybe that was what this relaxed sunshine-filled island did for you. They completed the dance and then he led Iris back to their table and finished with another bow. 'Thank you very much,' he said in the sincerest way Kate had ever heard the words uttered, then he went back to the bar to join his friends.

Kate leaned over the table. 'Get you!' she said to Iris.

'I don't think I've danced since 1987, when Geoff took me to a knees-up at the rugby club.' Iris looked pink-cheeked and happy. Her eyes shone.

'So, go on. Spill. Who is he?'

'His name is Errol and he's a local.'

'What else?'

'He likes going fishing at the weekends.'

'And?'

'His nephew is the founding pilot of the air-service company we took to get here. Small world, eh?'

'Small island. It's nice,' said Kate, glancing around, 'everyone seems to know each other. So, are you planning to catch up with him again?'

Iris laughed loudly. 'Oh, you are funny. We are here to get your information,' she said firmly. 'And on that note, this jet lag has really got to me. Time to call it a night?'

Kate agreed. Tomorrow was going to be a big day. A make-or-break day.

FIFTY-FIVE

Kate looked at herself critically in the mirror. There was a fine line between 'tourist' and 'professional in a hot climate'. The short-sleeved top was basic but had a collar, the shorts – correction, *culottes* – were often cited in style pages as *the* thing to wear in heat when working, and so what if they had a large flowery print on them, and on her feet were beaded two-strap sandals. Who was she kidding? They were flip-flops. Nice ones, but flip-flops, nonetheless. She didn't own anything smarter. It would have to do.

She went to knock on the interconnecting door and Iris answered in a pair of linen trousers and a blouse.

'Oh, hello, love. Are you about to get changed?'

'I *am* changed,' said Kate.

'Of course you are,' said Iris quickly. 'Don't mind me. I haven't got my glasses on.'

'Are we ready?' asked Kate.

'Lead the way.'

They had a different taxi driver this time, which added to Kate's nerves. She'd grown attached to Magic in the short time they'd known him, and she'd automatically expected him to be there again. It threw her when he wasn't.

The driver took them to The Valley, the island's tiny capital, where on the outskirts lay Crocus Hill, home to Government House. He dropped them off outside the building and they smoothed trousers and straightened blouses. As they walked up the white-stone steps, a smiling security guard held open the door. They stepped into an air-conditioned room dominated by a large curved wooden desk. On the top was a huge vase of frangipani in pink and yellow, their sweet tropical-fruit scent permeating the room. A uniformed lady stood up behind the desk. 'Good morning. How can I help you, ladies?'

'Ah, hello,' started Kate. 'I'm here with my . . . mother,' she said, indicating Iris, and was relieved to see Iris nod along, 'and we're looking to register our company here in this beautiful island. We have a few questions, though, and we would like to speak to the Registrar of Companies if he or she were available?'

'Do you have an appointment?'

'Not exactly . . . no. We were kind of hoping to be able to pop in.'

'He's very busy . . .'

'Of course! We realize he must be an *extremely* busy man but still . . . we were hopeful? It would only be for a few minutes.'

The receptionist deliberated for a bit and then said, 'I'll try his line. Would you like to take a seat?'

Iris and Kate each took a chair while the receptionist spoke on the phone. They tried to listen in but were too far away to make out what she was saying.

'Maybe he's looking for a nice distraction from work first thing on a Monday morning,' said Iris, optimistically.

'Maybe first thing on a Monday is just too annoying a time,' said Kate. 'We should have waited until after lunch when his belly will be full and he'll be in a good mood.'

The receptionist, still on the phone, looked over at them at that point and Iris smiled at her. 'Look confident,' she whispered to Kate under her breath.

The phone was replaced, and the receptionist walked over to them. 'He'll see you now,' she said, and Kate's heart leapt. 'If you just go down this corridor, it's the third door on the left,' she said, pointing them in the right direction.

Kate and Iris walked down the wide, carpeted corridor with its bright cream walls and large, white-painted doors until they got to the one that had a brass nameplate with the words 'Registrar of Companies' on it.

Kate took a breath then knocked with purpose. The door was opened wide and both Kate and Iris's bright, business-like smiles morphed into bewilderment.

'What an unexpected surprise,' said Errol, breaking the silence. Then, realizing they were all three just looking at each other, he beckoned them in. 'Please, do take a seat.'

He got them both a cup of water from the cooler in the corner of the room and then took a small chair next to them. 'How very nice to see you again. I had no idea you were here on business.'

Iris took a sip of her water. 'Ah, yes,' she said awkwardly, 'well, it's both. Business *and* pleasure.' She smiled at him, remembering her dance the night before.

'So, you are considering registering your company in our island?'

'Yes . . . well, it's Kate's really,' said Iris. 'I'm just here for moral support.'

Both Iris and Errol were looking at her. Kate cleared her throat. Tried to gather herself.

'Well, you see, the thing is . . .' started Kate.

'Yes?' said Errol.

'There's a particular question I had.'

'Go on.'

'Something I really need to know.'

He smiled. 'Hit me with it.'

Kate couldn't form the words and stared helplessly at him.

Iris sighed impatiently. 'Kate needs to know the listed director of a company registered here so that she can sue him or her for some really bad stuff that's been going on back home.'

Open-mouthed, Kate looked at her.

Iris shrugged. 'It's true, isn't it?' She turned to Errol. 'I didn't see any reason to beat around the bush.'

Errol sat back in his chair. 'I see. I'm sorry, ladies, but I am unable to give out any information. Even if I wanted to, I am not *allowed* to.'

Iris leaned forward earnestly. 'But what this person's responsible for . . . it's really bad, Errol. There's a little lad back home who's desperately ill with cancer. And he's not the only one.'

Errol paused, and a flicker of compassion crossed his face. 'Have you involved the police?'

'It's not as simple as that,' said Kate.

'I'm deeply sorry, truly I am—'

'The company's called Foxgold,' interrupted Kate.

Errol stopped still. Kate clocked his look of recognition and wondered if he was going to mention his error in emailing the forensic accountant, but he said nothing.

'I just need to know the name of the director. Please.'

Errol held up his hands. 'I am sorry, but I cannot help.'

'What about if you just got it up on your computer over there?' said Iris brightly, pointing at his desk. 'Then maybe you get an urge to go to the little boys' room . . . ?'

Amused, Errol shook his head. 'I have a very strong bladder.'

Iris held up her cup. 'Drink some water?'

Errol stood. 'Ladies,' he said firmly. 'I take it you don't have any questions about registering your own company?'

Neither needed to answer.

'It has been delightful to see you both again,' he said, looking at Iris, 'and if I can help in any other way, I am at your disposal.' He held Iris's hands and kissed the top gallantly.

Five minutes later, they were walking back down the front steps.

'So that's that,' said Iris. 'At least we tried.'

Kate's eyes gleamed. 'It's not over yet,' she said.

'What? But you heard him – he's not allowed to say a sausage. Probably breaking the law.'

'Yes, I heard him, but I also saw the way he was looking at you. You, Iris, are the key to this whole thing.'

'What?'

'I think you need to take him to dinner – I'll pay – talk to him, get to know him a bit, see if you can—'

'Are you pimping me out?' exclaimed Iris indignantly.

Kate feigned shock. 'What are you suggesting? I prefer, "using our persuasion tactics".'

Iris held her gaze for a moment and then, head held high, began to walk back to the waiting taxi.

Smiling, Kate quickly followed then took Iris's arm, gave it a squeeze. With Iris's help, this might just work.

FIFTY-SIX

'Now are you sure you're happy with this?' asked Kate. Iris was waiting outside the hotel for her taxi to take her to one of the island's restaurants, where she had arranged to meet Errol for dinner after she'd called him that afternoon.

'I'm a widow, he's a widower, we're both free to have dinner with whomever we want,' said Iris.

'You know I don't mean that.'

'I honestly don't think that me buying him a plate of lobster is going to make him change his mind. He made it perfectly clear earlier he couldn't say anything.'

'Not lobster, Iris, *you*. It's obvious he has a soft spot for *you*.'

'Pah,' said Iris, waving a hand dismissively.

'Could you just try?'

'I said I would, didn't I?'

Magic drove up to the front of the hotel, jumped out and opened the back door of the cab. 'Are you ready for your magical mystery tour?'

Iris climbed in and Magic shut the door. He looked at Kate in surprise.

'You're not coming?'

'Not tonight, she's not,' said Iris.

Kate leaned down to the open window and kissed Iris on the cheek. 'Thank you,' she said. 'I'll be waiting. Come and see me when you get back.'

Iris batted her away and Magic drove off. Kate watched the car go, and quietly crossed her fingers.

She had dinner alone in the hotel restaurant and then took a drink out to the pool area. Even at night, the temperature was in the high twenties, but the near-flat island meant there was always a cooling breeze.

Her phone beeped, and she looked to see if it was Iris, but it was Grace texting to say that there'd been a marked improvement in Arnie. *Thank God*, thought Kate, texting her back.

Afterwards, she sat there quiet and alone, listening to the waves end their journey on the beach. She wondered what Iris was doing right at that moment, what she was saying to Errol, what he was saying to her. She suddenly felt a desperate sense of panic, for although they'd casually asked Magic and one or two of the hotel staff what Errol was like, and they'd all glowed with respect when talking about him, she'd essentially sent Iris off alone with a strange man.

Once again, she'd found herself doing the unthinkable, realizing it long after the event and unable to undo it. It worried her that she had become so reckless, that she didn't know where her own boundaries lay anymore. She had a sudden overwhelming sense of wanting this all to end. To have the relief of a finish line.

Maybe they were having a great time.

Maybe Iris would perform a miracle.

'What time is it?' asked Iris as she walked back into the hotel later that night after being dropped off by Magic.

'Eleven thirty!' admonished Kate. 'I was about to jump in a cab and come and find you.' It was true: she'd come into the lobby an hour ago and had peered into the darkness beyond the hotel several times, looking hopefully for the lights of a car.

'Eleven thirty?' said Iris, astounded. 'Never!' She squinted at her watch, but unable to see properly, got her glasses out of her handbag. 'Is it really eleven thirty? Good Lord! The time's flown by.'

'You enjoyed yourself, then?'

'Oh, Kate, I did. He's such a good conversationalist.'

'What did you talk about?' Kate couldn't keep the hope from her voice.

Iris's face fell. 'I'm sorry. I tried, I really did, but he just said the same thing and then it got a bit awkward and I had to apologize and—' She saw Kate's face. 'I feel like I've let you down.'

'Don't be daft. Don't think that.' Kate squeezed her friend's hand tight.

'I'm suddenly very tired. Would you take me up to my room?'

Kate smiled. 'Of course.'

She accompanied Iris upstairs, waited while she went to the bathroom, then saw she got into bed. Iris closed her eyes and so Kate turned the light off at the doorway into her own room.

'Night,' she called into the dark.

'Goodnight, Kate,' said Iris.

Kate slipped into her room, cleaned her teeth then got under the sheets. She lay there for a while, not really thinking or planning, just letting the disappointment and the emptiness wash over her.

FIFTY-SEVEN

'Errol's invited us fishing,' said Iris, placing her linen napkin on her knee. They were sitting outside enjoying a late breakfast. Iris cut a piece from her sliced mango and ate it delicately.

'Fishing?'

'Yes, Errol wants to take us. Both of us.'

'When?'

'Tomorrow. He's got a half-day. He wants to pick us up in his car, drive to the beach and we'll go out in his boat.'

'But I don't know how to fish.'

Iris smiled. 'I'm sure it doesn't matter.' She continued to eat her breakfast leisurely.

Kate watched her, envious of how Iris was adapting to this island's way of life. Relaxed. Stress-free. Of course it didn't matter if she knew how to fish or not. She cut a piece of fresh pineapple on her plate. Put it in her mouth. Chewed it. *Relax. Enjoy. Take in the indescribably beautiful beach just a few metres from your table.* She swallowed hard. Took a sip of water to stop the coughing.

'Are you OK?' asked Iris.

'Fine,' grimaced Kate, hitting her sternum with a closed fist.

'It'll be lovely, they all have these colourful boats, apparently. Handmade.'

'OK.'

'There's just one thing,' said Iris.

'What?'

'I get seasick.'

'You do?' Kate thought about Iris's previous lack of travel. 'How do you know?'

'When I was a child, my mother took me to the Isle of Wight. On the ferry.'

'Maybe you've changed. It was a long time ago.'

'It was. But I don't think so.'

Kate stared. 'So why . . . You *agreed*?'

'Of course.'

'Why?'

'So we could still talk to him. Bend him to our will.'

Kate looked at her and started to laugh. 'You'd get seasick just to do that?'

'There's no just about it. It's very important.'

Kate smiled. 'So . . . a bit of sightseeing today?'

They decided to explore some of the island's history and took a taxi to the Heritage Museum, painstakingly curated by a local man, who took great pride in his work. The tiny museum was full of old photographs and artefacts that traced the island's history over the last four centuries, covering everything from the Anguilla Revolution to a visit by the Queen in the 1960s.

As they drove across the island, Kate was struck by how

relaxed it was. No casinos – none of the massive cruise ships stopped in Anguilla. It was totally unspoilt.

The next afternoon, Errol drove them out to Island Harbour, where numerous brightly coloured, hand-crafted fishing boats lined the quay. They were helped aboard Errol's blue-and-yellow boat and once they'd motored out of the small harbour, he hoisted the huge white sail. It thwacked in the breeze, driving the little boat along the flat turquoise sea.

'Are you OK?' Kate asked Iris, quietly.

'Fine!' said Iris. She gazed around. 'There are no waves, well, none to really speak of. That must be the difference between here and the Isle of Wight!'

'I thought we wouldn't go far today,' said Errol. 'Just half a mile north-west to a good spot I know. Take it nice and easy.'

Kate looked behind her at the shrinking island as they sailed away. A few chilled-out fishermen at the harbour waved to her and it was impossible not to smile and wave back. She brought her gaze back to the water, watching the boat cut through the clear blue. Then, to her amazement, she spotted something smooth and flat swim rapidly past. Two – three! – stingrays.

'Look!' she exclaimed and, smiling, Iris leaned over to see.

It wasn't long before Errol was slackening the sail and they were slowing down. Anguilla was now a small green jewel in the distance. Errol dropped the anchor and the little yellow-and-blue boat rocked gently on the water.

Kate listened: nothing.

The peace had its own beauty, had the power to move her as much as the aquamarine water or the warm sunshine. She closed her eyes for a moment, let it wash over her.

When she opened them, Errol had baited up two fishing lines. Iris took one and Kate watched as he instructed her how to use it, holding her arms as she cast off. He found a battered, sun-bleached cushion for her to sit on and made sure she had the place on the boat that was in the shade.

Then he turned to Kate, indicated the other line. 'Would you like to try?'

Actually, she didn't want to. She wanted to be still, to just be in this place.

He understood, and cast his line alongside Iris's. Kate could hear them talking in soft tones. Gentle, harmonious. Often, they were just quiet, too.

She leaned over the boat and let her hands fall into the clear water. It was so warm, it surprised her. Then, to her delight, a turtle – at least half a metre long – swam past her and under the boat.

It was gone before she could point it out and she looked up to see Iris lost in her own happiness.

'I might swim,' Kate suddenly announced.

'Go for it, love,' said Iris.

Kate stripped to her swimsuit and dived into the warm water. She looked down, feeling giddy at its clarity. She could see several metres below her, her feet suspended in a clear blue light. She swam away from the boat, rolling over in the water. An unidentified shoal of silvery fish swam alongside her and then, with a synchronized sharp turn, passed her.

What an incredible place this was. Surely somewhere like this could throw up a pearl. Surfacing, she looked back towards the boat, its yellow paint glistening in the sun. It was within the capability of the man just a few metres away to tell her a name. Just a single name that would allow her to do something good. Do what was right.

Tantalizingly close.

'Oh my giddy aunt!' exclaimed Iris and Errol jumped up to help as she had a bite on her line.

Kate swam back as Iris and Errol reeled in the fish. A silver kingfish, its iridescent skin reflecting pinks and blues. It gulped as Iris, eyes agog, held it.

'Wow,' said Kate, finding the little ladder Errol had thoughtfully put on the side of the boat for her and climbing up.

'Lunch?' said Errol, indicating the fish.

'Oh, I couldn't,' said Iris. 'I mean, I know I eat them and it's hypocritical, but can't we just let him go?'

Errol laughed, and Iris gently let the fish back over the side. They watched as it swam away, undeterred by its brush with death.

'Now that Iris has given our lunch back to the sea,' said Errol, with a twinkle, 'I'd better take you to Elvis's.'

He lifted the anchor and they headed back to the island.

Lunch was a not-so-lucky fish and salad, beneath a palm-leaf umbrella by the beach. The conversation remained in light, neutral territory and Kate wondered how best to raise the topic of Foxgold without sabotaging her chances – or the afternoon. The decision was made for her, when Iris went to the bathroom.

'Iris has told me everything,' said Errol, breaking the heavy silence. 'The whole story. You are an incredible woman.'

'Thank you but I don't need flattery, just a little help.'

'I wish I could.'

'You can. You just choose not to.'

'I could go to jail.'

They saw Iris heading back from the ladies' and stopped talking. Iris looked from one to the other.

'Everything OK?'

'I'm sorry, Iris. I am unable to help in the way you really want,' said Errol. 'Maybe there will be another way.'

'What do you mean?' asked Kate. Try as she might, she was unable to keep the scepticism out of her voice.

'This island, it is a special place. Sometimes I feel it can perform miracles.'

Yeah, great, thought Kate, and knew it was pointless pressing him any further.

Later, Errol drove them back to the hotel. Kate got out the car and waited for Errol to help Iris. He and Iris spoke privately before he drove off with a wave.

'What was that about?' murmured Kate as they watched him disappear out of the hotel grounds.

'He was wondering if I might be able to meet for dinner again one night,' said Iris. 'Before we go home.'

Iris was looking at her hopefully. Kate smiled. 'You don't need my permission.'

'No . . . but we're here together. And for a particular reason, that Errol is unable to help with. I feel . . . traitorous.'

'Don't,' said Kate quickly. 'Don't feel that.'

'Sometimes I'm quite angry with him . . . But I do so enjoy his company. It's been a long time since I've enjoyed a man's company so much.'

Kate smiled. 'I do believe this is what they call a holiday romance.'

Iris blushed. 'Don't be daft.'

Iris met with Errol not once but twice more before they went home, and on the last time tried again, but Errol just repeated his sorrow at not being able to help.

She and Kate packed their bags and Magic took them to the airport. On the plane, Iris put her hand over Kate's. 'You did your best, love. More than your best.'

Maybe, thought Kate, but it hadn't been good enough. *I'm sorry, Becky.*

Both women were quiet on the flight back to London. The taxi took Iris home first. Kate saw her inside and helped her unpack.

'Kate, I can't thank you enough. You've made an old woman very happy.'

'I'm just glad you came. Are you going to stay in touch with Errol?'

Iris didn't answer immediately, then shook her head. 'No. It was wonderful meeting him and, in another time, a younger time, things might have worked out differently. But he's so far away . . . and a little part of me can't quite forgive him. For not helping.'

Kate put Iris's empty suitcase back on top of the wardrobe. 'There. Till the next one, eh?'

'Thanks, love. Are you getting a cab home?'

'I'll get the bus.'

'Are you sure?'

Kate nodded. The five-star lifestyle was over. 'Back to reality for me now.'

As Kate approached her house, she felt herself growing wary. She took a moment before getting out her keys, checked the door for signs of entry. Then she let herself in and closed the door behind her. The air smelt stale, the light was fading, and the emptiness filled every room, every corner. She went from room to room looking for signs of intrusion, not getting any sense of comfort when she found none. For the first time since she'd moved in, it didn't feel like home.

She began to unpack. As she filed away her passport in the drawer, she came across a letter she'd stashed there. She took it out, opened it up. It had been sent to her soon after Becky had died, from her boss, Terence, at the newspaper. Her eyes fell on some of the words:

We were about to offer her a full reporter's position. I'm telling you this not to lament what could have been but to add to your raft of her achievements to be proud of.

A life unlived. Kate slowly replaced the letter. *You would have done it, Becky. You would have solved all this by now. Got justice for Arnie and the rest.* She'd had so much going for her, her daughter. More than she, Kate, ever had. 'I've let you down again,' she said out loud to the empty room.

A dark cloud started to settle over her and, afraid of where it would take her, Kate set about tidying the house. Threw out the mouldy food in the fridge, recycled the piles of shouty junk mail. Put on a wash. Tasks completed, she sat at the table. There was nothing to do.

It was over.

FIFTY-EIGHT

2016

'We're on "E"!' whispered Iris excitedly as she leaned into Kate, squeezing her arm. They were in a packed Royal Festival Hall, every one of the two thousand nine hundred seats taken by family and friends of University College London graduates. The graduates themselves were filling the large wooden stage, backdropped by the humungous organ, in a highly orchestrated manoeuvre that saw each of them get up to receive their certificate in turn. After 'East' and 'El-Kati', it was time.

'Miss Becky Ellis, journalism, first-class honours,' said the official and Kate watched as her clever, beautiful daughter walked across the stage in her academic robe with its black-and-red hood, and collected her certificate.

Then Becky turned, and her eyes flickered up to the huge audience. Kate knew she had a sense of where she and Iris were sitting but it would be almost impossible for her to pick them out in such a large sea of faces.

But then – yes! – she'd seen them and managed a quick wave before being directed along to allow for the next graduate.

Kate began to well up, overwhelmed with pride and love. Her little girl was all grown up. She turned to Iris and, seeing tears streaming down her face, the two of them laughed at each other and Iris pulled a packet of tissues out of her handbag. Noses blown, they each sighed and fixed their gazes back on Becky, drinking her in.

This is her time, her moment, thought Kate. Becky was about to be launched into the world. This was what she, Kate, had dreamed of for her when she'd been born in that hospital twenty-one years ago. Despite Kate's numerous cock-ups and inadequacies, her daughter had managed to make something of herself. Becky had heard only the previous week that she'd been offered a prestigious place at a respected national paper, the *Herald,* on one of their graduate traineeships, and would be starting at the end of the month. Everything lay ahead of her. *Her whole life*. She was right at the beginning. About to start a career in the field she'd wanted to work in since she was a child. So much to look forward to. So much to experience.

Kate couldn't help reflecting on what she'd been doing the summer she was twenty-one. She'd had a six-year-old – that same wonderful girl on the stage right now – and they'd taken their first holiday together, in a mobile home in Devon. God, it felt like a long time ago. She briefly wondered what her life might have been like if she'd stood on a stage like Becky, collecting a degree. Her parents looking on proudly from the audience. What might she have studied? What could she have achieved?

Then they were all throwing their hats into the air and

the whole auditorium was clapping and cheering. Kate stood with the rest, helping Iris to her feet. She tidied the past away and was filled with joy. Her daughter was so fiery, so passionate about what she wanted to do, Becky would likely achieve enough for the both of them.

The celebrations continued out on the roof terrace. The views were breathtaking. From the grassy lawn, Kate could see the London Eye rising above Iris's shoulder with its graceful slow turns, the pods dropping below the edge of the roof wall and then eventually rising up again, continuous and reliable. The grey-green river flowed and glistened in the sunlight, a myriad of boats passing through. Around them were the voices of the young, the air ringing with opportunity and optimism. Gowns were open in the warmth or had been discarded, and the new graduates, drinking from plastic glasses, spilled onto the grass and around the edges of the planters filled with deep yellow sunflowers and scarlet geraniums.

She saw Becky and her best friend from the course, Maria, head over to them, clutching cups of Pimm's and lemonade. They were deep in conversation about something. Becky was shaking her head, shamefaced.

'What are you two up to?' asked Kate, as they approached, handing out the cold, minty drinks.

'Becky has been managing unwanted amorous attention,' said Maria.

'Oh, yes?'

'Oh, don't, I feel bad,' said Becky.

'What do I say if he gets in touch, checks the number with me?' teased Maria.

'You can't give it to him,' pleaded Becky. 'Promise?'

Maria laughed and promised, then went off to find her own family, wishing them all a good summer and congratulating Becky again on her job. Maria herself was going to take up a journalism fellowship at Harvard.

Iris lifted her sunglasses and raised her plastic cup of Pimm's.

'To Becky,' she said proudly. 'You are going to make a fine journalist. Wily, smart, tenacious. And I should know, you would always find out where I'd hidden the chocolate biscuits.'

Kate smiled. 'To Becky,' she said and hugged her daughter tightly.

'And to Kate,' added Iris. 'A truly wonderful mother who made all this happen.'

Kate pulled a face. 'Don't be daft. I did nothing.'

'Not true,' said Iris. 'Not true at all.'

FIFTY-NINE

2018

Her phone was ringing. Dragging her up through sleep. She glanced at the screen through squinting eyes but didn't recognize the number.

'Hello?'

'Is that Kate?' said a male voice. Despite her sluggishness, Kate still registered – *what was it?* – tension in his tone.

'Yes?'

'It's Adam, Adam Langley. Becky's friend. We met at the Agrochemical Britain conference.'

Adam! Kate sat up quickly, tried to reorder her brain. 'Yes, yes . . .'

'I need to see you. After work. Today.'

'OK. Sure. Where?'

'Bushy Park. South side of Heron pond. Six thirty.'

She scrabbled around on the bedside table for a pen and scrap of paper. Wrote it down. 'I'll be there.'

'Don't tell anyone you're coming.'

'OK . . .'

'I mean it.'

'I won't. I promise.'

He waited a moment and she sensed him evaluating her trustworthiness, then he just said: 'Please don't be late,' and hung up.

She looked at the clock. It was seven thirty. She had to get to work.

The day dragged, as they all had since she'd returned from Anguilla a week ago. She felt Martin watching her, checking her attitude matched the company one – 'Here to help!' – and it took all of her effort not to walk out of the door. Her mind went round and round wondering why Adam wanted to see her. The last time she'd spoken to him he couldn't get away from her fast enough and had instructed his girlfriend, what was her name, Trixie, to drive off at speed.

As soon as her shift was over, she took the train to Hampton Court and then walked past the palace into Bushy Park. She made it to Heron pond at six twenty-three and looked around for Adam but couldn't see him. It wasn't that busy, just a few commuters walking home and some teenagers practising wheelies on their bikes. A few deer wandered about, noses to the ground as they grazed or stared nonchalantly at their fellow human park-dwellers.

'Keep your distance,' said a low voice from behind and Kate saw Adam pass her and head away from the pond towards the Oval plantation. She did as she was bid, walking in the same direction but staying back twenty metres or so, allowing herself one hesitant check over her shoulder to see if anyone was following them, but saw nothing.

Once he disappeared into the trees, she thought she'd lost him. She stepped through the crackly undergrowth, the fallen crisp leaves dusting the floor, feeling caught in a maze of tree trunks.

'I don't think anyone saw us,' said Adam from behind her.

She jumped. 'Adam.'

'We should talk quickly,' he said.

She nodded. She was alarmed by the way he looked. He'd changed since she'd seen him outside his office in the rain. It wasn't anything physical, nothing simple she could put her finger on, but there was something about his demeanour. He was nervous, tense.

'When Becky and I were seeing each other, I worked in the R&D department of Senerix. You understand what that means, right?'

'Yes, you were developing new products. Researching.'

'I remember when she first got in touch. I couldn't believe it. I'd liked her since university.' He paused, embarrassed. 'I'd keep all her texts, even the practical ones arranging times to meet, just to remind myself – me, geeky Adam – I was seeing *Becky*.'

Kate smiled.

'I was so fucking *stupid*.' He wrestled with something. 'I used to call her on my work phone. Something went wrong with it, can't remember what, now. IT took a look. I never got it back. Thought it odd at the time.'

Kate didn't follow.

'The messages from Becky were still on there,' said Adam.

424

Oh. 'Was there anything incriminating in them?' asked Kate.

'Her name was there. The fact she was a journalist. Then I got the sense I was being watched. Small things. I could've sworn a few of my emails were read before I opened them. The new phone they gave me – I believed it was bugged. I also believed they tracked my movements.'

He took a breath. 'At the end of February last year, I was offered a new job. In a different department. Genomics. You know, genetic engineering? Seeds and so on. They painted it as a promotion of sorts but . . .'

'You think they were deliberately moving you out of R&D?'

'Yes.'

'And do you think that's because you knew something that they didn't want you to tell anyone? To tell Becky?'

It took a moment before he could answer. 'Yes.'

Kate swallowed. 'Can you tell me what that thing is?'

'Not here.'

'But it's something about the use of herbicides? Near people?'

He nodded.

'A report? That you've read? About Crixus?'

He nodded again. 'A memo. I stumbled across it at the beginning of last year. I was in the middle of a research assignment and it suddenly appeared in amongst the files I was working on. Naturally, I read it. It disturbed me. It was clear the company knew stuff about their products that they were keeping secret. I couldn't forget about it so a couple of days later I raised it with my boss. He spun me some story about how it was still a work in progress, nothing conclusive – the company was changing formulas. I was reminded of how my work was confidential. When I got back to my desk, the document had disappeared from the server.'

She felt her breath quicken. *Think, think.*

'But this is something you read almost two years ago, right? Does it even still exist?'

'They may have destroyed it. I've certainly never seen it again. If it does still exist, only a select few would have access.'

Kate's excitement evaporated into the air. 'So, it would be your word against a multi-million-pound company. It's never going to stand up.'

'But, you see, I made a copy.'

She froze. 'You what?'

'Not electronic. I was afraid they'd know. Be able to trace the email if I sent it to my personal account. So, I just printed it. Before I went to see my boss. Then I smuggled it out in my coat pocket.'

'And where is this printout?' asked Kate, her heart in her mouth.

'Well, it was at home. In the cushions of my sofa.'

'Oh my God.'

He reached into his coat, pulled out a brown envelope. 'I want to give it to you.' His eyes were pained. 'I feel responsible. For letting them know about Becky.'

Kate took the envelope, immediately zipped it into her bag. 'It's not your fault, Adam. You didn't kill her.'

'I was going to hand it to her. We'd arranged to meet. She never turned up and I thought she'd lost interest. It wasn't until I saw you at the conference and you told me she'd been knocked off her bike . . . I was so scared.' Adam took a moment to compose himself. 'I wish it could have been different,' he said. 'She was amazing.' He nodded at her bag. 'Be careful, Kate. They'll do anything to stop that getting out.'

He gave her a half-smile and then walked back towards the park. After a short while, he left the trees and she lost him.

SIXTY

She clutched her bag on her lap all the way home, holding it tight against her chest where she could feel her heart going *thump, thump, thump*. The train was packed with commuters and she got a seat in a group of six, the middle of the facing-forward row. Arms jostled, and she felt an elbow in her ribs. She clutched her bag tighter. She glanced up and the man opposite her seemed – what? – intrigued? Curious? She quickly looked away.

Finally, she was off the train. Her bag over her shoulder, she followed the streams of people and they gradually dispersed as they walked further from the station. Then she was alone. She turned into her road and, as usual, approached her house warily.

She stopped. Maybe she'd just made a massive mistake bringing the papers back to her house and she should go to a cafe or something to read them. But then she dismissed the idea – it was not something to read in a public place.

Kate unlocked her front door, slowly pushing it open and listening out for sounds of a disturbance, an intruder. She could see into the shadowy hall, but was met with an empty silence. She slipped inside and did her usual check of the house, holding her bag close the whole time. Her nerves were on edge; the fridge kicking in with its loud hum made her jump. It seemed she was alone and, as far as she could tell, no one had been inside. She sat down at the kitchen table, unzipped her bag and took out the brown A4 envelope. Untucking the flap, she pulled out a handful of papers that were stapled together.

The memo was dated January 2016 and was marked highly confidential. It was written by Roger Harris – the same man whom Kate had spoken to at the conference – and it was addressed to the Director of Marketing.

Naomi,

In response to your query on Crixus and its safety record, and historical test results, I realize the authorities in Spain need assurances so they can license the product but you cannot categorically say that Crixus is not a carcinogen. We have undertaken testing on the product in the 2015 mouse study #2 (mid- and high-dose males and females), spraying the insides of cages and runs over a period of twelve months, which threw up concerning/negative results, with 67 per cent of mice contracting cancers (full test report and results below, including indications of tumours where present). As it is critical that we have our product accepted in the upcoming meeting, I would advise that you avoid any direct claims and frame your statement to imply that there is no reason to believe that Crixus can cause cancers. Dr Andrew Faber from this department is

currently reviewing the mice test tumours and will present
his evaluation to support exactly this statement – that
they are not related to Crixus. (I will have this report
available by next week, should it be required, but
hopefully it won't.)

    Can talk more at the drinks tonight if it helps,
    Roger

Stunned, Kate looked up from the documents. They
knew. They bloody knew all along and had done for years.
They'd also deliberately covered it up with lies and fake
science.

She pulled her cardigan closer, suddenly feeling cold. The
families at Ramsbourne had been regularly exposed to this
stuff – she'd seen the bottles of Crixus stacked up in the
farm's container. Each and every one of them was at risk
and the manufacturing company knew about it. This was it.
This was her smoking gun.

Hands shaking, she went to dial Adam's number. Then
stopped. Did she want her records to show she'd been calling him? She stuffed the document back in her bag and
hurried to the high street where she knew there was a public
phone box, praying it hadn't been vandalized as had so
often happened in the past. To her relief, although covered
in graffiti and littered with empty beer cans, it was working.
She tried Adam on both the number he'd called her from
that morning and the old number she had for him, but there
was no answer on either. She didn't dare leave a message.

Back home, she went through Becky's things, looking for

a diary, an address book, scraps of paper, anything that might give her a clue as to where he lived. She recalled Becky had been to his flat – they'd had a date and she'd waited for a cab there. And then she remembered. Becky had told her he lived in Clapham opposite somewhere. What was it, the Picture Palace? *No, the Picturehouse.* She found it easily enough on Google.

Kate slept fitfully that night, the papers hidden behind a loose panel at the back of one of the kitchen cupboards. In the morning, she rose early, took the train to Clapham and walked the short distance to the small cinema. She stood with her back to it and looked across the road. In front of her was a line of terraced Victorian house conversions.

Crossing the road, she walked up the path of the first building, but the curtains were still closed in all the windows. She tried to peer through a tiny sliver of a gap but could see nothing. Hurrying up the path to the next, again she couldn't see in any of the windows but, alongside the bright-red front door, there was a row of buzzers for each of the flats. The top one was for a Mr A. Langley.

She pressed it and waited for Adam to answer.

She pressed again.

And again.

It was only seven in the morning – surely, he hadn't left for work already? Maybe he was in the shower . . . ? Desperate, she tried a different doorbell, a Miss T. Evans.

'Hello?' answered a female voice.

'Oh, hi, it's –' Kate glanced at the names written against the keypads; the basement flat belonged to Andrea Gibson

– 'Andrea from downstairs. I've just locked myself out!'

The buzzer sounded satisfyingly, and Kate walked in. Then from the flat on the ground floor, a young woman suddenly appeared, dressed in short pyjamas, a floral wrap and fluffy slippers. It took a second and then Kate recognized her. It was Adam's girlfriend . . . what was her name? *Trixie*.

'You're not Andrea,' said Trixie suspiciously. Then she frowned. 'Hang on, I remember you. You came to talk to Adam . . . at his office.'

'That's right.'

'What are you doing here?'

'I'm looking for him.'

'Well, get to the back of the queue,' said Trixie, distinctly unimpressed. 'We'd all like to know where he is.'

Alarm bells were faintly sounding in Kate's ears. 'We?' she queried.

'There was a bloke here earlier this morning from his work. *Really* early. Six o'clock, he woke me. Wanted to speak to Adam. Knew I shouldn't have got the flat on the ground floor,' she grumbled.

'What did this man want him for?'

'Apparently something urgent had come up. Adam was needed in to sort it out.'

Kate's heart started beating faster. 'Did that not strike you as odd?' she asked.

'What do you mean?'

'That he was needed so early in the morning?'

Trixie pondered. 'Well, I suppose . . . I don't know really, he's always so secretive about what he does. Science research or something. I guess I never really thought about it.'

'Where did he go, this man?' asked Kate.

'Well, he went up to Adam's flat, tried to wake him.' Unease was starting to form on Trixie's face.

Kate raced up the stairs, Trixie following. Kate stopped abruptly at Adam's door. It was ajar, broken at the lock.

'Oh my God!' exclaimed Trixie. Kate gingerly pushed the door open further so she could see inside.

Papers were strewn across the hallway, spilling from the doorways of the rooms. She stepped in, catching her breath as she saw into the living room. Furniture had been over-turned or destroyed. Cushions lay slashed on the floor, drawers had been brutally tipped empty. Kate slowly walked around the flat. Nervously called Adam's name as she stepped through the debris of each devastated room, but the place was empty.

'We need to call the police!' declared Trixie.

Kate ignored her. 'What did the man look like?'

'Eh?'

'Who came this morning? What did he look like?'

'Oh. Big, you know, tall. Had a moustache, one of those long ones,' said Trixie, running her finger and thumb down either side of her mouth.

It was him. The same man I saw outside the courtroom and in the street in Ramsbourne. Kate tried to gather her thoughts. He knew something. If he found Adam – she hoped to God he hadn't already – she remembered what had happened to Justin. Maybe the man knew Adam had met her. Maybe he knew Adam had given her the document that was burning a hole inside the bag on her shoulder right now.

She suddenly knew she couldn't go home.

She was way, way out of her depth. Help, she needed help. There was only one person she could think of: Jill. The uber lawyer had already turned her down but now Kate had proof. Proof of what Crixus did to people. Surely Jill would listen? Know what to do? At the back of her mind was a dim recollection of needing to be at Greg's office for the PR session mid-morning but that would have to wait. She turned to leave.

Trixie had her phone out of her pocket and was about to dial when she cut Kate a quizzical look.

'You remind me of someone. This girl . . . you look a bit like her . . .'

Kate stopped at the doorway of the flat. 'Who?'

Trixie frowned, then shook her head. Dismissed it. 'I can't remember. No one . . .'

Kate raised herself up to her full five-foot-one height. Stared Trixie down. Her voice was strong, steeped in emotion. 'Her name is Becky Ellis. And she is not a no one.'

Then she turned away from Trixie's gawping face and left.

SIXTY-ONE

The heavy rain meant it was already dark when Becky packed up her things, turning off her laptop. She sent a brief text to her mum: 'Leaving now. See you (both!) soon. X' Then she put her phone and water bottle in her backpack, pulling out her helmet, ready to cycle to the station. The wind blew the rain hard against the office window, an irregular rhythm of cold and wet, and she groaned. She'd be absolutely soaked by the time she got home, would need a shower before she could show her face in front of Tim.

As she pushed her chair under her desk, Piers approached.

'Not in the mood,' she said, holding up her hand. She didn't have time for a run-in with him, she had to get back, didn't want to be late for her mum.

'Hey, I come in peace,' said Piers.

Becky ignored him. Slung her backpack over her shoulder.

'Seriously. I was going to offer you a lift.' He held up his car keys, a large shiny BMW badge dangling from them. 'It's pouring down. You're going to get drenched. Let me take you to the station.'

'Are you having a laugh?'

He looked bemused. 'Nope.'

Becky snapped. 'You do whatever you can to find out about my story, *stalk* me, in fact, and then you grass me up to Terence, telling him I've been bunking off work.'

'Ah, so that's what this hostility is all about.'

Exasperated, Becky flashed him a look and started to walk off.

'OK, guilty of first charge but definitely not the second. That wasn't me.' He put a hand on her arm. 'Promise,' he said, smiling at her.

She glared at him.

'For what it's worth, I told . . . the individual . . . to leave it be. I admired you ducking out of here. Stories are not going to come to us, are they?'

'Who?' she said suspiciously, not entirely believing him.

He said nothing, just kept smiling.

'Who was it?'

He dropped his hand. 'I'm not a grass.'

She rolled her eyes, amazed she'd almost fallen for it, and was about to walk off again when—

'Come on, let me drive you. Peace offering. First of many. Let's just say, I like you. That's why I've been winding you up.'

'Seriously. That's your idea of *flirting*?'

'Didn't work?' He smiled again, and Becky saw again how handsome he was. 'OK, sorry. I know – as you have rightly pointed out – I've been a dick.'

She looked at him. If she didn't know any better, she'd say his apology was genuine.

'Go on, let me drive you. It would be nice to chat in the car. In fact, I was hoping . . . I'd love for the chance to take you out properly. Nice restaurant.'

'You're forgetting something. I'm not the one who fancies you.'

'Ah, that. I've had a word with Darcy. Made it clear. Tactfully!' he added quickly at the look on Becky's face.

She said nothing, and he seemed to falter – but surely that wasn't possible, thought Becky. This was arrogant, cool Piers.

'Please? Becky?'

Becky! He'd called her Becky. She had to pick her chin up off the floor.

He held out a crooked arm. 'So, will you?'

She almost went then, almost thought, *sod it, the rain's terrible. I could do with a lift.*

'I've got my bike.'

'It'll fit in the back. I've got an estate,' he explained, 'for the dogs.' And she realized she knew nothing about him.

'Dogs?'

'Two. A working cocker and a lab.'

This seemed so out of character, her jaw fell open again. Did obnoxious people have dogs?

Becky hesitated. They were standing outside Terence's office and she remembered the conversation from earlier. How Piers had landed her in it.

'Nah, you're all right,' she said.

His face crumpled into such a look of disappointment she was taken aback.

'Oh,' he said.

She was embarrassed then, awkward. Then realized she was going to be late if she didn't get a move on.

'Another time, maybe,' she mumbled and headed for the lift that took her down to the garage. As she pressed the button, she shook her head, bewildered. What had happened back there? The lift reached the basement and she stepped out and saw Darcy getting into her car. Becky smiled and was just lifting a hand in goodbye when Darcy blanked her. Becky stared as Darcy drove away. What was all that about? Come to think of it, Darcy had kept her distance all afternoon. It suddenly hit her. It was *Darcy* who'd grassed her up. Darcy, who fancied Piers. Becky paused, in half a mind to go back upstairs and accept Piers's offer of a lift. But time was ticking. If she wasn't careful, she'd miss her train. Be late for the meet with Tim.

Becky quickly unlocked her bike and cycled out of the garage, the rain pelting her eyes immediately. She turned into Gray's Inn Road, not noticing a motorcyclist with a black visor pull in behind her. The rain was relentless, and the cars sped past, soaking her further. Becky turned off the main road as soon as she could, taking her usual route down the side streets.

It was better once she was away from the traffic and she relaxed a little. She was looking forward to the evening, meeting the man who had put a smile on her mum's face. It would be nice to forget about work for a few hours and just hang out at home. She'd grab a bottle of wine from the shop once she'd got off the train. Maybe something really nice to go with the fillet steak. Something special.

At a junction, she stopped to let a lorry pass. Then she turned left, following in its path. She kept her distance, knowing the spray from such a large vehicle would be severe. Becky didn't see the motorbike turn down another street and disappear into the night.

As she headed for the next junction, a gust of wind blew rain into her face. The same gust turned a woman's umbrella inside out and she glanced over as the woman on the pavement struggled to right it. Becky needed to go left at the junction and she stopped patiently behind the lorry, who had his indicator on, also turning left. She saw him check his mirrors, saw him acknowledge her with a friendly wave, and she lifted her arm, likewise.

Becky waited for the truck to turn, but he didn't move. She peered up through the rain and saw he was beckoning to her, indicating for *her* to go first. She double-checked this was the message he was giving. There was plenty of room to cycle down the side of the truck – he was one of the few drivers who actually left the obligatory 1.5 metres from the kerb for cyclists. There was no one behind her.

She double-checked again – yes – he had his thumb up, then waved his hand to signal 'you go, you go'. She stood on her pedal.

She cycled alongside him and was just midway past his vehicle when she sensed it move. Alarmed, she looked up. *Jesus, he was driving.* She was almost at the corner now and saw there were railings along the edge of the pavement. She was sandwiched between the truck and the railings. With a panicked burst she tried to cycle around the corner to safety but then the truck clipped her wheel and with a cry she fell from her bike and the huge, thundering metal machine was over her, the wheels bearing down on her, and then she felt unbelievable, excruciating pain. Confusion, agony. She tried to move, couldn't move. Somehow, deep in her mind, she knew why. The wheels were on top of her.

A woman rushed over, and Becky registered the horror on her face. Somehow that frightened her more, seeing her reaction.

'Oh my God, oh my God,' the woman kept on crying out, a twisted umbrella in her hand, which she suddenly dropped. 'An ambulance is on its way,' she said, visibly trying to pull it together.

Time slipped. Becky felt the woman take her hand. She heard someone else shout, 'Move! Move it forward!' and there were blue lights reflected in the windows of the buildings she could just see from under the truck. She suddenly realized what the lights were, and she saw legs in uniforms, a policeman bend down and say, 'We're going to get you out, love.' A thought streaked through her mind: *I'm going to be late for Mum.* Then the woman who'd taken her hand let go and she heard the engine rev and then everything went dark.

SIXTY-TWO

2018

Kate burst out of the communal front door and ran down the path onto the pavement, leaving the metal gate banging behind her. She looked anxiously up and down the street, then realized if anyone *was* watching, she was drawing attention to herself.

She headed back towards the Tube station, her pace quick but controlled. She forced herself not to keep checking over her shoulder until she needed to cross the road, which would give her an opportunity to stop and glance behind. It was peak commuter time in a busy part of south London, known for its upwardly mobile professionals. There were a lot of people about. Most of them seemed as intent on going about their business as she was. She checked for anyone who had stopped, was perhaps waiting for her to move on. There was a man in a brown jacket with his back to her, looking in an estate agent's window about ten metres away. Tall, broad. Could he be the man with the moustache? She watched for a moment, then he took a call on his mobile, and turned around. Not him.

The pedestrian lights changed, and Kate moved with the hordes towards the green man on the other side of the road, and then down the steps into the underground. The platform was busy, but she managed to get on a train and stood between the seats hanging onto a yellow side rail. The train doors closed, and it picked up speed. She wondered what had happened to Adam, where he'd gone. She prayed he was safe somewhere, that someone was looking out for him. With a pang, she wondered about his mother, what she knew. When she'd see him again.

Kate shook her head, expelling the thoughts. She had to focus on getting to Jill. She remembered from when she'd scoured Jill's website that she was based in Westminster – Horseferry Road. It was a short journey up the Northern line and then a couple of stations on the Jubilee. If all went well, she should be there – she checked her watch – in half an hour.

The train stopped at the next station; a few people got out, many more got in. It set off again, the same procedure at the next station, except this time many more exited – it was an intersection with another Tube line. As the doors closed again, Kate noticed the crowds had thinned a little, then she suddenly saw a man sitting three seats down, head bent over a newspaper. He had a moustache. Sweat started to form at the back of her neck. She shrank back, while still trying to get a better look. Then he glanced up and, for a moment, it was as if her heart stopped beating. But it wasn't him.

She looked at the map displayed above her head. Five more stations to go, then she'd change onto the Jubilee line.

She stared at the map, mentally urging her journey on. The train stopped. A few passengers off. More on. Was he amongst them? It was hard to see, the jostling of the crowd meant she couldn't catch each of their faces as they got on the train. The doors closed, and Kate suddenly felt trapped. She couldn't stand it on there a minute longer.

As the train pulled into the next station, Kate headed for the doors. The crowd engulfed her, and she had a sudden panic she wouldn't be able to get off. As the door-beeps sounded, she pushed herself through, just exiting the train as the doors shut behind her.

Desperate to get out of the station, she followed the throng, made her way through the gates and was suddenly in the open air. She got out her phone and opened up the maps app, realizing with much relief that she wasn't that far from Jill's office. She could walk.

Kate set off in the direction of the river. Again, she glanced behind her; the mill of commuters was ever-present.

Unnerved, she hurried on, through Cleaver Square with its white-painted, tall Georgian houses. It was quieter here and the central open communal space was lined with trees that could hide someone, so she quickened her step and then crossed Kennington Lane into busy Kennington Road. She sensed a man stride up behind her, making her heart thump as he gained on her. She raced on, not daring to risk a look behind, and then miraculously he passed her, intent on his journey, and her anxiety momentarily subsided.

Kate stopped and watched as he went up the road, telling herself she had to get a grip or she was going to be a nervous wreck by the time she got to Jill's office. She failed to see the car pull up alongside her and the passenger door open.

'Need a lift?' someone called out and she jumped, before realizing the voice was familiar. It was Greg. She leaned down, looked into the car.

'I thought it was you,' he said, smiling. 'I can take you to the office? You're not walking all the way, are you?' He glanced at the clock on his dashboard. 'You're early! We're not meeting until eleven.'

He meant the PR event. She thought quickly. 'I was actually going to see a friend first. In Westminster.'

'Let me give you a lift.'

'I'm OK. Fancy the walk.'

'Sure? It's no trouble.'

She looked at him, trying to see behind the smile. Who was he? Could she trust him? The cars behind Greg were beeping their horns and, agitated, Kate didn't know what to do.

Greg looked in his rear-view mirror. 'I'm in the way. Just jump in a sec, will you, and I'll pull over up there.' He nodded to further up the road. 'I can give you a copy of the press release to look at. I think it's good, but we won't send it out until you're happy.'

The driver in the car behind was doing one long continuous beep and, under pressure, she got into Greg's car. 'Thanks,' she said as she did up her seat belt, putting her bag at her feet. As they drove off, it suddenly occurred to her it was a coincidence, seeing Greg there, and she said as much.

'It's my usual route in,' he said. 'I live in Dulwich. Always cross the river here, then I'm practically at the office.'

It was true; it was the easiest route for him to take.

He smiled at her. 'You look well. Tanned. Been away?'

'Er . . . yes. I took your holiday.'

He laughed delightedly. 'You did? And how was it?'

Caught, she wondered whether to tell him she'd changed the destination. Something made her not do so. 'Lovely. Sunny!'

'The hotel?'

'Wonderful.'

'I've stayed there myself. It's amazing. Simone still working on the desk?'

She faltered. 'Yes . . .'

'Lovely lady. Can't do enough for you.'

Kate did a small laugh, which she hoped served to acknowledge Simone's top-notch hospitality.

Was he looking at her sceptically or was she imagining it? She tried to smile it off. An awkward moment that was blessedly interrupted by her phone ringing. It was Iris.

'Hi, everything OK?' asked Kate.

'Everything's fine. I had to ring, I got something in the post this morning.' Iris sounded excited, tense. 'The hotel wrote to me – you know, where we stayed in Anguilla . . .' Kate's heart skipped a beat and she avoided looking at Greg. Iris continued. 'A very polite, very apologetic letter, saying they were extremely sorry, it was most unusual for this to happen, and assuring me of their utmost commitment to high-quality service, and so on and so on.'

'Go on,' prompted Kate.

'They'd been handed an envelope to pass to me before we left – and they hadn't done it. Got put in the wrong pigeonhole or something. So, they posted it.'

'OK . . .' said Kate.

'Inside the envelope was a single piece of paper with a name on it.' Iris paused. 'It's from Errol, I know it is. He couldn't be seen to be telling me who the director of Foxgold is, so he left an anonymous note for when we flew back home.'

Kate suddenly realized she was holding her breath.

'I'm sorry, Kate, I don't think you're going to like this. It's Greg Hollander. He owns everything, Kate. The farm, the chemical company, the whole damn lot.'

Spasms of fear coursed through her body. The silence ticked on. *Say something.* But horror was splintering all her thoughts and she didn't know what to say. She was suddenly aware the fingers holding her phone had locked up and she flexed them.

'Where are you?' asked Iris.

Kate swallowed. 'That's right,' she said, trying to keep her voice pleasantly neutral, 'my friend Greg's giving me a lift into town.'

He glanced across and she tried to smile at him. She felt it falter, felt the sickness rise up in her throat. *Has he noticed?*

'Good God, get out of the car,' said Iris. 'I don't want you anywhere near that man.'

Kate felt her stomach tighten. She forced the rising panic back down.

'Are you doing it?' said Iris urgently.

Be careful what you say, her brain was screaming. *He's listening.* Her right hand was sweating and so she moved the phone into her left.

Think, think. You need to get out of the car. Then she suddenly realized he hadn't pulled over to let her get out again, as he'd said he would.

'Yes, shouldn't be long. We're just going up Black Prince Road. About to cross the bridge.'

'Oh, Kate, Kate. Get out of the car. You need to get out of the car!' shouted Iris.

Then Kate did something mad. She hung up the phone. She was terrified Greg could hear Iris shouting at her. Conscious he was looking across at her, she arranged her features into a neutral expression.

'Everything OK?' asked Greg.

She nodded, then realized she hadn't made eye contact so turned and smiled at him. 'Fine.'

'Was that your friend?'

'Who?' Dazed, she had answered automatically.

'That you're meeting,' he said, amused.

'Oh. Yes, it was.' She affected a light tone. 'Weren't you going to drop me off?'

'Oh! Yes, sorry. Got carried away hearing about the holiday. Like you just said, we're about to cross the bridge. Mind if we just get over? It'll be hell to stop now.'

Should she insist? Or was it better to act as if nothing was wrong? The traffic was flowing; if she opened the car door and flung herself out, she'd be hurt. That was if she managed to get away quick enough. Was this all just some kind of madness? Had she been doing this too long and she was losing her mind, imagining terrible things because she missed Becky?

As she fidgeted in her seat an uneasy thought suddenly caught up with her.

The coincidence hadn't been seeing Greg in Kennington. It was seeing him at that *exact moment*, when she, Kate, was walking along the road. *And he hadn't even questioned the unlikeliness of that happening.* Her phone was still in her hand. The phone Greg had given to her. Was he able to *track her*? The hairs went up on her arms. It meant he knew she'd been to Adam's flat that morning. He knew she'd been to Anguilla, not the Bahamas. God, he'd known every single one of her movements for *weeks*.

More madness. An overactive imagination?

They were almost at the roundabout that led onto the bridge. The first exit. Only a couple more minutes and he'd drop her off.

'The press release is in the glove compartment,' said Greg. 'Help yourself.'

She looked down and clicked open the hatch. Sure enough, inside was a folded sheet of paper. She opened it to see a printed-off press release on corporate headed paper. As she looked up again, she just noticed they'd passed the turn to the bridge.

'What the . . . ?' she started. 'You've missed the turning!'

'It was gridlocked,' said Greg, with a smile. 'Taking another route.'

She took this in, panic tightening in a ball in her stomach. Then an awful thought struck her. *What if he isn't taking me to Westminster?* She almost cried out then, a small gurgling noise, a sound of fear. *What is he going to do with me?*

They drove on in silence, Kate's mind racing out of control. A drop of sweat rolled down the side of her face and she resisted the urge to wipe it away.

They were moving away from the river now, in the opposite direction. Did Greg just glance at her bag that was resting at her feet? Rigid, she forced herself not to touch it.

Now they were heading towards Elephant and Castle. In a few minutes, they'd be on the A3, a faster road that would take them out of London. *Where is he going?*

She looked across at him, at his smooth, expensive suit, his air of supreme confidence, and was filled with a sudden clarity. He was a man who gave himself permission to do whatever he liked, whose motivation was power and excessive riches at the expense of others, who refused to tolerate anyone getting in his way. This was the man who had had her daughter killed. He'd taken away the only person who had really mattered to her.

Kate was suddenly consumed with revulsion and hatred. A black rage spread through her. She grabbed hold of the steering wheel and spun it hard to the right.

'What the . . . ?' started Greg as the car swerved across the road but he was silenced by an almighty crunch as his car smashed into a parked van. The deafening blare of alarms rang out.

Get out of the car!

Kate started fumbling for the seat-belt catch, it gave way, snaked its way back into the roller and she was free. Greg looked at her then, and in that split second she knew it was all true.

He grabbed her arm, but she wrenched it away and frantically fumbled at the door. Snatching her bag, she half stumbled out, aware that she'd bought herself precious seconds as Greg was trapped as his door was wedged against the crumpled van.

She saw people staring, bemused faces.

Run!

She dodged past onlookers and ran as fast as she could. Some were filming on their mobile phones but she had no time, no breath to stop and explain.

On she went, back towards the river. Ahead she could see Lambeth Bridge, its iconic red paint glowing in the morning sun. She risked a glance over her shoulder and, to her horror, saw Greg gaining on her. She wouldn't make it. Jill's office was too far, and Greg would get to her first.

She dodged down a side street, then another. Lungs heaving, she flung herself behind an industrial waste bin under the railway bridge and tried to catch her breath. A train thundered overhead, and she cursed; she needed to be able to hear if anyone was approaching.

Her phone rang.

Shit! She'd forgotten all about it, the fact Greg could track her. Frantic, she pulled it out of her bag, was about to smash it on the ground, when she saw the screen. It was Tim. She'd risk a few seconds.

'Tim, I'm under a railway bridge right near Lambeth Bridge. Greg is following me – he did it, he did everything,' she garbled, as quietly as she could.

'I know,' Tim said, urgently. 'Iris called me.'

'I need to get to the lawyer's office in Horseferry Road. It's so close but I don't know if I can make it.'

'Can you see him now?'

'I don't know . . . I don't think so. I need to get off the phone, Tim, he can track me. He'll find out where I am.'

'*Shit*. Head to Horseferry Road. I'm nearby. I'll come and find you.'

Another train thundered overhead. Kate hung up and, fingers shaking, smashed her phone on the ground. She listened hard but could hear nothing.

Very, very slowly, she crept from behind the bin. The tunnel was narrow and dark, lit by just a few strip lights. To her right, at the end of the tunnel, she could see daylight, the main road. Tentatively at first, she started to walk, then jog towards the light, looking back over her shoulder, but no one was there. When she reached the junction, she looked both ways, but couldn't see Greg.

She broke into another run, heading towards the river. Soon she was at the bridge and her flagging limbs were energized. *Not long now*. The Palace of Westminster loomed larger, beckoning her over the bridge. As she ran, she glanced backwards.

He was right behind her.

She let out a howl, nearly stumbled. She had about a hundred metres on him. *Faster, you have to go faster*. But her legs couldn't. As she crossed to the other side of the bridge, he'd narrowed the gap to fifty metres. She was on the right road, but the office was further up. *Come on.*

She could hear him get louder, closer, his feet thudding on the tarmac, the pump of his arms brushing against his jacket. Gasping, she knew he'd be on her in seconds. A few people were walking about, paying her no attention. The odd car passed by. City living. Everybody minding their own business. Greg would silence her scream in seconds. She'd fight him, though, she'd fight him like a tiger—

Kate suddenly felt a vast swoosh of air and, losing her balance, she stumbled onto the ground, stupefied with fear as a red bus mounted the pavement and came to a stop between her and Greg, taking out the wall of the adjacent building as it did so.

The driver jumped out.

Tim. Oh my God, it's Tim.

'Go! Go!' he shouted, gesturing blindly up the road. She saw Greg come around the side of the bus and she ran, sweating, lungs rasping for breath, until she reached Jill's building, then thundered up the steps and barged through the door.

'I need . . . to see . . . Jill Pattinson,' she gasped at a man sitting at a desk in the reception area.

'She's in a meeting right now,' said the young man, taken aback at Kate's appearance.

Kate shook her head in defiance, and, seeing him stand protectively in front of a door ahead of her marked with Jill's name, barrelled across the room to open it.

'Hey!' interjected the man but she was already in. Jill was sitting behind a large, sweeping wooden desk, examining some papers in front of her.

'Do not send me away,' gasped Kate. 'As I won't go.'

Jill looked up, astonished, and then slowly pushed her glasses onto the top of her head.

'Aren't you that student from—'

'Yes,' said Kate. 'Gloria Chapman's class.' She held out a sweaty hand. 'Kate Ellis.'

Jill looked at her proffered hand and smiled politely. 'Anil, could you please get Miss Ellis a glass of water?' she said to the young man and he nodded and disappeared out of the room.

'Well, this is a surprise,' said Jill. Kate held her gaze and the two women stared at each other for a moment. Kate stood her ground, her eyes burning.

Then Jill indicated a chair on the other side of the desk. 'You had better take a seat.'

SIXTY-THREE

Kate lowered herself into the chair. Placed her bag carefully at her feet.

'You look . . . hot,' said Jill.

'I ran.'

Jill nodded. Waited for Kate to speak. 'How can I help?' she prompted.

Kate was about to open her mouth when there was a short rap on the door and Anil appeared with a glass of water, which he placed on the desk, on a smooth marble coaster, before disappearing again. Kate downed the lot. Then she placed the glass back on the desk while Jill waited patiently.

'I need your help,' said Kate.

'I see,' said Jill.

Suddenly Kate was nervous. Nervous of Jill saying 'no'. Nervous of having to step back out of this cool office into – what? She was no longer safe.

'When I spoke to you a few months ago, I mentioned a case I was putting together for some people, as their litigation friend.' Kate saw Jill's eyes harden but she ploughed on. 'They've been subjected to pesticides and herbicides, in particular a product called Crixus, which is sprayed in their homes and gardens from the nearby farm. It's caused a number of serious illnesses. I'm trying to get them compensation.'

Jill sat forward. 'I really don't think—'

'Shut up,' said Kate, keeping her tone pleasant. 'Shut up and listen because this thing, what I'm about to tell you, is big.'

Jill had frozen and Kate could see she was on the verge of throwing her out. She smiled her friendliest, widest smile and held her breath, then, mercifully, Jill gave her a tight nod.

'I've been researching for months. Watertight evidence is hard to find. The company responsible hides it well. They threaten those who dare to challenge them. But yesterday I got actual proof that the manufacturer knew what they were doing was wrong.' Kate leaned down and unzipped her bag and put Adam's document on Jill's desk. As Jill flicked through it, Kate scrutinized her face for her reaction.

'Interesting,' said Jill, looking up at Kate.

Interesting? It's a great deal more than that!

'But now I need you to take over. To run this,' said Kate. 'I am way out of my comfort zone.'

Jill paused. Kate saw her expression turn into one of sympathy and she knew what was coming.

'Look, everything you've done here,' said Jill, 'it's really commendable—'

'I need you to make this happen,' said Kate urgently.

'But I'm rather full at the mo—'

'Please don't let me down.'

Jill spoke patiently, as if explaining to a child. 'As I was saying, a case like this is going to take a large amount of time—'

'Do you not feel ashamed?' snapped Kate. 'You are as bad as the companies. Companies who put profit above everything else, even if they *knowingly* make people ill to do it. This is about responsibility, transparency, public accountability, or in my book, actually giving a damn!'

Kate stood, moved to the front of Jill's desk and started jabbing her finger on its shiny, varnished surface as she spoke. 'I don't give a monkey's about these so-called laws that say it's OK to spray herbicides right up against gardens where small children are playing. The corporations *know* it's wrong. They are hiding behind rules that are wrong. *The rules have to change.*'

Jill went to speak, but Kate held up a hand. 'I haven't finished. I think I should bring these people here. Then you can explain to Arnie, a six-year-old boy who's spent nearly a quarter of his life in hospital because he happens to live near a field that's sprayed with chemicals, why you don't want to help. Or Abby, a twelve-year-old girl who's got to have part of her brain cut out because she happens to live near a field that's sprayed with chemicals. Or Sunita, who's ever fearful of her breast cancer coming back and leaving her two young children without a mother, all because she happens to live near a field that is sprayed with chemicals. I'll bring them all.'

Breathless and emotional, she paused. Pulled back her

shoulders in a dignified manner. 'My daughter died trying to expose this story. She was working as a trainee journalist, and on her way home one day she was deliberately knocked off her bike and killed by these people who see profit as more important than my daughter's life.'

The room fell silent. Jill was watching her. Neither said anything. Kate held her breath.

'So, what do you want to do – get compensation or change the rules?' asked Jill.

'Both.'

Jill nodded. 'OK.'

'OK, what?'

'OK . . . I'll do it. *If* there's a case, which it sounds like there might be, I'll do it.'

'They don't have any money,' said Kate fiercely.

'I get that. I'll do it on a pro-bono basis.'

It took a moment before Jill's words sank in. 'Seriously?'

'Seriously.'

'Oh my God.' Kate couldn't believe it. She suddenly collapsed back in her chair, swamped with relief and a rising euphoria.

'So now we have to go through everything you've done so far with a fine-tooth comb,' said Jill. She pulled out a yellow executive pad. 'Can you stay?'

Christ, she could hardly leave. Greg was still out there – and Tim . . .

Worried, Kate looked up. 'Yes, I think so. I mean, I just need to make a quick call first.' She indicated that she needed to leave the room and Jill nodded.

As Kate moved away, Jill spoke up: 'How's the little boy?'

Kate turned back.

'You mentioned a little boy who was sick. When we last met. I take it that's Arnie?'

She remembered. Kate smiled cautiously. 'It's looking good. He gave us all a scare a few weeks ago but he's on the mend again.' She opened Jill's office door, about to ask the PA if she could use his phone, when the words died on her lips.

Tim was sitting in a chair by the window, looking out onto the street. The PA was typing away, a faint *click, click* on his modern keyboard. Seeing Kate in the doorway, he suddenly stopped.

Tim turned his head. He jumped up and ran to her. 'Are you OK?'

Kate nodded, flinching as she saw his face. 'You?'

'Fine.' Tim gingerly touched his swollen eye. Smiled. 'You should see the other guy,' he drawled.

She let out a pained laugh. 'Where is Greg?'

'Police took him away. He punched one of them trying to do a runner. They've got him for assaulting a police officer. I also told them he'd kidnapped you.' Tim nodded back towards Jill's office. 'How did it go?'

Kate broke into a grin, eyes shining.

His eyes widened. 'Really? She's going to do it?'

'I found this document – well, I was given it. It's proof, Tim. Proof about Crixus and how dangerous it is.'

He hugged her so hard she could hardly breathe.

'Hey!' she gasped, and he let her go.

Kate smiled. 'You were amazing back there. You crashed the bus!' she said in awe. She started laughing. '*You crashed the bus!* What's work going to say?'

'I may be fired.'

'Oh, Tim . . .'

'Never mind.'

'I need to go back in . . .'

He looked at her proudly. 'I'll be waiting.'

SIXTY-FOUR

'Hey, Mum, don't you ever do anything like that again.'

'What?'

'Don't act the innocent. My God, I thought it was bad enough when you were challenging scrotes on the shop floor at B&Q. But then you go and get in a car with that murdering bastard, crash it . . . my God, anything could have happened.'

Becky was sitting on the branch of 'her' tree, looking down at Kate. *She looks too big for it now*, thought Kate: her legs were dangling almost to the next branch down.

'What else could I have done?'

'Walk away?'

'Never,' said Kate vehemently. 'I could never do that.'

'Wanna come up?' asked Becky, patting the bark next to her.

Kate grinned and climbed the tree, finding it surprisingly easy. In a matter of seconds, she was sitting next to her daughter. The view was astonishing, a green canvas as far as the eye could see. The light had a golden quality to it, and on the horizon, there was a silver-like shimmer that seemed to glow.

'What?' she exclaimed. 'Is that the *sea*? Since when have you been able to see the sea from Crawley?'

'It's different up here,' said Becky in a faraway voice. 'Not like Crawley.'

When Kate looked again, she could see. It *was* different.

'So, no more crazy stuff? You promise?'

Kate smiled. 'I think it's going to be OK now. There's Jill, she's going to take this to court. She's all fired up. She gets scary when she's like that.'

'Good. You did it. You're amazing. An amazing, *clever* Mum.' Becky nudged her shoulder and the two of them leaned into each other.

'I might have to climb higher,' said Becky, looking up into the canopy.

Kate raised her head. The branches appeared to go on far into the sky, the tree in full leaf, an abundance of optimism and life. She could see glimpses of blue sky, way up above. A sudden panic gripped her.

'I don't want you to go.'

Becky smiled. 'I won't fall, Mum. Not anymore.'

She lifted herself up and took hold of the tree trunk. Then she started to climb, higher and higher. Kate watched, tears pouring down her face, but she knew it was the way things were. Then Becky looked back down, meeting her gaze. She gave a little wave.

'I did it for you, you know,' called Kate.

'I know,' said Becky. 'And I love you for it.'

461

EPILOGUE

Jill arranged for a class action lawsuit to be served on Fox-gold Ltd and Greg Hollander, and a date was set by the court for the following summer. With Kate's research and Adam's document, Jill was able to prove a causal link between the actions of herbicide spraying and the claimants' illnesses.

The trial took two weeks and the judge ruled in favour of the claimants. The defendants were ordered to pay £57 million, divided amongst the families of Ramsbourne. The judge made the exceptional decision to make a provisional award of compensation to the claimants to allow them to reapply to the court should their health deteriorate significantly in the future.

Greg was arrested for assaulting a police officer, kidnap and soliciting to murder. He denied all knowledge of Becky's death being deliberate and organized. Bail was refused on the grounds that the crimes were of a very serious nature and the witness needed to be protected.

Janković was arrested for the murder of Justin Holmes.

Jed Craven was arrested for the murder of Becky Ellis.

Greg, Janković and Craven were all found guilty and sentenced to life imprisonment.

Abby's operation was a success, and, after further radio-therapy treatment, she is now in remission. With the damages awarded through the lawsuit, Rob was able to clear his mortgage and take his family on a much-deserved holiday.

Sunita is still clear of breast cancer. Her children never knew how ill she was. One day she plans to tell them.

Ian and Hazel followed their dream to move to Italy. He had eight years in the sun before the cancer took over. He died in his home in a small village in Umbria.

Arnie is still in remission, and for a seventh birthday present, he and his twin brother John received a puppy, who they called Rocket. Rocket regularly chews their Lego and occasionally deposits it while they're out walking – not through sprayed fields.

Adam fled to the continent, withdrawing as much cash as possible before he went. He stayed at a small B&B in a tiny village near the French–Swiss border until he learned of the news of Greg Hollander a few weeks after Greg's arrest. Only then did he return to the UK. The *Herald* sought an exclusive interview with him, with Terence running the story.

With the success of Kate's lawsuit, Dr Zayan was able to find a lawyer to file a case for the children of his village. They were also successful, winning significant compensation for all claimants. Dr Zayan's professional reputation, which had been in dispute following the damning reports written by Senerix scientists, was fully restored. He continues to write industry papers and articles on the human cost of pesticide and herbicide spraying and recently featured on a *Time* magazine cover.

Kate accepted Tim's proposal of marriage and they tied the knot in Shoal Bay in Anguilla. A small number of friends attended, including Iris, who reignited her friendship with Errol. To this day, Errol still denies ever leaving an envelope at their hotel.

Kate and Jill's case was a landmark ruling that triggered a snowball effect of similar cases in the UK, Europe and internationally, including some of the biggest compensation claims seen in the USA since the 1990s tobacco scandal. As a consequence, governments are being forced to review agricultural and horticultural pesticide-and-herbicide spray regulations.

Kate is still studying law and accepted a position at Jill's firm as a paralegal working towards a traineeship. They continue to advise numerous claimants and lawyers around the world who are seeking compensation for similar cases. She combines this with looking after her new baby son, born a year after her marriage.

AUTHOR'S NOTE

During the course of writing this novel, an extraordinary piece of news hit the headlines in the summer of 2018. In a stunning blow to one of the world's largest agrochemical companies, jurors in California told Monsanto that they must pay $289 million in damages to a man dying of cancer, which he alleges was caused by exposure to Roundup, one of the world's most popular herbicides. Lawyers for this man – who worked as a school groundskeeper, regularly spraying the sports fields – uncovered corporate documents that indicated that Monsanto had long known about, and covered up, the dangers in using their products. Monsanto is appealing. They argue that Roundup, a glyphosate-based product, is safe. They claim that the evidence has been misrepresented.

Despite Monsanto attempting to stop their internal emails and reports being available to the public during the course of the trial, the judge overruled them, and they can be found readily on the Internet. They make for sober – and astonishing – reading.

It's not just in the USA where stories of the dangers of herbicide and pesticide spraying are hitting the headlines.

Here in the UK, chemicals are regularly sprayed on fields, and there are numerous reports of the catastrophic harm it can cause to those living or working nearby. A simple search on the Internet will reveal a plethora of information on this highly contentious subject: everything from reports on agrochemical corporations' tactics to harass journalists, conspire with regulators and hide and distort scientific reports, to articles on those countries currently working to ban glyphosate or restrict its use. The personal testimonies of the dozens and dozens of people affected leave you with your heart in your mouth.

The characters and scenarios in this book are all a work of fiction but are drawn from interviews, evidence and reports on the use of pesticides and herbicides in our fields here in the UK, and around the world.

ACKNOWLEDGEMENTS

Thank you to my very special editor, Trish Jackson; I am forever grateful for your guidance and insight. Also to Jayne Osborne, Rosie Wilson, Mel Four, Sam Sharman, Eloise Wood, Karen Whitlock, Lucy Wai, Becky Lloyd, Stuart Dwyer, Rebecca Kellaway, Holly Martin, Andy Joannou and everyone at Pan Macmillan who worked so hard to get this book published.

Gaia Banks, I'm very lucky to have you as my agent. Also huge thanks to the wonderful Lucy Fawcett and Alba Arnau, Markus Hoffman and Joel Gotler.

I would like to express a very heartfelt thank you to everyone who helped me while I was researching this book. Georgina Downs, who tirelessly campaigns to change the law on pesticide and herbicide spraying on our fields. Hannah Price-Harries, thank you for all the time you gave up patiently answering my 'what if' litigation questions; you are a legal genius. Viki Hill and Soroya Thethi, your passion and steadfastness in cancer care is awe-inspiring. Anna Stimson, thank you so much for all the police procedural knowledge and advice. All the mothers, whose stories of campaigning for justice for their children have inspired me. Thank you also to both Nicholas Parton of Opus Pear Tree Forensic Accounting and Karim Kiffin of Kiffin Consulting for the insight into the world of forensic accounting, and I'm sorry, Karim, that the novel didn't end up in Jamaica!

As ever, a big thank you to my wonderful family for all their support – Mum, you are a one-woman publicity machine – also Dad, Sally, Rhys, Ettie, Neil, Tina, Leila and Brandt.

Finally, my husband, Jonny, and Livi and Clementine, for always believing in me.

THE
GIRL
FRIEND

A girl. A boy. His mother.
And the lie she'll wish she'd never told.

Laura has it all. A successful career, a long marriage to a rich husband, and a twenty-three-year-old son, Daniel, who is kind, handsome and talented.

Then Daniel meets Cherry. Cherry is young, beautiful and smart, but she hasn't had the same opportunities as Daniel. And she wants Laura's life.

Cherry comes to the family wide-eyed and wants to be welcomed with open arms, but Laura suspects she's not all she seems.

When tragedy strikes, one of them tells an unforgiveable lie – probably the worst lie anyone could tell. It is an act of desperation, but the fallout will change their lives forever.

THE
TEMP

No one was going to replace her.
Were they?

Carrie is a successful TV producer in a high-pressure job. She's talented, liked and well-respected. She and her husband, Adrian, an award-winning screenwriter, decided years before that they didn't want children. But now, just as they're both at the pinnacle of their careers, she has discovered she is pregnant, and is shocked to find that she wants to keep the baby. But in a competitive industry where time off is seen as a sign of weakness, Carrie looks on the prospect of maternity leave with trepidation.

Enter Emma, the temp, who is everything she could wish for as her cover: smart, willing and charming. Carrie fears that Emma is manoeuvring her way into Carrie's life, causing turmoil in both her marriage and her work as she does so. The problem is, everyone else adores her . . .

Increasingly isolated from Adrian and her colleagues, Carrie begins to believe Emma has an agenda. Does Emma want her job? Or is she after even more?